*E*ndless *L*ove

⌐God Shall Supply All Our Needs⌐

Written by

Elizabeth Anne Ryan

Endless Love
by Elizabeth Anne Ryan

Printed in the United States of America

ISBN 978-1-60266-936-9

Book One of the Endless Love Series

Be sure to read this book before reading the following books in this series.

Book Two – One More Moment in Time
Book Three – To Be announced in Book 2

Unless otherwise indicated, Bible quotations are taken from: The Good News Bible, Today's English Version, copyright 1988, by American Bible Society publisher.

The website addresses recommended throughout this book are offered as a resource to you. These websites are not intended in any way to be or imply an endorsement on the part of the author or publisher, nor do we vouch for their content for the life of this book.

"By Grace, we are saved, not of the works that we do, lest any man should boast." Ephesians 2:8-9

"I can do all things through Christ who strengthens me." Phil 4:13

"And with all his abundant wealth through Christ Jesus, my God will supply all your needs." Phil 4:19

www.xulonpress.com

~Words of Encouragement~

*C*url up by the fire and immerse yourself in this inspirational romantic story of passionate characters you will find yourself caring deeply about as the plot engages you in this compelling page-turner of spell-binding love.

— Justin and Jenny Janney

A sure-fire winner that inspires readers with a message of hope and healing through the power of unending love. God's unconditional, redemptive, all-consuming love. Draws you like a magnetic force to read the next mesmerizing chapter. Would love to see this book as a *major movie*.

— Faye R. Adams

Gripping, attention-grabbing story that keeps you on edge. A story with a purpose to allure you into compassion, forgiveness, faith, hope, and love. I could not put this book down.

— Robin Janney

Wow, wow, wow! This was so good. You kept me guessing in the direction the story would go, and how the results would turn out. I am very pleased with how you showed God's love, forgiveness, and faithfulness. Your information on educating people about the illnesses is very creative in the story. Wow, it was enjoyable to read. It stole my heart. I found myself emotionally attached to the characters as they went through their challenges (physically, mentally, and spiritually). God is good — yes, he supplies all our needs. Bless you.

— Teresa Manczyk

EXCELLENT BOOK!!! I enjoyed it very much!!!!! You are very talented Elizabeth! A faith-filled and faith-focused book!

— Kathleen A. Ford

Liz- God was in control through this entire book, not only through this book, but through the writer too. It was a pleasure to read and edit this book with such love for the Lord coming from the writer. Your book is a witness to all who believe and to those that need to believe. This book is a sure winner for the Hallmark channel. Thank you from the bottom of my heart for sharing this with me. This book has become a part of my life now, what a joy it has been to read. You have me in awe at your talent. You have a natural God given talent for writing. I have cried, laughed, been angry, sad, all the emotions that you would expect to read in a great novel, my compliments to you. I cannot tell you when I have been more intrigued by a book.

— Deborah Edwards

Liz- I am so proud of you. I knew this day would someday come, and it is finally here. All of your hard work has paid off. You have given Mark life, and so many people will be blessed as they read the pages you have written in Endless Love. I pray that God will bless you abundantly and that Endless Love will be a huge success, both in the bookstores and eventually on film (it should be on Lifetime). We have to celebrate! At long last, you can celebrate and yes, I would be honored to come along with you on book signings. I will help edit too, if you need me. Again, I am So proud of you! I love ya.

— Kittie McGuire

It is a great book, Liz
The characters seem so real and it is almost like viewing a movie. I can see the scenes in my mind because your wording is so descriptive. I very much enjoyed reading this book. Thank you for being obedient to God and having a heart bent toward Him.

— Betty Rogers

~Acknowledgements~

$\mathscr{I}$ want to extend my personal and sincere thanks to these wonderful people, their constant belief in this book made it happen:

To God – His constant love in my heart inspired this story. I shared my love for Him with others throughout this book. All the credit goes to God as He filled my heart with this story using me as His instrument.

My children, Robin, Justin, Bryan, and Nathan, who sacrificed time away from me while the book was being written and for their unconditional love and support in making this book possible. I dedicate this book to each one of them. You are my endless loves. I am honored to have you as my precious children.

My Grandchildren, Hannah Nicole, the apple of my eyes, and the twins, Madison and Stephon, the joys of my life. Thank you for giving up sitting in my lap while I wrote this book. Nana loves you.

Teresa Manczyk – My brilliant editor, who wrote words of unwavering enthusiasm to encourage me to share this book with others. I am proud to call her my friend. Her endless hours of editing are greatly appreciated. She is a treasure to have on my editing team.

Faye Adams – An amazing friend who was the first to read this book, and believed so passionately in it that she convinced me that this book should be published or made into a movie. She gave me hope and lifted me up when I felt overwhelmed.

<u>Melanie Williams</u> – My gifted editor. Truly a daughter of our King. Her sweet personality melts hearts for the Lord. I am blessed to have her in my life. Thanks Clint and Emma for giving up your precious time with Melanie so she could edit for me.

<u>Kathleen A. Ford</u> – A special editor that encouraged me to get the medical information correct. She gave generously of her time to edit for me. She was a valued member of my editing team.

<u>Deborah Edwards</u> – An extraordinary friend who encouraged me to believe in myself. Her daily editing e-mails were an inspiration as we edited the book. She continues to be optimistic that this book will one day be a movie on the Hallmark channel.

<u>Kittie McGuire</u> – A unique friend who edited the book and encouraged me to keep God first in every chapter. Kittie and her husband inspired me to believe that a marriage grows stronger when God is the center of it. When they look at each other, I see my characters.

<u>Suzy Schmitz</u> – My remarkable sister. She has supported me in all my endeavors. Her comments encouraged me to make this the best book possible. I am blessed to have a family who loves me. Thanks Barry and Janelle.

<u>Becky, Beth, Betty, Bonnie, Carolyn, Jenni, Laurie, Marcia, Marsha, Susan, and Sabrina,</u> and to all those who read the book, and gave me positive feedback to continue in my writing ambition to honor God. I am blessed to know these wonderful women.

<u>My Church Family at Believer's Church</u> – They showed me what genuine love is meant to be. I love each one of you. You are truly my family in Christ.

<u>Pastor Mark Evans, Clint Williams, and Scott Stringer</u> who shared God's message each Sunday and Wednesday and motivated me to be the best that I can be through Christ our Lord. Our website is: <u>bchurch.org</u>

In addition, to our praise team, their extraordinary God-given talents lifted me up with God's amazing Spirit through their faith-filled songs and special music. Our youth praise team and Bryan Price, their leader. The best of our youth! Continue your walk with Jesus.

To my students who attended <u>Noah's Ark Christian Academy</u> – I love you. Dale, Matthew, Hannah, Madison, Stephon, Breeanna, Chris, Lucas, Seth, Hannah, Marcus, Jessica, Evan, Caleb, Kaley and all those before you. Thank you parents.

<u>Joel Osteen's Book – Your Best Life Now</u>
This book taught me that God has a plan for my life and I was not to sell myself short of my dreams. Joel enlarged my vision for my life. His encouragement gave me the self-assurance to publish this book.

In addition, to all those who suffer from a blood disorder or illness. May God give you supernatural healing. May you discover that God has an extraordinary purpose for your life. Believe in the truth of God's Words found in the Bible. Claim life to the fullest and speak words of joy, peace, healing, and happiness over your life.

Lastly to Bob and Meghan, your life together was an inspiration to all those who knew you as a couple. In living and in death you will always be together in each other's hearts. Bob will be remembered for the outstanding individual that he was during his short life.

Each defining moment of our day can be significant; life is made up of small moments that we must treasure as gifts from God. Pursue your faith and find the courage and love to grasp deep within to find your God-given strengths no matter how difficult your circumstances.
Author unknown.

If you would like a copy of this book or would like information about this book, email this address:

endlesslovebookorders@yahoo.com
List your request as the one of the following:
Copy of Book 1 – Request
Information about Book 1 – Request

endlesslovebookcomments@yahoo.com
Comments about Book 1
Book signing requests
Speaking engagement requests

For information about Book 2, "One More Moment in Time"
endlesslovebookorders@yahoo.com
Copy of Book 2 - Request
Information about Book 2 – Request

Author will autograph any books purchased from this e-mail site.

~Endless Love Chapters~

Next Book in the series is:
One More Moment In Time – Book 2

CHAPTER ONE –
⌾Lost but Now Found⌾

*T*he chilly late December breeze was blowing the remaining autumn leaves off the trees, scattering them on the frozen ground below. At this late hour, the park was empty except for Mark Sanders, who sat peacefully on a park bench, watching the birds fly overhead as they headed south.

The squirrels busied themselves with gathering nuts, making rustling noises among the dry leaves. Mark smiled at their playfulness as he watched two of the squirrels engage in a game of tag as they jumped from tree to tree.

The gentle breeze blew his dark sandy blonde hair away from his tan face. Mark was an attractive, athletic young man. He stood six feet three inches tall and was in excellent physical shape. However, his hectic schedule was taking a toll on him and stress showed on his eye-catching face. It had been a long couple of days at the hospital, where he worked as an intern.

Only 24 years old, Mark had already advanced in his medical career much further than others had at his age. He had combined four years of college into two years.

His early years of private school had offered him academic training in many college courses. Mark was extremely intelligent. He had taken college courses every summer since he was in the ninth grade. Immediately after his graduation from college, he enrolled in medical school. He was not wasting any time at becoming an excellent doctor as quickly as possible.

Combined with his medical lectures and internship, he was also a professional football player. Mark had played college football as a quarterback, breaking several college records before going pro after medical school. He loved the game; it offered him a chance to relieve some of the daily stress in his life.

Mark started his morning early with hospital rounds and his many tasks as an intern. He had football practice in the evenings, and then he returned to the hospital at night when he was on-call.

Because he was the hometown football hero, he was given special privileges with his job, allowing him to leave work to practice. He never took advantage of the situation. Mark was considerate of his fellow interns, and worked extra hours for them during the off-season of football.

Finally, tonight, he had a night off from the hospital. Mark sat on a bench to collect his thoughts on how his life was progressing. His long days at the hospital left him feeling as if life was passing him by. He had passed by this same park everyday, never taking the time to stop and enjoy its peacefulness and beauty.

Earlier, he left the hospital to go to practice. When practice was over, he had previously planned to go back to his apartment to study. His apartment was across the street from the park. It was only out of his extreme exhaustion that he stopped here tonight. The park looked so inviting and calm. He needed the serenity it offered.

Mark was very tired but found his thoughts were making him too restless to sit. He decided to walk. In and out of the pine trees he weaved, bending down and picking up pinecones and tossing them like footballs through the air.

He bent down to pick up another pinecone, when he noticed the small shoes of a child under a bush. He could hear the soft sound of the child's whimpering, which sent a wave of confusion throughout his body.

Mystified, Mark moved closer to the bush and spread it apart. Surprise struck him as he revealed a small girl lying on the ground curled up in a ball, her arms wrapped tightly around her knees, her forehead resting on her arms. She was crying softly to herself. A runaway, Mark genuinely assumed sadly.

The lamppost provided a ray of light that shimmered down on her little body. Mark gently touched her tiny arm, not wanting to frighten her. She quickly looked up at him with her dirty tear-stained face, her deep clear blue eyes glaring at him as she studied his kind inviting face.

Frightened, she quickly scrambled to her feet and started to run. Mark turned and scampered after her. She tripped over a fallen tree branch and fell to the ground among the accumulated leaves, hitting her knee on a small rock.

Mark reached her, knelt down over her, and began evaluating her condition. Carefully, he turned her over. She did not move; she seemed dazed or scared or possibly playing possum with him. Mark noticed a small cut on her knee. She looked up into his kind face with wide eyes.

She appeared cold and was visibly frightened. All she had on was a tattered dress and an old worn out dingy gray jacket. She looked like a limp broken rag doll that badly needed attention.

Mark gently brushed her tangled dirty hair away from her face with his tender hand. He instantly felt compassion for her. The phrase, "what the cat dragged in," described her appearance, he thought sadly.

"Shhh, shhh, don't be afraid, I want to help you," he said kindly, hoping to relieve her fear of him. Her eyes remained wide as she watched him.

Mark quickly looked around and saw there was no one around to help him. The park was deserted and dark, except where the lampposts gave light. *Why is this abandoned child out here alone, dirty and scared?* Mark angrily questioned.

He gently spoke to her again, asking her where her parents were, but she would not answer him. Her eyes remained unchanged, wide open like an owl in the dark of the night.

He knew he urgently needed to get her to a warm place. He briefly thought of the hospital, but he decided that his apartment was closer. He could help her there and call for assistance. He reasoned that she would be less scared if he cared for her in a less frightening atmosphere like his apartment.

"I am going to take you to my apartment and fix up your knee," he spoke tenderly, and conveyed a reassuring smile across his face. She slightly nodded her head in agreement. She seemed willing to trust him. He took his leather jacket off and wrapped it around her.

Mark picked her up in his arms carefully and cuddled her next to his body. She did not protest as he gently wrapped his arms around her. He walked through the park to the sidewalk, crossed the paved street, and walked over to his apartment complex.

He had a knot in his stomach, thinking of all the possibilities that this child could have suffered if he had not rescued her from the night of the park. He prayed for her as he hurriedly carried her in his arms.

Mark took the elevator up to his apartment on the fourth floor. He struggled with his key to unlock his door but finally he managed to get the door open and he went inside.

The apartment included two bedrooms, a bath, and a kitchen area with a counter bar that separated the kitchen from the dining area, which opened into the living room. The room was neatly kept and was warmly furnished.

It was small compared to his own room at his parent's elaborate ranch house in the country. He only rented the apartment because it was conveniently located close to the hospital.

Mark gently set the little girl on his couch. He removed his jacket, grabbed the throw blanket, and wrapped it snuggly around her body. She remained in a dazed state.

He got a warm washcloth, knelt down in front of her, and carefully wiped the blood from her knee. He was relieved that the cut would not need stitches. She continued to stare at Mark, analyzing his every move as he cared for her. She looked frightened and confused, but thankfully, she did not need any additional medical attention.

"Are you lost; did someone take you?" She shook her head, no.

"It's alright; I'm not going to hurt you," Mark reassured her with his kind soft blue eyes and his gentle voice. *I have to earn her trust if I am going to help her.* He thought she must be a runaway.

She did not say anything as she proceeded to study Mark's kind face. *He looks concerned for me,* she thought with satisfaction.

He is kind, and oh so handsome looking, she thought to herself. *I guess I don't have to be afraid of him. He could be the Prince Charming I've been praying for, to rescue me. Did God send him to save me?*

Mark thought, *she must be hungry; soup would warm her insides, and warm soup might help me earn her trust so that she will tell me where she belongs and I can take her back there.*

"Are you hungry?" he asked her softly. Her face brightened some as she slowly shook her head yes. She had not realized how hungry she was until he mentioned food.

She began to study her surroundings and liked the warm feeling the apartment generously provided.

Mark went into the kitchen; he could watch her from there as he prepared the soup. She did not move; she just looked around the apartment, but her face looked less frightened.

She eventually stood up so that she could watch Mark at work in the kitchen. They exchanged pleasant looks, and then she sat back down and wrapped the blanket securely around herself. She was nervously combing her hair with her tiny fingers as she contemplated her situation.

Mark figured that it was time to find out more about her. He went over to the couch and sat next to her.

"What's your name?" Mark asked her softly. She shyly looked up at him.

"Sunflower," she said slowly, still twisting her hair with her fingers.

"That's a very nice name," he said as he smiled at her, and she returned the smile.

"Where do you live?" he asked gently.

"No where," she answered sadly as she lifted her chin up so that she could look straight into his face.

"How old are you, Sunflower?" he asked with softness in his voice.

"Six," she replied shyly.

"Did you run away from home, Sunflower?"

Sunflower looked away from him and wondered. *Hmmm, can I trust him?*

"How old are you; what's your name?" she mocked his questions to her, hoping he would not question her again about where she lived.

Mark smiled at her cleverness to avoid his questions. "I'm twenty-four, my name is Mark Sanders, and I am a doctor." He humored her.

She smiled at him, glad that he played along with her.

"Did you run away from home? It is ok to tell me."

She put her lips together in a funny way as if to keep from saying anything. She studied his kind face and widened her smile.

"You're cute, and I like your apartment," she announced in a sweet childish voice as she cleverly changed the subject again.

"Thank you, you are very pretty. Did you get all that blonde hair from your mother?" he asked her, hoping to get some kind of information from her. However, her face took on a look of sadness instead. She lowered her head so that her chin touched her neck.

"I ... I don't have no mom," she whispered sadly.

Mark felt his heart sink. "I'm sorry, what happened to her?" he inquired with concern.

"She died ... so did my dad ... I live in a foster home," she briefly paused, "the lady there is real mean to me. Her apartment's not nice like yours, it's old and messy," she informed him sadly, "I don't like it there."

"Where is your apartment?" Mark asked, realizing he had to be careful not to upset her any further, but he needed to know where to take her home.

"I ... I can't remember," she pretended as she looked away from him. When she looked away, Mark knew that she was not telling him the truth.

"Sure, you can remember; if you really wanted to tell me the truth."

"No, I can't ... I don't want to go back there anyhow, they don't want me!" she exclaimed with hurt in her eyes that cut into his heart.

"I am sure they are worried about you. Don't you think they want you to be home for Christmas?" Mark tried to sound persuasive.

"No, they're not, they don't believe in Christmas!" she said angrily. "Besides, her husband's gone and left her and she's out drunk on the couch. She don't even know I'm gone," she told him, as tears began to form in her sad eyes. "She won't wake up for days. She don't care when I leave; I do it all the time."

"Maybe I better call her just in case," he said, relieved somewhat that she was not lost or a missing child, but deeply saddened at the story he was hearing.

"NO! NO! Please, don't call her!" she yelled as she got excited and stood up on the couch so she could be face to face with Mark.

"Please, don't make me go back there; I hate it there!" she pleaded. "I will just run back to the park if you take me back. I'm never going back!" she cried out as she stared straight into Mark's concerned eyes.

She covered her face with her hands and cried into them. Mark felt sympathetic towards her. He moved closer to her with caution, knowing it was not wise for him to have any physical contact with her, yet he felt compelled to comfort her tears.

She quickly climbed into his arms, put her tiny arms around his neck, and held tight, sobbing on his shoulder. Mark hesitantly put his arms around her and hugged her.

Her affection surprised Mark. He awkwardly patted her back to comfort her. Her crying eased some and he let her go. He looked into her teary eyes and knew he would give her anything she asked for if it would make her smile again. She gently placed her head on his shoulder and held onto his neck.

What am I going to do now; she is not a stray animal on the ranch that I can bring home to my grandfather. I cannot just bring her here, give her a name, and keep her, as I did with all those homeless animals when I was a child.

Surely, someone cares about her. Is she really telling me the truth? He looked at her rags for clothes; someone was neglecting her, that was true. For now, she was safe with him.

"It's okay, Sunflower, I won't call them if you don't want me to," he said as he softly patted her back. She pulled away and looked him in the eyes.

"Please, can I live here with you?" she asked, begging him with her beautiful eyes. Her statement completely took Mark by surprise. He found himself captured by her desperate glare.

What is happening to my heart; what is she doing to me? Has she cast an irreversible spell on me? He smiled, thinking how easily he was falling for her charm.

"How do you know you would even like living here?" he smiled at her. She moved closer to him and touched his gentle face with the palms of her tiny hands and held them there, looking straight into his baby blue eyes. She had his undivided attention.

"Cause you're so handsome and nice to me," she giggled and then bent and touched the tip of his nose with her finger. Mark smiled at her. She wanted to win his heart, and she was doing a fantastic job of charming him. Then she looked over her shoulder with a puzzling discernment on her face.

"Don't you believe in Christmas either?" she asked as she looked around his undecorated apartment.

Mark realized that he had done nothing to prepare for Christmas Day. "I haven't had time to decorate yet," he explained.

They both laughed and Mark was glad that she was smiling again. He put his hands around her waist and lifted her up into the air as he stood up. Then he gently set her down on the floor.

What charm she has; someone has taught her how to be loving. How could she be so charming, if her life had been as bad as she claimed? Mark wondered with suspicion, as he raised his eyebrows.

"Let's go eat some of my delicious soup."

Sunflower followed him into the kitchen, and he lifted her up to the counter bar. She helped him set the bowls and napkins in place, humming a happy tune as she worked. She was so adorable. Watching her, Mark knew that she was about to steal his heart.

She folded her hands together and bowed her head. "Dear Lord, thank ya for this food and thank ya for finding this new home for me, Amen." She looked up at Mark, who had a surprised look on his face.

She knows God, things were not adding up, Mark thought puzzled and then grinned. "Amen. Sunflower, do you know God?"

"Oh yes, when I was at the children's home, I went to church with Sister Jessica. She told me all about God. God loves me. **God shall supply all my needs**. I prayed for someone like ya and God sent ya to find me," she said with a confident smile. Mark did not know how to respond.

Sunflower picked up her spoon and began to eat. She continued to smile at him as they ate. Mark knew she was trying to warm up to him, but he did not care.

How could a child this small be so smart and intelligent? What was it about her that made him feel the way he did? She reminded him of someone, perhaps some child from his past.

Mark was surprised how she had broken through his masculine character. He the professional football player, the bachelor, having chicken noodle soup with a six year old child; it was not something he would have done of his own choosing.

Where were the thick juicy steaks and a room full of fellow male companions, the poker table, and the colas? Mark laughed, thinking what a ridiculous sight he made sitting there with Sunny. If just one of his teammates came through his door unannounced, word would get out that he had turned completely soft.

Mark played with the children in the children's ward at the hospital but he was not in the habit of letting his heart feel this way. He loved his nephews and enjoyed being around them, but this was different, she was a little girl. Was he going to trade football games with the guys for dollhouses? He laughed again.

Sure, Mark had a kind nature about him. He would do anything for his friends, but there was that wall that he stayed behind, never letting any stranger get too close to his heart until he trusted them.

Mark always portrayed the tough guy image, the strong spirited resilient man. That was the man many knew him to be. How was he going to explain to the guys what was happening to him?

What was it about her that seemed to draw him to her? He stared at her as if he had seen her somewhere before.

"How did you get the name, Sunflower?"

"The hot dog man in the park gave it to me, 'cause he said my hair is the color of the sun and I look like a flower," she said as she twisted a strand of her golden hair with her hand. "My hair needs washin'," Sunflower added as her eyes searched Mark's face for signs of compassion for her.

"Are you finished eating?" he asked, anxious to move on.

"Yep, it was good, better than the soup at the mission. That's where I go when I am hungry. Thank you, Mark," she said sweetly, making sure that her words captured his sympathy for her.

She put her bowl in his and started to clean up the counter around them. Mark watched her with amazement. She certainly has cleaned up after herself before. Now that she had eaten, the next step was bathing. Mark dreaded the thought of a bath, but it had to be done.

"Do you know how to take a shower by yourself?" he asked, hoping that she did, but not sure if she was old enough to do it alone.

"Sure I do, silly," she giggled. Mark gave her a smile and was relieved that he would not have to bathe her. He leaned over and lifted her down.

He stood up, and she followed him to the bathroom. He turned on the water and felt the temperature. When it was just right, he turned to her.

"The soap is right here, the shampoo is here, you can use this towel, and I'll find you something to wear. Just call me when you are finished," he told her, feeling somewhat awkward.

"Does this mean I can stay with you?" Sunflower asked excitedly, using her witty facial expressions to get what she wanted.

"For tonight, since it's too late to do anything else with you," he smiled as she jumped around him in excitement. She folded her hands together as if to pray and held them out in front of her.

"Thank you, Jesus," her lips whispered.

"If ya let me stay here, I won't be no trouble. I can do all the housework. I'll be real good. Oh please, can I stay here with ya?" she pleaded with a serious look of desperation.

Mark placed his hand on her head. "We'll see, but you need a shower first. I'll be right outside if you need anything," Mark said as he turned and left the room.

Mark went into the living room and picked up the phone. He dialed the police department. He asked if anyone had reported a missing child, but no reports had been filed. He hung up the phone without giving them any information. He did not know why he had done it, he just had. It was as if his subconscious was speaking to him, telling him not to report finding Sunflower until he knew more about her.

Was it true no one was looking for her? Mark leaned against the back of the couch, trying to figure out this strange situation that he had gotten himself involved in.

He could hear Sunflower singing in the shower. "You are my sunshine, my only sunshine." She sang out in a beautiful voice much like his sister Rebecca's voice sounded when they were growing up.

Mark closed his eyes. He was so tired he would have drifted off to sleep if Sunflower had not called his name. He got off the couch and went to the bathroom. Sunflower was standing there wrapped in a towel.

"Let's get you dressed." She followed him into his bedroom. He pulled out a t-shirt from his dresser and handed it to her. He kept his back to her, so she could dress in private.

"Done," she informed him.

He turned to face her. What a sight she made, her hair all tangled, the t-shirt dragging the floor. Nevertheless, she was so beautiful, so innocent; he smiled at the silly sight of her.

Mark took a brush off the dresser and she stood in front of him as he sat on the side of his bed. He gently brushed her tangled hair until it was straight. She did not complain when he pulled the knots in her hair. Mark felt awkward and was thankful when he was done brushing her hair.

How could someone possibly mistreat this gift of God's?

Was she right, did God send him to the park tonight to find her, to save her, to give her what she deserved in life, he wondered.

Why me, Lord, why me? There is just no room in my life for a child. However, he knew better than to ask God. If this was God's plan, he would obey it. Besides, he had already fallen in love with this child.

"Let's get you to bed," Mark told her. She followed him into the spare bedroom. He pulled the covers back and helped her climb on the bed. She looked so small in the huge bed. She folded her hands together to pray.

"Thank you, God, thank you, God, thank you, God; uh, you know what for." She charmingly smiled up at Mark and winked. Mark knew he was in deep trouble now. How could he break her heart and send her away after she had asked God to get involved in this delicate situation? He knew he did not stand a chance against the two of them.

"Good night, Sunflower, if you need me, I will be in the other room." He touched her forehead with his hand. "We'll figure this all out in the morning." She nodded her head and closed her eyes.

Mark stood beside the bed and watched her fall asleep. How beautiful and peaceful she looked. Mark felt such compassion for this tiny girl he knew very little about. One thing he did know, she was the prettiest lost puppy he had ever brought home to keep. He smiled at himself; there was humor in this situation after all.

Then Mark went into his bedroom, picked up his medical books off the desk, and laid them on the bed. He leaned against the headboard and tried to study, but he kept thinking about Sunflower.

Someday he planned to get married and have a family. It was something that he looked forward to doing, when the time was right.

Mark knew that he was feeling emotions he had never felt before. Why was this little girl causing his heart to desire a family now?

He had always been unconquerable. Not a single woman had ever conquered his affections. It was true that women found him irresistible and flirted with him constantly. That came with being a public figure and of course, a doctor.

Mark had dated a few women but he had always kept his heart distant from them. He had resisted any type of serious commitment to any one woman. There was just no room in his life for an emotional relationship. Most importantly, he had not yet met the woman that he knew God had waiting for him.

His life as he knew it was about to change.

CHAPTER TWO –
⌒The Eyes of a Child⌒

*T*he sun was shining brightly outside, its soft rays poured in Mark's bedroom window. He had fallen asleep thinking about Sunflower; his book was still lying open and unread across his chest.

Mark opened his eyes. Wow, what a dream, he thought. He gave God praise for a new day. He lazily glanced over at the clock. It was six-thirty. He sat up quickly and stretched; he had rounds this morning. He thought he could smell the aroma of bacon cooking, and hurried out to the kitchen.

Maria, his parent's housekeeper, was standing at the stove cooking. She was in her late forties, dressed in her housekeeper's uniform with a white apron tied around her small waist. Her dark complexion and deep black hair reflected her beauty. Mark affectionately thought of her as a second mother.

"Good morning, Maria," Mark said to her warmly. She looked up at him with her brilliant brown eyes and a wide smile crossed her face.

"Good morning, Master Mark, look who I found here this morning when I got here," she said as she gave Mark a puzzled look.

Then out from behind the counter came Sunflower, still wearing Mark's t-shirt. Mark looked surprised; he had not been dreaming. Sunflower was real. She cutely waved to him and made her little giggle sound, her face lighting up as she saw him.

"Hi, Mark, me and Maria are cookin' ya some eggies and bacon," she said proudly. She ran to him and hugged his legs. Mark reached down and stroked Sunflower's hair as reality struck him.

I must think; what am I going to do? I have to get to the hospital. I need help here. I do not have time to figure this all out now, he thought as he looked at the clock on the wall.

"Maria, can you stay here this morning and watch Sunflower for me?" Mark asked her with the same adoring eyes that usually got him his way with her when he was a child.

Maria was a sucker for helping her employer's son out in all his many times of need, and he was praying this would be one of those times.

Maria was setting the table for Mark and Sunflower. She looked questioningly at him. "Sunflower tells me you found her in the park last night. Just what do you plan to do with her?" Maria inquired.

Mark sat down at the table and Sunflower sat next to him. Both waited for him to answer. Mark did not know what to say.

"He's gonna keep me, ain't ya, Mark?" Sunflower said with self-assurance. Mark made the mistake of looking into her big blue eyes. She gave him that smile he could not resist.

I have to be strong, as painful as that might be, he reasoned, trying to find some self-control against Sunny's overpowering eyes.

"First, you're going to take me to your home, and then we will decide what to do with you, but for now, I have to get going. Maria, will you watch Sunny for me?" Mark pleaded again in a soft gentle voice.

"Sure, I would be happy to do that for you, Master Mark," Maria said half-heartedly with a broad grin on her face to let Mark know he still owned her heart. "You explain to your mother why I'm not at the ranch this morning helping her get ready for Christmas Eve," she said with a smile.

"Thanks, Maria, I can always count on you," Mark said as he got up from the table and kissed her on the cheek.

Maria noticed that he had not eaten anything. She thought Mark looked like he had lost weight. Maria had taken care of Mark and fussed over him since he was a newborn, and she was concerned that he was not eating right. She frowned as she picked up his untouched plate from the table.

Mark did not stop to notice that Sunflower's face hung low, tears forming in her eyes. He turned and went back into his bedroom to get ready to leave. Sunflower, feeling rejected, crossed her arms across her chest and hugged herself. Maria noticed the sadness that had befallen Sunflower and felt great compassion for her.

Mark hurried back in the room with his backpack in his hand. Sunflower turned towards him, and then she jumped down from her seat and ran to him, grabbing both his legs tightly. "I don't wanna go back!" she yelled. "I'll run away again and come back here!"

Mark felt her awful pain and bent down to her level. He would just have to stay a little longer; she was too upset for him to leave her like this.

"Why did you run away?" he asked her sympathetically.

"I hated it! Sara and Bill were always fighting. They had a big one, and I was scared. Bill left this time, and Sara was so drunk. I had to get out of there; I had to!" Sunflower cried as she wrinkled her sad face.

"Who are Sara and Bill?" Mark asked as he led Sunflower into the living room so they could sit on the couch and talk. Maria stood watching them from the kitchen.

"They're my foster parents. I used to live at Blanche's, the home for kids, 'til the Stanleys came and got me," she took a deep breath so she could continue. "They only wanted me for the money. I heard them say it. Sara drinks a lot and she yells at me to do all her work so she ain't got to. She don't love me. She tells me to get lost … I don't got no place left to go," she cried as she covered her face with her hands and let the tears fall.

Mark picked her up, put her in his lap, and hugged her. He let her cry, tears forming in his own eyes. He gently rubbed her back trying to calm her. She continued to whimper and shake with the fear of having to go back to her foster home. Mark knew he had to say something to calm her fears and provide her comfort. Even Maria was brought to tears by Sunflower's sadness.

"It's going to be fine, Sunflower. I won't let anyone hurt you," he said softly. "You have me now. I will do whatever I can to help you."

Sunflower stopped crying and looked into his soft eyes.

"Nobody ever loved me," she sniffled, "Can't you and I live together?"

Mark had an amazing feeling of love for this desperate little girl come over him and he knew it was incurable; he could never deny her anything. Mark sucked in the tears crowding the corners of his eyes. Tears were not something that he easily let happen to him. So what were they doing invading his eyes now as his heart unintentionally responded?

"I love you, Sunny. I'll do whatever it takes to keep you here with me." He kissed her forehead, she kissed his face, and they hugged.

Then it hit him, what had he said, those hard-to-say words, "I love you?" Those words had just slipped out before he could think to hold them back. It had been a long time since he told anyone of his love for them. Not since the day his grandfather died, when he was just eight years old.

"I love you too, Mark. Oh, and I like the name Sunny. You can call me that," she told him with new hope in her voice.

Sunflower ran to Maria who was wiping the tears away from her own face. She was ready to pack Sunflower up and take her home with her.

"Did you hear? Mark loves me and I can stay here. Oh, isn't it just wonderful!" she exclaimed with excitement as she danced up and down.

"That is wonderful, Sunflower, but Master Mark has to go to the hospital now. You be a good girl and go watch TV in his bedroom," Maria told Sunflower. Sunflower ran to Mark for a good-bye kiss and went into the bedroom.

Maria stood looking at Mark doubtfully; she needed to have a serious talk with him. She gave him her stern face just as she had done so many times before while he was growing up; he knew that look all too well.

"I know what you're thinking, Maria."

"You shouldn't have made her promises you can't keep. Just how are you going to take care of a little girl?" she level-headedly asked him.

"I don't know. I will figure something out. One thing for sure, that little girl will never suffer another day of her life as long as she has me. Before I do anything, I'm going to find out the truth about her," Mark informed her. "I know how the system works. I see its failures at the hospital all the time. That little girl is not going to be a part of that flawed system. I am going to find out who is responsible for this mess," Mark determinedly expressed.

There was nothing more Maria could say to him. When Mark Sanders made up his mind to do something, nothing could stop him.

"I can watch her for you, go, get out of here," she volunteered. Mark gathered up his things and headed toward the door.

"Thanks, Maria, tell Sunny I will be back later," he said as he went out the door.

Mark went to do his morning rounds at the hospital. Since it was Christmas Eve, he did not have any lectures. He thought about Sunny, and contemplated what he should do next. He had seen the system fail so many other children he had treated in the hospital. Mark was not one to sit back and do nothing.

He hurried back to his apartment after rounds to talk to Sunny, who was excited to see him when he walked through the door. Mark sat down beside Sunny on the couch, where she had been watching old Christmas cartoons with Maria on the television.

"Sunny, I need you to let me talk to Sara. You have to tell me where to find her, so that I can help you." Sunny was reluctant, but he convinced her to tell him the address of her apartment. She refused to go with him, so he went alone.

It was an older building in bad need of repair and paint. Mark walked down the poorly lit hallway until he came to the number Sunny had given him. He knocked. No one answered. He could hear a TV blaring inside. He knocked harder which caused the door to open enough that he could see in. Sara Stanley was lying on the couch passed out. Mark cautiously entered the room.

There were beer and wine bottles lying on the floor in front of Sara. The room was absolutely filthy. It was just how Sunny had described it. Mark felt sick to his stomach knowing that Sunny had lived in this filth. He was feeling angry and disgusted as he stared at Sara.

"Sara!" he shouted. She did not move.

Mark really just wanted to leave her lying there, but he knew that he could not. The doctor instinct in him told him to make sure she was just intoxicated. He bent over, picked up her limp wrist, and felt for a pulse. He was somewhat relieved to find one. He let her arm drop, turned, and left the apartment.

Then on second thought, he turned back around, got out his notepad from his jacket, and wrote his name and number down with a brief message to call him when she woke up. He set it on the coffee table under a beer bottle.

How could anyone let the Stanleys be foster parents? Mark vowed he would never let the Stanleys get Sunflower back.

God spoke to him to place a blessing on Sara, so he obeyed. Mark asked God to deliver Sara out of her need for alcohol. "Make her desperate for You, Lord, instead. Turn her life around, Lord, give her mercy and grace in her life."

Even as angry as Mark was for the way that the Stanleys had cared for Sunny, his prayer spoke to his own heart to have compassion for Sara.

How could he ask God for grace on his own life, if he did not give it to others?

On his way home, he stopped at a department store to pick up some things he knew Sunflower would need. He did not know anything about choosing clothes for a little girl so he asked a salesclerk for help.

He hated shopping but tomorrow was Christmas and this little girl deserved to have one. He made several other stops before going back to the apartment.

When he got home, Sunny was excited to see him, and she jumped into his arms and hugged him. Mark explained his visit to Sunny's apartment to Maria and then after giving him a big hug for support, she left.

Sunny had on her old dress since Maria had washed it for her. Mark decided to let her wear it one more day. He would save his surprises for tomorrow, Christmas morning.

He gave her one of his sweatshirts and a pair of his long football socks to cover her legs and then he gave her his warm leather jacket to wear. She looked silly, with the jacket sleeves flopping at her sides. His jacket made her feel safe as she hugged it to her body.

He took her to the park and they walked around the pond. She cheerfully talked about how much she loved the birds and the animals that lived there in the park. She acted as if nothing in her life was wrong. She skipped and danced around and sang as if she was in a beautiful make-believe dreamland. Mark could feel nothing but sympathy for her young life of misfortune. *How much had she suffered?*

Watching her, he wondered how she could be so carefree and happy after all she had suffered. She was one brave little girl, or maybe she truly just found happiness in the joy of such simple things since she knew no other life.

She certainly did not know of the life of wealth that Mark had known as a child. Maybe he could learn more about life through her.

Is that what You want me to know, Lord? Do I need to look at life differently, like when I was a child? Come to Me like a child, is what God had told His people.

I have so much to be thankful for and yet I seem to keep drifting away from those who love me. Have I become like my earthly father once was? Am I losing who I was and what I believed in? Why do I do it to myself? Why is there no true peace in my life?

He knew the answer as soon as he asked. He had put God aside these last few months. He was thankful that God had not put him aside. He knew that God was walking right there with him and had not forsaken him. It was time he stopped and listened to God, again.

Mark hated that he missed church when his football team was out of town for the weekend. He was glad that he could get tapes of the service to listen to later in the week.

His thoughts were interrupted by Sunny's tugging. "Come on, push me," she said as she pointed toward the playground.

Sunny and Mark played on the swings. Her long hair blowing in the wind suddenly reminded him of that girl from his childhood, what was her name? Mark tried hard to recall her. He stood back and looked baffled.

His father's best friend, Dan, who was also Mark's godfather, used to bring her out to the ranch with him. Mark had been told they used to have good times together. His grandfather used to tease him about his little companion, but he really did not remember her. His memory of her was vague, yet being reminded of her warmed his heart.

They had been two special friends having fun together during summer breaks. That was so long ago, but why hadn't he thought about her before now? There were things in his younger life he did not want to remember. Like the mineshaft. However, she should not be one of those memories he wanted to forget. *I wonder whatever happened to her? Funny, Dan never mentions her.*

Sunny's laughter brought him back to the present. The joy in her voice and her spirit filled him with energy. Her very presence had given him new life. Let there be joy in everything you do, came to his mind. It felt so good to be alive and laugh again.

It had been a long time since he felt he could be free to open his heart completely. With Sunny, there were no walls he needed to hide behind; she was bringing out the warmness of his true character.

The sparkling Christmas lights turned on around the park. Sunny wanted to take Mark to her church where they were having a Christmas Eve program. She wanted him to meet her friend, Sister Jessica. He was not into things like children's plays, but if it made Sunny happy, he would go.

Sister Jessica's face lit up when she saw Sunflower walk in the church. She was extremely happy to see Sunflower and warmly embraced her.

When she looked up and saw Mark Sanders standing there by Sunflower, her face went totally white. Her head began spinning from the thoughts that quickly came to her mind about Mark.

"Sister Jessica, this is Mark. He found me in the park and wants to keep me," Sunny informed Sister Jessica with a joyful voice.

Mark held out his hand for Sister Jessica to shake. "It is a pleasure to meet you, Sister," Mark smiled warmly at her as he shook her hand. She stood there in silence, but nodded her head in agreement.

Mark doesn't remember me, she thought, *he has not gotten his memory back yet.*

Sunny tugged at her skirt and she looked down at Sunny. Sister Jessica wanted out of this awkward situation, having Mark this near to her was making it hard for her to breathe.

"Mark calls me Sunny; you can call me that too, if you want."

Sister Jessica asked Sunny to dress as an angel in their Christmas play. Sunny gleefully agreed and rushed backstage to put on her costume.

Sister Jessica excused herself and disappeared behind the stage. She had a lot more to think about than this Christmas play, as her mind raced with thoughts about Mark.

Mark sat down in a pew. The lights dimmed as more and more people gathered and sat down. Mark found himself enjoying watching Sunny play the part. She really was an angel. He smiled as Sunny made him laugh with her impromptu acting abilities.

Mark noticed all the parents who were enjoying watching their children. He felt sad that Sunny had no family to treasure moments like this in her life.

Afterwards, they enjoyed Christmas cookies and juice in the social hall of the church. Sunny beamed as she pretended that Mark was her father. Finally, she did not have to stand alone as she watched the other children interact with their parents; she had Mark at her side. She reached up and took his hand in hers. Their eyes met and Mark gave her his approval with his supportive smile.

Sunny noticed the boy named John Jr. standing alone in the corner. She had met John in the park. He told her that he had run away from home several times and gone to the park. Sunny thought that if John could do it, she could do it, too. And so began Sunny's getaways to the park when Sara and Bill were fighting.

John always appeared from out behind the trees when Sunny showed up at the park. She thought he was a special angel sent by God to watch out for her.

Sunny took some cookies off the table and went over to talk to John. Mark was touched by Sunny's kindness.

Sister Jessica came over to Mark. She wanted to know more about how he had found Sunflower. She was amazed at the story he told her. She found it even stranger that he had no clue who she was.

Sister Jessica told Mark that he had attended high school with her, but Mark did not have any recollection of her.

She told him that she had been a nun for the last six years. She worked with the children at the children's home, where Sunny had lived since she was a baby.

She briefly cast her eyes away from him as she spoke of things Mark did not remember about them. There was something strange about her voice that made him feel like she was not telling him something.

Sunny came back and joined them. Mark also noticed that Sister Jessica seemed very fond of Sunny. She was extremely affectionate and fussed over Sunny with motherly adoration. Mark could see that Sunny had gotten her kind heart from Sister Jessica. Sister Jessica had shared the love of Jesus with Sunny.

Mark looked into Sister Jessica's blue eyes as she shyly spoke to him. If Mark did not know better, he would have thought that Sister Jessica was Sunny's … hmmm. No, that could not be or could it?

Mark and Sunny stopped at a restaurant for dinner. This was the first time in her life that she had eaten out. The free hotdogs from the hotdog man in the park did not count.

After dinner, Mark took her ice-skating in the park. She learned to do it remarkably fast for someone her age. By the time they got home, it was late and he quickly got her ready for bed. Sunny politely thanked Mark for the evening of fun.

"Tomorrow, I have a big surprise for you," he told her as he kissed her goodnight.

Her eyes lit up. "Oh boy, what is it?" she asked excitedly.

"I can't tell you, silly, or it wouldn't be a surprise," he laughed at her as he pulled the covers softly over her. She bowed her head and put her hands together for prayer.

"Dear Lord, thank You for giving me Mark, Lord. Thank You for answering my prayers. Please, Lord, help Mark find a way to keep me here. I promise I won't be bad no more. I will love Ya, Lord. I don't want to be cold and hungry and all alone no more like I was. If 'n Ya can just watch over me, Lord, I would be thankful, amen. Oh and Lord, whatever made that sad look on Mark's face; please make it go away. Amen." Sunny smiled at herself.

She looked up at Mark, who was attentively studying her tiny face and listening to her sweet little voice. Her delicate words to God deeply touched his heart. His subdued face flashed a smile at her. His love for her radiated out in his tender voice as she looked up into his glimmering eyes.

"That was really beautiful, Sunny, but I want you to know that God loves you even when you are not good. He will answer your prayers if that is what is best for you, if that is His plan for your life. You cannot make deals with God. Do you understand? God loves you, Sunny. I love you, Sunny," he explained to her gently.

"I love you," she said sleepily, and then she lay down on her pillow and closed her eyes. She would think about what Mark had said.

Mark stood there in deep thought.

Poor little child, she does not even know the anticipation of it being Christmas Eve and Santa coming. Instead, she was worried about where she was going to get her next meal.

Mark choked up, and inhaled the tears that were threatening to fall. Just what was she doing to him, he thought as he felt a single tear slide down his cheek.

Mark called the police station again; there were no reports on file of a missing child. Again, he hung up. *Maybe Sara really does not care that Sunny had disappeared.*

Mark knew he would have to report Sunny to the local social worker soon. This weekend was his chance to give Sunny a better life and to figure out what he could do to adopt her. There, he said it.

"Whatever it takes, even my pro football career, I will give it all up for her." Those words would come back to him someday.

What he did not know was that the fight of his life was soon to come.

CHAPTER THREE –
◦Drifting into the Past◦

*M*ark called his father that night and informed him of his situation. He told his father that he wanted to become Sunny's foster father and eventually adopt her.

At first, Mark's father was firmly against the plan. After a lengthy conversation, Robert realized that Mark was committed and there was no changing his mind without risking his newly found relationship with his son. Robert agreed to take the case to his lawyers. However, he made no promises that they would be successful in solving this complicated matter.

Mark went into his bedroom and fell across the bed. It had been a long and emotional day. Mark felt as if he had raised Sunny. There was this unexplainable attachment towards Sunny that was becoming stronger each minute that he spent with her.

Is this what a true father would feel for his child? It was the same kind of love that he had shared with his grandfather so long ago. If only that were still true, if only he still had his grandfather's love, he thought as he drifted off to sleep.

Mark Sanders was from a wealthy family. His father, Robert, was the president of an extremely successful company, one that had been handed down to him by Mark's grandfather. Robert had also been a prominent lawyer and still had full control of his prodigious firm.

With all Robert's responsibilities, there was little time to spend with his family. He often spent the week in the city, staying at the family penthouse. Robert's priorities, however, were out of order; nothing seemed important to him, except his work.

Mark's mother Julia was a beautiful and elegant woman. She was president of many of the local charities, and she had a very busy social life. She was highly respected for all her accomplishments in their community.

She was an attractive woman of grace, with a warm heart, and a smile that could melt an entire room of guests. She attended the high society functions with her husband, but her heart was dedicated to helping with the charities.

Julia exposed Mark to the needs of others at a very early age. Her gentleness and compassion was apparent in everything that she did. Mark had a very close relationship with his mother. He had her gentle ways, her compassion and her concern for others.

When Mark was a young boy, he missed her terribly when she stayed in the city with his father. Mark resented him for taking away his mother when he was younger.

Mark had one sister, Rebecca, who was four years older. She was now married to Steven Martin. Steven was a brilliant doctor, known for his exceptional abilities as a surgeon. Rebecca was a nurse. They had two sons, six-year-old Brad and four-year-old James Robert. They lived on the families' ranch in the west wing of the enormous ranch house.

Mark and Rebecca shared a very special bond and had a caring relationship growing up together as brother and sister. Rebecca had hovered over Mark his entire life. Mark loved her sons and they adored him. He was their hero, of course.

The most important person in Mark's life had been his grandfather. His grandfather had purchased the large ranch estate after retiring at the age of 45. It was here on the ranch that Mark lived as a child after his grandfather insisted that the city was no place to raise his grandson.

The city was only 35 minutes from the ranch, but Mark's father used a helicopter for transportation between their two homes and his businesses.

The elaborate ranch was enormous, with all the state-of-the-art equipment needed to breed horses and raise beef cattle. There were several stables, barns and bunkhouses.

The bunkhouses were fully furnished mini apartments that were made available for the majority of the ranch hands that chose to live on the ranch. The Sanders treated their employees with respect and saw that they had all the modern accommodations.

The ranch foreman was Pedro; he saw to the daily operations of the ranch. His wife Maria was in charge of maintaining the house and the household staff as well as assisting Julia. They had a son Mark's age, Carlo. They lived on the ranch in a small home where Mark spent a great deal of his time during his summer vacations. Growing up, Carlo and Mark pretended to be brothers. As the years passed, they developed a mutual respect for one another.

Old Charlie, a full-blooded Native American with long graying white hair, was in charge of the stables. He was an older man of small build, yet strong and wise. Charlie was a kindhearted man and was well respected by all the ranch hands.

Mark treasured his special friendship with Charlie. As a boy, Mark enjoyed hanging around the stables shadowing Charlie as he worked on the ranch. Charlie taught Mark all there was to know about ranching and instilled in Mark a love for the land and the animals.

Charlie had been with young Mark when Mark's horse, Thunder, was born. Charlie spent hours helping Mark train Thunder. It was also Charlie's responsibility to keep an eye on Mark when he was in the stables as a young boy.

The household staff included Thomas, the family butler. He too had to keep a close eye on young Master Mark, as everyone called him. His wife Martha was the head cook.

Thomas and Martha had rooms off the servant's area of the main house. Since they had no children of their own, they enjoyed spending time with Mark and Rebecca as they grew up.

Maria, Mark's Grandmother Ella and Martha were in charge of Mark's care while Mark was at the ranch without his parents. They were very fond of the youngster but were quick to provide discipline should Mark need to be reprimanded.

From his Grandmother Ella, Mark learned about God, as she was the strong spiritual leader of the entire family. One of Mark's favorite memories growing up was sitting on a church pew between his grandparents, worshipping God. Mark could bellow out a worship song as he had an excellent voice, inherited from his mother.

His grandfather taught Mark to love nature. They took many camping trips by horseback where Mark learned about fishing, hunting, tracking animals, and how to survive in the wilderness.

His grandfather was kindhearted, unlike his son, Robert. His grandfather made Mark feel worthwhile. Their love for each other was unconditional and they were inseparable.

Mark had a strong compassion for animals. He was always bringing a homeless or hurt animal home to his grandfather to be mended. Mark usually had a collection of them recuperating in the old barn, his make-believe hospital.

His father disapproved of Mark having a pet. A pet would make Mark soft and spineless; Robert had told his wife, Julia.

Life growing up on the ranch was satisfying except for the lack of love from the one person Mark needed it from the most, his father.

Robert believed in strict discipline. He did not show any sensitivity or emotions towards Mark. Robert had expected Mark to be the impeccable son. He would not tolerate anything less from Mark than perfection. He had to prepare Mark to take over the family businesses, and there was no room for weakness.

Robert's firm grip on Mark had caused Mark to rebel against him when they were together. It was not so much in being disobedient as it was in a rebellion against the businesses that took his father's attention away from him.

Robert was intensely overpowering towards Mark. He thought camping trips, nature, and God were a waste of Mark's time. Mark's adventurous spirit was not to be tolerated, Robert demanded.

While Robert was in the city working, Mark was spending most of his time at the ranch. All that stored-up energy from being cooped up with his father, in the city, made him even more adventurous at the ranch, when his father was away.

All the ranch hands were aware of Mark's risky and precarious behavior and tried to keep a close eye on him.

Mark did not seem to understand the meaning of danger. Thank goodness, Julia could call on their family friend and Mark's godfather, Dr. Dan Morgan, for body repairs when Mark found himself injured.

Then it happened, on a warm summer day. Eight-year-old Mark had left the house before anyone was awake. He had planned an outdoor adventure. Carlo had tried to talk him out of it, but Mark was determined to test his survival skills on his own. Mark rode Thunder bareback out into the wilderness to find the lost mines.

Maria was the first to discover that Mark's bed was empty. She thought he had gone to feed his collection of homeless animals in the old barn. Julia had missed him at breakfast; however, it was not unusual for Mark to eat in the kitchen with Martha.

It was Charlie who noticed Thunder was not in his stall and began to ask the other hands if they had seen Mark. When no one had, he sent word to the house for the foreman, Pedro, to come to the stables.

When Pedro arrived, Old Charlie was panicking; his fatherly intuitions had spoken to him. Mark was in serious danger. Pedro formed a search team among the ranch hands, because he thought it too early to panic the family.

Pedro was on his way to the main house to question Carlo and Rebecca when Thunder raced into the yard without a rider. It was now time to alert the family. Mark was somewhere out there and most likely in trouble.

An urgent call was made to Robert. He was in an important business meeting. "I do not have time for this foolishness; call me when you find him, and I will deal with him later," Robert angrily told Pedro and went back to his meeting.

The next call was made to Dr. Dan Morgan at the hospital. Dan quickly grabbed his medical bag and other supplies they might need and rushed to the ranch in a panic.

Dan was extremely fond of young Mark. Dan had been at Mark's delivery and held him as a tiny infant. He later became Mark's godfather. Dan thought of Mark as his own son, the son he never had.

It was Dan that had rescued Mark from Principal Quarterman's office on several occasions when Mark had gotten into some mischievous predicaments at school. Usually Mark's insubordination involved the influence of an older boy named Jeffery Kirkland.

Dan shook his head firmly at Mark on one such occasion. "Mark, if you and Jeffery ever become good friends, the world will be in serious trouble."

"But Uncle Dan, if Jeff hadn't missed the biscuit I threw, it wouldn't hit old Quarterman in the head. It was an accident." Dan tried not to smile at Mark's innocent explanation.

"I suppose it was an accident when you put the frog in the girl's toilet."

"It had a broken leg! You didn't expect me to leave it at home with a broken leg? And besides, A, put it in the girl's toilet, not me."

"Don't blame April for your behavior, Mark. You have to take responsibility for your actions." Dan held his grin at the blue-eyed boy.

There was nothing Mark could scheme up that Dan was not ready to show him grace. Mark's imaginative mind brought many smiles to Dan's face. Like the time Mark had put a note in the suggestion box, at the church, that Father Paul had read aloud to the congregation, one Sunday.

"Father Paul, Sir, if you want more people to eat your communion, you need to serve chocolate waffles; those ones of yours are stale." Father Paul smiled at Mark. "I will consider that, Mark."

Mark sat up proud, "Thank you, Sir." Robert had turned ten shades of red. But Dan, he had to hold his hand over his mouth to keep from laughing.

Dan's heart raced as he drove to the ranch to see what had happened to Mark this time.

Charlie and Mark's grandfather picked up Thunder's trail. It was not long before they found Mark in the mines where Carlo had said Mark had gone. Mark had fallen into an abandoned mineshaft. It would take hours to rescue him. Rescue workers were called there to help free Mark from his horrifying tomb.

Julia pleaded for Robert to come as she held tight to Mark's grandfather for comfort. Two hours later, the sound of Robert's helicopter was heard.

The helicopter landed in a field not far from the site where Mark was trapped. Once Robert saw the expressions on everyone's faces, he realized that this time Mark was in a serious predicament. The family gathered outside the mine and waited. They continued to hold hands and pray as the rescue efforts continued.

Grandmother Ella was beside herself so Dan sent her to the hospital where she could be monitored for her heart condition.

Twelve-year-old Rebecca and eight-year-old Carlo sat together in the family den, holding hands and praying with Maria. The entire household staff was nervously trying to find things to do. The thought of Mark embalmed in the mine took a toll on everyone who loved him.

Mark's condition was unknown. He had stopped screaming for them to rescue him hours ago. His frightened voice had torn the hearts out of those who had heard his horrifying cries, but at least they knew that he was still alive. His stillness now was unnerving. They all prayed that God had delivered him into a peaceful sleep.

The shaft was extremely wet and bone chilling cold. Dan feared Mark would have hypothermia by the time he was rescued. Dan also feared the toxins in the shaft might make Mark very sick.

Six hours later, a loud cheer was heard inside the mine and moments later, the small boy was carried out on a backboard. He was limp, dirty, wet and so cold, but he was breathing. Dan took immediate charge of his care.

Julia cried and hugged his tiny body, before the backboard was lifted into the awaiting helicopter and rushed to the hospital.

Everyone who had been at the mine gathered in a circle and joined hands as they gave thanks to God for Mark's successful rescue.

CHAPTER FOUR –
⌒The Departure⌒

$\mathscr{O}$nce at the hospital Dan assessed Mark's condition. Mark was suffering from a broken leg, abrasions, and bite marks on his legs. All realized what a horrifying experience it had been for young Mark.

Mark was extremely restless in his hospital room. He had panic attacks, screaming uncontrollably as he kicked at the bed sheets encircling his legs. He claimed that the walls were closing in on him and would tightly hold his hands over his eyes. He had terrible nightmares, but he adamantly refused to tell anyone about them.

He screamed in escalating fear as they put him in the CAT scan machine to scan his broken leg. He needed to be sedated to complete the scan. He pulled out the IV's in his arms when he felt like they were tying him down. He fretfully scratched at his arms and legs until they bled. He wanted out of the hospital immediately.

It was all Julia and Dan could do to restrain Mark and keep him in his bed. It emotionally drained them as they dealt with Mark's extreme anxiety. Dan suggested that Mark see Dr. Gina Price, a psychiatrist at the hospital.

Dr. Price explained to them that Mark was suffering from post-traumatic stress disorder and recommended therapy. She explained that Mark's outbursts were caused when he was actually re-living the traumatic experience of being trapped in the mine and seeing it unfold before his eyes or in nightmares.

Only when Mark was in the safe arms of his grandfather would he calm down. Many nights at the hospital, his grandfather slept beside him and held Mark in his comforting arms.

The ordeal of being trapped in the mine left Mark extremely fearful of small places. After ten days in the hospital, Mark was sent home with his broken leg. Even the confinement of the helicopter ride home made him fidget.

This was the turning point of Robert's intolerance for Mark's recklessness. Robert was appalled at his son's anxious behavior and his broken body. Mark no longer was a work of perfection.

Julia, however, was pampering Mark. Her heart was aching from the thought that she had almost lost him. She moved Mark into the bedroom suite next to her bedroom. It was far too large for such a young boy, but Mark felt overwhelmed in the smaller bedroom.

Rebecca sneaked into Mark's room at night and climbed into bed with him. Rebecca was determined to protect her little brother from anymore harm. She could not bear the thought of losing Mark. She believed that it was her fault that Mark had been hurt, *a burden she would carry in her heart the rest of her life.*

The staff continuously fussed over Mark. Martha and Maria brought him cookies and treats from the kitchen and the ranch hands visited him daily. All were thankful that God had taken care of him while he was in the mine.

His grandfather stayed with him during the day. He would bring Mark's homeless pets into his room. Grandma Ella cuddled next to Mark and read to him at night. His mother was never more than a few steps away from his room.

Throughout all the attention he received, Mark remained quiet and subdued, locked in a shell, refusing to return to the energetic youngster he once was. He never spoke unless he was answering a question and even then, his voice was barely audible. Mark never spoke about what had happened to him in the mine that day.

Dan came to the ranch with his eight-year-old niece to visit Mark at least three times a week after his accident in the mine. When she entered the room, Mark's face lit up seeing her standing there in the doorway. She did not have to say anything; he could read her mind as she twisted her long blonde hair with her fingers as she stared at him.

She cuddled next to him on the bed and watched cartoons with him. She was the only one who could make him smile and laugh. She would wrap her arm around his shoulder and hold his hand with her other hand. She was his little companion and a faithful friend.

Dan had been bringing her to the ranch for the past several years so that she and Mark could spend time growing up together. April was the daughter that Dan never had.

April and Mark had a very special friendship. Mark was extremely protective of her; no harm would come to her as long as he was around to protect her.

Mark shared his deepest secrets with her while they sat together in his tree house. She was the only one who understood just how he was feeling inside, yet she was also someone he could pal around with in the dirt or chase fireflies with in the warmth of a summer evening.

Carlo knew he took a backseat when she and Mark were together, but Mark always made sure he included Carlo in their adventures when she and Carlo were both there.

For weeks, Mark waited for his father to enter his room for a visit, but sadly, Robert never came. The longer Mark waited the more withdrawn he became. Mark thought he was a disappointment to his father, but he held his sorrowful thoughts inside.

The cast was finally removed and painful therapy began. Mark never complained about the pain as he worked hard to strengthen his leg. He was determined to prove to his father that he was completely healed, even better than before his accident.

It was not Mark's leg that hurt; it was his heart. His father had taken Thunder away and forbidden Mark to go to the stables. There would be no more playing with Carlo or Dan's niece.

Mark would spend hours by himself throwing a football through an old tire swing. The more he threw the football, the better he became. He had the arm of a quarterback after the summer was over.

Mark ran as fast as he could around the stables to gain more strength in his legs. Around and around he went as Charlie stood watching him. "Poor little fellow." Charlie thought as Mark peeked into the stable to see his beloved Thunder.

Several times a week Charlie put Thunder in the outside corral so that Mark could sneak a private moment with his horse.

Just before school was about to start, Robert announced that Mark would not be attending the public school. Robert had enrolled him in a private boy's school where he would live, except on holidays and summer breaks.

Robert insisted that this would teach Mark to learn respect and stop all his intolerable behavior. The pampering was turning him into a weak-willed child and he would not have his son behave in that matter.

No one could understand how Robert could say those things about Mark. Mark was respectful and well mannered. Mark was thoughtful, humble, and kind and everyone there loved him. There was nothing weak about him.

Julia and Mark's grandfather protested against the private school on Mark's behalf but Robert would not hear of it.

Dr. Price advised them not to remove Mark from the ranch. She was afraid that if they sent Mark away it would have severe consequences on Mark's emotional state of mind. Nevertheless, Robert rejected her advice without a thought. He decided that Mark would leave in two weeks.

The household filled with sorrow as the days passed by. No one could swallow the thought of losing Mark from the household.

Mark spent most of his remaining time at the ranch with his grandfather, doing all the things he wished his father would do with him.

Mark's heart was so heavy, but he shed not a tear; he would not give his father the satisfaction of seeing him be a weak child. He would face this head on; he would show his father he was strong. He was only eight years old; his father's decision to send him away was more than he could understand.

Mark said his heart wrenching good-bye to the girl behind the church building on a hot summer morning after they attended church. She had cried on his shoulder, each tear touching his heart and falling deep within his soul. He would have done anything to make her smile again. He never wanted her to cry again. Someday he vowed, he would protect her from all harm.

"Don't forget to keep the cross you made in vacation Bible school. When you miss me, read the back of your cross." She reminded him tearfully.

"I will. I know you gave your cross to your dad, but someday he will give it back to you, and you will think of me."

Little did they know how important that simple cross they made in vacation Bible school would be to them someday in their distant future, when it reappeared unexpectedly.

On the day of departure, Mark's grandfather took Mark for a walk down to the stables to say good-bye to Thunder. "I want you to listen carefully to me, Mark. Your father loves you; he only wants what is best for you." His grandfather exhaled deeply.

"I know you don't understand that right now, but someday you will. Your father works hard for you. Someday the family business will be yours, all of this will be yours, the house, the ranch, everything." His grandfather gently spoke to him.

"You will go to the best schools and get the formal education you need to take over everything, just like your father took over these things from me."

"Your father has huge responsibilities to this family, and you should be grateful; do not forget that. You be proud of the Sanders' name, for it is my name that I have passed on to you."

"Do not disgrace your name out of vindictiveness for your father; you will only hurt yourself and those who love you. Do you understand me, Mark?" His grandfather looked him sternly in the eyes to make sure that Mark understood him. Mark nodded his head in agreement.

"I love you, Mark. I never had a chance to love my son as I have loved you, my grandson. I am going to miss you very much. I will think of you everyday and pray for your happiness. Life is what you make of it, Mark. You must find happiness in your life."

"Whatever happens, know that God is in control; do not ask yourself why God does the things He does. God brings no suffering, do you understand? I want you to remember that, Mark, tell me you will remember that?" he had cried as he held Mark with both hands on Mark's shoulders. Mark promised he would remember and obey his words.

He had hugged Mark as if it were their last hug. Mark was taken back by the soothing words of his papa. Out of the unconditional love he had for his papa, Mark would remember those words, etching them deep in his heart. He vowed he would honor them for the rest of his life.

They walked back to the main house. Everyone that lived or worked on the ranch had gathered there on the front porch to bid Mark farewell.

Sadness filled the air. Mark heard the sniffling of those weeping. Mark gave them a gentle wave as he past by them.

His mother was standing by the car, trying hard not to cry. Grandma Ella gave Mark a tearful hug. She turned and leaned on her husband for support. Mark bravely walked towards the car.

Robert wanted to take the helicopter but Julia insisted that Mark was not comfortable with its confinement. Mark needed more time to adjust to having been trapped underground. Robert reluctantly gave in and allowed them to leave by the limo.

Mark turned to look at his papa. When Mark saw him crying, he ran back to him. "I can't leave you, I can't," Mark pleaded tearfully. Mark held onto his legs securely. Robert sternly walked over to them and pulled Mark's arms away and forced Mark to let go.

Mark gave in and without any further protesting, he got into the car's back seat. Robert and Julia got into the car and the doors were shut. Everything that Mark loved dearly was locked outside the doors of that limo.

Mark turned around and looked out the back window as they drove away. He saw his heartbroken grandparents hugging each other. His grandfather turned and headed back towards the stable, his shoulders hunched as he walked slowly. Each unsteady step took them further away from each other.

This was the first time Mark had seen him look so old and broken. *Papa won't be able to live without me*, Mark thought to himself. Mark lifted his small hand to wave a final good-bye. "I love you, Papa," he whispered softly.

Would things ever be the same again? Mark wondered.

CHAPTER FIVE –
⸙Thanksgiving Mourning⸙

*M*ark had gone that day and left behind the only true friends he had: the girl and his grandfather. It was true that so many at the ranch loved him, but not like his grandfather and not like the girl. No one could take his grandfather's or her place in his heart.

Dan visited the school at least twice a month to check on Mark. He was grateful that Mark was making great progress at the school.

Mark was well-liked by his instructors and classmates. He had an amazingly positive attitude for a child who had been through so much.

Mark proudly showed Dan around the school. His favorite spot was in the meadow where the horses were kept. Dan was amazed at the way the horses came to the fence when Mark called to them.

Julia had gone to visit Mark on weekends, but it was not the same. Mark missed everyone and everything at the ranch. Julia promised that he could come home for Thanksgiving break.

The days seemed to drag by slowly as the Thanksgiving holiday approached. Finally, Mark was going home. Mark was overjoyed that he was returning home to see his grandfather and everyone he missed. He was very impatient as he rode in the limo with his mother. He asked a million questions about everyone.

When the limo finally pulled into the driveway in front of the main house, Mark eagerly looked out the window and saw everyone standing there to welcome him home. He searched through the crowd but he did not see his grandfather. He was puzzled. *Where's Papa?* he wondered restlessly.

Mark jumped out of the car and ran towards the house. Everyone wanted a hug from him, but he really just wanted to find his grandfather. He stood in the entranceway and called for him.

51

"Papa, I'm here!" Mark shouted, looking in all directions. The others came in and stood quietly. Sadness covered their faces. Mark was getting anxious. Something was terribly wrong; he could read it on all of their faces.

It was his father that came to him. Robert touched Mark's shoulders and spoke. "Mark, come with me, I need to talk to you," he spoke calmly. Mark had never heard him speak in such a soft voice. He could tell something was terribly wrong by the strained look on his father's face.

His mother came to him and wrapped her loving arms around him. Now Mark was sure that something was wrong, and he knew it had to do with his grandfather.

Mark pulled away from his mother's arms and ran into the living room, shouting his grandfather's name. He was fearful as he shouted again, "Papa, Papa, where are you?" He frantically paced the floor, desperately wanting his grandfather to answer his calls.

Julia and Robert came towards him and Mark backed away from them angrily. "What have you done with my Papa?" Mark screamed at them as he narrowed his eyes in anger.

"Your grandfather has taken ill, Mark. He is in his room. Mark, your grandfather is not going to make it through this illness; he is going to die." Robert tried to explain to him. Mark shook his head at his father.

"No! No! That's not true! Why would you say that?" Mark screamed angrily, shaking his head back and forth in disbelief. Hatred showed on his young face.

Julia put her arms around him to comfort him. "I'm so sorry, Mark, but it is true. He does not have much time left," she said softly as tears formed in her sad eyes. Mark's face tightened and he looked at his father with such hatred.

"It's all your fault! He's sick because he was so lonely without me. He needed me. There was nothing for him to live for when I was gone. You did this to him!" Mark shouted angrily at his father.

"Mark, settle down," Robert sternly told him. Mark pulled away from his mother; his face was red with anger.

"Why didn't you tell me Papa was sick? Why didn't you come get me?" he yelled with his lips askew.

"Mark …" his mother tried to say, but Mark shook his head at her and then he faced his father.

"Why did you send me away? I won't go back there! I will stay here with Papa and make him better, you'll see!" Mark said with determination. All the emotions he had bottled up inside his heart started to show as tears formed in his eyes and his lips quivered.

"Mark, stop that. Crying will not help your grandfather; he is going to die, and you will return to school. It's time you accept the way things are around here," Robert told him harshly. But in truth, this was one situation where Robert felt compassion for his son.

"No!" Mark shouted through his tears, "I won't leave my papa; he needs me! You can't send me away; I won't go!" Mark screamed as he ran out of the room.

Mark ran to his grandfather's room; he hesitantly opened the door, and saw his grandfather lying on his bed sleeping. A nurse was sitting by the bed reading a book. She looked up sympathetically as Mark entered the room.

"Hello, you must be Mark," she said kindly. Mark shook his head slowly as he stared at his grandfather.

"Your grandfather boasts about you all the time. He's been asking for you, so I'll leave you alone with him," she said to Mark and then left the room.

Mark moved slowly over to the bed. He sat on the edge beside his grandfather and placed his head on his grandfather's chest and started to cry, first softly and then in streams.

"Oh Papa ... I love you ... I won't leave you ... I will never leave you ... he can't make me go ... I hate him ... I'll always hate him," Mark spoke softly, choking on his words as the tears streamed down his cheeks.

Mark was unaware that his grandfather had awakened and had been listening to his heartbreaking words. His grandfather had scarcely been able to talk but he knew he had to soothe Mark's tears.

"Mark, listen to me," he spoke quietly. Mark raised his head slowly and looked into his grandfather's loving eyes.

"Your father loves you, Mark ... you must always love him for me. He is my son, just as you are his son. The love is there, you just have to find it. ... Do what your father tells you, respect him ... you promised to remember what we talked about ... I love you ... you have made me very proud." His eyes watered and a single tear fell. Mark threw his arms around his grandfather's body and placed his head against him.

"I love you, too; please don't leave me," Mark cried, his tears slowly falling down his damp face.

His grandfather placed his arms around Mark's back and held him. He drew a final breath, knowing his end was near. *My precious Mark.*

"It will be okay, Mark … just remember … follow your dreams … and let your spirit fly," he said very weakly, trying to hold on for the young boy.

After his pleas to Mark, his eyes closed and his arms slowly lost their hold on Mark as the life drained from his tired body. Mark realized what was happening and panicked; he quickly looked up and began shaking his grandfather's shoulders.

"Oh Papa, please don't leave me!" he cried, "I need you!" The tears were streaming down his face uncontrollably. "I love you …... I love you." Mark put his head down on his grandfather's chest and wept. "I love you … you can't leave me," he cried with such heartache that his whole body trembled. He sobbed until his face was swollen.

Robert was standing in the doorway watching his father and his son share in their last moments together. Robert did not say anything; he turned and left the doorway, only stopping to tell the nurse it was over, his father was dead.

Robert had known for a long time that his father was dying of a blood disorder that had turned into cancer. That was one of the real reasons that Robert had sent Mark away. Robert had wanted to spare Mark the pain of watching the man that he worshiped and loved so much, suffer and die. Robert knew that no one could take the place of his father in Mark's heart.

Robert had even hoped that his father would die before Mark came back. Nevertheless, his father refused to die without saying good-bye to Mark; there was no other explanation for why he had not died weeks ago.

His father had gotten his wish; he and Mark had said their final good-byes. In doing so, he had left the boy with a broken heart. Would Mark ever get over this last moment in time they had shared?

Mark will just have to learn to be brave and deal with it, we all will. This will be the beginning of a lifelong trail of painful events in that boy's life, and it is my responsibility as his father to teach him to be strong, just as my father taught me, Robert thought. He did not realize he had just spoken words over his son that would haunt him one day.

Now it is up to me to raise my son, Robert thought fearfully, *can I teach him all the things he really needs to know?*

Chapter Six –
Mark's Last Tear

*D*an was the one who entered the room and stood over Mark, gently whispering kind words of reassurance. Dan patiently waited until Mark had shed his last tear.

Then, very carefully, Dan instinctively lifted the distraught child up in his safe arms and held him tightly against his chest. Mark was limp from the emotions of letting go. Mark had been defeated. There was nothing more he could do; his Papa was not coming back.

Dan gently carried Mark to his bedroom and lay beside him on the bed. Dan softly stroked the child's back as he continued to whimper. It was not long before the small boy fell asleep with an empty heart.

"Comfort him, God," Dan whispered, "Give this little boy some peace."

Dan would have given anything to take the pain away from this special child, that he thought of as his own son. He gently kissed Mark's forehead and quietly slid off the bed and went to check on the rest of the family.

Ella was sitting by her husband saying her good-byes. She appeared calm and at peace as she hummed her husband's favorite hymn. Her marriage to Mark's grandfather had been a loving relationship, one that Mark wanted for himself someday when he fell in love.

Julia was in the kitchen talking to the staff. There were many details that they needed to take care of in the coming days.

It was Robert that needed Dan's attention. He was in his office, sitting with his head bent over on his desk, agonizing over all the wasted years of pain. Dan would wait until Robert had finished grieving in private before he spoke to him.

They had been friends since childhood. Dan was familiar with Robert's tendency to hide emotions. It served Robert well in the courtroom, but Dan was troubled by the coldness Robert had shown towards his family.

Sadly, Robert had felt the lack of love from his own father. In recent years, Robert and his father had hardly spoken to each other. They had an understanding between each other that neither would step over.

It was the wealthy positions they both held. Those positions had certain guidelines or statutes that had to be executed, or so they both thought. The two men would not allow themselves frivolous emotions; at least that is the way they both had perceived it.

If only they had known that prominent, wealthy businessmen could love and live a life with emotional attachments without losing their status quota.

Mark's grandfather had found Christ in his later years when he retired from the family businesses. After years of Ella's persistence, he begrudgingly began attending Sunday church services. There, he found what he had been looking for. He received Christ with arms wide open and was able to establish a loving relationship with God.

The joyful event of Mark's birth had provided the reconnection between the two men for a brief time. Mark was welcomed as the heir to the Sanders' empire. However, Robert would seek to give wealth to Mark and his father would choose to seek love and wisdom for Mark. Both quickly disagreed on how Mark should be raised.

Robert's father had chosen to seek God and live a simpler life on the ranch, and teach Mark with gentleness. Robert had chosen to seek earthly possessions and lived a complex life. He kept a firm hand on Mark.

Before Dan could offer any comforting words to Robert, Maria was heard screaming for Robert to come. It was Mark. She was frantically screaming, "It's Mark, something is awful wrong with him, dear Jesus, come quick!" Dan and Robert rushed to Mark's room.

Julia was trying to calm Mark, but he was having such a fit, tossing wildly on the bed, tears streaked his face. He kept repeating in a terrified voice, "Get me out of here! Get me out of here!"

It did not make sense; he acted as if he was not in his bedroom. He did not seem to acknowledge anyone was in the room with him. The more they all tried to calm him, the more he tossed about wildly and kicked at them with his feet.

"Get them off me!" he screamed in a petrified voice, as he kicked, slapping his legs wildly with his hands.

"He's in the mineshaft; he thinks he's trapped in the mineshaft!" Maria exclaimed. All agreed. Everyone was extremely tense. It was so painful to watch Mark suffering. Nothing they did or said seemed to bring Mark any comfort.

"Help me ... I can't breathe ... I'm going to die ... I can't breathe!" he screamed frantically as he held his arms tightly across his chest.

"Mark, you are safe now, feel my hands on you," Julia tried to tell him.

Robert turned to Dan. Robert was grieving for his son. "Make him stop; give him something. I can't stand this, just make him stop!" Robert demanded as he grabbed Mark in a bear hug so that Mark could not hurt Julia with his wild jerking.

Dan left the room and quickly returned with his medical bag. He took a syringe and a bottle of medication out from his bag, and then he carefully measured the dose.

"Hold him still," Dan instructed and then he gave Mark the injection. As Mark calmed down, Julia took Mark from Robert and cuddled him safely in her arms on the bed. "He will sleep now," Dan told them as he felt Mark's pulse.

Dan motioned for the others to leave the room. Rebecca had been standing against the wall agonizing over her brother's torment. She crossed the room and joined her mother on the bed.

Robert sat down and they all hugged. Mark would never know of the bond his family shared in his bedroom; he was asleep.

Mark had recovered from his outburst; he had no memory of it. Over the next few days, he spent most of his time in the stables with Charlie and Thunder.

Rebecca was always nearby ready to offer Mark a hug when she saw tears form in his eyes; however, the tears never fell. To everyone's disbelief, Mark never cried again for his grandfather after that first day. They all anxiously held their breath for his next outburst.

The tailor had driven out to the ranch and fitted Mark with a black suit with a matching tie. Mark instantly hated the imprisonment of the suit and tugged at the tie to loosen its restriction on his airway.

The day of the funeral arrived. First, there was the dreaded long memorial service in their little country church. Mark sat on the pew beside his Grandmother Ella. When Mark looked to his right where his grandfather had always sat, he felt miserable as he realized that his grandfather would never again sit beside him as he had done all those years.

Where is Papa sitting now? He always said he was going to sit at the right hand of his heavenly father. Was he sitting there now?

Mark looked at the casket in the front of the church, and he hung his head so his chin touched his neck. Sadness filled his empty heart as the Mass continued. Rebecca reached her hand out and took Mark's hand in hers, but he would not look up at her.

What was it his father had told him that morning? Real men never show their emotions. He crunched his teeth together; no tears would fall from his eyes, he thought angrily, as he fought with determination to hold back his tears.

Next came the silent ride in the limo to the gravesite. Mark just took it all in stride, showing no emotions. Concerned eyes constantly watched over him.

At the gravesite, Mark stood tall beside his father, staring towards the casket as if in a trance. His father had told him what was to be expected of him, and he had been obedient thus far.

Mark could not hear the Priest's voice. His own mind was in another world remembering some of the times he and his grandfather had shared together.

Then Mark remembered the time he had waved good-bye from the limo as it drove away from the ranch and he had seen his grandfather crying for him.

Did my Papa know that would be our last time together? Was that why he gave me that long lecture in the stable? Is that why he wanted me to know that God does not bring suffering? Mark thought.

Mark wanted to scream out how unfair this was. If he had known his grandfather was ill, he would have stayed. Nothing could have made him leave. The anger was building up inside of him. The pain hit hard in his chest; he wanted to burst. He was desperately trying to hold back the tears that were threatening to fall.

Mark looked up at his father; there were no emotions on his father's rigid face. *I bet he's glad Papa is dead,* Mark thought angrily, as he bit his bottom lip with his teeth.

Robert felt Mark's squirming and gave him a stern look. Mark took a deep breath; he was determined that he would never let his father see him cry again. *I'll just pretend I'm not here.* He stood straight again as he rolled his eyes and kept them focused on the clouds in the sky.

Rebecca and Mark were given roses and together they walked forward and placed them on the casket. Mark heard Rebecca's crying; he had to shut her tears out of his mind. He looked up into the blue sky and saw a dove fly overhead.

"Good-bye, Papa, let your spirit fly," Mark whispered softly as he set his grandfather free. A light cool breeze blew Mark's hair away from his face. Mark took a memory of his grandfather and wrapped it around his heart. Then Mark locked his heart shut and made a decision never to love anyone as much as he had loved his grandfather.

Julia took his hand in hers and led him away. Robert took Rebecca's hand and they followed. Dan helped Ella from her chair and they followed behind Robert.

Mark turned back and took one last look at the casket. *Papa is all alone now. I'll never see him again.* As much as it hurt, still no tears would he let fall.

The entire ride home Mark never said a word. The minute the car stopped and Thomas opened the door, he quickly jumped out. He had all he could take. He was going to the stable to be alone, away from all these insane people.

"Mark!" his father called after him, "You need to come in the house; we have guests coming to pay their respects."

Mark stopped and slowly turned around to face his father. He put his hands on his hips and gave his father a hateful look. *Surely, he doesn't expect me to greet guests.* The look on his father's stern face told him his answer. Mark begrudgingly walked back to the house with his father.

When they went in to the house, Mark was surprised to see the large number of people inside, carrying food plates, talking and laughing. Mark weaved his way through the crowd and sat down on the stairs. He watched as people came in and out of the house.

What is this, a party? Doesn't anybody know my Papa just died? He thought angrily.

He did not understand what was going on, but one thing was sure, he did not like it!

Then he saw his Grandmother Ella sitting in a chair in the main room. She was gracefully speaking to everyone who passed by her.

Poor Grandmother, why don't these people go home and leave her alone? How can she find that peace she was talking about if no one will shut up?

Before he knew what had happened, his father grabbed his arm and pulled him into the main room and told him to stand beside him. Now all these crazy people were talking to him. They would say things like, "you are so handsome," or "you are so cute," "aren't you just adorable in that little suit." "Robert, you must be so proud of this nice young gentleman of yours."

Mark detested it all. *If just one more of those old ladies pinches my cute little cheeks, I'm going to ….* He did not get to finish that thought; Robert had nudged for him to stand up straight.

Mark turned to Rebecca; surely, she would take his side. He whispered to her, "If one more person touches me, I'm going to scream."

Her eye widened, "Hush, Mark," she told him. Disapproving eyes fell on him.

Then Mark saw her, Auntie Isabella, her hand reaching out to touch his face. "That's it; I'm outta here!" Mark started his move, but Robert grabbed the back of his collar and pulled him back. Mark was mad; his face was blowing up. *I hate this*, he thought as he squinted his eyes in anger.

Then it was Dan to the rescue. Dan was kneeling down in front of him. If anyone cared, it would be him. Before Mark knew it, he had fallen into Dan's arms and put his arms around his neck. Dan held Mark with affection, wishing with all his heart that he could take away Mark's pain.

"Uncle Dan, my grandfather's dead, doesn't anyone care? I don't want to be here; take me away from here," Mark pitifully pleaded, his tears were just begging for him to let them spill from his eyes. Dan's agonizing heart was instantly torn by Mark's broken heart. Dan's eyes filled with heartfelt tears for the young boy.

Dan looked up at Robert and then stood up to face him. "Robert, I think Mark has had enough, why don't I take him home with me for awhile?" Dan asked Robert with great concern for Mark's emotional state.

"Mark's place is here with his family," Robert replied firmly.

That was it; that was really it, no more! Mark steamed. "No, it's not, I hate this! Why don't you people all go home and leave us alone!" he had yelled as he ran from the room. This time his father was unable to grab him. Instead, Robert looked back to the guests who were staring at him.

"I apologize; my son is very upset about his grandfather's death." Everyone shook their heads in agreement; "poor child" was heard throughout the room.

Mark had run out to the stables. He tore off the insufferable jacket and tie, and angrily threw them in a heap on the hay. He opened the door to Thunder's stall. Thunder was resting in the hay.

"You miss Papa, too, don't ya, boy?" Mark sat down in the hay and rubbed Thunder's neck. Thunder seemed to sense Mark's excruciating pain and bent his head towards Mark and then nudged Mark with his wet nose. Mark wrapped his arms around Thunder's neck and hugged him.

There came a dainty voice. "Mark." Mark turned to see Dan's niece standing there looking down at him. Her face was covered with compassion as she looked into his heartbroken eyes.

The brilliant rays of sunlight peeking in from the window above fell on her gently, making her appear as an angel as she stood there waiting for Mark to reply. She pulled her long blonde hair to her back and stepped into the stall with Mark. She quietly knelt down by him; she too started rubbing Thunder's mane.

She did not have to say anything. Their blue eyes met and each shared the pain of losing one so dear to them both. Mark leaned over and embraced his dear friend.

This would be the last time he would openly cry about his grandfather's death. She held him in her loving arms and he let the tears fall one at a time down his cheeks. She wished with all her heart that she could take his pain away.

Her tenderness at that very moment would not be forgotten by his heart. *For she alone would own his heart forever.*

If two children could have loved each other while so young, their special love for each other would have lasted them a lifetime. If only this had not been their last childhood encounter together, life would have been so different for Mark, and for her.

In Mark's mountain of pain, he was determined never to let anyone claim his heart again. But for her, no matter where Mark was, or how far away he went, her heart would follow after him, he would be *"forever in her heart."*

Once again, Dr. Gina Price asked the Sanders to reconsider and let Mark return home where those that loved him could nurture his broken heart. She stressed that Mark had suffered a terrible loss, and it was sure to add to the anxiety he was already experiencing. Robert disagreed; Mark needed to move on with his life, not stay at the ranch and dwell on his loss.

Mark returned to the boarding school the following Monday. He did not care; there was nothing left at the ranch for him. It would be too painful living on the ranch without his grandfather to share it with him.

And the girl, as much as he was afraid of loving her, she still held a special spot in his heart. No matter how hard his mind would try to forget her, his heart would never let her go. She would be *"forever in his heart."*

Besides, the boarding school was what his father wanted and he had promised his grandfather he would respect his father's wishes. He willingly left, only to return for vacations. The bitterness he felt consumed a part of his heart he would never let anyone enter into.

Mark had been an excellent student and excelled at everything he did. He developed his love for sports in the fourth grade. By the beginning of his eighth grade, he had surpassed the other students in academics and in sports. He had a drive for greatness that controlled everything he did, yet he did it with amazing humbleness.

It was decided by his father that Mark should take summer classes at the local college to further advance his knowledge.

The painful memory of his grandfather's death seemed to be fading as the years passed. Mark did not have time to think about that painful time in his life. He would fill his life to the fullest to keep out the pain.

Mark had only one goal: to be more successful than his father. He would make his grandfather proud. He would show them all.

CHAPTER SEVEN –

❧Returning the Son❧

It was growing harder on Julia and Rebecca to be apart from Mark.
Julia had become fragile and emotional. Her heart cried out for the
little boy Mark once was. Mark seemed so different, so grown up, so sure
of himself and independent.

Julia worried about the pressure Mark was under from Robert to be
successful. She wanted Mark to have a more normal life. She wanted to
teach him to love again. He was to come home, she demanded of Robert
after Mark's eighth grade graduation.

Rebecca and Mark had stayed close during his vacations at home. She
had deeply missed Mark while he was away at school. It was as if half her
heart was missing when he was gone.

Now she was going off to nursing school. Rebecca worried about her
mother's fragile condition and approached her father about Mark returning
home.

It was decided, much against Robert's approval, to allow Mark to
come home in his freshman year and he was enrolled at the local high
school in August. Mark was under strict requirements and guidelines from
his father and warned not to disobey, or he would be sent back to the
boarding school.

Robert's company was in the beginning stage of a merger, and he spent
most of his time now in the city. This allowed Mark his freedom to make
his own decisions about what he wanted to do at the ranch.

Mark joined the football team in his freshman year and was quickly
given the position of starting quarterback. It was not long before he was
breaking team records, and articles about his achievements were printed

in the local newspaper. He excelled in basketball and baseball. He maintained a 4.0 grade point average as well.

Although he was the top athlete, and exceedingly good-looking and popular, Mark never let his success go to his head. He was meek, kind and humble. He was a good friend to everyone at the school and showed no discrimination. His closest friends tended to mimic his gentle nature with other students.

Mark was known for tutoring his classmates who needed extra help. If another student was tormenting a classmate, Mark stood up and defended the underdog. Because of Mark's tall athletic build, most bullies backed down from him instead of risking a fight with him. Mark was not a fighter, but he would defend what he thought was right.

The coaches were astonished at Mark's physical strength and his natural abilities. He had the leadership skills and the virtue the team had lacked.

The other players respected Mark's dedication to the team and admired his devotion to them. They voted him the team captain in every sport he played, a responsibility Mark took very seriously. *It was not unusual for Mark to continue playing after an injury that would sideline most players.* He would not let his team down no matter what.

The old country church had closed and Mark went to a new church with his Grandmother Ella. This Christian church was different from his old church. People of all denominations and backgrounds gathered to worship God in a way that Mark had never experienced.

There was plenty of love among the members. It felt like one big happy family when everyone gathered. The youth group was outgoing and the fellowship among them was a great inspiration to Mark.

God began speaking to his heart, and he accepted the Lord as his savior. With that decision, he found a new relationship with God. The bitterness in his heart completely disappeared and he glowed with the joy of having God first in his life. He wanted the Holy Spirit to live within him.

He also wanted his friends to know the Lord as he did. He wanted to be a good example to his friends so they would join his youth group. If his friends saw all the things God was doing in his life, he hoped that they would want what he had and make the same decision to be saved. It was not long before his church youth group grew larger.

It was Julia and Dan who supported Mark in all his different sports, going to all his games to cheer for him. It was not unusual for his cheering section to include Pedro and Maria, Thomas and Martha, and Charlie. Mark felt honored to have them in attendance. Their love and support meant a great deal to him.

Robert was never in attendance, but Robert could read. Everyone in his office had either seen Mark play or had read about him in the papers, and Mark's achievements were the talk of the office. Mark was their hometown hero. What better way to impress your boss than to speak highly of his son, his employees thought?

Robert would have demanded that Mark spend more time studying and less time in sports but with all the commotion about Mark in his office, he was forced to allow Mark to continue. Deep down Robert was proud, but he would not acknowledge it.

By Mark's junior year of football, college offers for scholarships were pouring in. TV stations were asking for interviews. He had received all kinds of outstanding awards. Through all the attention, Mark remained humble. He always gave rightful credit to God and his teammates.

Mark was even described by his teammates as being extremely shy. Mark did not like all the attention he was receiving. He wanted to stay out of the commotion and remain private. He did what he did because he loved it, not to get attention.

Without seeming conceited, Mark had also made it clear to his friends how he felt about smoking, drugs, and drinking. If you are living for God, then those things did not fit into your life anymore, he would tell them. This was his personal choice, but since he cared deeply about his friends, he hoped they too would choose to refrain.

Mark added that he had worked too hard in sports to mess it up with those things. That reasoning, he thought, would relate more to the players who had not found the Lord yet. He never passed judgment on those who did stray. Instead, he prayed for his friends daily, as he grew each day in knowing the Lord, himself. He still had a lot to learn.

There were other things in life one could get high on, and Carlo had introduced it to Mark soon after he had returned home. Mark put his horse aside and learned how to ride motorcycles. During the summer months, Carlo and Mark would ride together.

Once again, Mark also had a natural talent in his ability to ride. He started entering races with Carlo. Even though Carlo had been racing for years, Mark was soon beating him.

Mark had no fear; he let out his uncontrollable urge to be reckless when he rode. There was something about the openness that drew him to this sport. His wild side for adventure was renewed when he rode.

Many times, he rode in the pastures with no helmet, letting the wind blow his hair away from his tan face. He would even take his hands off the handlebars, hold them out shoulder length and declare his freedom.

Carlo was afraid of Mark's fearlessness and his wild actions. Mark had not been this wild since childhood. *I guess he can't be serious in everything he does,* thought Carlo. Still, Carlo did not like the fact that Mark took too many dangerous chances.

One day Mark's lack of caution would cause an accident, Carlo feared.

Thank goodness, Mark had not even gotten a scratch, *so far.*

CHAPTER EIGHT –
↬Remember When↫

*I*t was just before Mark's senior year started. Football practice was in full swing. Mark had moved up into a higher dirt bike class and even had sponsors paying for his ride. Life seemed great. He had learned to relax more and enjoyed the things he was doing.

To keep his father happy, Mark had continued his classes at the local college during the summer. He spent time with Dan at the hospital after deciding that he might want to go into medicine.

Mark followed Dan around as if Mark was an intern. Mark conducted himself very professionally for a seventeen year old. He soon earned the respect of the many doctors he would later shadow.

Besides racing, Mark had not had time to hang out with the gang. Carlo had been away with his cousins most of the summer. Mark was ready to catch up on all the news from his friends and wanted to spend some time with Carlo now that he was back.

After practice, Mark and his friends had gone to Bryan's Pizza Joint. Bryan's was the main hangout for the high school crowd. The players sat at a round table, laughing, talking, and watching the girls who entered. Pitchers of cola and round pans of pizza covered the table.

The guys kept talking about the new good-looking girl on the cheerleading squad. She was new at the school; she had come from a private girl's school. Her dad was some weird wealthy man; Carlo had informed them. Mark did not seem interested in this conversation; he was busy eating his third piece of pizza.

Although they had all asked her out, she had turned them all down flat. Heads turned towards Mark, and they laughed and pointed at him with devilish intentions. All of them had asked her out except one - Mark Sanders.

"What?" Mark looked at them questioningly and they just smiled at him. Mark could hear the mischievous planning going on inside their clever minds.

"Oh, no way. I don't have time for some girl whose dad is a maniac," Mark informed them with a half laugh, as he continued to eat his pizza.

"But you haven't seen this girl yet," Carlo said as if he knew something more about her. The rest agreed with Carlo and smirked at Mark.

"I'm not going out with her!" Mark tried to convince them firmly. He contemptuously raised his eyebrows in disapproval of their teasing.

"Don't be so sure; you'll be surprised when you meet her," Carlo grinned and gave the other guys a thumbs-up when Mark wasn't looking in his direction.

The other guys continued to smile in an amusing way as they whispered to each other. They were obviously taking pleasure in whatever they were planning against Mark. Mark just smirked at them as he ate his pizza. He knew he would have to watch his back; he knew these guys all too well.

Mark and Carlo had left together and had driven back out to the ranch.

"Let's go horseback riding this weekend," Carlo suggested.

"Sure, it will give us some time alone to catch up. I'll meet you at the stables at ten o'clock," Mark had agreed.

Saturday came and Mark waited in front of the stables for Carlo. *What is taking him so long?* Mark wondered as he placed his cowboy hat on his head.

He wore a skintight long sleeve t-shirt that well-defined his muscular shoulders and the biceps of his arms. He had on blue jeans and cowboy boots. In his hands, he held his thick leather riding gloves to protect his quarterback hands.

He looked up towards the main house and saw a limo approaching the driveway in front of the house. *That's odd, why does Tony have the limo out today?*

Then Mark saw Carlo get out of the limo followed by two teenage girls. One of them Mark knew, Sharon Johnson, Carlo's new girlfriend. Mark did not recognize the other girl.

Even from where he was standing, he thought she was beautifully shaped in her tight blue jeans. Then it hit him, he knew what Carlo was doing. *Okay, so I've been setup, this must be the new cheerleader*, Mark speculated with a humorous smile.

As they walked closer, Mark noticed that she seemed very shy. She glanced at the ground a lot as they walked towards him. Her long blonde hair flowed out from under her cowboy hat, down her tiny shoulders, hiding her face somewhat.

When she got closer to him, she slowly raised her face to meet his and pushed her hair back. She was standing there face to face with him. No words were said. Mark was astounded; he could never have forgotten those gentle blue eyes. They took his breath away the second he looked into them.

It had been ten years, but there was no mistake, this beautiful young woman was his childhood love, Dan's niece, April Morgan.

She certainly was not the pigtailed tomboy he remembered. Had it really been ten years since they shared that private affectionate hug in the stable?

April was refined and proper looking, and yes, she was not a little girl any longer. She was stunning and had grown into a beautiful young woman. What had that private girl's school done to her? Would she be the same girl he had loved as a young boy? He certainly hoped so as his heart beat faster with the anticipation of renewing their friendship.

They continued to stare at one another, each thinking about times spent with each other as children. They had their precious memories locked in their hearts. Her eyes were holding the key to unlocking the love he instantly felt for her.

Sharon approached Mark for a hug, her arms embraced him, but his arms remained at his side as his eyes stayed locked on April. Sharon retreated from Mark's rejection and gave Carlo a smug look to tell him to stop grinning from the pleasure of knowing he had brought Mark and April together again.

Finally, Carlo broke the ice. "Are you just going to stand there and stare? Say something, Mark," Carlo urged as he nudged Mark in the ribs with his elbow.

"I can't believe it's you, A," was all Mark could manage to say as he continued to admire April's graceful beauty. April smiled sweetly and extended her arms out to him and they embraced. The hug seemed awkward to Mark. He was flooded with feelings for her that he never expected.

"It's so good to see you again, Mark," she said softly as she let go. Just feeling Mark's muscular arms around her told her that he was not the little boy in the stables. He was a young man. He was so handsome and so strong looking. He was flat out irresistible. She just wanted to melt.

"Ok, this isn't going anywhere; let's go ride horses," Carlo declared, afraid that if he did not do something, Mark and April would stand there all day gawking at each other.

They all went into the stable where Charlie had four horses saddled and ready. *First Tony, now Charlie, who all was in on this plot to bring April and I back together? Yes, probably Dan, too,* Mark wondered. Mark raised his eyebrows and smiled.

Mark was the perfect gentleman as he helped April mount her horse. He felt her tiny waist in his hands as he lifted her up onto the saddle. He knew he was in deep trouble as the very touch of her flooded him with emotions. She politely thanked him.

They followed the trails out into the woodlands. At least this gave them time to think. Talking had been so awkward. Boy, did Mark need time to think. He was sure April was doing the same.

She rode in front of him. Her long blonde hair shining, like pure gold, was blowing in the wind. She had him mesmerized by her beauty. He could not wait to be closer to her.

Mark tipped his cowboy hat sideways as he held the reins with one hand; a wide grin crossed his face. He smiled deeply thinking that the guys had finally pulled one over on him, and this time, he was not going to object.

The guys had been right; he was about to step out and claim her as his own. He gently kicked his horse to move forward so that he could ride along side of her. Her bashful eyes greeted him.

Mark remembered their close relationship as children. April's long blonde hair and beautiful blue eyes had captured his attention even then. How *sweet-natured* April had always been with him. They had been insep-arable as children. Would that happen again?

Mark remembered the look on April's face that she gave him when he did not get his way. That look of hers always put him in his place, Mark thought with a smile. Mark would gladly have her look at him that way again.

Could they reclaim their relationship with each other or had they grown up into two different people? Where had she been all this time? Why had Dan never mentioned her? His special little companion was what Dan and Grandfather had called her. He suddenly realized how much he had missed her all these years.

When they arrived back at the stables, Mark quickly dismounted his horse, took her reins from her, and reached up to help her down from her horse. She slid into his strong arms, her body touching his as he held her briefly against him and then he let her feet touch the ground. Their eyes were so close that he felt his body quiver as she knocked down his walls and opened up his heart to love again.

He was no longer afraid. He was older now, and he wanted her friendship more than the fresh air that surrounded his lungs. He took her in his arms and confessed how much he had missed her.

She politely smiled and stepped back. His touch against her delicate skin sent waves throughout her body. She could not let him step over the line of being just friends, at least not today.

He walked next to her as they headed back to the house. They exchanged memories of their past life together with laughter. Mark asked her where she was attending church and invited her to his church. When they reached the limo, she politely thanked him for the wonderful time she had horseback riding.

Tony held the limo door open and she bent and got inside. Tony shut the door and she was gone. Mark stood there, not knowing if he could breathe without her.

Mark had wanted her to stay so they could talk, but she insisted that she and Sharon had to return to her home together. What was the big deal, Mark wondered? Why had she acted so mysterious when he questioned her about her life? Rebuilding their friendship was not going to be an easy task if she acted as reserved as she had today.

Mark found out that Sharon's brother Phil was married to April's sister, Debbie. The marriage had met with the disapproval of April's father, Paul.

Paul was Dan's brother, although the two were nothing alike. Paul was ruthless and disagreeable. His business was considered mob-like, and it was speculated that he might be involved in illegal actions.

Dan had taken April under his wings when she was younger just as he had done with Mark. Both youngsters had lacked the love of their fathers and needed Dan to step in and love them.

Dan had brought them together in hopes that they could share their heartaches and become friends.

April had been sent away to a girl's boarding school not long after Mark had been sent away by his father. Paul had prohibited Dan from taking April to the ranch when she returned home during her summer breaks.

Paul would not allow April to attend church anymore with her Uncle Dan. Once the old church closed, Dan had moved his membership to the same church as the Sanders. Paul had moved his family to a different church.

When April got older, Paul had forbidden April to date anyone without his approval. Paul even had April followed by one of his assistants to ensure she was not sneaking around as her sister Debbie had done when she was April's age.

Once high school classes began, Mark found ways to corner April in the hallways so they could talk. He would meet her at her locker between classes. She would lean against the lockers as he stood over her with one hand placed on the locker above her head.

Gradually April eased up to him and let her guard down. They sat together at lunch and talked. At football practice, they began meeting at the water fountain to see each other.

She joined his church youth group on Wednesday nights. It was not long before Mark convinced her to give her heart to Jesus.

They found ways to be together without anyone knowing so that they could talk. Often, they met and sat on the football stadium bleachers. Mark would fill her in on his pastor's latest message. It was not long before they could share their deepest thoughts with each other just as they had done as children.

It was the perfect friendship between a gal and a guy, nothing more. Mark was very careful not to put them in a situation that would change their friendship.

Although as time passed and their friendship grew deeper, his feelings for her changed. He now longed to hold her and kiss her tender lips, but he retreated before temptation became too great. Neither spoke of their secret desires of wanting more than friendship from the other one.

Mark could not call her house, but when she was at her sister's house, she called him and they talked for hours. April insisted that their friendship must be kept secret from her father. Why, Mark wondered? Would he not meet with her father's approval? However, Mark was glad to have any time with her that he could get.

April was deeply in love with Mark, but she kept things between them subtle. She did not want to emotionally hurt him or have her father physically hurt him. She knew Mark did not meet with her father's approval.

A hotshot jock is what her father had called Mark, when Paul read about Mark in the newspaper at their breakfast table one morning.

He sternly looked over at April. "That is Robert Sanders' kid, and I do not want you hanging out with him!" April had been warned, and she knew her dad meant it. She would have to be more careful when she went to Mark's youth group meetings.

In the past, Robert Sanders and Paul Morgan had unpleasant business deals with each other. The feeling for each other was mutual: hatred. There was never to be anymore talking about Mark Sanders in his home. Even if Mark was the spoiled kid his brother, Dan, seemed to care about, Paul wanted none of Mark.

April had been heartbroken, but she would never tell Mark how her father felt. She knew he was already hurt by his own father's rejection. She would stay best friends with him, but never encourage anything else between them.

Mark knew he was in love with April since the day she arrived at the stables. He could not get her off his mind. Sharing his faith with her was very important to him. She was eager to grow in her relationship with God, and they felt comfortable talking about God with each other.

It soon became harder and harder to be just her friend as their relationship continued to deepen. He finally asked her out on a real date. But she refused to go on a date unless the entire gang tagged along with them, and they went only as friends.

This insistence on being just friends and only going out if they were with a group of friends was not going to work. Most of his friends acted immature when they went out as a group. Mark wanted to act mature when he was with April. He took his love for her seriously.

Seeing April everyday at school only made it harder as he fell deeper in love with her. He wanted more, something as simple as holding her hand and letting the whole world know they were a couple.

Once at lunchtime, he reached out to take her hand, and she pulled it back from him as she looked away from his confused eyes.

"Mark, please, let's just be friends," she insisted despondently as she gently pulled her hand from his, got up from the table, and left him there feeling rejected.

From that day on, the only thing Mark could do was avoid her. It hurt his heart too deeply, only having half of her in his life. Besides, he reasoned, he had to keep his mind on football; too much was riding on his success this year.

However, when football season was over, whether April Morgan liked it or not, he was going to pursue her. He would win her heart.

CHAPTER NINE –
⮜Eternal Flame⮞

*M*ark had qualified for the state finals in motorcycle racing. It was quite a shock to Mark's mother when he finally told her that he had been secretly racing his motorcycle for the last three years. All this time, she thought Mark had been going with Carlo as part of his racing team. She had not realized that Mark was racing his own motorcycle.

Julia nearly fainted, when she thought of the danger Mark had been in. It was bad enough worrying about Carlo, but now Mark. For the first time, Julia interfered and begged Robert to stop Mark's racing.

Surprisingly, Robert had not said anything to Mark. Carlo's father, Pedro, and Robert had already discussed Mark's racing. Robert had put Pedro in charge of monitoring him.

Robert had read all the articles about Mark's accomplishments in sports in the local paper. The football team was heading for the state play-offs. Mark's picture had been on the front of the paper on several occasions.

Dan had been putting pressure on Robert to attend Mark's games. It was time he got involved in the things that were important to Mark, Dan had told Robert. Mark's eighteenth birthday was approaching; there would not be much time left before Mark was off to college, Dan had warned Robert.

After that conversation, Robert had been secretly attending Mark's football games with Dan. Robert would even sit on the visitor's side of the field so he could go undetected. Robert was proud of Mark. Nevertheless, he still could not surrender his pride and admit to Mark that he had been wrong about football.

Robert was still determined to have Mark follow in his footsteps. Mark had expressed his desire to be a doctor like Dan and had even taken classes in the medical field during the summer. He also spent more time at the hospital with Dan, who was thrilled to have Mark at his side at the hospital.

Robert's goals for Mark were not about to change. He did not want Mark to take a football scholarship; he wanted Mark to take one of the many academic scholarships Mark had been offered.

With professional football teams making offers, Robert was fearful that Mark would pass up college and go pro. Robert could not encourage that. Football was not an option for his son. Even the thought of Mark going to medical school did not satisfy Robert.

Another thought concerned Robert. Mark was inheriting millions of dollars and the entire ranch from his grandfather, on his eighteenth birthday. Mark's grandfather had turned over his business assets to Robert but everything else would soon belong to Mark.

Mark had no idea that he was about to become very wealthy. He would have the responsibility of operating the ranch and managing his wealth all too soon.

Robert had known this since the reading of his father's will. Robert would oversee Mark's inheritances until Mark reached eighteen. He had been afraid of telling Mark before his eighteenth birthday, because he feared that Mark would take control of his own life before he turned eighteen.

Friday night after Mark had led his team to another victory, he joined his friends at Bryan's Pizza Joint to celebrate. They were all wearing their football jackets and having a great time, laughing it up, reliving the game and stuffing themselves with pizza.

The cheerleaders came in and joined them. April had made eye contact with Mark, but said nothing. How could he eat with April across from him; his heart ached to be alone with her. He had missed their long conversations on the football bleachers.

If only he could get April away from Sharon, Christy and Jessica, he might stand a chance with her. Frustrated, he threw his pizza down on his plate and looked away. If he could have gotten up and left, he would have, but he did not want to appear rude. He felt uncomfortable for the rest of the evening.

When Mark got home, his father was waiting for him. Mark walked in and saw his father standing there. The last thing Mark wanted was a lecture about being so late; he was definitely not in the mood for another one of his dad's dull lectures.

"I'm sorry I'm late, Sir. Carlo and the guys wanted me to go out with them after the game to celebrate our win tonight," Mark said calmly. "I guess I lost track of time."

"Have you been drinking?" Robert inquired sternly, as he looked Mark over from head to toe and frowned.

"Of course not," Mark assured him. He hated it when his father disapproved of his clothes. They had had many discussions about his football jacket and blue jeans. They certainly were not the desired clothing for someone of the Sanders' status in the community to be wearing; Robert had enlightened Mark on several occasions.

"I just wanted to remind you of the social gathering your mother and I have planned for your birthday. All our close friends and my business associates will be there. This will be your introduction into the business," Robert informed him.

"Sir, I told you, I am not going into the family business right away. I've decided to play college football and go to medical school," Mark reminded Robert as he stuck his fingers in the pockets of his football jacket and stood to one side.

From the look on his father's disapproving face, Mark knew they were about to argue. Mark hated confrontations with his father; they were pointless. Robert frowned at him, and Mark submissively stood up straight.

"The party is at eight," Robert evenly said. Mark was surprised at his father's unusual calmness.

"I had plans to go out with the guys for pizza that night," Mark told him politely, not wanting to provoke his father's unreasonable temperament.

"Change them; I want you to meet these important people. You will be eighteen, Mark. It is time that you meet the people you will be dealing with when you join the company or the firm," Robert's voice raised a notch as he sternly made his point.

"But ....," Mark tried to say as he lifted one shoulder.

"Those friends of yours are beneath you. It is time that you stop wasting your time doing foolish things with them. I will expect you to wear your tuxedo and be prompt, do you understand?" Robert expressed firmly, his eyebrows lifted forming stress lines across his forehead.

"Yes, Sir." Mark caved in with a quiet moan. He turned and left the room, ending their conversation. Just as he thought, it was pointless trying to talk to his father.

At times like this, Mark wished that he had not made those promises to his grandfather so many years ago. He remembered that emotional moment in the stable like it was yesterday, and he had not forgotten his grandfather's wise words.

What more would he have to do to earn his father's approval? Mark was not going to give up his friends. It would serve his father right if he went out drinking with them instead of going to his father's glorified social party.

I have tried to be the perfect son, and that was not good enough for him. Maybe it is time that I act like kids my own age and live a little. It is time for him to see what I could have been doing with my life all this time. That would really give him something to disapprove of, Mark thought sorrowfully.

As quickly as those thoughts came, Mark was reminded of his grandfather's wise words about vindictiveness. Once again, Mark would decide to honor those words given to him by his grandfather. They were the last words he had heard cross his grandfather's lips.

Mark thought of that painful day as he lay across his bed in the dark. He turned on his side, placed his pillows around him, and hugged a pillow against his chest. He had to fight back the tears as he thought about his grandfather. Then he thought about his distant relationship with April.

Mark could not sleep, as his feeling of loss tore at his heart. In the last ten years, he had refused to shed a single tear. There was no way, tonight, that he would give into the tender heart that God had restored when he had been saved. Crying was still not an option. "Yeah, Dad, real men don't cry."

He silently sneaked out of the house and drove to the cemetery. He reached into the glove compartment and got a flashlight.

The iron gates had been locked so he climbed up the brick wall and flung himself over the top and jumped down on the other side. He looked around to see if anyone had seen him. Then he ran between the tombstones until he reached his grandfather's marker.

He rubbed his hand tenderly over his grandfather's engraved name as he bent down on both knees and faced the stone before him. He sat back on his legs, bowed his head and prayed.

Single teardrops softly trickled down his face as he closed his eyes, and thought of the man who had helped form him into the man he was becoming. The unfairness of his grandfather's death when he was so young still hurt deeply. He angrily brushed away the uninvited tears.

The wall that he had placed around his heart threatened to rebuild itself as he pondered his father's comments about real men never showing their emotions.

Mark sat down and leaned against the back of the stone, and that was where the groundskeeper found him sleeping the next morning.

Mark had done the honorable thing and precisely at eight o'clock, he appeared in his tuxedo. His dark blonde hair had been cut and styled. Mark was handsome and distinctive looking as he entered the room and took his rightful place at his father's side.

Robert held up his hands to get everyone's attention. "I'd like to thank everyone for coming here tonight for my son's eighteenth birthday. Most of you know Mark already, but for those of you that have not had the pleasure; I would like to introduce you to my son, Robert Mark Sanders, the third." The guests clapped as Mark gave them a wave of acknowledgement.

Mark's eyes met his father's eyes. This was the first time Mark could remember his father publicly acknowledging to being his father. Uncertain feelings took him by surprise. Just as Mark thought his father might actually have feelings for him; Robert held out his hand for Mark to shake. It had been, what appeared to be, a gentlemen's handshake, nothing more.

"Happy Birthday, Son," Robert conveyed formally.

"Thank you, Sir," Mark responded politely, still in awe. They looked into each other's searching eyes. Most of all, Robert wanted to tell Mark how much he loved him. However, the words would not come, and Mark feeling rejected, had already turned away.

Robert had admired the way Mark had conducted himself so maturely. Mark had taken his rightful place among the power and wealth of their guests.

From across the room, Mark saw Dan, but it was not Dan that caught his full attention, it was April. At that heart-stopping moment, she turned and looked straight at Mark.

She was breathtaking in an exquisite white gown that wrapped tightly around her tiny waist in a fitted bodice and gently tapered to a flared skirt that draped down to the floor. It was sleeveless with tiny straps that went over her soft shoulders. The gown was delicately embroidered and detailed in beading.

He saw the soft rays of light, from the decorative chandeliers above her, dancing across her body. As the light caught each curve, her silhouette echoed the reflections of light in the beads on her gown. She was truly a revelation of a princess and *she was in his castle*.

Mark thought his heart was going to jump out of his chest. He had never seen such beauty and elegance. There was no stopping him, as he knew that this young woman would soon belong solely to him.

The soft romantic music began to play. Mark gracefully crossed the room to April. He looked lovingly into her sparkling eyes. Then he took her hand gently in his and led her to the middle of the room. Mark knew how to dance well; Julia had taught him when he was just a child.

At first, they danced with open arms, looking into each other's glowing eyes. She was mesmerized by his very being. She melted as his loving eyes pierced her heart. April could feel Mark's warm breath when he held her closer to his shoulder.

There was no need for words. The magic of the music floating all around them was all they needed to express the way they felt for each other.

Mark was lost in her captivating eyes as she took him to the stars and then to heaven. His heart was exploding from the love he felt for her. All his walls came tumbling down as she opened the doors to his heart. He knew that this was a love deeper than he had ever known, and he would never let go of their love as he held April in his heart.

How elegant and romantic the pair looked as they danced with such grace. Neither noticed that they were the only ones dancing on the dance floor. Each step they took together was refined and beautiful. The truth of their love was seen in their eyes.

The entire room of guests stood admiring the young couple. Dan was tearful, Julia was crying, and Robert smiled proudly.

Neither spoke. They did not have to say anything; their eyes did all the talking. Mark gathered her in his engaging arms, putting his hand around her tiny waist and drew her closer to him. The softness of her body embraced his body. Her warm breath on his neck filled the deepest part of his soul with pure joy. No longer did they feel awkward, for they were joined as one, in perfect harmony. April prayed the music would never end.

April lifted her head from his shoulder and looked up into his warm inviting eyes. Her perfect, alluring lips spoke to him, and he bent his head close to hers. "May I kiss you?" he asked so tenderly. April shook her head in agreement. Their warm lips touched softly, joining them together in an unimaginable bliss. Her first kiss, she was about to faint. He seemed to sense her legs going weak and held her tightly in his secure arms.

He touched the side of her face with his fingertips and slowly slid them softly down her tender cheek. He was so in love with her. He wanted to spend the rest of his life holding her in his arms.

The sweet taste of her kiss, her soft hair against his cheek, her enchanting eyes and their hips slowly swaying as one to the passion of the music were igniting his desire to belong solely to her. There was no turning back his feelings as he bent and asked for a second kiss to seal their love forever.

April felt like a princess at a ball. Her *prince* was in her arms. Oh, how many times had she dreamed of a moment like this with him? How many times had she cried herself to sleep thinking she would never have the man she truly loved with all her heart?

Could Mark hear or feel her rapid heartbeat against his chest? Did he know that her heart beat to the same rhythm as his? He lifted her fingers to his moist lips and kissed them. Did he know that the touch of his hand against her skin, his deep blue eyes that pierced her heart, the delightful smell of his skin, was what took her breath away as she leaned into his kiss? *Please do not let this feeling end*, she prayed.

If only it could last forever. If April's father found out that her Uncle Dan had escorted her to this social party they would both be punished. April would not have dared to come if her Uncle Dan had not insisted.

April had exposed her true feelings for Mark to her uncle. She knew of Dan's special relationship with Mark, and she trusted her uncle with her feelings. If anyone could bring them together, it would be her Uncle Dan.

These last few weeks without Mark's friendship had torn her heart into a million pieces.

The love that the two had shared as children was reunited during this blissful moment. Their love filled the room as they danced cheek to cheek. The magic of the music filled their hearts with their *endless love* for each other.

They never spoke the words they were feeling for each other. When the music was over, April backed away and politely thanked Mark for the dance, and excused herself. She quickly turned away from him and rushed tearfully into the arms of her Uncle Dan.

The other young women bidding for a dance with him quickly surrounded Mark. He was desperately looking in the crowd for April as one of the girls named Jessica took him hostage and joined his resistant hands into hers, forcing him to dance with her.

April knew deep down that Mark could never be hers. She had stepped over the line and allowed him to steal her heart. No longer could they just be friends; she had taken that away from them when she had allowed him to kiss her. April knew that she had to let him go to save them both.

Robert had seen the approval on everyone's faces as they watched Mark hold April in his arms. Mark had won over his friends with ease that night and had conducted himself maturely. *Why can't I just tell Mark how much I love him?* Robert thought, feeling disappointed in himself.

Mark looked over at his father and saw him staring at him with that worried expression on his face. *Don't worry, Father,* Mark thought to himself angrily, *I won't embarrass you in front of your friends.*

Mark resented the way his father was scrutinizing him. If only each of them had known what the other was feeling. If only Mark knew how wrong he was about his father's feelings for him.

Mark broke Jessica's hold on him and politely excused himself from her. He stood on the dance floor looking around for April but she had disappeared. She had left without even saying good-bye. She may have gone, but the warmth of her lips against his still remained. His first kiss would not be forgotten, he thought.

Mark disappeared from the party and went to join his friends.

Chapter Ten –
The Night He Might Never Remember

*T*hree weeks later, it was the State Championship Football game. Mark was so pumped for it. But since his birthday, he had been feeling uneasy. He was restless and could not sleep. So many important things were happening in his life that it was hard to focus.

Mark had not talked to April since the night of his party. She was avoiding him, leaving his troubled heart vulnerable. April intentionally did not invite Mark to her eighteenth birthday party. That had been a direct hit on Mark's dejected heart and knocked the wind out of him, until Carlo told him that during the cutting of her birthday cake, April had burst into tears and left her party.

Could her unguarded tears have belonged to him, he wondered with the slightest surge of hope. Maybe she had thought of their romantic birthday dance together and profoundly missed him at that moment.

Mark anxiously waited for her to join him for lunch but she never came to their favorite table. Her face seemed sad and withdrawn as he secretly observed her from a distance.

Sharon sadly advised Mark to give April some space while she figured out her emotions concerning him. Sharon also returned the unopened notes Mark had written to April.

No matter where April was, she was still in his heart and constantly on his mind. April filled his thoughts as he lay on his bed in the dark trying to figure out what had happened to them.

She had stolen his world, right out from under him, and there was no patching up the empty hole he felt inside, without her. She was a mystery that he just could not figure out. *What am I doing wrong?* he agonized. Mark needed to know; he needed April back in his life.

Mark dreamed of holding her securely in his arms and talking to her for hours as they shared their innermost feelings for one another. He had a memory of her etched in his soul, and not an hour passed by that he did not affectionately think of her.

Then just before the Championship game, April had come to the locker room door in her cheerleading outfit and waited for Mark. The second he looked into her deep blue eyes, he was pulled into her very soul. Tears formed in her eyes as she timidly spoke to him and leaned so close to him that she sent his mind spinning out of control with his love for her. She wished him luck in the game and was gone before he could utter a word.

Excitement filled the cool air. This was it; this was to be Mark's final high school football game. The game was on local TV. Reporters had swarmed Mark all week long. College scouts had met with his coaches. Professional football scouts would be there. The stands were overflowing. Mark's entire family was coming; even the ranch hands would be there.

Mark knew his entire football career was on the line tonight. He was excited as he waited for the game to start. Finally, he would prove to his father how good he was. He was laughing and getting the players pumped for the game.

The coach told Mark that Julia was outside the locker room and needed to speak to him. Mark knew the second he looked into her disappointed eyes that something was wrong.

She regretfully informed Mark that his father had been called out of town to an emergency business meeting with William Triplett. Robert had sent his best wishes for Mark to have a great game, she told him as she gave him a supportive hug.

Sure he did, Mark thought angrily. *I have worked my whole life to prove to him that I am worth taking the time for, and he cannot show up to see me play in a State Championship Football game. The whole world is here to see me play, but not my father!* Mark thought with such resentful anger.

Mark was so infuriated with his father that he slammed one of the lockers with his fist. His teammates were confused by his sudden anger. Mark rarely got angry at anything. Mark was always in a good mood and cool-headed. Nothing seemed to bother him. He was not conducting himself as he normally did before a game. What had changed, his teammates wondered.

Something was definitely not right with Mark, his teammates thought, as they watched Mark continue to act frustrated. Would he get himself together before they went out on the field?

Someone had better have a talk with Mark; where was Carlo? However, Mark had already bluntly told Carlo to mind his own business when he had tried to talk to Mark. Mark had never spoken that way to anyone before.

When the team came together in the pre-game huddle, the coach asked Mark to pray. Mark said the prayer with little emotion, but he gave the team a full blessing. His teammates were even more concerned for Mark.

What were they going to do if Mark did not get his act together? They realized now, how much they depended on Mark to be the backbone of their team.

It was time to take the field. The team lined up around their coach for last minute instructions. They could hear the screaming fans from the locker room as they made their way out of the room.

Just as they feared, Mark played with no passion in the first quarter. He did not attempt to pump his team up, as he normally would have done during a game. He stood quietly on the sideline, his hands firmly placed on his hips, while the other team had the ball.

Julia anxiously took hold of Dan's hand and prayed for her son. Robert deserting Mark, tonight of all nights, was inexcusable, she thought with great sadness. Dan's eyes showed the same unfathomable concern for his godson, wishing that his presence at the game could have been enough for Mark.

The defense on Mark's team began struggling against the other team's offense. The coach angrily called Mark over to him. Mark quickly obeyed and respectfully faced him. The frustrated coach began screaming in Mark's face to make something happen with his team.

After the defense gave the opposing team another first down, the coach grabbed Mark's helmet and yelled, "You're the captain of this team; get us out of this mess!" Mark could see the anger in his coach's eyes as he held Mark's helmet. "The stands are full of scouts, Mark! You have to turn this game around."

Mark understood the coach's frustration. Mark knew the coach would need him to excel at offense to keep the game close.

Mark paced back and forth on the sideline. He was frustrated that the opposing team was having such a negative impact on his team. Mark said nothing, but he was obviously discouraged, which was something the other players had never seen him express.

Mark's devotion to the game and to the team had always been what took them that extra yard. It was unusual that their most valued player did not seem to have his head in the game.

It was not that Mark played poorly; he was doing very well. He just did not exert himself as the team leader as he normally did. There was no excitement in his voice as he called the plays. There were no encouraging words. He was strictly business, angrily telling the other players to do their job and get themselves out of this mess.

When Mark threw an incredible forty-five-yard pass for a touchdown, he did not celebrate it. He walked off the field and went over to the water jug. Grabbing a cup of water, he gulped it down and threw the cup in the trashcan angrily. *Dad missed that one*, he thought with anguish in his heart that his father was not there.

April had noticed how subdued Mark was acting. She felt it might have something to do with her and knew she had to talk to him. She waited until he had sat down on the bench away from the team.

Mark had taken his helmet off and was sitting there thinking about the game. He felt bad that he was letting his anger come to the surface during such a crucial time. He realized that he was the one that was holding the team back. Instantly his heart sunk, and he felt remorse. Still, his heart missed the one person that he had hoped to impress. He had wanted with all his heart to gain his father's respect tonight.

April came up to the bench and stood behind him.

"Mark, is something wrong?" she asked tenderly. He turned and looked at April. There was concern in her warm eyes for him.

"Only you would understand," he said to her. She remembered other times in his younger life when he had been unresponsive.

"It's your father. He's not here, is he?" she responded sympathetically.

"Nope," Mark replied with frustration. "He didn't show up."

"But I did … I love you, Mark Sanders," she said as a tear fell from the corner of her eye. She had exposed her heart to the man she loved more than her life.

Mark stood up and faced her. His heart filled with joy when he heard those tender words cross her lips. Without thinking, he put his hand behind her head and pulled her to him. He kissed her lips softly, savoring the sweetness of them against his. Love was glowing in his eyes as he let her go. April had lit his flame, and he was on fire. She was all that mattered to him now.

"Meet me after the game, in the park," he said eagerly. She bit her lip, and then nervously nodded in agreement.

Mark was thrilled she had agreed. That simple nod of her head injected his veins with pure jubilation. Her love had saved him and not a minute too soon as he recaptured his dreams of winning her and this game.

She smiled at Mark, and that very smile gave him the boost he needed to get his head back in the game. Mark returned her smile and excitedly turned to join his team on the sideline.

April stood stunned. She hoped that her father's assistant, Lewis, had gone to get a hotdog and had missed her kiss with Mark, otherwise, she knew she was in deep trouble. However, at this particular moment, she really did not care because she loved Mark Sanders.

"What's wrong with you guys? You look like a bunch of deadbeats; let's get pumped," Mark shouted at his teammates. "We've got a State Championship game to win!"

That promissory kiss was all it took. Mark played the best game he had ever played. His team won the State Championship, and Mark had been the hero of the game.

Mark stopped briefly, knelt down on one knee, and thanked God. He knew his victory tonight belonged to God alone.

It was time to celebrate. Mark was so pumped. Nothing mattered. He had won the game for his team, and April had agreed to meet him in the park. Life did not get any better than this!

Mark had not planned what happened that night after the football game, which would change his life forever. He and his friends had celebrated all night long, breaking all the rules that Mark firmly believed.

Mark would not remember all of the events that occurred that night, not until much later in his life, when his memory would come back to haunt him.

CHAPTER ELEVEN –
⌒The Race to Finding a Son⌒

*S*aturday afternoon, Mark woke up on his bed, not knowing how he had gotten there. He had no memory of what had happened the night before. His head hurt, his body hurt. He stumbled when he tried to walk and ended up falling back across his bed.

How did I end up like this? he wondered with disbelief. *Why did I let myself get plastered last night?* Mark had no memory of the night after the game. In fact, he was not sure who he was at this appalling moment. He thankfully passed out again as a wave of pain struck his head.

Thomas and Martha were glad that Robert was not expected to be home until Sunday morning. Julia was visiting her parents and would not be back until Sunday afternoon.

Martha covered Mark with a blanket as Thomas removed Mark's boots. Thomas grinned remembering the first time he had gotten a wee too tipsy at Mark's age. He was surprised that Mark had not found himself in this delicate situation before now. Robert surely could drive the best of them to drinking.

Sunday was the day of the State Motocross Championship Race in which Mark would participate. Carlo was pulling Mark out of bed at six a.m. and drowning him in the shower, clothes and all. Mark loudly protested as the stone cold water hit him in the face.

Next came the black coffee, which Mark threw up soon afterwards. Dan had been called at seven a.m. to come doctor him. Dan skipped the lectures on drinking, skipping church, and went straight to treating Mark's condition. By noon, Mark was feeling well enough to leave for the motor-cycle track.

Dan had stayed behind at the ranch to wait on Robert so they could attend the race together. He looked down at his watch anxiously and frowned. *Would Robert disappoint Mark again? How many more rejections could Mark take?*

Round One of the qualifying races was about to begin. Mark was ready to do what he had to do to win this race. Carlo helped him adjust his helmet and put his gloves on.

Mark wanted to win the first race to get a good starting position in the final Championship race. The noise of the motorcycles was deafening as they lined up at the starting line.

Mark looked up in the stands where Dan always sat. He had hoped that Dan would bring his father with him. He did not see them anywhere and felt a rage of disappointment. *Even Dan has abandoned me.* His heart was pounding but not from the excitement of the race.

Unwisely, Mark did not care about his life anymore. *I am going to win this race if it kills me. Who would care anyways?* he thought despondently. The blood in his veins was pumping as the starting gun went off, and he exploded with full force down the track.

Mark raced dangerously, taking chances that could have been disastrous, to advance his position in the race. The crowd stood on their feet cheering as he crossed the finish line in first place. Mark gave Carlo the thumbs-up as he crossed the finish line.

Carlo looked faint as Mark came back to the holding area. "Are you crazy?" Carlo yelled at Mark, "You are going to get yourself killed if you race like that again!"

Mark totally ignored him as he threw his gloves and helmet on the bench and kicked the dirt on the ground with his boot in frustration. Carlo frowned at Mark as he began checking the bike over and preparing it for the next race.

Mark went over and sat on the back of the trailer to gather his thoughts. A dove landed in front of him and walked around the dusty ground without any fear of Mark's presence. Mark intensely watched as the dove circled around on the ground. A cool breeze blew through his hair, and Mark felt peace for those brief minutes as he watched the *Dove*.

Rebecca and her husband, Steven, were watching the race on ESPN at the hospital in the Emergency Room. Excitement filled the room as Mark won the first race and the doctors and nurses cheered wildly. Rebecca did not share their enthusiasm as she left the room. She only felt relief that the race had ended, and Mark had survived in one piece.

Dan and Robert had taken their seats in the stands just before the race had ended. They gave each other a high five as Mark crossed the finish line.

Dan and Robert sat down, waiting for the next race.

"Mark really missed you Friday night at the game," Dan explained to Robert, hoping to put guilt where it belonged.

"I wish I could have been there," Robert expressed with deep regret. "There wasn't any way that William and I could have missed that important meeting." Robert failed to mention that the meeting had caused Dan's brother, Paul Morgan, a million dollar loss in his company.

"Mark was hoping that you would come to this race."

"Why? I mean nothing to him. He doesn't even care if I'm alive. It's you, Dan, that Mark wants here cheering him on."

"That is not true; Mark wanted your approval before your father died. Mark needs your love now more than ever. Don't put it on my shoulders because you are failing as a father; do something about it, Robert."

"I just don't know how to relate to Mark. I love him, but I can't seem to say it when I am with him," Robert reflected with sadness.

"Admitting love is not a sign of weakness. Mark is your son, Robert. When are you going to start believing that is the truth?" Dan responded as the two men searched each other's eyes, knowing exactly what that statement had actually meant.

"When I look into those sad eyes of his, I see how disappointed he is in me as a father. He never looked at his grandfather that way; Mark really loved my father. I could never be what my father was to him," Robert expressed with disappointment.

"Don't let your pride stand in the way, Robert. Tell Mark you love him, let him know you stand behind him, or you may lose him completely someday," Dan warned Robert. "Mark does love you. He would forgive you, Robert, if you would just put your pride aside and ask him."

Robert remembered the night of his son's birthday. He remembered the way Mark had appeared that night in his tuxedo. Robert had known that all Mark had really wanted to do, that night, was to go out with his own friends and celebrate his birthday. Just like Mark, he had been obedient. He had honored his father's wishes.

Robert had been proud of Mark's noble behavior among his associates. He realized that he had feelings for Mark that he had never let himself admit, as he stood back and admired the man that Mark had become.

Robert had been jealous of his father, even more jealous of Dan, for the relationships they had developed with Mark. Mark was his son, he loved him and it was time that he showed it.

Robert knew how important this race was to Mark. For the first time in his life, he wanted Mark to know he was there supporting him. *Maybe somehow if Mark knew I was here, he would want to win even more*, Robert thought. *This time I will not let Mark down.* Robert stood up as the race was about to begin.

The sound of the starting gun went off and the race began.

"I have to let Mark know I'm here," Robert told Dan as he started to make his way down to the bottom of the grandstands, with Dan chasing after him.

The race was exciting. Mark finally gained the lead after some daredevil moves. The crowd jumped up and stood on their feet.

Mark leaned the bike completely sideways as he rounded the curves, dragging his boot in the dirt. Then he shot down the track at full speed, flying over the hills like a jet airplane.

At the hospital, Rebecca covered her eyes for a second until Steven told her Mark had made it out in front. Many of the ER staff were standing there watching the race on the television in the emergency room. Most of them knew Mark and cheered him on.

Robert and Dan made it to the edge of the track. Carlo spotted them and waved them over to where he was standing so they could get a better view. Mark passed again and nearly skidded his bike into the tires that surrounded the track's edge.

"He's too reckless, Dan; he's going to hurt himself!" Robert yelled over the noise of the bikes. Robert was becoming anxious as he watched Mark dangerously race. Suddenly he felt frightened for his son's life. Winning was no longer important to him.

There was one lap left. Mark was neck and neck now with another rider, with several riders close behind him. They were racing around the corner, kicking up dirt into the air and headed for a steep jump. They shot off the hill high into the air. Mark knew he had the win. He looked over for Carlo as he always did.

Dan and Robert were at the sideline by the final jump. Robert was leaning over the ropes and yelling as he waved his hands back and forth to get Mark's attention. Mark had pulled ahead and was about to win as he flew high over the final hill into the air. He was feeling exhilarated seeing the checkered flag waving at him.

"Mark, be careful!" Robert yelled. Mark did not hear him. But as Mark looked for Carlo to give him the thumbs-up for winning, he thought he saw his father. In that split second, Mark turned his head back to get another look.

Confused, Mark lost his concentration and forgot about his landing. He came down forcibly, losing control of his bike. He flew over the handlebars and slammed to the ground at the bottom of the hill just past the finish line.

The bikers behind Mark could not avoid him and they struck him with extreme force, landing on top of his defenseless body.

At the hospital, Rebecca screamed and then fainted when she saw what had happened. Everyone in the room was in shock.

"NO! MARK! NO!" Robert screamed, as he watched in horror as the other bikes battered Mark.

The racetrack workers rushed onto the track, waving off the remaining bikers. But the damage was done. Mark's crumpled body lay motionless in the dirt.

Robert's heart was pounding, what was only seconds seemed like eternity as he frantically reached his son's side. Carlo had beaten him to Mark and slid to the ground beside his friend. Carlo was in disbelief, as he feared for Mark's life.

"Don't touch him!" Dan yelled after Robert, as he hurried to Mark.

God, please let him be alive, Robert prayed.

"Don't move him! Someone get the ambulance over here now!" Dan instructed. Carlo jumped up and went for help.

Mark was lying over on his side; he was in extreme agony. The pain was relentless. He tried to move, but the slightest movement caused him to scream in pain. Robert and Dan knelt over him, trying to keep him from moving.

"Mark, can you hear me? Dan, do something!" Robert yelled. Dan was carefully examining Mark for injuries the best he could as Mark screamed out in pain with every touch of Dan's hands.

Mark was struggling with his breathing. His helmet was in an awkward position and was cutting off his airway. Dan knew he had no choice but to remove Mark's helmet so that he could provide Mark with an open airway.

"Get the backboard and a neck brace," Dan ordered the track attendants, who quickly brought them to him. The paramedics were helping Dan. Robert held Mark's helmet in place as Dan instructed him, as the others held him tight.

John Andrews, one of the paramedics, placed the neck brace around Mark's neck carefully. Then Dan was extremely careful as he slowly removed Mark's helmet while everyone held Mark steady. Once they had enough clearance for the neck brace they secured it in place. Then Dan removed the helmet completely.

They placed the backboard beside Mark. "Watch his left arm and left leg; they are broken," Dan directed his orders to the men.

"Don't touch me!" Mark screamed as Dan held Mark's neck while the others took their positions.

"On the count of three ... one, two, three!" Dan instructed.

Slowly they turned Mark over onto the board. It was not slow enough for Mark as he screamed in anguish. Dan lifted Mark's jersey to listen to his heartbeat and to listen to his lungs; a worried look came over his face. Mark's face was strained with excruciating pain.

Robert moved closer to Mark so that Mark could see he was there. Mark saw the tears welling up in his father's eyes. Mark had difficulty talking; the pain he was experiencing was heard in his winced voice.

"I guess ... I ... finally found it," Mark spoke softly as his emotions escaped, remembering what his grandfather had told him about finding his father's love.

"Grandfather ... said ...," Mark had tried to explain, but before he could finish, he lost consciousness. Robert panicked.

"Dan, is he alive?" Robert shouted with a fearful voice. Dan was already rechecking Mark's vital signs, little relief showed on his face as he looked at Robert.

"He's alive, but we have to get him out of here fast or he is not going to make it." Dan went over to the ambulance and called Life Star on the radio. Then he hurried back to Mark's side.

"I've called Life Star; they are on their way. Let's move him into the ambulance so I can start working on him."

Together they lifted the backboard with Mark on it and carefully put him in the ambulance.

Dan placed an oxygen mask over Mark's face. Then he took the large scissors and cut through Mark's motorcycle jersey. He hooked Mark up to the EKG machine and started an intravenous line in the vein in Mark's right arm.

John struggled to remove Mark's protective gear as Dan cut through Mark's motorcycle pants. When Dan saw the broken bone in Mark's upper left leg, he was thankful that Mark was unconscious. There was a lot of blood pouring down the side of Mark's leg, so Dan quickly slowed the bleeding.

John started to remove Mark's left boot, but once he discovered blood inside of it, he decided to wait until they were at the hospital. He put a splint on Mark's broken arm.

Thank God, Mark had on protective gear; he never would have survived if he had not had it on, Dan thought. *Would Mark survive? It was up to God now.*

Dan removed Mark's motorcycle gloves and out fell Mark's bracelet. Dan held Mark's penicillin allergy medical bracelet in his hand and squeezed it, then he began praying for Mark.

The hospital's helicopter landed, and Mark was quickly loaded into it. Dan went with him. Mark was rushed to the hospital where Dan worked. When they arrived at the hospital, Rebecca and Steven met them on the landing pad. A team of nurses and doctors were ready for him in the trauma room.

Robert had called his helicopter pilot, and instructed him to bring Julia to the racetrack, before he picked up Carlo and himself. When they landed at the hospital, they rushed to the emergency room.

They waited impatiently outside Mark's exam room as the minutes ticked by on the wall clock. It seemed like hours, as they stood there eager for word on their injured son.

Rebecca came out with an update on Mark's condition. She had to catch her breath before she could speak, but instead of words, tears erupted. Robert sympathetically held Rebecca in his arms and let her cry. "Mark is hurt so bad," she cried as her heart ripped into tiny pieces for her younger brother.

The elevator doors opened and their butler, Thomas and his wife Martha, followed by Pedro and Maria, came out. Charlie stayed behind with Grandmother Ella at the ranch, while Ella called all her friends, to start a prayer chain for Mark, before she and Charlie went to the hospital.

Finally, Dan came out of the room. He looked exhausted and his face was wet with perspiration. Mark's bloodstains were on his clothes from when he had worked on Mark in the ambulance.

Dan instantly embraced Julia when she came to him. She placed her hands on the blood stains, knowing the blood belonged to her son.

"His left arm is broken, he has a compound fracture in his left leg and ankle, several ribs are fractured and he has a punctured lung. It is not good; as soon as we can get a CT scan, we will know more and get him into surgery for repairs." Dan broke the devastating news to them with a strained face.

Dan was concerned about other potential complications but he felt it better not to tell them until he knew more. They were still waiting to get Mark to CT scan.

"Can we see him?" Julia pleaded as she tried to stay calm.

"He goes in and out of consciousness. They are preparing him for surgery, but I'll let you see him for just a minute," Dan said as he opened the door so they could look in and see Mark. Steven was attending to Mark as Rebecca held onto her brother's right hand.

Mark lay motionless. Robert scanned Mark's body, which was only covered from his lower waist to above his knees. Oxygen prongs were in his nose. IV lines were in his arm. Drainage tubes punctured his chest. His left arm was splinted. His left leg was wrapped in thick bloodstained gauze and lay in a splint. His ankle was wrapped in an ace bandage that was covered with blood.

Robert held Julia around the waist, afraid that she might faint when she saw Mark. Slowly they moved forward. The others stood at the door.

Mark was semi-conscious when they went to stand beside him. Rebecca gave Mark's hand to her father. Mark opened his weak eyes. He tried to move his head back and forth, but the brace held him in place. His forehead had been taped to the backboard.

"Mark, don't move your head," Steven told him sternly.

Julia bent over his face, and he was finally able to focus his eyes on her. She tried to keep from crying, but the tears dropped slowly.

"Don't cry, Mom," Mark said softly, the pain was still heard in his voice. He turned his eyes and looked at Robert.

"Thanks for … coming to … the race," he choked out.

"We love you, Mark," Julia told him as she leaned over and kissed his forehead.

"I love you, Mark," Robert said with a lump in his throat. Mark noticed the tears forming in his father's eyes. "I love you, Son, please just hold on and fight," Robert said as he patted Mark's hand with his.

Mark had never seen such compassion on his father's face. Mark remembered the words his father said to him many times in the past, "Real men do not show their emotions."

"Dad …" Mark tried to talk but the pain he felt at that exact moment overtook him and he had to draw a deep breath to recover. A tear trickled down his face as he tried to squeeze out the pain. He tried desperately to hold back his tears in front of his father.

"Dad, it hurts … it really hurts … bad," Mark finally managed to say, slurring his speech, thinking his tears would disappoint his father and make him think he was being weak.

Robert wiped the tears off Mark's cheeks. "I know, Son," Robert said gently, "it is all right to cry, Son."

Julia bent down, brushed back his hair and kissed Mark's forehead again.

Rebecca wiped the tears from her eyes as she witnessed this heart-wrenching scene. She watched as Steven ran a needle down the bottom of Mark's right bare foot. There had been no movement. Steven and Dan exchanged fearful looks.

"Mark, what hurts?" Dan asked him, puzzled.

"My arm, chest and my head." That had been Mark's response; he did not mention his mangled leg and ankle. They had not given him enough pain medication to stop his pain entirely. They became extremely worried that Mark was becoming paralyzed. Dan's heart sank as Mark continued to deteriorate before his eyes.

"I'll go call CT scan again, and see what is taking them so long," Steven said to Dan, trying not to alarm anyone in the room.

Mark seemed to be less alert. He began struggling with his breathing. When he opened his eyes, they showed panic. He reached his right hand up to his forehead. His teeth clenched together, he squeezed his eyes tightly closed. He was quiet then. Robert watched the monitors for any signs of distress.

What is taking Steven so long, thought Dan. Five minutes passed. Mark opened his eyes quickly. Terror was written all over his face as he became restless. Dan feared a panic attack and quickly moved to hold his head in place.

"I don't deserve to live …!" Mark screamed, "What have I done to A …."

"Don't say that, Mark; why would you think such a thing?" Robert asked.

"I didn't mean it …" Mark exclaimed remorseful.

"Mean what?" Julia questioned him. He was not making any sense.

"I just want to die … let me die!" Mark shouted. He was wrenched with guilt. He was becoming combative. Dan held his head tighter. Mark was twisting his chest up and down. Dan feared a brain injury. "Get me out of here!" Mark screamed at them, as he imagined the dark wet walls around him.

"Mark, you have to calm down and be still," Dan cautioned him sternly. Julia covered her face with her hands in anguish. Mark continued to battle them with his violent jerking. The nurses struggled to hold him down on the gurney.

Steven had reentered the room, and when he saw what was happening, he grabbed Mark's arms firmly and restrained them to the gurney. Mark tried to pull free of the right arm restraint. "Get them off of me!" Mark screamed through clenched teeth. In his mind, he was kicking his feet violently, yet they never moved off the bed.

"Get them off me!" he continued to scream as if something was attacking his legs.

Steven quickly spoke to the nurse. She handed him a syringe, and Steven injected it into Mark's IV. Slowly, Mark stopped jerking and lay still.

The monitor keeping track of his oxygen level went off; Mark was having trouble breathing. Everyone rushed into place. Mark lost consciousness.

Rebecca took her parents' hands and led them outside the room. She did not want them to see the doctor inserting an endotracheal tube down Mark's throat to help Mark breathe.

"Is Mark going to be all right?" Robert asked Rebecca.

"They will put a tube down his throat to help him breathe," she informed him through her tears.

They waited by the door. The hallway and waiting room had quickly filled up with concerned students, teachers, coaches, family members and church family. Word had quickly spread about Mark's accident. Many had seen it live on TV.

The football players stood together in unity, but none spoke. The girls from the cheerleading squad also huddled together. April stood alone in the back, leaning against a wall for support.

"God, I can't breathe," April prayed. "I can't lose him. My heart is ripping in two." She slid down the wall slowly and hid her face in her knees.

She had seen the accident on TV: the young man she loved, hit repeatedly, until he lay lifeless. "God, please don't let Mark die; I can't live without him," April said through her tears as she twisted the ring that hung on a gold chain around her neck. She was riddled with guilt, thinking this was all her fault. Sharon, Christy and Jessica came over to her and offered her comfort.

Dan came out and spoke softly to Robert and Julia.

"Mark is stable. We are taking him to have a CT scan, and then we will take him to surgery to repair his broken bones," Dan informed them. "You can wait in my office; I see the waiting room is full. You can call your parents from my office and update them on Mark's current condition."

Mark was wheeled out into the hallway. Julia bent and kissed Mark's forehead. The nurse was squeezing the ambu bag, delivering oxygen into Mark's lungs through his breathing tube. Robert patted Mark's shoulder. Then Mark was quickly taken from them. Julia buried her face against Robert and cried.

A surgeon came to explain one of the surgeries Mark needed. It was called an open reduction internal fixation of the left leg. This surgery involved the use of metallic devices inserted into or through his bone to hold the fracture in a set position and alignment while it healed. There was a danger of infection and soft tissue damage.

The surgeons would work jointly to put Mark back together. All knew how important it was to restore Mark's body back to normal so that he could pursue his promising football career. They gathered in prayer before the surgeries began.

Mark was in surgery for six agonizing hours. The waiting room remained full until word came that Mark was in the recovery room. The surgeries were successful. He was in stable condition.

Their prayers had been answered.

CHAPTER TWELVE –
A Father's Guilt

Six hours was a long time for Robert to wait. He paced the floor in Dan's office and walked the halls. He was beside himself. He finally turned to Julia who had been resting on the couch in Dan's office.

Robert looked at his wife, Julia, with anguish written upon his face. "It's all my fault!" She looked up at him and shook her head no.

"Yes, it is, I called to him … he was looking at me when he wrecked. I caused this to happen to him! Don't you see, he was so shocked to see me there, that he lost his concentration and crashed," Robert told her in anguish as he paced back and forth.

"Robert, stop," Julia spoke softly.

"I wish I were on that table; it should be me, not Mark!" Robert admitted as he pounded his fist on Dan's desk.

"Robert, this is hard enough, don't blame yourself," Julia replied as tears welled up in her eyes. She wished that her parents would arrive quickly; she could not handle the thought of losing Mark or deal with Robert's insaneness by herself.

"If Mark lives, he will never forgive me for making him crash and ending up here all broken up," Robert continued.

"Don't say that; Mark would never blame you for this," Julia responded as a tear escaped from the corner of her right eye and slid softly down the side of her face.

"Why did I have to wait till now to tell him I loved him? Did you see the look in his sad eyes? They cut through me like a dagger, to see all that pain pouring out, pain I caused him. What have I done to my only son?" Robert went on and on, guilt ridden.

"Oh, please, Robert, say no more," Julia cried in a desperate whisper. She covered her face with her hands and wept into them.

Robert continued to pace the floor, shaking his head back and forth, trying to reason with his conscience.

"What was he talking about, wanting to die? He said he did not mean to. What was he talking about?" Robert inquired. "Did he think he was in the mine again?" Julia did not answer; she had wondered the same thing.

Mark had not had a panic attack for a long time. He had seen Dr. Price when he was younger and learned how to deal with his feelings when he felt an attack coming on. Julia did not think that Mark was remembering the mine; he was very upset about something else. *But what could Mark have done to be remorseful for doing? Had something happened they did not know about?*

"All I wanted him to say was how much he loved me. I wanted to hear it for the first time since he was a young boy. I wanted to know my son loved me, but he did not say it," Robert said as he wiped his eyebrow with his trembling fingers. If Mark died, he would never know if his son had forgiven him.

Julia looked at him. "Mark loves you; I know he loves you," she tried to convince her tormented husband.

"No, Julia, he loves you, he loves Rebecca and Steven, he loves everyone and everyone loves him!" Robert held up his arm and pointed towards the hallway. "Didn't you see all those people out there praying for him? I have never given him the chance to love me. I let Dan be his father. Mark wants to be a doctor like Dan, not a corporate executive like his father. I just drove him away," Robert conceded as he continued to pace back and forth.

"Stop it right now!" Julia screamed at him as she stood up and faced him. "I do not want to hear any more of this kind of talk. Let's pray together, Robert," she said to him with eyes filled with pain.

"I cannot ask God to listen to my prayers now. He doesn't even know my voice. I have done nothing but warm the pew I have sat on all these years." The muscles in his jaw tensed up as he spoke.

Before Julia could tell him how wrong he was about God, he had left the room. She was too weak to follow him.

She let herself slump into a chair and placed her hands together to pray. She would not just pray for Mark on Robert's behalf; she would pray for Robert to find comfort in the Lord.

Even though Robert thought the Lord would not listen to him, Julia knew that the Lord was waiting patiently for Robert to come to Him.

Robert had gone to a bar across the street from the hospital. He found a table in a dark corner and ordered a drink. He had never been a drinking man, except socially at business meetings or at social gatherings. But he wanted to drown out his emotions in order to feel nothing. He could not think of any better way to do it than this.

After several drinks, he still felt heartache and now more guilt for leaving his fragile wife alone in Dan's office. *Dan would be there for Julia*; he reasoned as he continued to drink. *Dan was always there for Julia and the kids. Let Dan be there for Mark and Julia now*, Robert thought resentfully, thinking of the day that he had left Julia in Dan's consoling arms twenty-five years ago.

Mark does not want me at his side. I will only bring him more harm. Mark is being punished because of my mistakes. God is punishing Mark because of me.

Robert got up to leave. He called his pilot, Tony, and told him to pick him up at the helipad. He paid his tab and walked out into the cold dark night. Robert was running away from himself, not from Mark. He was a broken man, out of his mind with guilt.

As they flew over the ranch, Robert looked out the window of the helicopter. The ranch was all lit up around the main house and the stables. He thought he had it all. He had every materialistic thing he could possibly want. There it was, in front of him, but what he wanted more than all of this, was his son back.

The house was unnervingly quiet; everyone was still at the hospital. Robert went to his office and turned on the light. "Where did I go wrong?" he asked himself. He picked up a picture frame of his father from the bookcase.

"Why did Mark always love you, Father, always you? Mark never came to me, he always went to you. He worshiped the ground that you walked on."

Robert looked around his office. His exquisite leather law books stared back at him. His many distinctive awards hanging in place on the walls seemed to scream out at him. None of these things meant anything to him now. He had always justified his hard work and long hours by telling himself he was doing all of this for his son. That statement had been nothing more than a lie; he had done it for himself, not for Mark.

Then it finally occurred to him: his son never wanted or asked for any of this. All Mark ever wanted was a father. Mark did not want the business; Mark wanted his father's attention and love. He did not deserve a treasure like Mark as a son.

Where had he put Mark in his life while he was working? Did he get those Super Bowl tickets for Mark's birthday? No, he had broken his promise to Mark and gone on a business trip instead. Now Mark was lying in a hospital bed because of him. *I have taken away Mark's dream of being an NFL quarterback someday.*

Mark does not have the personality to be an executive, like me. He is too kind-hearted and gentle, too concerned about other's feelings. He is the pride of his mother and has all of her wonderful characteristics. Mark has always cared for everyone else; he would make a wonderful doctor.

"Why now, why have I never seen these qualities before in Mark? Lord, are You talking to me? Did Mark send You here to talk to me? I am finally listening, Lord; You have my attention," Robert said in tears.

"Please Lord, please forgive me; please don't take my son away because I have not deserved to call him my son. Mark wants to belong to You, Lord, are You going to take him? Give me another chance to make things right," Robert pleaded, and then he sat at his desk and broke down and cried.

If only Robert knew that God does not punish us by causing us pain. God would never punish us by hurting the ones we love, because God loves them far greater than we do.

Two days later, Dan went out to the ranch to check on Robert. Dan found him in his office, passed out. Robert had been drinking.

"Robert, get up!" Dan said, as he tossed the liquor bottle in the trashcan. Robert sat up weakly and looked up at Dan with a heavy heart.

Dan told Robert to stop feeling sorry for himself. He convinced Robert that drinking would solve nothing; it would not bring Mark healing.

Dan reminded Robert that he had warned him to make things right with Mark. But Dan also reassured Robert that it was not too late to be a father to his son.

"Mark loves you no matter what you have done to him in the past. It is the special power of love between a father and son. You may fail each other sometimes, but you can never break the bond of love that you share with each other. It is up to you, Robert. Go to Mark, and ask him for forgiveness," Dan said as he assured Robert with a stern pat on the shoulder.

Robert and Dan headed to the hospital. When Robert saw the dreadful condition that Mark was in, it was too much for him to accept. How could Mark ever forgive him? It was not possible, Robert thought.

Dan knew that Mark had already forgiven his father. That was just like Mark. All Robert had to do was believe in his son.

CHAPTER THIRTEEN –
⌒The Recovery⌒

For the next thirty days, Mark remained in very serious condition in the intensive care unit. His left arm and left leg were in casts. Inserted into his chest was a triple lumen catheter. Tubes and wires connected him to their life controlling machines. The cardiac monitor was beating away. He had a percutaneous endoscopic gastrostomy (PEG) feeding tube.

They had removed the airway tube from his throat after two weeks. An oxygen mask was over his nose. His chest drainage tubes had also been removed.

Mark had been placed in a back brace to protect a slight fracture in his spine. The CT scan revealed swelling in his spine, but doctors were hopeful that he would regain feeling once the swelling was reduced. The doctors had a hard time finding a drug to reduce the swelling because Mark was extremely allergic to the medications he needed.

The doctors would not know how much control Mark would have in his legs until he came out of the coma he had lapsed into while in the emergency room.

Blood and cerebrospinal fluid had accumulated in his brain, which put pressure on it. Even though he had a helmet on, his brain had banged against the inside of his skull when the motorcycle had crashed against it. A catheter had been implanted to drain the fluids. A gauge had monitored the pressure inside his brain. They had been removed once the pressure returned to normal.

Dan had felt helpless as he monitored Mark's recovery. There was nothing more anyone could do but wait for Mark to respond to them. Mark was in the loving hands of God, which was the only comforting thought they had as the days passed by and Mark did not open his eyes.

Even though Dan had seen the accident first hand, he had not realized the impact of it until the local news showed it in slow motion. It made Dan physically sick to watch the footage.

Reporters had swarmed the hospital for a human-interest story. The hometown hero, who had led his football team to a State Championship, who had won the State Motocross Race seconds before crashing, was now in a coma, fighting for his life.

Would Mark ever walk; would he ever play football again?

Christmas had come and gone. The Sanders family faithfully observed the birth of Jesus, but there were no joyous holiday celebrations at the ranch. They wanted to wait for Mark to recover before they celebrated with presents, decorations and a tree.

Julia stayed in the city so that she could be with Mark each day. Robert came as often as he could. He was still guilt-ridden and the sight of Mark was more than he could emotionally handle. He did the only thing he knew to do; he threw himself into his work even though William volunteered to manage the company for him.

Rebecca, Mark's sister, and Sally Johnson took turns as his nurse. Sally was the mother of April's friend, Sharon Johnson.

Sally was very kind and compassionate to Mark. She had cared for Mark years ago when he had fallen into the mineshaft. It was then that she had grown attached to him and understood all his fears about being in the hospital as a patient.

April had come to the hospital, often at night when Mark's family had gone home. She looked around to make sure that no one had followed her, and then she went to his room. She stood outside the sliding glass doors to his room just staring in at him.

Sally kindly allowed her to sit by his bed. Many nights April held Mark's hand in hers and prayed desperately for him to wake up. Sally felt April's sorrow, and she worried about her as the weeks passed and Mark remained the same.

After school let out, there was always a group of his friends to visit Mark. The nurses allowed only his best friends in his room, one at a time, as the others watched from the glass door, a few at a time.

Normally, the hospital would not have allowed all these students in the ICU, but the doctors hoped that one of them might be the key to waking Mark out of his coma.

Julia sat beside Mark's bed holding his fingers in hers. She closed her eyes as she thought about how small his hands used to be.

When he first started to walk, he would reach up to her with his tiny fingers waving back and forth, as if to say, "Pick me up, Mommy." She would reach out, hold his hand and help him walk, just a few steps at a time, before picking him up in her arms.

Everyday she prayed that he would open his eyes and return to them. She promised God that she would do whatever it took to help him take his first steps back to recovery.

Julia knew Mark had many friends willing to support him, too. It was evident by the get-well cards covering the walls of his room. She had lovingly read each one to him in hopes that hearing her voice would cause him to wake up.

Rebecca came into the room. She removed the oxygen mask, took a washcloth and wiped Mark's face. As she wiped his brow, he moved his face. Joy overtook her.

"Mother, Mark moved!" Rebecca said excitedly.

Julia stood up close to Mark's face and touched his forehead softly with her hand.

"Mark, wake up!" Julia spoke loudly, praying that he would hear her. She lifted his hand in hers and held it up to her heart. "Please, dear God, send Mark back to us."

He tried to move his head back and forth, but the brace would not allow him to move. He blinked his eyes several times and acted as if he was going to wake up, but he never did.

Julia immediately called Dan. He reassured her that it was a good sign that Mark showed movement. Over the next few days, Mark opened his eyes for brief moments. He was now termed as being in a stupor, a deep sleep-like state, where they could awaken him briefly by vigorous stimulation, such as loudly calling his name. He still only responded to pain above his waist.

Each day he stayed awake longer. As he regained his strength, his doctor gave orders for his neck brace to be removed. His breathing gradually improved, and he no longer required oxygen. The back brace was removed a few days later. He had a blank look on his face as if he was in deep thought. Everyone continued to pray that he would snap out of his fog and return to normal.

113

Julia had just arrived in his room, when she noticed he was stirring. She went over to his bed and loudly called his name.

"Mark, wake up!" Julia called out to him as she touched his shoulder and leaned down to his face. "Mark, I need you to wake up. Please, Mark, do it for your mother."

He opened his eyes slowly. He looked around the room, as if gathering information. Then his eyes met hers; he looked straight into her heart. She smiled at him and took a deep breath of joy, as she saw his connection to her. Julia was overjoyed that her son had finally returned to them.

He tried to talk but the words would not come out. He looked around again in confusion. Julia wiped the happy tears from her eyes so that she could speak to him.

"You are in the hospital; Mark, you had a bad motorcycle accident," she informed him, as the warm tears trickled down her cheeks.

Mark quickly turned his head back to her. "What?" He spoke hoarsely, giving her a dreadful look.

"The State Championship Race, do you remember?" she asked him. He shook his head no. He was confused, and panic was setting in as he tried to figure out what his mother was trying to tell him.

"You had a motorcycle accident, don't you remember?"

Mark shook his head no. He looked at her deeply trying to figure it all out. Why was he here, and why was his mother crying? Nothing made any sense to him.

"Do you remember the State Football Championship game?" she asked, not understanding why Mark was so clueless.

He shook his head no; he was in deep thought trying to figure it all out. Why was he here in the hospital; what had happened to him, he continued to wonder. He held up his right arm and looked at the IV line. Then he looked over at his left arm in the cast.

"You broke your arm and your leg," she told him compassionately.

He looked down at his legs. After gathering the information about his broken leg, he tried to move his body for a better look. His chest was sore. Alarm showed in his eyes. He moved his right arm down to his legs. Julia knew that he was concerned about his legs.

"I don't feel my legs!" he yelled out, "What's wrong with my legs?" Panic stressed his face. "Oh, God, what happened to my legs?"

Mark was struggling to sit up, reaching for his legs. He was frantically grabbing at them, trying to make them move with no outcome. Julia was begging him to calm down as she held onto his upper arm and encouraged him to lie back down.

Rebecca had heard Mark's panic-stricken voice from the nurse's station and quickly entered the room. Julia was upset, not knowing what to do or what to tell Mark. Rebecca went back out and called for Dan to come quickly.

"It's okay, Mark, Rebecca is here, and Dan is on his way." Julia had hoped to calm him. He was terrified that he had lost his legs and continued to grab at them.

"I can't feel my legs, oh God, what happened to my legs?" he cried out intensely.

"Calm down, Mark," Julia pleaded with him.

Rebecca tried to ease his bare shoulders back onto the bed, but Mark was determined to hold his legs. He was desperately trying to make them move. Dan came into the room in a hurry. He took a hold of Mark's shoulders.

"Mark, I want you to lie back down. You have to stay calm," Dan advised him. But Mark continued to struggle. He was determined he was going to get out of the bed and walk. Dan had to hold him around the shoulders to keep him from leaving the bed.

Rebecca had gone to the nurse's station and returned with a syringe. Dan held Mark while she injected it into his IV. In less than a minute, Mark was sluggish.

Mark wrapped his arms around Dan's back and lay his head on Dan's shoulder. They embraced each other, and then Dan gently lowered him on the bed.

Mark looked at Dan with pitiful eyes, and in a tear-jerking voice, he spoke. "I can't feel my legs, Dan." Then Mark closed his eyes and was asleep.

Mark had reached out for Dan to rescue him, just as Dan had done so many times in the past. This was one time he could not help Mark.

Dan was heartbroken; the tears slowly trickled down his face. He looked away to gather his composure. As far as Dan was concerned, Mark was his son and he loved him deeply.

Dan was reminded of the little boy with the scraped knees. Mark was the little fellow that he could hold in his arms and make everything better. Dan felt helpless. He could not make Mark better this time; it was up to Mark and God.

Julia rubbed Mark's hair gently. Tears were streaming down her face. She knew that Mark might never be the same son she had just a few months ago. How was she going to help him survive this ordeal, she cried. Would Mark accept his handicap?

She feared that his lifetime dreams, which God had planted in his life, were gone. Mark would never play college football or win the Super Bowl someday.

"He should sleep now, Mother," Rebecca told her mother compassionately as she took Mark's hand in hers.

"He seemed so frightened," Julia spoke softly as she looked at her helpless son and felt sorrow.

"I'm sure he was frightened when he woke up and found himself here," Rebecca said, trying to reassure her mother that Mark's reaction was normal for his circumstance. She gave her mother an encouraging hug. "Try not to worry; Mark is going to be fine."

Rebecca's stomach was in knots knowing Mark might never walk again. Mark's life was never going to be the same again. Would his faith in God see him through this darkness?

Dan was taking Mark's vital signs. He listened to Mark's heart and lungs. He felt his chest carefully, checking for signs of damage from Mark's struggle. Relief showed on his face.

Mark seemed to be sleeping restlessly. Dan stood back and watched Mark lying there helpless. "Please, God, show him your favor and heal him," Dan prayed. "Mark is your friend … Lord, he loves You … embrace him, Lord."

"Mark did not remember the accident or the football game, Dan," Julia informed him with a look of concern.

"That's not unusual, it is very common for a person with a traumatic brain injury such as his to have some memory lost," Dan tried to enlighten her. "I am sure Mark will be fine. He did remember all of us, which is encouraging. Things will be cloudy for him for awhile, and then they should clear up."

Dan let Julia fall into his comforting arms as she cried hopelessly on his shoulder. How could she ask God for another miracle? God had just given Mark back to her, and for that, she was eternally grateful.

Mark drifted in and out of unconsciousness for the next two days. April had been at his side when he had awoken; he stared right through her and said nothing. She worried that if he had forgotten the game and the race that he may have forgotten her as well. She left the room in tears when her fears proved true.

On the third day, Mark was conscious but lightly sedated to keep him calm. Dan wanted to talk to him about his condition. It was a troublesome conversation; it pained Dan that Mark was not regaining feeling in his legs. Dan explained the accident to him. Then he told Mark what the accident had done to his body.

Dan told Mark that he needed to be calm and be patient as he waited for his healing. God was in charge, and they needed to let Him handle this. Dan reminded him that he should be thankful that he was alive.

Mark politely thanked Dan for saving his life. He had kept his composure during the conversation. He was not about to accept his handicap, and as soon as Dan left the room, he began to pray.

He was confident that he would receive God's supernatural healing; he was sure that it would happen. Mark knew that God rewards people who seek after him. He believed he would be better than he was before the accident, when God made him perfect.

At that very moment, a feeling of calmness filled the room, and he peacefully drifted off to sleep.

Chapter Fourteen –
∽Saying Good-bye∼

*L*ate one night Dan was leaving Mark's room. April was standing by the glass door staring into his room. She touched the object that she had hidden under the sweater that she wore. It was a round symbol of Mark's love for her.

Dan was surprised to see her. He gave her a warm hug as he noticed that she looked troubled.

"Hello, sweetheart, what are you doing out here? Why aren't you in there with Mark?" Dan questioned April.

"That's ok; I'm fine standing out here. I just wanted to see if Mark was doing all right. I heard that he was better," she said without much emotion, her face blank. She seemed so far off in her thoughts.

Dan knew that something was bothering her. "Did you and Mark have a lover's quarrel before his accident?" Dan asked with concern, his heart reaching out to her.

"We don't have that kind of relationship, Uncle Dan," she tried to sound convincing as she continued staring at Mark through the glass door, wishing with all her heart that she was in his arms.

"What happened after Mark's birthday dance with the two of you?" he quizzed her as he remembered that magical night.

"Nothing, we are just friends, remember. Mark never got serious about me; he was too hung up in all that football game stuff," she said quietly without any hint of anger.

Her heart was so broken, it was sure to splatter all over the floor if she did not take a long deep breath and take control of her true feelings. Feelings that she could tell no one, not even the uncle she had trusted with all her other secrets.

"I thought Debbie told me that you were the Homecoming Queen and Mark was the King?" He was baffled that she was making no big deal of her relationship with Mark. He knew there was much more to their relationship than she was letting on.

"We were … but we did not go to the dance together, he took … uh … uh … Jessica, and I went with, uh … Sharon and Carlo," she stated with hesitation and then sighed quietly.

"What gives, April, I know you had a crush on Mark. You told me." Dan was not buying her story.

"I got over it; he was too arrogant for me. It just took me awhile to figure that out," she said nervously.

"Arrogant? I have never known Mark to be arrogant," Dan said puzzled. None of her answers were making any sense.

"It was all that attention Mark got from the media; it really went to his head," she said without looking at her uncle.

"I don't get it? Just a few months ago you would have given anything to be with Mark." Dan continued to try to figure out what was going on.

"Don't ever say that, Uncle Dan, please don't tell anyone that! Promise me that you will never tell my father about Mark and me!" she exclaimed fearfully, finally looking into Dan's face and then quickly turning back to stare at Mark. *My father must never find out*, April worried.

"April, calm down. You know I would never tell your father our conversations. Why are you so uptight about your father knowing about you and Mark?"

"You know how Dad feels about the Sanders'; he warned me against dating Mark. He cannot know that we were even friends," she said in a panic. Dan detected the shakiness in her voice.

"Does this have anything to do with what happened after the game?" Dan interrogated her. April's face got pale and her eyes wide.

"What do you mean?" she asked in a scared voice.

"Did you go out drinking with Mark and his friends?"

"No, I swear, uh, I never saw Mark after the game. He went out with his friends," she said in a panicked voice.

"Are you sure? You know that you can trust me," Dan assured her with an understanding voice, hoping to gain her trust and finally get to the truth.

"I wasn't with him ... uh ... that is why I am so mad at him. Mark promised to meet me and, and ... he never showed up," she said unsteadily at first, but then firmly.

"Stood you up, did he?" Dan questioned her, not believing her story. Mark was extremely dependable.

"He did," she said, unable to look him in the face.

"So why are you here, staring at him? This is not the first time I've seen you at this door," Dan questioned her, knowing there was more to her story and wanting April to come clean. April made a quick sweep with her eyes around them to make sure no one was watching or listening.

"He's still my friend. I was worried about him. Just because I'm mad at him doesn't mean I don't care about him anymore," she said without looking at him.

Dan heard the sadness in April's voice. "If that's what you say," Dan said, still unconvinced that April was telling him the truth.

"Is he going to be all right? I mean really, he doesn't seem to be all there." She fumbled with her words.

"He has a long recovery ahead of him; it is up to God now."

"Will he get his memory back, you know, about the accident and the game?" she wanted to know.

"Not likely, people with traumatic events like his tend to suppress them. On top of that, he suffered a brain injury. I doubt Mark will ever remember that weekend. We can be thankful that his mind seems to be undamaged otherwise."

"Is there any way to make Mark remember that night?" She raised her eyebrows as if her whole life depended on Dan's answer.

"I'm sorry, April. Dr. Price has advised us not to push Mark into remembering that weekend. She said Mark could suffer from posttraumatic stress disorder. It could be extremely dangerous to him."

"What is that; how could it hurt him?"

"If Mark is exposed to cues that symbolize or resemble the events of that night, he could persistently re-experience that night through intrusive thoughts, dreams or flashbacks. He could have difficulty sleeping and eating. He would experience irritability or angry outbursts, even feelings of guilt. Even worse, April, he could become detached from us. Dr. Price advised us to let Mark remember things on his own and not for us to force him to remember."

"But, Dan … he doesn't remember me!" She cried out as a tremor made its way through April's veins and into her heart. Tears formed quickly, and there was no holding them back as they spilled over.

Dan compassionately wrapped both arms around her. "Shhh, sweetheart, Mark will remember you … just give him time … you have to be strong for him right now, sweetheart. I am so sorry this is so painful for you."

April broke their bond and stood back with her head hanging down. Dan placed both hands on her shoulders and looked down in her swollen eyes. She slowly faced him and met his concerned eyes.

"He will remember, sweetheart, he loves you more than anyone in this world; you have to know that in your heart, April. You cannot give up on him, but right now, it is better that you let him recover on his own."

"You are right," she exhaled and wiped the final tears away. Dan gave her a hug.

"I have other patients to see. I love you, April. If you ever need to talk, come see me," he said lovingly as he hugged her again. He turned and walked away. Dan knew that Mark had a form of *dissociative amnesia*. No one could understand why his memory of April seemed deeply buried within his mind. They prayed that his memories of her would resurface on their own soon.

April stood at the glass door and looked in at Mark, who was sleeping. She wanted to go in there, take him in her arms and hold him. Maybe this time he would remember her. But she knew that she did not dare go in there. Someone might see her and tell her father; she could not risk it. She wrapped her arms around her stomach.

"Good-bye, Mark, I will always love you. Forever you will be a part of me," she whispered, as the tears fell softly down her cheeks.

She said her silent tearful good-bye to him there, wondering if they would ever see each other again.

CHAPTER FIFTEEN –
∾The Forgiveness∾

*T*he doctors decided to give Mark a light sedative and anxiety medication to keep him calm, for fear that Mark would develop another episode of his panic attacks.

Dr. Price was concerned that the motorcycle accident and the extended hospital stay would cause Mark to relapse from his progress with coping with the traumatic event of being trapped in the mineshaft when he was only eight-years old.

When Mark was eight, he developed high levels of anxiety and panic attacks. The Sanders' had put him into therapy with Dr. Gina Price. Although Mark had learned to deal successfully with the onset of the panic attacks, he had not opened up about that day in the mine during therapy sessions. Whatever happened remained Mark's unspoken secret.

Dr. Price had been concerned when Julia told her that Robert was sending Mark off to a boarding school as punishment for his stunt in the mine. The last thing Mark needed was to be sent away from the safety of his home at a time like this, she had told Julia.

Dr. Price stressed to Robert that a normal eight-year-old would have emotional issues with being sent away from home. Mark was at a higher risk since he was already suffering from anxiety due to the accident. However, Robert insisted that Mark needed a firm hand and was uncompromising.

When Mark's grandfather died a few months later, Dr. Price again spoke to the Sanders' and challenged them to keep Mark at home where those who loved him could nurture his broken heart. She warned them that Mark could develop a case of posttraumatic stress disorder and that his panic attacks would likely return.

Over the next few years, Dr. Price met with Mark and determined that he was quick to become angry in situations that he could not control. They worked on controlling his anxiety levels.

Thankfully, Mark had a stronger healer in God, and he used God to control his emotions. Mark's character of gentleness and meekness surpassed the anger he held inside. Mark was remarkably intelligent and able to compensate in situations that caused him stress by using successful reasoning instead of anger.

Weakness was not a word that described Mark. He had high standards for himself and became an overachiever.

Losing the use of his legs would surely cause Mark to go back over the edge. Once again, everyone was nervously waiting for Mark to show signs of stress as the days passed, and the feeling did not return to his legs.

Dr. Price felt that Mark's paralysis might be the result of a psychological problem caused by his repressed memories.

Mark and God were spending many hours together, and he was in agreement with God that he would regain the feeling in his legs, all in God's time. Mark would have to let God be in control, which would not be an easy thing for Mark to do. He wanted his healing yesterday, and with each day that passed, he felt his life, as he knew it, being swept away. Yet his faithful prayers claimed every promise that God had spoken.

Mark's pastor provided him with Bible verses to hang on to while Mark waited for his healing. Mark would be a prisoner of hope. God would give him the endurance to fight this battle. Mark humbled his heart and thanked God for each day he woke up to another day. Life is what you make of it; his grandfather had told him.

Robert had been out of town when Mark came out of his coma. He cut his business trip short and flew home to see his son.

Robert stopped in front of the glass doors and looked inside Mark's room. Mark was sitting up talking calmly to his mother. Would his son really forgive him? Dan had told Robert that Mark did not remember anything about the accident.

Still Robert was worried about facing his son. He was apprehensive that their jaded past would keep Mark from forgiving him.

Julia saw Robert standing at the door and motioned for him to enter the room. He slowly opened the glass door and stepped inside. Robert absorbed the condition that Mark was in and was thankful that Mark looked better. Mark's arm and leg were still in casts. He was scheduled to get them off at the end of the week. Mark had a gentle look on his face.

Julia came over and hugged Robert. "Mark is really okay; he doesn't have anymore pain," Julia informed Robert with a reassuring smile.

"You look awful, Dad," Mark said jokingly.

Robert smiled; he was glad that Mark had made the first move and had not called him father. Robert went to Mark and stood beside his son's bed.

Julia had told Mark that his father was having an extremely difficult time dealing with his accident, blaming himself for his condition.

"You look better than the last time I saw you," Robert said as he extended his hand out for them to shake. Mark took his hand, but it was not Robert's hand that Mark wanted.

"I'd give you my left hand if I could," Mark joked with him. There was no hatred in Mark's eyes, as he looked into his father's eyes, only love. Robert was overwhelmed. How could Mark just forgive him and hold no ill feelings for the way he had treated him as a son in the past? Robert did not understand it as he looked into Mark's merciful eyes.

Through tears, Robert managed to say it, "I love you, Mark. I know I do not deserve your love …" Tears welled in his eyes as he tried to speak.

"I love you too, Dad," Mark whispered as he welcomed his father into his heart. The words were easily said as if they had been on the end of Mark's tongue just waiting for an opportunity to speak them to his father.

Robert leaned over the bed and hugged Mark as the tears fell down his cheeks. The hardness in Robert's heart was completely gone and replaced with love. Robert would never be the same man again. Mark had shown him what true forgiveness was all about.

"Thank you, Lord, for giving me my son back," Robert said before he let go of Mark, stood up, and faced Mark's glassy eyes.

"There is so much I need to explain to you, Mark. I hope you will give me the chance," Robert said. Mark brushed back the tears that had fallen. Mark had waited a long time to hear his father's words of love for him.

"I'm not going anywhere so I guess now is as good a time as any." Mark smiled, hoping to relieve some of his father's tension.

It was on that day that the father and son found each other and began a new and loving relationship. Robert took a leave from work in order to spend time at the hospital with Mark.

Robert could not stop thinking about the mercy his son had shown him that day. Mark's serene attitude was a true testimony on seeking God in a desperate situation. Mark would claim healing and would not settle for anything less than a perfect body.

Three days later, in the hospital chapel, Robert humbly gave his heart over to God and repented for all the heartache that he had caused his son and family. Robert let go of the old so that he could receive the new. God's mercy is fresh and renewed each day, and Robert was ready to receive his new beginning with God.

When Robert went to tell Mark the good news, he saw his family and friends tearfully hugging each other in Mark's room. Robert felt his heart sink, thinking something awful had happened to Mark. As he dreadfully wondered what all the commotion was about, he stood frozen at the entrance to the room.

The others, seeing Robert, slowly parted the room so that Robert was directly facing Mark. Mark's face lit up when he saw his father, and he moved his toes. Everyone gleefully clapped for Mark as Robert fell to his knees and thanked God.

The day that the father gave his heart to Jesus was the same day that his son received his supernatural healing. Robert had a lot more to learn about the God that had shown him mercy, grace and forgiveness for his sins.

When Rebecca had come into the room with a wheelchair for the first time, Mark refused to have it in his room. He was not leaving the hospital in a wheelchair; he was going to walk again.

Once they stopped the sedatives, Mark became extremely restless. He immediately wanted to leave the hospital but Dan refused to let him go home. His blood counts had been low and he was still very weak. A few days later, he caught a lung infection and struggled with his breathing. This did not help the damage already done to his lungs from the accident.

His body needed time to heal. Mark was not agreeable to any of this. The walls were caving in on him and the nurses were smothering him. Nevertheless, over the following weeks, Mark regained most of his strength and he found the courage to rehabilitate himself. He continued to pray for patience as he struggled with his fear of small places.

The feeling had returned to his legs, which was very painful. He had an operation to remove the devices in his leg. It was the beginning of a painful process of learning how to walk again. He was sent to a rehabilitation center for the next few weeks. His determination to be completely healed was accomplished in record time. He did not even have a limp. It was nothing less than a miracle from God.

Robert was at his side when Mark returned home and even took up jogging with Mark. Robert thanked God daily for giving his son a second chance to walk. Robert would never forget what God had done to save his son.

Mark's memory of the accident only returned in nightmares. He would dream he was lying on the track with motorcycles bearing down on him. He would wake up in a cold sweat. He could not remember the actual accident even though he saw it on film; he could not recall any details.

Mark had no memory of the State Championship Football game either. He regretted that something so important in his life had no meaning to him. He watched the game on tape and it was like watching a stranger.

Something else bothered him; he had no memory of the girl who had come to see him while he was in the hospital. Julia had told him that April was Dan's niece and that they had grown up together at the ranch.

It was as if she was right there in his mind yet he knew nothing about her. He could not understand why she had been upset when she left his room crying. Later, Dan told him that April had moved away to California with her family. That deeply pained him, but he did not understand why. There was an emptiness in his heart he could not explain. He found himself thinking about her, and she appeared in his dreams. But there was nothing real about her to him.

There was no time to think about anything; he had to concentrate on his complete recovery. He wanted to race motorcycles again and play college football as soon as he got stronger.

Dan advised him to give up professional bike racing because of the extensive damage to his lung. Mark agreed for the time being and put his extra racing bike in a stall in the stable.

Dan wanted Mark to give up football as well, but it was useless; Mark would not give up football. He planned to go all the way, become a professional football player, and win the Super Bowl someday. It would be a dream that he would strive for as he drove himself to be the best he could be in his life.

The doctors had warned him about flying or doing underwater sports because of his lung damage. In time, he hoped that his lungs would be one hundred percent again.

When he rode in the helicopter, he sometimes had to be on oxygen. But other than that, he had no lasting effects from his accident.

His parents hired a private teacher to work with him while he was in the hospital. By March, Mark was back in high school. He was named the most valuable player in baseball.

In June, Mark graduated at the top of his class. The speaker spoke of all Mark's accomplishments before introducing him to the crowd.

When Mark stood up to walk, yes walk, to the podium to give his speech, the crowd stood and clapped loudly.

With a humble heart Mark spoke. Mark thanked God for all his accomplishments and for his healing. He told the crowd that God can turn anything around as long as you keep the vision for your victory. He told how God plants seeds in our hearts for goodness and greatness and that it is up to us to guard those treasures inside of us. God works on the inside of our hearts so that on the outside we bring forth good things. He asked that everyone learn to love one another as God loves them.

Mark thanked his parents for their support and love. He thanked his teachers and friends for standing by him. He thanked Dan for being his encourager. There was not a dry eye in the audience. It was a day that all rejoiced in having Mark for a friend.

Robert wanted more time at home with his family, so he turned his company over to his vice-president, William Triplett, to run it for him while he was on leave. He did most of his law practice work at the ranch house so that he could spend more time with Mark.

Each day Mark and Robert came to understand each other better. Their close relationship developed into a meaningful friendship. Robert encouraged Mark to follow his dream of being a doctor.

Despite Mark's accident, many colleges continued to offer him football scholarships. Mark decided to play football for the same university that his father and grandfather had attended. The university was right there in their city.

He could also study medicine and work at the same hospital with Dan and Steven. Dan was thrilled that Mark would be under his wings.

That fall Mark entered the university, and he moved into his own apartment to be closer to it. He had finished college in just two years, because of all the classes that he had already taken while he was still in high school. He started medical school soon after that.

He played college football and went pro. His father never missed a home game. Mark's goal of playing in the Super Bowl was just a few weeks away, and Robert planned to treasure his son's dream on that special day.

Mark had found that his lungs needed extra oxygen when he over-exerted himself, but he continued to be very successful and broke many records.

He did not have a lot of spare time to visit his parents. Therefore, when they got together for dinner once in awhile, it was a special time for all of them.

His mother called to check on him almost daily. It had been her idea to have Maria clean for Mark. Mark was also thankful for the homemade meals Martha filled his refrigerator with each week.

Mark was now 24 years old and had many things going on in his busy life, but he tried to remember that the most important part of his life was living for God.

He had all the money he could ever want. He would never have to work a day of his life if he chose not to work. Nevertheless, that was not how he wanted to live. He wanted to be a doctor and help people with the gifts God had given him.

To those Mark met and cared for, he would be a blessing. His tender heart was like that of his mother's, and he planned to spend time helping those who could not afford to get medical treatment when he finished with his medical training.

Mark wanted to open a free clinic on the Indian Reservation someday. Charlie had been an important person in his life, and he wanted to repay Charlie by taking care of his people.

Now unexpectedly, Sunflower had entered into his demanding life. That poor child, she really knew what hard knocks were. Mark was amazed at the way she took everything in stride and smiled through all her hardships. He had a lot to learn from her.

Mark believed that somehow the Lord had given Sunflower to him. He still could not figure out why the Lord had chosen him. Nevertheless, when the Lord called him to do something, he would obey.

Life had seemed to be passing him by lately, until the day he found Sunflower. He had forgotten the simple joys of life that he had once cherished.

Sunflower had put him back in his place and reminded him that life was more than work and football, and with her around to remind him, he would never forget that.

ᴄGive and Receive the Blessingᴄ

"Get up, get up!" Sunflower said as she shook Mark. He opened his drowsy eyes to find Sunflower sitting on his chest.

"It's Christmas," Mark said sleepily. What a restless night, he thought, as he stretched out his arms.

"Come on, Mark, get up!" she begged sweetly.

"Oh, all right. You win, what do you want to do today?" he asked sleepily as he looked up into her cheerful face.

"First we have to wait 'til my dress is dry, and then we can go get me another one at the mission," she told him, as if this was an everyday occurrence in her life.

"How did your dress get wet?" he asked, puzzled, as he let out a sleepy yawn and wiped the sleep from his eyes.

"I washed it in the sink, silly," she laughed and giggled.

"You don't have to wash your dress, Sunny," Mark told her.

"I wanta look all pretty for you," she said with a smile that brightened the room.

"You already are pretty to me," he smiled, as he tickled her and made her laugh. Her laughter filled the empty room as the sun split through the curtains.

"Remember last night I told you I had a surprise for you?" he teased as he playfully stuffed his pillow over her and made her giggle again.

"Yes, what is it?" she asked excitedly. Mark rolled over and got off the bed.

"Let's go in the living room," he told her as she jumped off the bed into his open arms, and he set her feet on the floor. He watched as she skipped into the living room. Her eyes got big as she saw the small Christmas tree

131

in the corner with presents under it. She went to get a closer look. Her mouth dropped wide open and a brilliant expression crossed her childish face; one would have thought the tree was ten feet tall, not a mere four feet.

The few gifts under the tree caught her attention, and she bent down and ran her fingertip across one of them. For just a second Mark saw a hint of sadness cross her face. He understood; she had not been the recipient of Christmas gifts in her past. He knelt down on one knee, picked up a gift and handed it out to her.

"These are for you," he told her with his radiant smile.

"All of them?" she asked in disbelief, her blue eyes shimmering.

"All of them," he said, taking great joy watching her glow with happiness.

"Oh boy, I've never had any presents before, but, but, can I share them with Katie?" Mark's heart felt for her; she was just as giving as he had been when he was a child. She had told him briefly about Katie, the girl who had watched over her at the Children's Home.

"We'll go shopping tomorrow and get Katie whatever you want her to have," he promised her.

"Oh, thank you, Mark," she said as she hugged him.

He handed her the first box. She carefully unwrapped it, trying not to rip the pretty paper. The box contained a pink dress with bows, a pair of white tights, pink buckled shoes and matching hair ribbons. Sunflower's eyes sparkled as she let out a big breath of air.

"Oh, Mark, they're beautiful," Sunny cried with tears of joy.

He handed her another box. She opened it and pulled out socks, underwear, and two nightgowns. The third box contained jeans and shirts.

"I can't believe these are for me," she said cheerfully.

"There is more." He handed her another box. This one contained tennis shoes and snow boots.

"If they don't fit, we can take them back and get you some that fit," he told her as he sat on the floor.

"Wait 'til Katie sees me in these," she squealed in delight.

"Here, open this one." He handed it to her. There was a white sweater and a jacket with a matching scarf, hat and some gloves.

"I want you to wear that jacket every time you go out."

"I like wearing your jacket," she smiled at him.

"Here, when I first saw you that night, you reminded me of this," he said as he handed her the last big box. It contained a Raggedy Ann doll.

"Oh, Mark, thank you, thank you," she said as she kissed his cheek and he kissed her forehead.

"I want to be your little girl; please can I be your girl?" she asked with anticipation, using her irresistible charm on him.

"I sure hope so, Sunny, but that may not be up to you and me to decide. I am not married and you need a mother," he told her kindheartedly.

"I don't need anyone but you, and I can take care of myself," she reassured him.

"You don't understand, I work at the hospital and I play football. I am hardly ever home. You need someone to look after you while I'm gone," he said, hoping not to disappoint her.

"No one has ever watched me before, except Katie. She can watch me while you are gone," she said, thinking she had solved the problem.

"How old is Katie?"

"She's 15. I told you about her; she lives at the children's home."

"Where is the children's home?"

"Close to the park, can I stay here with you forever?" She asked in a tiny voice that sent waves of compassion into Mark's fragile heart.

"We'll see; I still have to work out all the details." He was tender with his words as his heart was trying to absorb the sadness of her past life. He wished at this moment he could change all that for her and give her what she deserved in life.

She looked straight into his face and the corners of her mouth formed a smile. Her eyes took on a sparkle as she giggled.

Whatever she is thinking must be pretty amusing, he thought as he joined her in a warm smile. Then she hit him squarely between the eyes.

"Let's find you a wife," she said in a matter-of-fact way with a big smile on her face.

Mark grabbed a breath of air. "Oh no, not me," he laughed, shocked that she would think of that. "It will take a pretty special lady to tame me," he added with a grin as he rubbed his forehead.

"I will pray God finds you one," she smiled back at him with determination.

"You are all I can handle for now, Sunny. Don't marry me off just yet," he laughed and reached out and tickled her.

"You are so marvelous," she laughed.

"Why, thank you, Sunny, now go change into your new dress and model it for me," he told her. She grabbed it and went into the bedroom.

Mark dropped back against the floor and laughed. A wife was not the answer he was looking for, at least not yet. Nevertheless, without a wife Mark knew he was facing the impossible.

However, with God's help, all things are possible, and Mark knew he would strongly need to claim that Bible verse if he intended to keep Sunny.

The doorbell rang and Mark got up and answered it. It was Rose Brown from across the hall. She and her husband, Joe, were retired. Their son Kevin was one of Mark's teammates. She was the motherly type, who liked to bring Mark homemade goodies. Mark was very fond of Rose and Joe. They thought of him as another son.

"I thought you might like some of my freshly baked Christmas cookies," she merrily said as she handed them to him.

"You know I would. Come on in, there is someone I want you to meet." He placed the cookies on the counter. Rose saw all the boxes on the floor.

"What's all this? It looks like Christmas in here," she said.

Sunny came bouncing into the room in her new dress, and she modeled it for Mark and Mrs. Brown.

"Rose, this is my new friend, Sunflower. I call her Sunny," Mark introduced them, as he admired Sunny's cheerfulness.

"Hello! My my, but you are a sweet looking little girl. Mark, wherever did you find her?" Rose asked him, thinking Sunny must be his niece.

"He found me under a bush in the park," Sunny stated. "Now I am going to live with him." Sunny beamed with happiness.

Mrs. Brown looked a little puzzled. "Oh, really?" she laughed, thinking surely this was all in fun.

"She's telling the truth; I did find her," Mark told her with a sly smile, knowing this was a hard story to believe.

"Well, goodness gracious, Mark Sanders, just what have you gotten yourself into now?"

"Believe me, I am just as in shock as you are. Sunny is from the children's home. I am going to try to adopt her. First, I need to work out a few details. Do you think you could baby-sit Sunny while I'm working or at practice?" he asked hopefully.

"Why sure, I'd love to baby-sit anytime you need me. Oh, Joe won't believe this! We miss having a little one around to spoil. He will love having a little girl to do things with; just wait 'til I tell him," she said as she went to the door.

"Good-bye, Sunny, you be a good girl for Mark."

"Thank you for the cookies; I will be calling you," Mark told her as he placed a kiss on her cheek and she touched his cheek with affection. Mark closed the door and turned to Sunny.

"I have to change out of these clothes and take a shower. We are going out to the ranch for Christmas dinner," Mark told Sunny and then he went to take a shower.

CHAPTER SEVENTEEN

Meeting the Family

*M*ark was excited that Sunny would soon be meeting his parents, Robert and Julia, his sister Rebecca, her husband, Steven, and their two boys: six year old Brad and four year old James Robert. His grandparents, Ella Sanders, Everett and Victoria Tate would also be there.

When they got to the ranch, Thomas opened the door to let them into the foyer.

"Hello, Thomas," Mark said warmly as they went in. Thomas was pleased to see Mark, and the two of them shook hands in friendship.

"It's so good to see you, Master Mark, and who is this charming little girl?" Thomas asked formally, as he helped Mark remove his winter coat.

"I'm Sunflower. Why do you wear that silly looking outfit?" she asked Thomas curiously, as Mark took Sunny's coat off her.

Thomas blushed. Mark just grinned at him and handed him Sunny's coat.

"I'm the butler, of course," Thomas answered her kindly.

"What's a butler do?" she asked shyly.

"We answer doors," Thomas replied, with a grin on his face.

"Oh, how strange," Sunflower said, still puzzled.

"Where are my parents?" Mark asked, hoping to free Thomas from any more questions. Mark took his sports jacket off and handed it to Thomas.

"I believe, Sir, they are in the sitting room," Thomas replied.

"What's a sitting room?" Sunflower asked with another one of her puzzled looks.

"It's a place where people sit and drink coffee or tea and have a conversation," Thomas informed her.

"Oh, let's go do that," she said excitedly. Mark smiled at Thomas as if to thank him for answering all of Sunflower's intriguing questions. Then he took a hold of Sunny's tiny hand and led her to the sitting room.

"Hello, Father," Mark said as he warmly shook hands with his father. Then he went to his mother who remained sitting.

"Hello, Mother, Merry Christmas," he said warmly as he bent down and kissed her cheek.

She took his hand in hers and held it. She was thankful to have her son standing there before her. The memory of his motorcycle accident at Christmas time still haunted her. She took a good look at Mark as they exchanged a hug with each other.

Julia noticed Mark's weight loss as his dress slacks hung loose around his hips. Maria was right; Mark was not taking care of himself, Julia thought as she frowned in concern for her son's health.

Sunflower stood back watching, and then she went over to Robert and held her hand out to him.

"Hello, Mark's father," she said sweetly. Robert took her hand and kissed it. Sunflower was surprised and giggled. Mark stood back and watched Sunflower apply her irresistible charm that was sure to capture his parent's affection.

"You look handsome in that jacket," she said to Robert and he smiled at her.

"You are looking very lovely too, Sunflower," Robert said with a warm smile.

"How did you know my name?"

"Mark told me all about you. He told me how beautiful you were; now I can see for myself that he was right," Robert smiled at her.

"Thank you," she said sweetly and looked over at Mark for approval.

"Sunflower, my father's name is Mr. Sanders," Mark informed her. They had gone over some of the words that she had been mispronouncing as they drove to the ranch.

"Hello, Mr. Sanders, I'm happy to meet you," she said, trying to act grown up. She turned and looked at Julia who had been smiling at her. Sunflower had never seen anyone as pretty as Julia.

"Hello, you're very pretty," Sunflower expressed shyly.

"I'm Julia. Here, come and sit with me." Julia opened her arms and Sunflower climbed on to her lap.

"Dad, what have you been able to find out about Sunny?" Mark asked him somewhat apprehensively.

Robert stood up and motioned for Mark to follow him, and they went into Robert's office.

"First of all, Mrs. Stanley called the police department and reported Sunflower's disappearance this morning," Robert informed him.

"I cannot believe it took her this long!" *How convenient that Sara missed Sunflower on Christmas Day*, Mark thought angrily.

"I had already spoken to my friend, Captain Grant Nelson about your situation with finding Sunflower. Grant explained to Mrs. Stanley that Sunflower was under the care of another family. Grant is investigating my report regarding child neglect on behalf of Sunflower."

"There is no doubt about it; Sunny has been neglected for some time." The thought of how much turned Mark's stomach in knots.

"It seems that Mrs. Wilson, the social worker, was called out of town on another matter and left instructions for Captain Nelson to handle this case until she gets back."

"Normally Sunflower would have gone back to the children's home, but they are filled to the max. With this being Christmas, Grant agreed to leave Sunflower in your care until they can sort this whole mess out. We have one week to make a case before Mrs. Wilson gets back in town. I will have to prove to her that you will be a suitable foster father to Sunny until this case can go to court," Robert explained to Mark.

"I told you that I want to adopt her," Mark said firmly.

"This case is going to be complicated, Mark, since you are so young and unmarried," Robert stressed to Mark.

"You will just have to do it. Did you find out anymore about Sunny?"

"The police department has a record of abandonment on her. Sunflower was left in a basket at the children's home. Her real parents were never found so she became a ward of the state. One of the officers found a note hidden in her baby sweater; it claimed her real name was Jessica Parker. However, there are no records of her birth in this county or the surrounding area," Robert informed Mark as he listened intently.

"This means that her mother is still alive. Sunflower was raised in the children's home until a few months ago when the Stanleys became her foster parents," Robert informed him. Mark was still pondering the fact that Sunflower had parents out there somewhere.

"She thinks her parents are dead," Mark told him with concern.

"You know, Mark, Sunflower's parents could come back and claim her," Robert warned Mark.

"I do not care if her parents are out there; they gave her up. I am adopting her. She belongs with me!" Mark said strongly, as he felt threatened by Sunny's real parents. There was no changing Mark's mind about the adoption; his heart was set on having Sunny as his child.

"One step at a time," Robert said, trying to calm Mark down. He knew that Mark would be heartbroken if Sunny's real parents came back to claim her, which was a strong possibility.

Julia came in and told them that her parents had arrived, and everyone was now present to have Christmas dinner. It was a feast of all feasts; Martha and the staff had outdone themselves this year.

Sunny was so polite at the table. Even if she could not figure out all the different silverware, she was well mannered. Mark figured Sister Jessica must have taught Sunny her table manners.

Sunny talked about Sister Jessica all the time. Sister Jessica had even called Mark to check on her. Mark was thankful that at least Sister Jessica had helped raise Sunny.

After dinner was over Sunny went to play with Rebecca's boys. It reminded Mark of the many times Rebecca and he had run off to play with their new toys after Christmas dinner.

The adults gathered in the sitting room for a cup of coffee. Julia's parents, Everett and Victoria Tate, wanted to hear all about Sunny from Mark. Living 75 miles from the ranch made it difficult for them to see their grandchildren and great-grandchildren as often as they wished.

It was difficult for them to visit with Mark because of his busy schedule, so they took this opportunity to cherish their time with him.

Later, Mark took Sunny out to the stables and let her ride in front of him on Thunder. He had a strange feeling come over him as if he had ridden with another blonde haired girl on Thunder before. She must have been Dan's niece, April, he thought. He had heard stories about the two of them when they were kids. He did not know why, but he felt sad thinking about her.

Mark decided to spend the night at the ranch since he did not have football practice that night, and he felt too tired to drive back into the city.

Besides, Sunny was having such a good time getting to know everyone. She had won many hearts that day with her irresistible charm.

Julia rearranged the first room that Mark had as a child for Sunny. The room was next to Mark's bedroom suite, and he left the doors open in case Sunny needed him during the night.

Saturday morning Mark had football practice. He woke up at seven o'clock with another aggravating nosebleed. It made him feel tired and frustrated as he returned to his bed, fell on it facedown, and covered his head with a pillow.

Pre-game physicals were in an hour. Practice was at nine, he thought dreadfully.

Mark really did not feel up to going to practice but they were only two games away from playing in the AFC Divisional Playoff game, so he forced himself to get up again and sluggishly headed to the bathroom for a shower.

He looked at the clock after he got out of the shower. He lay down across the bed on his back, wrapped only in his towel and closed his eyes. Finally, at eight o'clock he got up and got dressed. He knew it would take 45 minutes to drive to the stadium.

Sunny was already up playing with the boys in the playroom. Mark found his parents in the sitting room drinking coffee. They wanted him to join them.

Julia noticed the paleness of Mark's face and became even more concerned.

"Mark, are you feeling all right?" she asked him. "Sit down and have coffee with us and I will have Martha bring you something to eat."

"What I really need right now is for you and Dad to baby-sit so I can go to my football practice at nine. Don't forget we have a game tomorrow," Mark said as he bent and gave his mother a kiss, reassuring her that he was fine.

"I'll call Tony; he can take you there by helicopter so you won't have to drive." Robert picked up his phone and called Tony.

Mark looked at his watch, noting he needed to kill some more time before heading to the stadium. He went and played with Sunny and the boys in the playroom. Then he told Sunny his plans for the rest of the day and went to football practice.

The team was on the field when Mark arrived, so he hurried and got dressed out and joined the team. It was not like Mark to be this late, the coach thought when he saw Mark take his place with the other quarterbacks.

When practice was over, Tony flew Mark back to the ranch. Sunflower had a good time at the ranch that morning. She excitedly filled Mark in on everything she had done.

Mark had Tony fly them back into town for the afternoon. He took Sunny shopping and let her pick out several gifts for Katie. He bought Sunny a few more outfits, games, puzzles, storybooks, and a few toys. They ate lunch together at the park, where Sunny introduced Mark to her friend, the hot dog man. The man insisted on treating them to a free meal. After they finished eating, they fed the ducks down by the pond.

Then Mark took her to the movies to see *Snow White*. After it was over, they flew back to the ranch to have dinner with his entire family. Rebecca was so taken with Sunny. She had always wished that she had a daughter.

The two of them ended up spending the night at the ranch. Again, Sunny slept in the room next to his. Mark was very tired; entertaining a child with as much energy as Sunny was hard work.

The next morning they all flew into the city for church. Sunny was scared when Mark had trouble breathing and had to put on an oxygen mask. Julia calmed her and told her that Mark had punctured his lung when he was younger and sometimes when they flew, it was hard for him to breathe.

However, Julia was concerned too. Mark seemed so tired and looked pale. He lay back against his seat and closed his eyes while he remained on oxygen. Julia worried that Mark was over-extending himself.

After church, Mark told Sunny she would be staying with his parents while he was at the football game. Then Mark left with Carlo to go to the team luncheon.

Robert told Sunny that they were all going to the game, the whole family. She was so excited. She really liked Rebecca and the boys, and Brad was just about her age.

Mark was surprised when he looked up into the families' stadium box and saw everyone there. He played exceptionally well. He wanted Sunflower to be proud of him, although he doubted she knew anything about football.

At halftime, Mark had gone up to speak to her and found her asleep in his father's arms. The sight of his father holding Sunny warmed his heart.

Dan had joined them, as he always did when the team had home games. Mark's friend Jeff was there as well.

Mark managed to make it through the whole game without being hurt, which was a big relief to his parents. The memories of his motorcycle accident were still too clear; they prayed that he would never be seriously injured in a football game.

Since his accident, Mark had games where he became breathless and would have to sit on the sideline while they gave him oxygen. It was not unusual for him to play with an injury that would sideline most players.

Lately, he had been getting bloody noses. Mark had them before when he was younger so he was not too worried about them.

Mark flew back to the ranch with his family to celebrate the team win. Everyone was excited that Mark was one-step closer to seeing his dream come true. Mark started making plans for attending the Super Bowl game and booked an entire floor of a hotel for his family. He would surprise them later, but right now, he was concerned about another matter.

They all sat down to a family dinner. Sunflower had easily won everyone's heart that day. Mark was proud of her as he watched her interact with his family.

Mark and Sunny drove back into the city. She fell asleep in his car on the way there, so he had to carry her into the apartment. He laid her on her bed and covered her up with a blanket. She was sleeping so peacefully, he thought, as he laid her new doll back in her arms. That doll had not been out of her arms since he gave it to her.

Mark wondered how many nights she had gone to bed without anyone being there to say good night. He knew what that had felt like when he had gone away to boarding school. It was lonely and scary. He never wanted Sunny to feel that way again; he wanted her to feel loved and secure. He would shield her from all harm.

Mark knew that he loved Sunny like a daughter. She was a breath of fresh air to him. He enjoyed every minute they had together.

He remembered how proud he was of her when they had gone to church that morning. Many of Mark's friends were surprised to see him with a child. After talking to her, they understood why he seemed so devoted to her. She was charming and delightful with everyone.

The service was very meaningful and uplifting. Sunny sat still and listened carefully as her doll sat in her lap. Mark felt so proud of her. She was, without a doubt, his gift from God; he was sure now more than ever.

This was meant to be. He was not quite sure why, but he knew God would reveal the answer to him soon.

CHAPTER EIGHTEEN –
⋗The Ring⋖

*M*ark spent every spare moment he had that week with Sunflower. Their love for each other grew stronger each day. Mark hated having to leave her at night with the Browns, while he went to football practice or when he was on call for the night at the hospital.

Mrs. Brown let Sunny go play with her friend Katie in the park. John Jr. was there and joined the girls, pushing Sunny on the swings. They learned that John Jr. lived with his father, John Andrews, who was a fire-fighter and paramedic. John did not want to talk much about his mother. Sunflower noted the sadness in John's voice as he mentioned her. Sunny wondered why he didn't even tell them his mother's name.

Katie promised to walk Sunny back to the apartment at two o'clock. As Katie and Sunny were walking towards the apartment, they were talking.

"You sure are lucky, Sunflower, to have someone as sweet as Mark," Katie told her. Katie had really appreciated and loved all the things Mark and Sunflower had bought her after Christmas.

"He is so wonderful to me," Sunny exclaimed with love in her voice for Mark. Just thinking about him put a smile on her face.

"I miss you at the home," Katie said sadly.

"I miss you, too. Maybe you could play with me at the apartment today."

"I can't. I have to watch the kids today. Blanche is on the war path because of you," Katie explained as she looked over at Sunflower.

"What did I do?" Sunny asked with a frown as she kicked a rock on the sidewalk.

145

"I don't know. Blanche and the Stanleys had this big conference about you the other day, and I heard Blanche say she would get you back," Katie informed her.

Sunny stopped in her tracks and looked up at Katie for answers. "Do you think she will?" Sunny asked fearfully.

Katie gave her a reassuring smile and pulled something out of her pocket.

"It's okay, Sunflower, look what I have," Katie said as she held up a high school class ring on a gold chain and showed it to Sunflower.

"What is it?" Sunny asked.

"It's yours. I found it in your baby sweater that first day you were dropped off at the home, and I hid it from Blanche and the police," Katie informed her, thinking back to when she had only been ten years old. On that day, Katie had opened the door to the children's home and saw Sister Jessica standing there holding a basket with a baby in it.

"I don't understand," Sunny said as she took a closer look at the ring.

"This ring must have belonged to your mother," Katie informed her. Sunny's eyes got wide as she looked at the ring and then she quickly handed it back to Katie.

"You keep it," Sunny said, showing no interest in the ring.

"Why, Sunflower? This ring could tell us who your real father is. Don't you see, it is a man's ring? Your mother must have gotten it from your dad and then they gave it to you when you were born," Katie said with excitement, knowing they could find Sunflower's real parents.

Sunny cried in a panic, "My mother and father are dead. I want Mark to be my father! I love Mark!" Tears swelled in her eyes.

"But Sunflower, we could find out who your real parents are and they could come get you. This man's ring is from my high school. I could find out who he is for you," Katie told her compassionately.

"Get rid of that ring! I told you, Mark is my father now. If my parents are alive, they didn't want me and … I don't want them. I want Mark and Mark wants me," Sunny pleaded tearfully.

"Okay Sunflower, but I will keep it just in case you change your mind." Katie put the ring back in her pocket.

They were standing in front of the apartment building.

"I'll see you tomorrow, Sunflower," Katie said as she kissed her. Sunny gave her a hug. Katie was the one who had cared for Sunny as a baby, and Katie would always protect her. Katie watched as Sunny entered the building and then she sadly walked away. "Poor Sunflower," Katie whispered.

Sunny went in and went to Mrs. Brown's apartment. The ring had really upset her. She did not want her old parents. She wanted Mark, and this could ruin everything if someone else found out about the ring, she thought fearfully, her tiny face somber.

Mrs. Brown greeted Sunny cheerfully at the door.

"Hello, sweetheart, I have your cookies and milk waiting," Mrs. Brown told Sunny as she walked in the door, but Sunny walked right by her, sat on the edge of the couch, and stared into space. Mrs. Brown could tell something was wrong.

"What's the matter, honey?" she asked as she sat down beside Sunny. But Sunny did not answer. Mrs. Brown felt Sunny's forehead; it was warm. She jumped up in a panic and looked at her husband who was reading the newspaper.

"Oh dear, Joe, I think she has a fever. I better call Mark at the hospital."

Mark came right over, dressed in his hospital scrubs. Mrs. Brown let him in the door. He went quickly to Sunny, who was now lying down on the couch. Sunny looked scared and was tearful. Mark knelt down by the couch in front of her. She sat up and put her little arms around his neck.

"What's the matter, Sunny?" he asked with deep concern as he felt her forehead for a fever.

"I wanted you," she cried as she lay her head against his chest.

"I'm right here, honey, now lay back and let me have a look at you," Mark told her, as he took his stethoscope from around his neck. He listened to her heart and lungs, and then he looked in her throat and ears.

"She seems fine; she might be coming down with a cold," Mark told the Browns, who were standing over him, watching with concern.

"Thank goodness," Mrs. Brown said with a sigh of relief.

"I have to go back to the hospital," Mark told Sunny gently, aware that her pitiful eyes were encasing his heart.

"Don't go, Mark, don't leave me!" Sunny cried in a panicked voice as she hung onto Mark's neck tightly, nearly choking him.

"What's the matter, Sunny?" he asked as he rubbed her long silky blonde hair on her back, trying to calm her.

"Katie said they are going to take me away from you," she cried harder. Mark instantly shook his head no. No one was taking Sunny away from him as long as he had a say in the matter.

"No one is going to take you away from me, do you understand?" he assured her with compassion as he patted her back softly with the end of his fingers.

"I love you, Mark," she said through her tears and hugged him tightly. *Please God, don't let anyone find out who my real father is. I want Mark,* she prayed to herself

"I love you too. I don't want to leave you, but I have to get back to work. I'll be back here in two hours and we'll eat together before I go to practice, okay?" he asked her with regret. Mark really wanted to take her home with him and comfort all her fears.

"Okay ... but hurry back," Sunny said softly, wiping the tears from her eyes.

"You be a good girl for Mrs. Brown," Mark told her as he kissed her forehead.

"She is always a good girl."

Mark kissed Sunny good-bye at the door and left. He really hated to leave her, but he had to get back to work. He thought back to the many times his father had left him when he had needed him. Mark was beginning to understand what his grandfather had tried to tell him. Sometimes work had to come first. The choice was not his, and he hated it.

Mark came back two hours later, and they had supper together and played games until he had to go to practice. Sunny was such a joy to be around as she made him constantly laugh at her silliness.

Mrs. Brown came to watch Sunny so that Mark could go to practice. She would put Sunny to bed before Mark got home so he said good night to Sunny before he left.

Mark wished that he could be the one to put her to bed and listen to her prayers. His heart ached as he knew Monday was coming up, and he worried he might not ever have the chance to be with her again.

Sister Jessica came over to the apartment that night and asked if she could read to Sunflower before Mrs. Brown put Sunflower to bed. Mrs. Brown thought that would be fine.

She lifted Sunflower on to her lap and read the Bible story about Moses as a baby. His mother and sister had placed him in a basket in the Nile River where Pharaoh's daughter found him.

Sunflower liked the part where Moses' mother got to care for him even though no one knew she was Moses' real mother. Sister Jessica told Sunflower never to forget that story.

She held Sunflower tight and gave her a kiss. When Sunflower grabbed her around the neck, she accidentally pulled Sister Jessica's veil off her head and her long blonde hair fell to her shoulders. Sunflower touched Sister Jessica's beautiful hair with her tiny hands and smiled at her.

"You have pretty hair just like me," Sunflower remarked as Sister Jessica carefully wrapped her hair back in a bun and put her veil back on. Sister Jessica gave Sunflower another hug and stood up to leave. Her heart ached with the secret she could never tell about Sunflower.

Thursday was New Year's Eve. Mark had been invited to several parties, but he was extremely tired from his busy week at the hospital. After he got off work that morning, he took Sunny out to the ranch. He decided to spend the rest of the day there so Sunny could play with the boys and he could relax some.

Mark lay down on the couch and watched Sunny play with the boys. It was not like Mark to lounge around on a day like today; normally, he would have ridden his motorcycle or Thunder, or hung out with Charlie in the stables. When he fell asleep, Julia covered him with a blanket and told the children to play in another room.

Mark had hospital rounds on Friday morning. After rounds, he worked a few hours before he flew back to the ranch to check on Sunny. He had an away football game and the team left that night to travel to the game.

He had missed New Year's Day with Sunny. However, Mark was thankful she had fun with the boys at the ranch while he was at work. Before he left to catch his flight, Sunny wished him luck as they hugged and kissed. Sunny loved to see Mark all dressed up in his sports jacket and slacks.

"You're gonna make me one handsome daddy someday," she informed him with her charming smile. That was one request that Mark prayed would come true and soon.

Sunny watched Mark's game on TV with his parents. She still did not know anything about football, but one thing she did know: Mark was good-looking in his football uniform, and she could not wait until he was her daddy.

After the game was over, Mark was interviewed on TV. Sunny attentively stood at the TV and touched his face with her hand. Julia and Robert exchanged a look of sadness; they both knew Mark was facing a complicated hearing on Monday; it was possible he would lose Sunny and break her heart.

Mark came back Sunday night and drove out to the ranch to pick up Sunny. Even though it was late, he wanted to spend time with her before the hearing took place tomorrow. However, he was too tired to drive back into the city so they spent the night at the ranch.

Mark stood over Sunny's bed and watched her sleeping peacefully; he knelt down and prayed for favor over her. "Lord, place Your hand of protection on her. I am declaring the blood of the Lamb over her life; the devil has no power over her life. I believe it and receive it." Then he stood up, bent, and kissed her forehead.

As he lay on his bed, he wondered if tomorrow would bring them happiness or deep sorrow. He knew that it was very possible that Sunny would not be allowed to live with him any longer.

Mark picked up his Bible and read from it. One line caught his attention: John 1:32, *"I saw the Spirit come down like a dove from heaven and stay on him."*

It gave him the peace he needed to fall asleep.

CHAPTER NINETEEN –
∼The Hearing∽

*M*onday morning Mark and Sunny sat at the breakfast table at the ranch with Julia and Robert. Julia was deeply concerned by the paleness and the grave look Mark held on his face. She wanted to touch his forehead and see if he had a fever but he read her thoughts.

"I'm fine, Mom, stop worrying," he spoke gently as he quit stirring his coffee with the spoon that he had held for the last ten minutes. He stood up from the table. He was unable to eat anything; his stomach was giving him a fit. He bent over, kissed his mother's cheek, and then looked at his father.

"I'll see you later at the meeting, Dad. Sunny, we have to go now," Mark said as he held his eyes on his father's face for that reassuring look that he needed. Sunny walked over to Julia and Robert and hugged them before following Mark out the door.

Mark had planned to drive Sunny to school. Instead, he drove them to the park. Mark was worried about the hearing. He wanted to spend as much time as he could with her just in case things did not turn out the way he hoped.

Sunny held Mark's hand as they walked over to the very same bench where he had found her lying behind, on that cold night. Sunny proudly called the bench, *"Mark's Bench."*

However, today the bench belonged to a single *dove* who sat on the armrest. Sunny held her hands up to try and gather the dove but it flew up to the lamppost next to the bench.

Sunny could feel Mark's tension as they sat down. Mark still could not believe how one little girl could have changed his whole outlook on life.

He no longer wanted to be single; he wanted a family of his own. He could not imagine losing Sunny without tears forming in his eyes.

"It's gonna be okay," she said softly as she reached out to squeeze Mark's hand. Her tiny fingers weaved in between his fingers. He weakly smiled down at her.

"I can't lie to you, Sunny; it might not turn out like we want it," he said doubtingly as he took a deep breath. "My father had to pull an awful lot of strings to keep you with me this long," Mark told her gently.

"I believe, just like the princess in my book, that you will save me, 'cause you're my *prince,* ain't nothin' gonna keep us apart," Sunny proclaimed with certainty from her heart.

Mark stood up abruptly. "I'm your prince." He was not saying those words to Sunny; he was saying them to himself.

He had heard those words before, but who had called him that? He tried to think. The word "prince" touched something deep within his heart to rise into a warm feeling but he did not understand why.

"Mark," Sunny said as she pulled on his jacket to get his attention. From the look on his face, she knew he was somewhere far away.

"Mark!" she repeated. This time he looked down at her with distant eyes.

"What?" he asked, still in thought about how his heart was feeling about the word prince.

"I said that you are my prince," she laughed at him.

"You are my princess," he smiled at her as he picked her up in his arms and held her. He wished that he could be as brave as she was trying to be for him.

Mark took her out for lunch and then he took her to school. He had arranged earlier for Katie to walk her back to the apartment after school.

Mark met his father at Mrs. Wilson's office. Mark took his father's hands in his and prayed with him before they went inside.

Blanche from the children's home was there. She gave them an evil eye as they entered the room.

"Good morning, Mr. Sanders, won't you and your son please have a seat so we can get started," Mrs. Wilson said as she looked over at Mark and saw the grave look on his face.

Everyone sat down. Robert touched Mark's knee to let him know he was there for him.

"Mark, your father and I have already talked several times on the phone. I think I understand the situation, but I would really like to hear it from you," Mrs. Wilson addressed him.

Mark explained how he had found Sunflower in the park. He told Mrs. Wilson that he had called the police department and found out that no one had filed a missing report on Sunflower. He thought the best thing to do, for the time being, was to care for her until he found out more about her situation.

He shared how he had cared for her and how much they had grown attached to each other. He expressed that he wanted to be her foster father until he could legally adopt her.

"I just cannot believe that the Stanleys were allowed to be foster parents. With Sara being an alcoholic, she was so drunk, she didn't even realize that Sunflower was missing until she had been gone for several days," Mark emphasized strongly.

"I know Mrs. Stanley; she's a good hard working woman," Blanche butted in. "She certainly is not an alcoholic; she was not feeling well at the time, Mr. Sanders!"

"Where was Mr. Stanley, and what does he do to support the family?" Robert questioned Blanche.

"I don't know where he was during those few days. I'm sure he was working on a job; he's a carpenter," Blanche replied.

"Just for the record, Mrs. Wilson, my sources have informed me that Mr. Stanley was fired from his job six months ago." Robert informed her as he produced documents from his briefcase and handed them to Mrs. Wilson.

"It was because of a misunderstanding. Times are hard, and jobs aren't as easy to find; you certainly can't hold that against him," Blanche added and aimed a discerning look at Robert.

"Sunflower claims Mr. Stanley left the household after a bad argument," Robert added back; he was not about to be intimidated by her facial expressions. Blanche seemed agitated as she looked over at Robert again.

"All couples have disagreements, and I'm sure it was no more than that. I assure you, Mrs. Wilson, the Stanleys are happily married. They have provided a decent home for Sunflower, and Mr. Sanders has no right to imply they are not fit foster parents. Why, this all started because Mrs. Stanley wouldn't let that spoiled child have her own way, so she ran away," Blanche bellowed.

Mark was furious at what Blanche had said about Sunny and stood up quickly to face her down in Sunny's defense. Robert grabbed Mark's shirtsleeve and indicated for him to sit down.

"That's not true!" Mark shouted at Blanche. He looked at Mrs. Wilson. "Sunflower is not a spoiled child; she is very *sweet natured*. She ran away because the Stanleys were abusing her." No one would talk ugly about Sunny as long as he was around to protect her, Mark thought angrily.

"Well, if they were abusing her as you say, then tell me why she is so sweet natured?" Blanche asked smartly with a crooked mouth that made Mark scrunch his eyebrows at her.

"She certainly did not get it from the Stanleys. I told you, I've been to their apartment and it isn't fit for rats to live in, let alone an innocent little girl," Mark said as Blanche's lies were agitating him.

"Well! Just because the Stanleys aren't as wealthy as you mighty Sanders is no reason to bad mouth them!" she yelled back at Mark. Before Mark could say anything back, Robert eyed him sharply to remain quiet.

"Let's calm down. I can see you both share a different opinion about the Stanley's eligibility as foster parents. I will be investigating their credibility and situation myself, and I will determine if they are still suitable. Until then, Sunflower will not be returning to their home," Mrs. Wilson said. Mark let out a big sigh of relief and relaxed back in his seat.

"I want Sunflower returned to my children's home," Blanche said quickly.

"No way, Sunflower should remain with me!" Mark said strongly as he sat back on the edge of his seat, ready for a fight.

"You can't do that, Mrs. Wilson, he's a single male and that is clearly against the foster care rules. It is inappropriate for her to be with him. You cannot allow that to happen," Blanche fumed.

"We understand the regulations, Blanche, but this is an entirely different situation," Robert added as he held his hand across Mark's chest to prevent him from coming out of his chair. Mark thankfully backed off, keeping his eyes glued to Mrs. Wilson, watching for her reaction to what was being said.

"Why, because you have money, Mr. Sanders? Do you really think you are above the regulations?" Blanche retorted smartly.

"Mr. Sanders, I'm afraid Blanche is right; the regulations are clear. I understand that Mark is willing to provide care for the child, and I am sure he is more than suitable to do so, but I simply cannot break the rules," Mrs. Wilson stated firmly.

Mark was speechless, as if a knife had passed through his heart. Mrs. Wilson looked at Mark's pained face and felt compassion for him.

"Mark, I know that you have given Sunflower a good home, but if I gave her to you, there could be all kinds of legal problems. The facts remain: you are single and male. I hope that you will understand my position on this matter," Mrs. Wilson warmly added.

It did not matter how she said it, it hurt more than anything he had ever felt.

Mark was shaking his head in disbelief. Robert held his hand up to keep Mark from speaking. Blanche looked pleased with Mrs. Wilson's decision.

"Mrs. Wilson, my son intends to file for custody of Sunflower, and we were hoping that you could grant Mark temporary custody until we can get a court hearing to give him full custody."

"You cannot be certain that the Judge will grant Mark custody; the odds are not in his favor."

"I will get custody of Sunflower, no matter how long it takes," Mark argued as his voice faded. Nevertheless, it was clear his heart was broken from the look on his face.

"Mark, I know that you have become attached to Sunflower, but in all fairness to the child I cannot give you temporary custody. It would not be fair to get her hopes up that you will get custody. Besides, you will have to take the custody issue up in the courts. Until then, I want you to return Sunflower to the children's home by three o'clock today."

"No, she cannot go back there!" Mark protested in distress as he jumped up from his seat, ready to fight for Sunny.

"She will be in good hands with Blanche until this issue is settled. I have already broken the rules by letting you keep her this long, a mistake I should not have made. Therefore, my decision is final. Thank you both for coming," Mrs. Wilson said as she gathered the papers off the desk.

Robert stood up beside Mark.

"No, this isn't fair!" Mark said with tearful emotions, "You can't separate that little girl from me ... it will break her heart."

"I am sorry, there isn't anything else I can do," Mrs. Wilson said as she left the room.

Mark's father held his arm. "Mark, we will take this case to court, it is not over yet." Mark anxiously ran his fingers through his hair in disbelief that he had lost Sunny.

Blanche gave Mark a smug look. "You rich people are all the same, always thinking you can get your way, regardless of the law," Blanche retorted toward Mark.

"Why did you do this? Why did you stick up for people like the Stanleys when you know I can give Sunflower everything she needs?" Mark asked her in torment.

"Because you rich people never help anyone but yourselves," she shouted as she left the room, leaving a very angry Mark behind.

Blanche wiped the sweat from her forehead, thankful that the meeting was over. *Why did Mark have to go and choose Sunflower? If only Mark could have picked some other kid in the home, I would have gladly let him have that kid*, she thought anxiously as she quickly fled the building.

Mark turned towards his father. "I cannot believe what just happened," Mark said angrily. "How in the world am I going to break the news to Sunny?" Mark looked down at the floor.

"The look on your face will tell her all she needs to know," Robert calmly replied as he reached out and gathered Mark in his arms.

CHAPTER TWENTY –
∞Broken Hearts∞

*R*obert did not want Mark to drive so he insisted that they take the limo back to Mark's apartment. Robert watched as Mark stared blankly out the limo window. He knew there was nothing he could say to mend Mark's broken heart.

Mark looked down at his watch as they walked into the quiet apartment. Sunny was still at school. Mark walked in Sunny's bedroom and looked around the room as he took in a big breath. He exhaled as he began to gather up her clothes. He picked up her rag doll and held it to his torn heart. Then gently, he laid the doll on top of the clothes. He left everything on her bed.

He went into the living room where Robert was seated waiting patiently to offer Mark moral support. Mark sat down across from him and hung his head between his knees. It was clear that depression had set in as his gaze fell to the floor. Robert was pained seeing Mark so miserable.

"It is not over yet, Mark, we'll have our day in court. I'll file for a court hearing, and we'll start an investigation of the children's home and Blanche," Robert informed him with a soothing voice, trying to give his son some hope. Mark did not appear to be listening.

"My investigator's report said that Sara's neighbors told him that Sara once lived in her apartment with a small boy, a few years older than Sunny. Shortly after she remarried, the young boy disappeared. No one knows what happened to the boy."

Robert thought about the strange way that Blanche had acted in the meeting. It was part of her job to place the children in her home with an adoptive family. So, other than Mark being single, why did she go out of her way to keep Mark from Sunny?

"There is something strange going on with Blanche and I plan to find out what she is up to at the children's home that is not legal."

Mark's eyes widened, "I just wanted to reach out and grab that woman by the neck and ..." Mark said with clenched fists.

"I am glad you refrained yourself from doing so, Mark, or you would have lost any chance of obtaining custody," Robert warned him. "You will have to watch your every move until the court hearing is over. Do not give them any grounds to determine you are lacking any essential qualifications for being a competent parent."

The door opened and Sunny came in. She swiftly ran to Mark and jumped into his lap.

"Well, what happened, am I yours, am I?" she asked with excitement in her voice.

"Give me a big hug," Mark told her as he gathered her into his arms and held her close. He did not want to let her go, but she pushed away from him and looked into his grieving eyes.

"Why aren't you happy, Mark?" she asked softly, realizing that Mark was upset. Although she asked, she knew in her heart why he looked the way he did.

Mark could not find the words. His heart was breaking; he wanted to scream. But he knew he had to keep himself together for Sunny's sake. He would have to be strong for her.

"Things didn't go ok, did they?" she asked softly. Mark shook his head no; he looked down at the floor unable to face her sad eyes, knowing they would split his heart in half.

"You mean I can't live here no more?" she asked as tears formed in her downcast eyes.

Mark could not say anything; he was so broken inside.

"It's okay, Mark, I know you tried," she whimpered.

Mark snatched her up in his arms and held her tight. He could feel her body quiver as she cried. The tears were trickling down his own face as he tried to suppress his own emotions. He rubbed the back of her long silky hair and tried to console her.

"It is okay, Sunny," he said softly to her, "I love you, and ... I am going to get you back ... no matter what."

She pulled away, wiped the tears from her red swollen cheeks and looked at Mark for reassurance. "But, why can't I live with you?" she sobbed, her chin quivering, as her crumpled voice tore deep into his mangled heart.

There was no way he could let her go. He would have given anything to keep her safe with him. He held his hand to his chest, sure that his heart was about to explode. It hurt to breathe in, so he took a short breath and exhaled. His world was fading away and there was nothing he could do to stop it.

He cleared his throat so that he could speak, and then he drew in his tears with a deep breath that sent a sharp pain through his chest. How could he explain this to her when he did not understand it himself?

"You and I talked about this ... remember?" He took another deep breath, "You know they don't let little girls like you ... live with unmarried guys like me," he sympathetically told her as his tears continued to cloud his vision.

"Then you'll just have to get married ... oh please, Mark!" she begged anxiously, her eyes wide with hope that she had the simple answer to this problem. Mark shook his head no, taking away her hope and causing her to frown.

"It's not that easy, Sunny. I do not love anyone special enough to marry her," he informed her sadly.

"But I am still praying you will meet her. You just wait and see. God shall supply all our needs, remember?" she said with such fortitude.

Robert came over to them and took Sunny out of Mark's arms. He feared that Mark was about to breakdown and let out all his emotions if he did not do something to prevent it from happening.

With Sunny's back to him, Mark quickly brushed the tears from his face and exchanged a look of understanding with his father.

"Sunny, Mark is not going to get married anytime soon. We have to face the facts that this may not turn out the way we want it, but I am sure you are right. God does have a plan for us all," he explained to her kindly. "It is three o'clock, Mark; let's get this over with and get Sunny to Blanche's."

Robert put Sunny back down. Sunny ran to Mark, who had stood up and was leaning against the bookcase with one hand. He was desperately trying to hold it together for Sunny's sake. This time he did not pick her up. He clenched his teeth together as he turned and faced her.

"Father is right, Sunny, we have to be brave right now. The fact is ... you have to live at the children's home until ... well, until," Mark told her with a shaky voice and looked away from her pleading eyes.

"It's okay, Mark, I'll get my things," she said numbly, hung her head and walked slowly to her room. Mark heard her shut the door to her bedroom. He knew she did not want him to hear her cry.

The unfairness of the situation was more than he could handle as he looked at his father, searching his face for answers. His heart had had enough, his life was falling apart, and there was nothing he could do to stop it.

"I just can't stand it!" Mark shouted in anguish as he pointed to Sunny's room. "I love that child in there like she was my own little girl! I can't just stand here and let her go to that filthy children's home!"

He angrily picked up a vase off the coffee table. He was seriously thinking about throwing it across the room at the wall, but then he saw his father's eyes staring at him with disapproval. As much as he wanted to let out his intense anxiety, he felt compelled to set it back down on the table.

Robert gave a sigh of relief. He would have to remember to lock up Mark's motorcycle when he got back to the ranch; he did not want a repeat of the last time Mark was distressed. Robert regretted that he had passed down his temper to Mark.

When Robert got back to the ranch, he planned to give Dr. Gina Price, Mark's psychiatrist, a call and let her know how anxious all of this was making Mark.

Sunny appeared in the doorway, her face sullen.

"I'm ready," she said with little emotion. Robert looked at his watch, and then he met Mark's eyes.

"We better go, Son." Mark walked over to her and took the bag she had hanging at her side.

"Where are your new clothes?" he asked her softly as he thumbed through the bag.

"I won't need those fancy clothes at the home," she said sadly.

Mark looked back in the bag. She had taken the t-shirt of Mark's that she had used as a nightgown, her old dress and her old shoes. Under her arm was the rag doll he had given her. Mark's heart was breaking. He found her new jacket and knelt down to face her.

"You will need your jacket, Sunny. It is cold out there," he said lovingly. He helped her put on the jacket. He turned to his father.

"I am going to walk her to the home. I'll be back, and you can take me to get my car."

Robert bent down to Sunny. "You be a good girl. Mrs. Sanders and I will come visit you," he told her and gave her a hug and a kiss.

Sunny and Mark left the apartment building. He held her tiny soft hand in his. Mark's legs felt heavy with every step closer to the children's home. How could he just hand her over?

As they walked, he saw her hand reach up and wipe a fallen tear. He squeezed her other hand to give her comfort, but he did not know what to say.

"Will you come and visit me?" she asked with such sadness in her voice.

"Everyday that I can," he said, and then he had new hope in his voice.

That's it! I will visit her when I get off work, take her to the park, and do things just as we were doing before. Why didn't I think of that earlier?

They had arrived in front of the home. They hesitated as they stood there and looked at each other. Blanche came out the door. Mark stopped Sunny at the bottom of the steps.

"I'll be here everyday to visit you, and I want you to remember that I'm just down the street if you need me. You know my telephone number so you can call me. I love you and I don't ever want you to forget that," he stressed to her using his gentle voice.

"I won't; I love you, too," she replied sadly.

They hugged each other and kissed. Then hand in hand, they climbed to the top of the steps where Blanche was standing with her arms crossed against her chest.

"You are late, run inside, Sunflower," she said as she opened the door.

Sunny let go of Mark's hand and went to the door. She turned around and waved a last good-bye before she went inside. Blanche closed the door behind her and faced Mark.

"Now I don't want you coming around here bothering her, do you understand?" Blanche said sternly to Mark.

"I'll be here everyday at four to pick her up, and there is nothing you can do about that," he informed her, trying not to let his frustration show.

"Well!" she puffed. "You shouldn't visit her, she needs to be separated from you so she can adjust to living here again. We don't have all the fancy things you've been spoiling her with."

"I intend to give her all the things that you do not."

"Why can't you just leave her alone and go about your own life?"

"Because Sunny is a part of my heart now. I am not about to give her up to you or anyone!"

"You are only going to hurt her," Blanche bolted at him.

"Never, I could never hurt her!" Mark retaliated.

"What do you know about raising a little girl?"

"What do you know?" Mark reacted smartly.

"Just what is that supposed to mean? I run a respectable clean home here." She put her hands on her hips in anger.

"Is that so?" Mark said, raising his eyebrow at her.

"It is clear you know nothing about the job I do; it isn't easy, you know. I get all the kids around here that no one else wants."

"And you lend them out to people like the Stanleys," Mark said sarcastically. For an instant, he had knocked the wind out of her.

"Well, uh, I can't be choosy about foster parents because no one else wants these kids. I try my best to find decent people, but people don't want kids like these. I try to find them an empty bed; that's the best I can do." The sweat was running down her forehead.

"I wanted Sunny, but you put a stop to me getting her. I don't understand why?" Mark asked her, the pain he felt was clearly heard in his voice. For just a second she might have felt sorry for him, as her face lost its hardness.

"I have enough problems around here. You just don't understand nothing." She expressed more calmly.

"I'm really sorry about all your problems." He took out his wallet and handed her two hundred dollars.

"I want you to buy food with this money. I will give you money every week to feed and take care of Sunny. If I find out you are not using the money on her, I will cut you off."

"I don't need your help; Sunflower's done fine without you all these years, and she'll do fine now. You've done your good deed, now please leave and don't come back!" She turned and stomped inside, slamming the door.

Mark had gone back to his apartment and his father took him to get his car. They hugged each other as Mark said good-bye to him.

Robert hated the thought of Mark being alone at a time when he needed support from his family. This was one of those troublesome moments when a parent wants to shelter their child from the heartaches of life. Robert wanted to shelter Mark and Mark wanted to shelter Sunny. Robert turned to God for them both.

Mark drove back to his apartment; however, when he arrived he could not remember driving there. His mind was consumed with distressing thoughts of Sunny.

He looked over at the park and decided that he would go there to think this all out. He was more depressed than ever; he needed some quiet time with the only person he knew to turn to.

Mark knew that he needed his quiet time to include God. Only God could bring him comfort.

Chapter Twenty-One –
~God Shall Supply All Our Needs~

*M*ark had gone to the park to think. He was walking around in a circle in deep thought as his heart swelled. Sunny deserved a better life than this, he thought crossly. None of this made any sense to him. *God, are You listening? This is not fair.*

It was remarkable how emotionally strong Sunny was after the kind of life she had endured. Sunny sure had a sweet natured personality that she certainly did not inherit from Blanche.

It had been Sister Jessica and Katie that had influenced her and been mother figures to Sunny. Mark was thankful that Sister Jessica seemed especially attached to Sunny. He still could not remember her from high school. Maybe she had been one of the cheerleaders, he wondered.

He sat down on their bench, *"Mark's Bench,"* and thought to himself about all the things he and Sunny had done together. The love they had for each other had been unexpected and taken him by complete surprise. Once again, he felt chest pains. If he were not a doctor, he would have thought he was having a heart attack.

He thought adopting Sunny was what God wanted. "God, if You wanted us to be together, then why, why isn't she here with me?" An avalanche of pain hit his empty stomach with sheer force. He raked his fingers through his hair in frustration.

He had not realized how long he had sat there trying to figure it all out. Then it hit him, God did not want him to figure it out by himself. Mark shook his head as he understood, and he began listening to God speak to his heart.

God wants to restore everything that has been stolen from you; Mark heard his pastor's voice saying to him. Blanche had taken Sunny away from him. Mark knew that God would work it all out and he would receive twice the blessings back. He patiently would have to trust God.

Mark repented that he had put God aside while he had taken control of his own life. He knew that once he put God first and let God have control, his life would have peace. He repented for the anger that he had let into his life. He genuinely prayed for Blanche.

By now, it was getting dark and cold. An eerie feeling that had haunted Mark since he was eight came over him like a tidal wave. He leaned forward, placed his elbows on his knees, placed his head in his hands, and covered his eyes. He knew it was the work of the devil speaking to him now, putting fear where comfort had come just moments ago.

He knew he had promised to trust God. However, the reality of the situation and his fear of losing Sunny continued to crush his heart as he sat there thinking about what he needed to do to get Sunny back.

"God, tell me what I need to do to get her back. I can't do this by myself."

As the fear of losing her forever crept over him, he became even more determined to do something to get Sunny back safe with him. Patience was not a virtue Mark owned; it was something that the devil still held over him.

I have to get her back, he said to himself. He jumped up quickly without looking in front of him. He bumped into a woman jogger, knocking her to the ground. Mark quickly leaned over her to see if he could help her.

"I'm so sorry; did I hurt you?" he asked with concern.

She was rubbing her ankle and without looking up at him, she said. "I think I twisted my ankle." She continued to rub her ankle.

"Here, let me help you up. You can sit on the bench while I take a look at it," he offered kindly.

His familiar voice startled her heart. She quickly turned to face him and looked shocked when she saw his face. From her stunned reaction, he thought she was scared of him.

"It's okay. I am a doctor," his tone was gentle, which did not seem to bring her any comfort at all. She looked mystified as she stared at him.

He lifted her arm gently so she could stand. She did not say anything. He helped her to the bench, bent down, and took a hold of her ankle to exam it. She continued to stare at him, her mouth partly open.

"Really, I am a doctor. You look like you have seen a ghost," he told her with a reassuring smile. "I think your ankle will be fine, but if you think you need an x-ray, I can give you a lift to the hospital," Mark offered as he stared into her captivating blue eyes. She was so beautiful his heart missed a beat.

"It's fine. I should be going," she said as her stomach did a flip-flop and her eyes locked on his.

Mark had gotten up and sat beside her. He admired how incredibly beautiful she was. Mark felt warmth in his heart when he looked into those deep blue eyes of hers. Her eyes gave him a peaceful feeling and sent his heart soaring.

"Can I give you a lift home? My car is not far from here. I could go get it," he offered kindly.

"No, thank you, I live close by," she said as she angled her head and studied his gentle face as he continued to stare at her.

Mark was speechless as he searched her face for answers. There was an air of electricity surrounding them.

"Why are you staring at me like that?" she asked as she fell deep in his eyes. Her mind was going a hundred miles an hour now. She flashed him a familiar grin.

"I just can't believe how much you look like a little girl I found right here. You have the same eyes and same hair as she does," he told her and now he knew that she was focused on him.

"You found a little girl, right here?" she asked confused.

"It's a long story," he told her. His mind was searching for an answer for the way that she was making him feel. They continued to stare at each other. Finally, she got up the courage to say what it was that she really wanted to say to him.

"You look like a guy I once knew," she said to him softly, her voice barely audible.

"My name is Mark ... Mark Sanders."

She already knew that, but hearing him say his name out loud startled her heart. She looked bewildered and her face seemed to go pale as she stood up quickly. Tears clouded her vision. It was far too painful to be with him; she quickly tried to get a grip on her emotions.

"I've got to go," she said sadly, as she turned to leave but Mark softly grabbed her arm and held her there. Their eyes met for just a brief moment before she turned her face downward.

"What is wrong?" he asked confused, "Who are you?"

She looked back into his warm eyes. "I'm ... April Morgan," she said softly as her eyes misted over.

She waited for him to hug her, but he just gave her a puzzled look. He was more confused than before.

"Are you related to Dr. Dan Morgan?" he asked, baffled.

"He's my uncle," she said as her eyes fell, disappointed he still did not remember her.

"Now I know where I've seen you before," he said, relieved and smiled.

"Where?" she asked with a surge of hope in her voice, praying that he did finally remember her.

"Your picture is on your uncle's desk at the hospital."

"Is that all you remember about me?" She was let down that he still had no clue of their past relationship. *I was your faithful best friend and your constant companion,* she thought with resentment, but she did not share that thought with him.

"Didn't your family move to California a few years ago?"

"We did; do you remember that?" she asked with continual hope that something would spark his memory of them.

"Your uncle told me. What are you doing here?"

"I just moved back," she said softly.

"Weren't we in high school together?" he asked her, feeling as if he knew her from somewhere else.

"Yes," her voice was so soft he could hardly hear her and she hung her head down and was looking at the ground.

"Is something wrong?" he asked with concern.

"No, I should be going," she said without facing him.

"Would you like to have dinner with me tonight?" Mark asked as he tried to find her eyes while she avoided looking at him.

"Maybe some other time. I have a lot of unpacking to do."

"May I at least walk you home? I feel so bad about hurting your ankle."

He had not changed; he was still considerate, April thought with a half smile.

"I'm fine, really, you don't have to bother."

"Your uncle would never forgive me if I let something happen to you." He could not understand why she was making him feel the way he did at that moment. His heart was beating so fast. He wanted to know more about her. He was not ready for her to end their conversation.

"All right, you can walk me to my apartment building," she agreed, as she pointed in the direction they had to go. He offered her his arm to help her up from the bench. He supported her with one hand until she indicated that her ankle was fine.

His nearness to her stirred memories of him that she held locked in her heart. He certainly did not appear to have the key anymore or he would have remembered her, she thought with conviction.

April walked quietly. Mark could feel the tension. He was surprised when she stopped in front of his apartment building.

"This is my apartment complex," she said.

He had a sly grin on his face. "Mine, too," Mark laughed. What luck, he thought, unable to contain his happiness.

"Oh, what floor?" she asked with a beautiful smile.

The smile without warning sent his mind, body and soul whirling around in circles, causing his heart to miss another beat.

"Fourth, uh, four B," he told her with his handsome grin.

"Second, two C," she smiled again and Mark liked her smile. *Was she glad that we share the same building*, he thought. He certainly was glad.

She sensed the effect that she was having on him. The expression on his face was unmistakable; it was a look of adoration for her. She had seen that the same look many years ago.

They went into the building. Mark pushed the elevator button for the second floor. April was speechless, so Mark did not say anything either. They glanced at each other and shared a simple smile. The elevator stopped at the second floor. April quickly got off and turned to face him.

"Thanks," she said abruptly as she quickly left him standing there with his mouth half-open ready to bid her farewell, but no sound escaped his lips before she was gone.

Mark thought her exit and behavior was strange. *Why was she in such a hurry to be free of me? She must be tired,* he thought, giving her the benefit of uncertainty.

He went to his own apartment. It seemed so empty now that Sunny was not there to greet him. He went into her vacant bedroom; anger split his heart as he imagined her lying alone in a bed at the children's home. She definitely would be crying for him. Tears stung at his eyes as an overwhelming sadness settled like a wet blanket over his heart. He had failed to rescue her tonight.

Once again, he was thankful that God had stopped him from doing something that he might have regretted later by side tracking him with April at the park. He would have to keep his head on straight and control his temper if he wanted to get full-custody of Sunny.

He slumped down on the couch and started to think. Who was this woman he had just met? What beautiful eyes she had. She made him have feelings he certainly had not anticipated. His heart was still beating too fast.

He laughed thinking about what Sunny had said about, "God supplying all his needs." *Was April the woman Sunny had been praying God would send me? God sure did not waste any time delivering her to me.* Mark laughed again with his brilliant smile as he thought of April. "God, you sure know how to pick a pretty gal."

On a serious note, April had touched his heart deeply. Was God responsible for the feelings he had for her when they had been together in the park? He had prayed for years that God would send him the woman that God had intended for him. *Could April be her? Did God send her to me tonight on purpose?*

April said she had gone to high school with him but he did not remember her. Was April the girl his mother tried to tell him about while he was in the hospital? Was she the girl that visited him at the hospital after his accident, the one they said he had grown up with at the ranch?

He got up, pulled his dusty senior yearbook off the shelf, and started looking through it. Most of that year was still a lost memory. Dr. Price told Mark that he was suppressing certain details in his life because they were too painful to remember. *How could someone like April be too painful to remember?*

He flipped through the pages. He looked under Morgan. There she was, in her class picture. Wow, she was as beautiful as she was now; she had not changed at all. How was it possible that he had forgotten her, he asked himself, as he looked at her picture more carefully.

Then he saw a picture of Sister Jessica, only she was Jessica Morton. He held the book closer in confusion. *What is going on?* The two girls favored each other much like sisters would.

Then he remembered how Jessica had tagged after him when he returned to school after his accident. Jessica had danced with him at his eighteenth birthday party or so she said. He did not remember dancing with her but she had reminded him of the things they had done together in high school when she talked to him the other night at the church. Other memories came to mind as he looked at the pictures in the yearbook.

He continued to turn the pages, searching for answers and memories. April, Jessica, Sharon, and Christy were cheerleaders. *Sister Jessica must have become a nun soon after graduating,* Mark thought puzzled, *from a cheerleader to a nun, but why?*

He turned the pages. April was Homecoming Queen, and what .... there he was with her, his arm around her waist. He had been the King. They were looking into each other's eyes and there was no mistaking it, it was a look of pure love. Mark was confused now as he nervously held the book closer.

"I don't remember any of this." But there they were together, staring him in the face, under the title, "Mark and April Forever."

So much of that year, he would never get back, or would he?

CHAPTER TWENTY-TWO –
∽Letting Go of the Past∽

*T*he phone was ringing and Mark answered it. It was Dan. Just hearing Dan's voice gave Mark the comfort he needed at this confusing moment. Dan always knew just what to say to Mark.

"I just met your niece, Dan." Mark informed him.

"Really? That is why I called. I thought maybe you could take her out and introduce her to some of your friends."

"Sure, if she'll agree to it," Mark said with some doubt in his voice.

"That should not be too hard. Don't you remember the crush you guys had on each other? Now she lives right there in your apartment complex," Dan said with a hint of satisfaction.

"I suppose you had nothing to do with that coincidence," Mark said with humor in his voice, knowing full well that Dan was guilty.

"Well, maybe. She asked if I knew of any place close to the hospital, and I just happened to think of your apartment complex," Dan replied, thankful that Mark could not see the wide grin on his matchmaker face.

"You said we had a crush on each other?"

"Sure, don't you remember?"

"I still don't remember much of my senior year."

"She came to visit you in the hospital after your motorcycle accident. She was your childhood companion. Don't you remember her?"

"I've heard stories, but I can't recall much about her. Why haven't you said anything about her to me before?"

"You suffered some memory loss after your accident, but I thought it would all come back to you. Dr. Price said to let you remember things on your own and advised us not to force you to remember things. Unfortunately that included April."

"I wish I could remember everything about April. She sounded upset at me and I don't understand why," Mark said puzzled.

"She was really crazy about you; she just has a bruised ego. I would not worry too much about it. Now is your chance to make it up to her and ask her out to dinner."

"I already did. She turned me down flat."

"Well, don't give up; she'll come around," Dan encouraged him.

"I hope so."

"Your father told me about Sunflower. You must be feeling pretty low." Dan's heart was breaking knowing Mark was emotionally suffering. Sunflower was special to all of them; she reminded Dan of April when she was smaller.

"I am. Sunny stole my heart, and I can't get her off my mind."

"I will be praying for you," Dan said with compassion.

"Thanks, I can use all the help I can get."

"If I were you, Mark, I would go straighten things out with April."

"How can I straighten things out if I can't even remember her?"

"Your memories of her will all come back to you, just like the other things did. You just have to spend some quality time with her, Mark."

"Don't tell her about this, okay?"

"All right. I am on my way to see her now. I'll be there in ten minutes. I'll see you tomorrow."

"Thanks, Dan."

Mark hung up and went back to looking at the yearbook. April had moved away shortly before he had gone back to school. That was when he was busy trying to get his life back in order and learning how to walk. Had he been selfish and not included her in his life because he was too busy with everything else, he wondered?

Meanwhile at April's apartment, she was carefully unpacking glasses and dinnerware, thinking to herself.

"I just cannot believe Mark did not remember me. How can you forget what we shared? Darn him. I never forgot about him no matter how hard I tried," she said aloud with deep sorrow.

The phone rang and she answered it.

"Hello."

"April, I thought I told you never to return home again. Why did you leave like this without telling your mother and me where you were going?" he demanded.

"I'm tired, Dad, I do not want to talk to you right now. I thought I made myself clear; you cannot run my life any longer."

"I am coming to get you and bring you back here where you belong," he shouted.

"Please, Dad, just leave me alone!" she shouted back and then she slammed the phone down. Her hands were trembling.

"Oh, great! Now what am I going to do? When will he learn he cannot control my life any longer?"

The doorbell rang.

"What is this; can't I just be left alone?" she asked as she went to the door and swung it open. It was her Uncle Dan and she let out a sigh of relief.

"Uncle Dan, I'm so glad to see you, come in," she said with excitement as she gave him a warm hug. They went into the living room.

"Your father called me; he told me you had forgotten to give him your new phone number."

"Oh, so that's how he got my number."

"What's going on, April?"

"The fact is I did not tell him I had moved back here."

"What? I cannot believe that. Are you and your father having problems?"

"You know Dad; he's always trying to run my life. Well, not anymore. I have had it. I'm on my own now, and that's the way it is going to stay."

"So that is why you called me for a job?"

"Not just a job, Uncle Dan, I wanted to be home. I needed to be near you, Grandma and Grandpa Parker and my sister Debbie and her husband, Phil, and their children, Jeffery and Kevin, and my brother Todd. I have missed them all so much," she said close to tears.

"We've missed you too, sweetheart. Todd is over at the college now so I see him more, but Debbie does not come over very often. She travels with Phil to his baseball games."

"Great, then it's settled. I'm staying here."

"I've missed all our heart-to-heart talks that we used to have."

"Oh, me too, you always understood me and listened to me."

175

"I was heartbroken when your Dad just picked up and moved so suddenly."

"That's Dad for you. He knew he could run his company in California better if he were there to oversee it," she said as she looked away from Dan.

"I guess, but it sure was a shock to us all. I wanted to visit you but Paul always came up with a reason for me not to come."

"I missed you; I am sorry I didn't call more or write."

"Well, you are here now; that's what counts."

"Thanks for getting me the nurses' job. I'm so excited I will be able to work with you," she said warmly as she changed the subject.

"Several of your old friends work at the hospital. Do you remember Mark Sanders?" he asked as he watched for her reaction to Mark's name. April turned away and got up and went over to the boxes she was unpacking. Dan was puzzled at her reaction.

"Mark lives right here in this building. I'm sure you will run into him." Dan acted as if he did not already know that she knew that.

"He already ran into me and nearly broke my ankle doing it!" she said somewhat crossly.

"You don't seem too excited about seeing Mark," Dan said puzzled.

"Why should I?" she said sulking.

"If I remember right, you were crazy about him."

"That was a long time ago; I don't even remember."

"Six years is not so long ago."

"Well, he certainly did not remember me!" she pouted.

"It's not Mark's fault he cannot remember. That accident he had was very serious; he almost died. He lost some of his memory around the time of the accident. By the time he returned to school, you had moved away. He was so busy trying to catch up on everything in his life that I suppose he forgot about you," Dan told her kindly, hoping to make her understand that it really was not Mark's fault he had forgotten her.

"I guess our relationship was not important enough for him to remember!" she said bitterly.

"What's bothering you, April? This kind of attitude is so unlike the April I remember."

"Oh, it's nothing. I'm just tired; it has been a long day."

"Why don't you give Mark another chance and forget about the past?"

"Why should I?" She looked at him with a frown.

"Because he is very special to me, just like you are, April," Dan informed her with love in his voice.

"What's so special about him?" she puffed.

"He's a nice young man, sensitive, smart and he doesn't go around chasing my nurses like my other interns do. Besides all the nurses like him, and it will only be a matter of time before one of them snatches him," Dan informed her.

"Good for her. She can have him," April said smartly.

"Oh come on, stop that and be fair," Dan said, as he smiled at her and she broke down and let a smile show.

"Well, maybe. I can see you want to play matchmaker, so I'll be nice to him, but that is all," she said as she grinned at him. Dan had a way of bringing out the best in her.

She just needed more time before she ran into Mark Sanders again. Having him in this apartment building was like having him in the next room. Whether she liked having him in the same building or the same room was still up for debate in her mind and in her heart.

Chapter Twenty-Three –
⟨No Longer Strangers⟩

The doorbell rang, and she glided over to answer it. She was baffled, who would show up at her door at this hour? She opened the door. It was none other than Mark.

Of course, she should have known. He pretentiously held a bunch of flowers in front of him, the precise flowers she had seen in the apartment lobby earlier that day. *He thinks he is pretty clever;* she smiled to herself.

"Before you slam the door in my face, I want you to have these, a peace offering for whatever I did that upset you earlier," he said as he smiled down at her and held the flowers out to her. April just stood there speechless, as if she was in some sort of a trance.

Dan had gotten up and gone over to the door. If his plan to bring these two together was going to work, he would have to get more involved in the matchmaking process, which was apparent from the way the two just stood there speechless. Dan grabbed Mark's arm and pulled him into the room.

"Come on in, Mark, I was just leaving," he invited Mark, as he kissed April on the cheek.

"I'll see you later, sweetheart. Remember what I told you," he whispered to her and then he turned to Mark.

"Good night, Mark," he said with an amusing smile on his face, and then he closed the door behind him as he left.

April stood still facing the man who had astounded her just an hour ago.

"April, are you alright?" Mark asked her with a smile that lit up the room around him.

"Oh, I'm sorry. I just didn't think I'd be seeing you again this soon," she expressed as she swallowed the lump in her throat. She could feel her heart thumping and she was sure he heard it.

He handed her the flowers. She was speechless as she looked down at them. She stood frozen in deep thought, feeling her knees going weak. She was not emotionally ready to be in the same room with him. She was torn in half: her mind was annoyed with him and the other half of her, being her heart, was still in love with him.

"April?" Mark whispered to her not wanting to startle her. With a jolt, she came back to life.

"Oh, uh, have a seat, while I put these in water," she said as she finally took the flowers from him.

Mark did not have the heart to tell her that the flowers were plastic. He chuckled and grinned to himself as he sat down and watched her every move. Noting just how beautiful she was even in her oversized t-shirt, old worn out blue jeans, her hair pulled back in a ponytail, and to finish her radiant look, a loose strand of hair outlined her attractive face. He smiled with approval.

"How is your ankle?" he asked with concern. He watched her fill a water vase and then she plopped the flowers in it. He just smiled, grinning ear to ear, trying hard not to laugh out loud.

"I am ... just fine," she stuttered as she came back into the room and sat down across from him. She seemed to be off in the distance, thinking. Then her eyes got big as she thought about what she had just done. *Did I really just put plastic flowers in a vase of water?* Her cheeks blushed in embarrassment, as she understood the laughter in Mark's eyes.

"I'm really sorry I bumped into you. Uh, I mean, I am sorry I hurt your ankle. I was thinking about that little girl I had found there by that same bench. Guess I wasn't paying attention to what was going on around me," Mark apologized to her tenderly.

"Was she lost?" She faced him with sudden interest.

Finally, he had her attention. "She was running away from her foster parents," Mark said sadly, as his gut tightened and he stressfully rubbed the back of his neck. Talking about Sunny at this moment sucked the breath from his chest.

"That is so heartbreaking," April said with compassion.

His face was torn and his voice filled with heartache. "I ended up taking her home with me. She told me this awful story about her life, and I fell instantly in love with her. I have been taking care of her, that was, until today. The child welfare worker sent her back to the children's home."

"Why did they take her away from you?" A combination of feelings consumed her heart as Mark told her his story. She bit her lip as she waited to hear more about this little girl.

"They have a rule about unmarried males being foster parents. It is tearing my heart apart, thinking about her being in that dreadful children's home, all alone tonight," he said, feeling miserable as he thought about Sunny. He had experienced that same scary feeling when he went away to school as a child.

"I'm sorry, you must be feeling awful," she said quietly. Mark noticed the crystal-clear sadness on her face.

"She is such a brave little girl. She is so loving and trusting; you would really like her," Mark told her, as he felt a strong connection to April as they talked.

"I would love to meet her sometime," April said tenderly. Mark thankfully shook his head.

April's understanding eyes grabbed at his heart. It was as if she had solved other tribulations in his life before tonight. What had Dan called her, his buddy? No, she was his little companion. Tonight of all nights, he needed a companion. He knew God had a hand in bringing them back together tonight; it was no accident that he had found her, Mark thought as he stared into her inviting eyes.

"I'm sorry; I cannot seem to remember much about you. Dan thinks it is because of the accident I had." He looked into her warm eyes intensely, trying to figure her out.

He studied her face, her eyes, her voice, and the way she smiled at him. Mark's eyes had been innocently unwrapping her soul like a package, as he desperately tried to figure out why she seemed so familiar to him. *God, help me remember her*, his mind begged.

It seemed like he was just inches from recalling her in his mind, yet he could not place her in his past life. Not remembering her was driving him insane. He ran his fingers through his hair nervously.

He closed his eyes for a brief moment and tried to picture her in his mind as a teenager. Nevertheless, no picture appeared. Was she lost to him deep inside the darkness of his mind; would he be unable to retrieve her?

He opened his eyes to the vision of her sitting there across from him. It was clear that his heart had not lost her after all this time; he knew she was what his heart had been missing. At this tender moment, he was falling genuinely in love with her.

"Do you remember anything about me?" she asked wishfully, noting the softness that filled his eyes when he looked at her.

"Not really, but I have these unexplainable feelings for you, a closeness. I feel like I know you, but I don't. Do you remember much about me?" he asked as he studied her memorable eyes.

"I was a cheerleader so I watched you play football. You were terrific; in fact, you still are." Her pleasant voice filled with excitement. Finally, she showed some spirit.

"You've seen me play pro ball?" he asked with enthusiasm in his voice as the corner of his mouth lifted into a warm smile.

"Only the games that were on TV." The truth was; she never missed a chance to watch him play when his team was on TV.

Mark Sanders was not just her childhood companion; he was a well-known celebrity. She had read several magazine articles that featured him as America's most eligible sportsperson. She had saved every article, every picture of him, in a scrapbook.

"You will have to come to one of my games," he invited her.

"That would be fun," she answered with a shy smile.

"Do you remember my accident?"

"I came to see you while you were in the hospital but you were really out of it," she said with sadness as she remembered that awful day when her world had come to a complete standstill.

"I must have been out of it, if I didn't remember you," he said as he smiled at her warmly. She instantly blushed and turned away from him briefly, to gather her thoughts.

"My family moved a few months after that, before you returned to school," she said as she stared back into his tender eyes. She had once loved those eyes that were intensely drawing her to him. She twisted her fingers together nervously.

"Dan told me you had moved; he really missed you."

Their eyes continued to hold on to each other's and unspoken words of affection were exchanged between them. She realized it and looked down; she seemed to be blushing again.

Mark felt unknowingly comfortable sitting there talking to her as if they were old friends. He liked the warm feelings she provided.

"You have such a pretty smile," he spoke sincerely. Now she was blushing; he was sure she was. His heart was becoming increasingly warm as she became more and more familiar to him.

"Thank you," she said shyly, feeling like a teenager on her first date. But then, Mark had been the only one she had ever dated, if one could call what they did in the past, dating.

"I just can't believe I can't remember you. You are so beautiful; you are not the kind of lady that could easily be forgotten. I just don't understand this." Mark was desperately trying to recall her.

Was it possible those eyes of hers had struck a chord with his heart years ago? Were her musical eyes playing the same tune with him now? His heart was unmistakably skipping beats.

"Don't worry about it; that was a long time ago. Besides, maybe it is better that … you do not remember," she said softly, casting her tearful eyes to the floor.

If only, if only things could have been different, she thought. The room suddenly became silent, the only sound being the breath she took to hold back her tears. If only she could take back … what she had done.

"Why would you say that?" Mark asked confused, pushing for more information, uncertain why her mood and her tone of voice had changed so suddenly. What had caused her tears, he wondered as his heart took on a different beat of uneasiness when he saw her first teardrop land on her jeans.

Her mood had changed back to being reserved as she thought of something in her past. She was now restraining from volunteering any further knowledge of their past relationship. It was a time in their life that had to remain forgotten, she thought.

Mark watched her collecting her thoughts and waited for her to speak. He thoughtfully looked for a box of tissues, but saw none. The silence was unbearable as the apprehension built between them.

"Why, April, why don't you want me to remember our past?"

"No reason." She shrugged her shoulders as she exhaled a breath of air. "I just believe in looking ahead in life, not backwards," she said as she nervously twisted her hair with her fingers. She had new tears forming in her eyes and she was trembling slightly; she refused to look back at him. The quiet tears fell slowly onto her jeans as she bent over to hide her face from his troubled eyes.

"Something is wrong. Is there anything I can do to help you?" he asked kindheartedly. He wanted to reach out and take a hold of her hand to reassure her that he was sincere, but he restrained cautiously, afraid he might instead embarrass her.

"Don't mind me," she sighed as she wiped away a few tears that had escaped the corners of her eyes, and she lifted her face slightly to steal a look at him. She was aware that Mark was attentively staring at her. Once again, she bowed her face, wiped the tears away with the palms of her hands, and took in a long deep breath. *Please, God, help me get through this*, she quietly prayed.

Each tear she shed sent a wave of pain to his heart. "I want to help, if you'll let me," Mark volunteered with a voice that melted her soul.

She briefly looked back at him and saw the look of compassion on his gentle face. She took a deep breath in hopes of regaining her composure. Her heart was vulnerable, and she wanted him to move closer to her. She wanted to feel his comforting arms around her. She wanted him to tell her that no matter what she had done in her past, he would understand. He was all she had ever wanted even when he had been off limits.

But how, how could she forget why she could not let him capture her heart again? How could she tell him the truth of her tears and not have him walk out of her life again?

God answered her. Tell him the truth. She bravely faced him and found the strength to open up to him.

"It's just life ... in California ... was unbearable for me. I was hoping ... I could get my life back together by ... coming back here. ... I thought somehow ... I could ... forget what happened ... but then ... but then...," she said with a shaky voice.

But then what? But then, she had run into him, and all that changed, is what she wanted to say. However, the truth was far from her tongue, as she faced him and silence fell on them.

"Sounds like you are running away from your problems. If you really want to solve your problems, you have to face them head on and then turn them over to God," he advised her, but she misread his words as egotistical.

"What?" She looked over at him with pain-filled eyes and gave him a not-so-friendly look. How dare he think it was that uncomplicated to forget the pain he had put her through, she thought as his words assaulted her mind.

"Maybe I was running away. I guess I did not realize my real problem was right here in my hometown. I certainly was not prepared to face it, so soon," she said as she looked away from him, fighting back the urge to tell him everything that had happened.

She was determined not to lose her self-control, no matter how upset she was. What she had to tell him would have to wait until she could trust him.

Mark had the feeling that she was trying to tell him that he was her problem. Nevertheless, he did not intend to confront her about it right now while she was feeling so distant.

"I hope you can work out your problems. I wish I knew how to help." He spoke with such sincerity that she instantly felt remorse for her anger towards him.

Suddenly she remembered what it felt like when they were sitting in his tree house when they were just kids. Not once had he ever caused her to cry. He had always wiped away her tears when she had been upset.

There was a brief moment of silence; they both could feel the tension as she refused to acknowledge him, knowing that her heart wanted to open up to him just as she had done so many years ago.

Nevertheless, she had changed her mind; she was determined not to follow her heart. Instead, she would keep things platonic between them. Maybe they could be casual companions just as they had been so long ago, but absolutely nothing more than that.

If they were just friends then she would not have to share the truth with him. The instant she looked up into his sad puppy dog eyes, her heart begged her to reconsider.

The little voice in her mind spoke, "Be strong, you have to be strong. Keep your head; he can't have your heart, he can't." She had to move away from him if she was going to let her mind win this battle. Her heart was racing entirely too fast as his pitiful look of rejection tried to trap her into forgiving him.

She finally got up and headed towards the kitchen area, leaving him to wonder what on earth she was trying to do to them. Why was she acting so strangely towards him? Why was she pushing him away when all he wanted to do was help her?

"Can I get you something to drink? I'm sorry, but I do not have any beer," she said somewhat smartly, as a memory struck her.

"Water would be fine. I don't drink," he informed her, wondering why she would think he would drink.

She looked over at him and feverishly thought about his answer. She mumbled something under her breath and then she spoke to him. "I'm glad. I prefer men who do not drink," she told him bluntly with a heavy sigh. She came back with the water glasses and handed him one as she sat down beside him.

"Thank you," he said kindly to her. Their eyes held each other's briefly, but this time Mark saw the hurt in them. It took everything he had not to reach out to her. He formed a fist to reduce the advancement of his fingers from touching her. He did not want to receive an unwelcome response from her.

"Let's talk more about the little girl you found. What are you going to do?" she asked halfheartedly.

She seemed so interested in his story about Sunny, which sparked his heart in the direction of her once again. It was as if she shared a common concern with him. Could talking about Sunny bring them back on the right track with each other?

"She is six years old, although she looks extremely small for her age. She has long blonde hair and blue eyes, in fact she looks a lot like you, she is very beautiful," he said tenderly hoping to lighten up her mood. He winked at her and raised his eyebrows. He deliberately shined her a smile to open up her heart.

He witnessed a small smile form on her face, even if she thought she was concealing it from him. He finally had her attention back. He directed another one of his irresistible smiles at her, making it impossible for her not to let her reluctant smile grow into a full-blown smile and then they both laughed.

"That's a lot better." She blushed again as she shook her head at him in a playful way. "A woman as pretty as you should smile all the time," he said warmly, hoping to take away some of the tension that surrounded them.

Her eyes drifted away from him as he looked intently her way. *Darn him, he is doing it to me again. Why do I let him win?* She thought good-humoredly, feeling her cheeks become warm.

"I bet you say that line to all the women you meet." She shyly glanced up at him, knowing he was using his overpowering charm on her, just as he had done in the tree house. Well, two could play that game, she thought as she sent him the eyes that once put him in his place.

"Only to Sunny. Her real name is Sunflower, but I call her Sunny."

"Oh, sure, just her?" she asked with a smile as her cheekbones rose. She was intoxicating when her eyes shined playfully at him. Mark felt dizzy just looking at her.

"It's the truth. She is the only woman in my life, but she is willing to share me, uh ...say, uh, if I found the right woman," he stuttered as they gazed into each other's eyes. He could tell she was melting like butter in his hands. "What do you say, you and me, could we be friends and forget about the past?" he begged tenderly.

"Sure," she said somewhat apprehensively, regretting that she had encouraged him with her eyes; that sure had backfired on her. How could she deny him when she was drowning in his appealing eyes?

"I promise I will not rush you into anything more than friendship," he assured her. However, his inviting smile and engaging eyes told a completely different story. He was not seeking a platonic relationship.

"I guess we could be friends," she said softly as she cleared her throat. His arousing eyes were cutting through her very soul as she tried to resist her true feelings for him. It was hard to breathe when he leaned closer to her. She took a few slow deep breaths to keep from hyperventilating.

"Good," Mark said with enthusiasm as he was about to reach for her hand.

She retreated and moved slightly out of his reach. She was definitely not ready to control her feelings for him; it was time to change the subject and put space between them, or she would be in his tempting arms and tasting his magnificent lips with hers.

"What do you plan to do about Sunny?" she inquired again, before he had a chance to conquer her emotions completely.

"I plan to adopt her and raise her," he spoke with assurance.

She looked stunned. "What ... adopt her ... she is ... that important to you?" she stumbled to speak, as a bombshell exploded in her heart. A look of confusion covered her grave face, knowing that it was six years too late to find out that he would want a child. It was too late, her heart cried out. *Oh, God forgive me!*

"Sunny's my life. For the last 13 days, she has brought me more happiness than I could have ever imagined," he said emotionally as he looked away, fighting the tears that were collecting as he spoke.

"The hardest thing I've ever had to do was to give her up today when she needed me and I needed her. Forever losing her would be inconceivable to me." He took a deep breath to keep his tears in check.

His eyes watered as he thought about the memory of what had happened that very afternoon. He looked over at April again and was surprised to see tears streaming down her face as she silently cried. He was touched by her sensitivity with regard to his feelings and his situation. He sympathetically reached out to her.

"I'm sorry, April. I didn't mean to upset you, too," he said compassionately. But she pulled away from him angrily, stood up, walked over to the door and opened it.

"I really ... am tired ... would you mind ... leaving?" Her voice was shaky; she made no eye contact with him as she looked down at the tile floor.

Mark was in shock as he stood up slowly and went to the door.

"Are you alright, April?" he asked with concern. He searched for her eyes as she concealed them from him. He was not sure what was going on in her mind. He wanted to take her in his arms and comfort her. But did he dare do it?

"Fine ... I'm fine," she said without looking at him.

Mark was stunned, just minutes ago, they had declared friendship and now she was practically throwing him out the door and he did not understand why.

"If you need anything or need someone to talk to, I'm just upstairs," he sincerely offered.

"Thanks," she choked out, "Good night."

"Good night, April," he said as he went out the door. She closed it behind him. Mark leaned against the door, still confused by the intense emotional reaction April had displayed towards him.

April was leaning against the door on the other side. She was overwhelmed with heartache. Her face was red from the heat of her sorrow. Her heart was pounding with grief.

"Where were you when I needed you?" she screamed out, "Where were you?" She ran to the couch, flung herself down on it, and cried.

Mark could hear her crying. He turned and faced the door. He leaned forward with both the palms of his hands reached out over his head against the door.

He wanted to split open the door and go back in there. His heart ached for April as she cried. He wanted to share her burdens and encourage her with his faith, anything to make her stop crying.

He knew something was terribly wrong, spiritual warfare, pure and simple, but she had made it clear, she did not want his help.

All he could do was pray that she would overcome her problems with God's help, hopefully soon, so that they could start a new friendship.

Even with all the mixed up emotions April had displayed towards him, he knew that something very special was going to happen between the two of them. He knew he loved her the very first moment he saw her in the park.

Finally, he backed away from the door and returned to his apartment. He had a hard time falling asleep that night. He was worried about Sunny. He was worried about April. Finally he did his nightly Bible reading, and then he turned April and Sunny over to the Lord and closed his eyes.

Whatever had happened in her past to bring her heartache kept her in bondage from having complete joy in her life. Until she learned to give her problems over to God, her life would lack the sovereignty to enjoy life to the fullest, as God intended for her, Mark thought just before he drifted off.

God was bigger than any problem she had. She needed to find peace in the midst of her storm so that God could work supernaturally in her life. Most importantly, would Mark open up her heart to all God had in store for her?

Would Mark Sanders win her heart and her soul?

CHAPTER TWENTY-FOUR

⁓Open My Heart to the Past⁓

*M*ark was tired when he got up at 2:30 A.M. to do his twelve-hour shift. He arrived at the hospital just before 3 A.M. and clocked in. He dragged through the entire shift, which was unusual for the energetic person he had always been. Late nights had never been a problem for him before. However, for some reason, it was all he could do to stay awake.

When Mark finished work, he walked over to the children's home to get Sunflower. He went up the steps and rang the bell. Blanche answered the door with a big frown on her face.

"I've been expecting you, but I was really hoping you would not show up," she said smartly, giving him her evil eyes.

"I've come to see Sunny," Mark politely informed her, wishing she would go get Sunny and leave him alone. The last thing he wanted was a confrontation with her.

"You can't do that," she declared as she handed him a court order. She placed her hands on her hips and looked pleased.

"What is this?" Mark asked as he looked at the papers.

"It says you can't visit Sunflower here, in the best interest of the child, it says," she stated with great satisfaction.

His chest instantly tightened. Mark looked up quickly at her in disbelief; his eyes glared at her.

"Like heck, it is!" he said as he moved forward to go inside, determined to get Sunny out of there. Blanche pushed him back with her oversized hands.

"You take one more step and I'll call the police and have you arrested!" she warned him. Mark looked at her with contempt. He remembered what his father had said about not doing anything that would cause him to lose custody of Sunny, so he backed down.

"I'll be back; you can count on that!" he howled at her as he turned and left. *That woman is not going to keep me from Sunny,* he thought as a feeling of weariness settled over him.

What Mark did not know was that Sunflower was looking out the upstairs bedroom window. Her little face was pressed against the glass pane. When she saw Mark leaving, she began to cry.

She pressed her tiny hands against the pane and cried out for him. "Mark, don't leave me, come back … please." Mark did not hear or see her as he walked away feeling helpless.

Mark went back to his apartment to call his father. His father told him that he had filed for a court hearing with Judge Thompson. The hearing would not be for another three weeks.

Mr. Sanders said he would try to get the restraining orders reversed, but he also told Mark not to get his hopes up, and he warned Mark not to go back to the children's home.

The orders only said Mark could not visit Sunny at the home. That left the door wide open to other possibilities to see her, Mark cleverly thought.

Mark could not stand the thought of not seeing Sunny for three whole weeks. What would she think; would she think he had abandoned her? He wanted to twist the pillow he was holding in two but instead he stopped and prayed.

He had come to his senses and realized that anger would not bring her back, only the prayers that he lifted up for her would. He needed to fight his downfall of letting anger consume him when he faced troubled times.

Mark got April's number from Dan and he tried to call her, but her answering machine was on. He left a brief message and his phone number on her machine. "April, hey, it's Mark, please return my call. My number's, 837-9910, thanks."

Mark waited as long as he could for April to call him back, but it was getting late and he had to leave for football practice. He was hopeful that she would leave him a message while he was gone.

Then he went to football practice. At least practice gave him some physical relief. He played aggressively to prove to everyone that he had his head in the game and to prove to himself that there was nothing physically wrong with him.

He looked in control as he called the plays and challenged his teammates to do their best. He was running all over the field making sure that everyone knew the plays.

An hour into practice, he had another unexplained nosebleed. He was getting fed up with these nosebleeds. The blood poured uncontrollably down the front of his jersey. This time it was harder to stop the bleeding. He almost fainted as the Doc and the trainer escorted him into the locker room and helped him on the exam table. Doc's daughter Paige who was doing her internship with her father held a towel out to Mark.

"What happened out there?" Doc quizzed him.

"I caught an elbow," Mark said as he leaned over the container Paige held out in front of his face.

Doc got all over Mark for missing his scheduled team physicals. Mark was apologetic, blaming it on his hectic work schedule.

"I'd give you a physical right now if I did not have a class to teach tonight at the college. See to it that you report to your next physical." Doc warned Mark not to let it happen again as he tossed the pile of blood soaked towels into the trashcan and then headed out the door.

Paige gave Mark a warm look and headed back into her dad's office.

Frustrated, Mark hopped off the exam table and headed to the showers. Mark held his hands against the wall, as he felt dizzy. He felt like he was on a rollercoaster ride; he closed his eyes and prayed the ride would stop as the water sprayed across his back.

When he finished with his shower, he left the locker room without so much as a good-bye to any of the players. A worried look crossed Carlo's face as he watched Mark depart.

Mark slowly drove by the children's home, hoping to catch a glimpse of Sunny. He knew he could not go three weeks without seeing her. Sunny was nowhere to be seen. His heart was inconsolable as he thought how awful that place was.

Once home, he tried to study but he could not concentrate. He felt tired and depressed as he lay across his bed with medical books piled around him. One book caught his attention, and he thumbed through it until he found the subject he was searching. Once he finished reading, he tossed it carelessly back in the pile.

He tried to call April but he got her answering machine again. He called her back several times just to hear her familiar voice on the machine, hoping to spark some memory of her.

When the phone rang his heart stopped, thinking it might be April finally calling him back. Instead, it was his father calling to tell him that Judge Thompson had been called out of town and would not be back until Friday.

Mr. Sanders warned Mark not to break the restraining order, or Blanche would have him arrested and that would not help his case.

Mark leaned back against the headboard, even more exhausted and depressed than before. He had never felt so powerless and out of control in any situation. He wanted to fall asleep but his mind would not shut down. He got up, went into the living room, and paced the floor in deep thought.

April had him baffled. At first, they had felt comfortable together, like an old pair of football cleats.

Why won't she call me back? What's going on with her, anyways? Was it something I did? What did we mean to each other so long ago?

Mark pulled the yearbook off the coffee table where he had left it. He stared at the picture of them together, searching his mind for answers. He ran his fingers over the picture; he could feel something within his soul as he touched the picture of her, and then he felt a strong vibration pass through his body. He knew he had loved April a long time ago. It had to be true, there was no other explanation for the way she made him feel.

He flopped down on the couch and leaned against the soft leather back. He propped his feet up on the coffee table and laid the open book across his chest. His thoughts were on his first encounter with April in the park. Her arrow had scored a direct hit on his heart and knocked the wind out of him. He wanted to know everything there was to know about her. He yawned and stretched his arms out above his head.

He desperately wanted to fall asleep as Sunny came to mind. "I love you, Sunny, good night," he whispered softly as his eyes welled up and he took a long deep breath. "God, protect her tonight for me." He closed his eyes before a tear could fall. It was not long before he was semi-unconscious and drifting off into a dream.

There was a chilling flash in his mind. He was at the cemetery. He was just a child, dressed in a suit that was a size too small. He yanked and pulled at the suit so that he could breathe.

A thunderstorm was threatening nearby as the strong winds tossed his hair wildly around his forehead. It was getting dark as the rain clouds moved across the sky above him.

He was standing over an open grave holding a single yellow rose; he tossed it high into the sky and watched it gliding around and around until it fell into the grave.

His grandfather's peaceful face was staring into his, and then his face slowly faded away until Mark could no longer see him. "Papa, come back!" he cried. Mark fell to his knees and reached out his small arms, begging his grandfather to come back. "Mark!" his father's voice sternly called to him. "Mark!" The voice cut into him like a sharp knife and he sobbed.

The grave was covered up with a mound of dirt piled on top. Mark frantically dug his fingers in the dirt like a rake. He clawed at the dirt, desperately trying to uncover his grandfather, as buckets of tears dropped where he dug.

The wind blew the dirt up into his tear soaked face, and he held his tiny hands up to protect it. He was very angry, as his shoulders shook violently.

He picked up a handful of dirt and angrily threw it at the grave. "I hate you, devil, why did you take my grandfather away from me? I want him back, right now! Do you hear me, God? Tell the devil to give Papa back to me!" He screamed the words as he shook his fists at the sky.

The sunshine came out so bright that Mark had to shield his eyes. In the distance, a double rainbow appeared across the sky. Then a dove landed on a tree branch above Mark. Mark looked up, stared at the dove, and knew that his God had come to bring him peace.

Then Mark felt a tender touch on his shoulder, and he slowly looked up into her compassionate face. She bent and gathered him in her protective arms. He was crying; she was comforting him. Every fiber of anger fled his body as she held him. He thought she was an angel sent from God. Heaven was shining down on him as he joined his heart to hers.

Her long blonde hair felt so soft as he wrapped his arms around her. "Shhh, Mark, it's okay, I got you." He looked up into her blue eyes. "A, I need you." His voice was fragile as he brushed his cheek against her cheek, as they came together once more.

"Please, don't let me go." But as soon as the words crossed his lips she faded away, leaving him standing there in the graveyard alone and frightened. Darkness fell all around him; he wrapped his arms around his trembling body and closed his eyes. *Where has she gone, why did she leave me? I trusted her.*

Mark's body jerked and he abruptly opened his eyes and looked around the room, trying to gather his bearings. He lay down, pulled the throw blanket over him in one swift movement, closed his eyes and quickly fell back asleep. His dreaming continued.

He was a teenager; he was riding on Thunder with a girl wrapped in his left arm in front of him as they rode. Her long blonde hair flying in the wind blew against his shoulders. He could not see her face, but he knew the shape of her body well as he felt her contoured shape against his. He held the reins with his other hand in front of them as Thunder soared off into the sunset at a full gallop.

Then it was his eighteenth birthday party … she was in his arms … they were dancing to the magic of the music. The side of her face was underneath his chin, her face hidden from his view.

He could hear the romantic music, he could feel her soft touch, and he could smell her inviting perfume. Her soft delicate hand was wrapped in his as he spun her around to capture her face, but she disappeared from him during the spinning.

He was left standing alone, looking in every direction for her, searching the room as it spun around him. Faster and faster, he spun until he dropped to his knees and closed his eyes in defeat.

His heart was racing as he dreamed. Mark fell into a deeper sleep.

He dreamed he was holding A in his arms and kissing her. She had her hair up in a ponytail and had on her cheerleading outfit. She had on his football jacket.

She ran from him and stood under the lamppost alone, just out of his reach. She held her hand out for him to join her, but he stood frozen; he could not walk; his legs would not move. He could not feel his legs; he looked down at them in a panic.

They were in the park; it was very dark. His head was spinning; he grabbed his head with both hands trying to make the spinning stop. His stomach burned and he felt ill.

It was getting darker, darker, and cold. The wind picked up and blew the leaves around in a violent whirlwind. A was crying desperately for him; someone was hurting her. Mark could not find her as he fought the wind and the leaves pounding against him with his hands. "April, where are you ... A?" he cried out.

"Mark!" her voice screamed out with such torment. "Mark!" Mark was helpless and could not save her from whatever it was that was causing her sickening screams.

Mark woke up in a cold sweat and sat straight up in a panic. His breathing was heavy. He felt sick to his stomach.

What had happened to April in the park? Something awful must have happened. Chills went down Mark's spine.

Did she blame me because I did not save her in the park that night? Was that why she cried out, where were you when I needed you, the other night when I was at her apartment? Was this what was causing her to act the way she was acting? Was whatever happened that night to her, what she was not ready to talk to me about yet?

His mind was filled with unanswered questions.

He was confused; he did not remember kissing April in the park. He did not remember letting her wear his football jacket. However, he did remember that he had called her A instead of April so long ago when they were just kids.

It was all nothing more than a bad dream. Sure, that was it. My subconscious is playing tricks on me. The devil is putting fear where there should be none. Dr. Price forewarned me about these types of distorted dreams. None of those things happened; it was all just a bad dream, he tried to convince himself.

Why was he feeling this way about her? He did not even know her; he could not remember her. Yet there she was in his dreams when he closed his eyes. She appeared so real he could almost touch her.

His feelings were not all warm. He still felt frightened and uneasy. Something was not right; something between them had happened. But what? Had they had a big fight, is that why she reacted to him like she had, he wondered? Had he chosen football and motorcycle racing over her?

Had he dated another girl instead of her? Did he date someone like Sister Jessica, and April had been jealous of them?

Had April wanted more in their relationship and he had been blinded? Mark picked up the yearbook again and stared at the picture of them. Was he in love with the picture or the girl? He thought he could hear her soft little laugh, her delicate soft voice. He felt his body go warm, thinking about her. He laid the book across his chest and closed his eyes again.

What was it about April that stimulated his mind with faded memories of her in his dreams, he wondered as he fell asleep.

April sat on her couch with her knees drawn up to her chest and her arms wrapped around her legs. She was in deep thought about Mark. She could not get him out of her mind since the night he had come over.

This was not the puppy love she had felt for him so many years ago. She wondered if all the dreams she had about him could now possibly come true.

Could they really fall in love? Were they in love back then? She had thought they were. No, it was only in her imagination that they were in love; he did not love her.

I did not mean anything to him or he would have remembered me, she thought. *He was so firm in his beliefs that maybe I never measured up to his standards.*

No matter how many times she told herself that he had not loved her, her heart refused to believe that. She remembered the look in his eyes when they had danced together. His eyes were starry and filled with warmth and love towards her. Her first kiss with him was so warm and gentle. On the other hand, was that just what she wanted to believe because she was so in love with him?

Was her mind playing tricks on her? Had she seen that same look in his eyes the other night when he sat on her couch and stared into her eyes? A warm feeling spread through her heart as she pictured his dimpled smile light up as he laughed.

She thought she had worked out all her feelings about him while she was in California. She thought she could stop blaming him for all the pain she felt. It really was not his fault. There was nothing he could have done without risking his life for her. Besides, they never had a chance to work things out before her father had discreetly moved her away.

After all, Mark had been in that awful accident that almost killed him. His doctor had been adamant – do not force Mark into remembering the events surrounding his memory loss or his memories might become distorted, fearful, or cause him horrible nightmares.

She could not blame him for what happened that night, not when she spent so much time dreaming of the day they would be together again.

She had not been prepared to feel the way she did when they met again that night in the same park.

Her thoughts were overwhelming her mind and her heart. She had to be stronger, she told herself.

She pressed the play button on her answering machine. "You have three old messages." April pressed skip. "Message two."

"April, it's me again, I just called to see how you are doing. April, I am worried about you; please call me so we can talk. I just got home from practice. 837-9910, Mark."

Beep. "Message three."

"April, please call me, I'm sorry if I upset you, let's talk about it. Give me a call. Mark."

The sound of his concerned voice on her answering machine deepened the feelings she had for him. She would have to fight from going to him. She knew she could not tell him what she had done; he would never understand or forgive her.

Next time, if there was a next time, she would make sure she did not melt in his eyes and let him take control of her heart, until she was ready.

She opened the box that was sitting on the coffee table, with her photographs inside. The scrapbook that held all the articles about Mark was on top. She opened it up and stared at the pictures.

No longer was Mark Sanders larger than life, a football hero. He was just the boy from a long time ago that she had shared all her secrets with on so many warm summer days in a tree house.

He was the boy that had taken her heart away when she was eight years old. He was the young man that had swept her off her feet at eighteen. He was the one that had led her to the Lord. He was the man that just wanted to be her friend and start a new relationship with her. A tear slowly slid down her cheek.

Everything in the past, well, it just never happened. *If he can forget, so can I.* Today is a new day. As far as she was concerned, they had never met, they had no past, just maybe tomorrows.

She promised she would be nicer the next time she saw him. After all, she knew how much pain he was in because of losing Sunny. She knew how that felt, so she would try to be more sympathetic.

She tucked the scrapbook under some magazines on the coffee table. It was time to start a new scrapbook of them, she thought.

Which direction was her heart traveling? Tomorrow was a new day, and she hoped that he would discover her along the road and persuade her to join him in what would be a new beginning for the two of them.

Only this time, she prayed it would last them a lifetime.

CHAPTER TWENTY-FIVE –
❧Risking it All❧

*M*ark slept a few hours and was back at the hospital by three A.M..
He worked all night long, attended a lecture that morning, and went back to work all afternoon, putting in two extra hours instead of going home to an empty apartment.

He grabbed two hours of sleep and then he went to football practice for two hours. Once again, he had a nosebleed. Mark was thankful that Doc was not at the practice. He hoped that Paige would not say anything to her dad about his nosebleed.

His coach had been concerned because of the lack of energy Mark had shown during practice. He summed it up to Mark's busy schedule.

When Mark got home, the apartment was too empty for him to stay there so he decided to take a walk to the park and do his thinking there.

Mark sat on "Mark's Bench," where he had been when he met April just two days ago. He put his elbows on his knees and bent his head forward, resting his head on the palms of his hands. He was exhausted. "God, You can do the impossible," he spoke.

"I knew you would come!" He heard a small voice say excitedly. Mark looked up quickly and saw Sunflower standing there in front of him. His face lit up. He grabbed her, hugged her, and held her close to him. It felt so good to have her in his arms.

Then he realized what time it was. He held her back, and looked seriously into her baby blue eyes.

"What are you doing here, Sunny? It is nine o'clock," he asked her as he tried to stay calm and not frighten her.

"I came to see you. Why did you leave me the other day when you came to see me? You broke your promise," she sorrowfully pouted.

"I'm so sorry, Sunny. I didn't want to break my promise to you but Blanche made me break it. She won't let me see you," Mark told her softly as he pulled her jacket edges together so he could button it.

"Why not?" Sunny demanded tearfully.

"I really do not know why," Mark said sympathetically.

"I want to go home with you, now!" she begged, as she cuddled against his body and held on to him.

"Blanche must be real worried about you."

"She don't know I'm gone. She puts us to bed at seven and she don't check on us after that. Katie helped me sneak out to see you," she said cleverly.

Mark's stomach turned knowing the danger that Sunny had put herself in by coming to the park in the dark. "You should not have done that Sunny; it is not safe for you to be here at night alone. Do you understand me?" he warned her sternly as he held her by both arms and looked her straight in the eyes.

"I hid in the bushes; no one knew I was here. Can we go home now?" Mark hesitated in answering her, remembering what his father had said.

"Please, Mark? I want to go home with you." Her eyes were pleading for him to give in to her. Mark shook his head no. Sunny touched his cheeks.

"I have to take you back right now."

"Oh please, Mark, I want you. I don't want to go back there." She started to tear up and grabbed him around the neck with both arms. "I wanted you to come get me away from there; please hold me!"

Mark was angry that Blanche had not kept a closer watch on Sunny. Mark knew he could not turn Sunny down, even if he knew he should. If he were caught, he would blame it on Blanche. If Sunny was discovered missing, it would be Blanche's fault, not his, he reasoned.

Mrs. Wilson had promised him that Sunny would be safe in Blanche's care. He would just have to have a little talk with Mrs. Wilson in the morning, after he returned Sunny, he thought angrily.

"All right, you win. But listen to me closely; you have to go back to Blanche's first thing in the morning before she knows you were gone," he said firmly.

"But …" she started to say.

"No buts. That is the way it has to be, okay?" he said as he looked firmly into her eyes.

"Oh, okay," she said as she hugged her rag doll.

Mark held her hand as they walked towards his apartment. She skipped along. He knew that she was feeling as happy as he was. Right now, he did not care that he was risking going to jail.

Just before they reached the edge of the street, Sunny saw the boy named John standing next to a tree. He slowly lifted his hand and waved at her as their eyes met.

Once they got to the apartment, Mark fixed them a snack, then they sat down, and he read her a book. She got out her pink dress and dressed up in it. She danced around the room, singing and laughing. Mark watched her with delight in his eyes. She jumped up onto the coffee table.

"I'm your fairy Godmother, and I am going to give you one wish. What ya gonna wish for?" she asked with a big smile.

"I wish I had a little girl with long shiny blonde hair and big baby blue eyes," he joked with her, wishing that it could come true.

"Your wish will come true. Close your eyes, and wish real hard," she promised him. Mark closed his eyes. Sunny climbed into his lap.

"You can open your eyes, now," she giggled.

"Sunny, is it you?" he laughed.

"It's me! I'm your wish."

"I wish that were true, but first the courts have to decide if it can come true," Mark told her sadly.

"Why, I want to be the one to decide," she said all grown up.

"Sunny, it is really late. Why don't you go get ready for bed. I left your pj's on your dresser."

"Okay," she said as she bounced off his lap and ran into his bedroom. She took a t-shirt from his drawer and headed to her room.

All I have to do is take Sunny to Judge Thompson and let her do all the talking. Who could look into her adorable eyes and not give in to her every wish? This thought made him feel good. It had to work.

He went in the bedroom. Sunny was on the floor saying her prayers. Mark noticed his t-shirt on her and smiled warmly at her.

"God, thank You for giving me Mark. Please take care of him, let me stay with him, and find him a wife quick," she prayed. Then she got into bed. Mark pulled the sheets up and kissed her on the cheek.

"I love you, Sunny," he said softly with love in his voice.

"I love you too, Mark," she said sleepily. He bent down, kissed her forehead, and watched her fall asleep. If he went to jail, this moment had been worth it.

Mark took a shower. It felt so good. He just leaned against the wall and let the water spray on him. He knew he had risked it all for one more moment of loving this child. He prayed he would not have to face the consequences in the morning if someone found out.

Then Mark noticed tiny reddish purple dots on his arms and bruises on his legs. He knew that something was up with his body. *I don't have time for this; I have to get some sleep.*

Mark got out of the shower, put on his robe, and went into the bedroom. He set the alarm for five o'clock. *That should give me enough time to return Sunny without anyone knowing she was gone.*

Mark decided he would go out to the ranch the next morning, see his parents, and talk to his father about his idea of letting Sunny talk to the judge.

Then he would have to go to his lectures, do rounds at the hospital, work his shift, and finally end his day with football practice. The thought of all that made him extremely exhausted.

Mark talked with God as he usually did before going to sleep. Then he closed his eyes and hoped that he could get some well-needed sleep, even if it would only be for a short time.

CHAPTER TWENTY-SIX –
∽Out of Control∽

$\mathcal{T}$he alarm blared at five. Mark did not move; his whole body ached to claim the sleep he desperately needed. He ignored the ear-piercing alarm and it mysteriously stopped. Seconds after the silence, he felt Sunflower tugging at his robe.

"Mark! Mark! Time to get up!" she said loudly. Mark sleepily opened his eyes, rolled over on his back, and looked up at Sunflower. He playfully put his pillow over his head. Sunflower climbed on the bed and tugged at the pillow, giggling.

"You silly bear, we're gonna be late. The alarm went off," she told him as they played tug-of-war with the pillow.

"Okay, I give in." He grabbed Sunflower and tickled her. She laughed at his playfulness.

Suddenly Mark saw a flash of April; he was tickling her. They were on the ground. He was kissing her lips. Then the flash was gone. Once again, he was baffled as a discerning chill went down his spine. Frustration once again claimed his mind.

Mark stopped tickling Sunflower and moved off the bed. *Why am I having these flashbacks?* he thought frustrated. His face drew a long frown as he ran his fingers through his hair and around the back of his stiff neck.

"What's the matter, Mark?" Sunflower asked as she started jumping up and down on the bed trying to gain a smile from him.

"Don't do that. You are going to fall." He grabbed her around the waist and set her on the floor.

"Go get ready to go," he told her sternly. She lowered her lips and quickly did what he told her to do.

Mark was puzzled – why was he having these flashbacks? He was so frustrated. He could not believe that he had talked himself into keeping Sunny overnight.

"What was I thinking?" he said as he headed quickly to the bathroom to change.

Mark silently drove Sunny to Blanche's home. He hugged Sunny good-bye and kissed her forehead. His heart ached as he looked into her sad eyes. He would have to find some way to be brave and strong for his little princess. *God, help me let her go*, he prayed.

"You be a good girl, Sunny, and don't let Blanche find out you came to see me, or we will both get into serious trouble," he warned her sternly. He had to be firm or she would not take him seriously.

"Can I come see you tonight?" she asked sadly.

"No, you can't do this again ... do not go to the park alone." He had to warn her; the park was far too dangerous for her to be there unsupervised. She hung her head in disappointment as she witnessed his unwavering eyes.

"Oh please, Mark, I wanna be with you!" she pleaded with a sliver of hope that he might change his mind if she persisted.

"Listen to me, Sunny, this is not a game. I know you do not like it, but you have to stay here until I come and get you. Do you understand me?" he said firmly, using his stern expression to make her fully understand that she had to obey him.

"Yes," she said very softly, her lips turned down with disappointment. Tears were fogging her vision.

"Okay, then. You better go before someone sees us together." He was regretting that he had let her stay the night and was putting them both through this difficult departure.

He opened the car door for her and she got out. Slowly she climbed the steps to the front door. She turned, looked back at Mark, and sadly waved good-bye before she went inside.

Mark suddenly had a flashback of himself waving good-bye to his grandfather when he was eight. Mark took a deep breath as the pain hit his heart.

Mark dreaded leaving Sunny. He had not gotten out of the car to walk her up to the door because he feared she would cling onto him and cry. Her outburst would have given them away.

He was heartbroken as he drove to the ranch. Sunny should never have to live in that house. Mark felt as if his life was out of his control. The pressure of his internship, studying for his boards, football, Sunny, and April were all clouding his reasoning. *I need some sleep*, he thought feeling his eyelids becoming heavy as he drove.

He put in one of his worship tapes and turned the volume up. He rolled the window down so that the cool blasts of winter air would blow in his face and keep him awake.

It was not long before he was singing the tunes to the praise music. "Help me know You are near," he sang.

The world was just waking up as the sun appeared in the sky. It felt refreshing to see a new day begin as the sun came up in all its glory. It reminded Mark of who was really in charge of this magnificent world all around him.

Every day is a gift from God. He rejoiced, refusing to let the confusing circumstances surrounding him control the rest of his day. He said a thankful prayer and repented for his earlier hopeless thoughts. With God's love, there was nothing he could not endure. He would find something positive in its outcome.

It was still too early to wake up his parents so Mark decided to visit his old friend in the stable. He went in and just as he thought, old Charlie was caring for the horses.

"Hello, Charlie," Mark caringly called to him. Charlie looked up in surprise. A warm glow came over Charlie's face as he looked at Mark with true admiration.

"Well, I'll be, if 'n it ain't my friend Mark." Charlie smiled and gave Mark a big bear hug and they shook hands. The closeness the pair shared was apparent. Sometimes it was hard for Charlie's heart to see Mark as a man and not as the little boy that not so long ago had shadowed him.

"It is good to see you, Charlie," Mark said warmly to his trusted friend. Sadness hit Mark's heart as he saw the stiffness in Charlie's bowed legs.

"Whatcha doin' down here at this here hour?" Charlie asked him with a sparkle in his eyes, as he treasured this moment in the stable with Mark.

"Came to see my father, but first I thought I'd give my motorcycle a short spin through the woods," Mark told him.

Charlie pondered that thought. Not one he liked. *Sure wish I could talk him out of that,* Charlie thought. They walked over to where Mark kept his motorcycle and gear.

"Thought you's given it up, since you's ain't ridden any races in a long time," Charlie said, wishing Mark would leave the bike right where it was. That bike haunted them all.

"I just haven't had the time, but I am going to give this old gal a spin," Mark said as he patted his bike on the gas tank. Mark put on his leather riding jacket and helmet and pushed the bike outside. He swung his leg over the seat and got on it.

"I'll be back in thirty minutes," he said to Charlie.

"You be mighty careful," Charlie said with concern for his friend and boss. Charlie watched as Mark started up the noisy bike and headed off, then he shook his head and went back into the stable.

Charlie looked over at the protective motorcycle gear Mark had left behind, and a bad feeling hit him. He ran back out of the stable to ask Mark to reconsider and have a cup of coffee with him instead.

Mark started up the noisy bike. That should wake up everyone, he thought mischievously with a lifted eyebrow.

At first, he rode carefully out to the woods. He knew Charlie was watching him like a hawk.

But as he got closer to the woods, he could feel the blood in his veins churning for excitement. He found himself going faster and faster as the elevation of his blood rose to its spirit of venture. It was passing through his body like a dominant force. He pulled back on the handlebars causing the front wheel to lift off the ground and into the air. He felt totally in control.

He could not and would not hold back now. The freedom he felt being in control in the face of danger was overwhelming. Fearlessly he dodged trees, flew over hills, twisted in and around bushes. A dust trail followed behind him as the tires spun against the ground. He had done this a thousand times in the past, and it had always felt great.

He let his spirit fly, as his grandfather had called it. He flew off a hill up into the sky and twisted his bike sideways in the air. He landed back on the ground and gunned the engine as he flew towards the next hill. His heart began racing faster as he took the bike to its limit. He was soaring through the air like an eagle.

The death of his grandfather passed through his mind. He closed his eyes as the memories of his grandfather walking away from the limo cut deep into his heart. He remembered the casket, the gravesite, then the military school as a young boy, and the lonely nights he spent there. He remembered the endless condemnation of his father as he grew up, the memories of their futile arguments surfaced in his mind.

Sunny's pitiful face appeared and his body shook thinking of her pain. He had made her promises that he could not keep. Anger drove him around a sharp curve as he nearly laid the bike completely sideways, and dirt flew all over him.

He bit his lip and pushed the bike harder, trying to shut out all his tormenting memories of his childhood. The memories disappeared the faster he went, and he flew through the woods with no fear. "No, devil, you can't have my mind! I am not afraid of anything you put against me!"

The sweat was running down his forehead. How sensational it felt to release all the stress and heartache he had suffered in the last week. *I can conquer it all*, he thought. *I can do it ... I can fly ... I believe I can have it all*. He let out all his emotions and was free. A dove flew out of a tree in front of him as the sunshine hit his face.

Mark let go of the handlebars and raised his fists to the clouds in victory. It felt so good to let it all out. He let out a yell of victory and shook his fists at the sky. He was flying free; he was in total control of his life at that very second.

Then without any warning, the front wheel fell into a deep hole, forcefully hurling Mark over the handlebars, and flinging him into a tree. The left side of his chest took most of the impact before he bounced off the tree and fell to the cold hard ground unconscious.

When he finally came to, his body was limp. He stared up into the trees and saw the rays of sunlight shining through. It was too painful to move. His body was cold; his bare hands frozen. It hurt to breathe. He groaned in pain.

The reality of his desperate situation was sinking in. He cringed as he removed his helmet as the pain in his chest screamed out. He cursed at himself as he slowly and carefully stood up, holding his chest with one hand and grabbing hold of a tree for support with the other. He looked up into the blue sky.

"Okay, Lord, what's the message You are trying to send me?" he said, but then he was remorseful for trying to blame his recklessness on the Lord. He would not let that happen again. God was not responsible for his foolish choices. He had no one to blame but himself.

Any suffering he felt, he would have to tolerate it; he had too many other things to concentrate on this week. This was nothing new; he knew how to suppress pain, and that is exactly what he intended to do.

He looked over at the mangled tire on his bike and frowned. *That's just great*, he thought. Let the devil have a good laugh. Mark was not going to give in to his seemingly impossible situation.

He put on his armor of protection from God and took a painful step forward. He would walk out of the woods and all the way back to the house if he had to do it. All he had to do was follow God's footsteps, he thought.

Mark did just that; he walked out of the woods. He stopped at the long path leading back to the ranch. He saw a pick-up truck quickly coming in his direction. It was Charlie. He stopped the truck in front of Mark, jumped out, and hurried to Mark in a panic.

Charlie had known something had happened; he always did when Mark had been hurt. They all thought that Charlie was sent to them by God as Mark's guardian angel. Charlie knew he was right when he saw Mark staggering out of the woods. Mark's clothes were covered with dirt; something awful had happened.

"I was a waitin' and you ain't come back, so I felt somethin' was not right, so I came a lookin'. What happened to you?" he asked with concern written on his face. Nevertheless, he was careful not to make Mark feel embarrassed in this awkward situation.

True to form, Mark smiled wide at Charlie to let him know there was no need for him to worry.

"Just got a flat tire and took a little spill, but I am all right. How about giving me a lift back to the house?" Mark asked as he tried to brush off the dirt on his leather jacket and his jeans, making light of the situation.

"What ya gonna do about your bike?" Charlie asked.

"Leave it right where it is. I am through with that sport," Mark said with a grin hoping to satisfy his friend. They exchanged a look of understanding.

"If 'n you say so," Charlie answered, relieved that Mark had finally given up his motorcycle.

Mark got into the pick-up truck, and old Charlie drove them back to the ranch. Mark rubbed his side and took a deep breath to hide the pain he felt as the truck bumped around on the dirt road. However, he was not fooling Charlie.

Mark went inside the house to find his parents. He saw the clock on the wall; it was eight o'clock. He would be late to his lecture if he did not hurry. The Sanders were sitting at the table in the dining room having coffee. They looked up at Mark as he entered the room. His mother gasped at the sight of him.

"Mark, what happened to you?" she fretted. Panic showed in her eyes.

"Nothing, Mother," he said and quickly turned his attention to his father.

"Dad, I came here to see if you could arrange a meeting with Judge Thompson as soon as possible. I want him to talk directly to Sunny. She'll tell him how she feels and what she wants and convince him to grant me custody," Mark said with assurance.

"It is not going to be that easy. Mrs. Wilson has informed me that the Stanleys have also filed for custody. They claim they love Sunny, and since they cannot have their own children they want to adopt her." Robert gently broke the latest news to Mark.

"That is crazy!" Mark was outraged at the thought of Sunny spending one second with the Stanleys.

"Mrs. Wilson does not want them to get custody. Nevertheless, she does not want you to get custody either. She thinks that Sunny deserves a family. She wants her to have a mother, and right now, you cannot give her that. I will try to arrange a meeting with Judge Thompson, and hopefully he will listen to what Sunny has to say about you," Robert said to Mark's displeased face.

"I hope you can adopt Sunny. Robert and I would love to have a grand-daughter," Julia said warmly, as she absorbed Mark's pain in her own heart for that innocent little girl that had won their hearts.

Mark looked at the clock on the wall. "I've got to go. I am running late. Thanks for your help," he said as he bent to kiss his mother good-bye. He gritted his teeth as pain struck him. "I'll call you later, Dad," he said as he rushed out of the room holding his ribs.

"Mark looked so tired, Robert. I am worried about him."

"I could see that, but he will be all right once we get everything settled with Sunny," Robert assured her. Still, he was very worried himself. Mark had been the main subject of his prayers lately.

Mark was extremely upset with himself for being reckless with his motorcycle. Now was not the time to be irresponsible; he had so many things he needed to do.

First, I let Sunny talk me into letting her stay with me and risk jail time. Now I wreck my motorcycle. What was I thinking? What is my problem; have I gone completely irrational? he thought. *I've got to get it together, Lord.*

He had the AFC Divisional playoffs, the AFC Championship Football Game and the Super Bowl Game coming up. He would not punish his team for something he had done to himself. It was his responsibility to lead his team to victories, not to hold them back. He owed it to them to be the best he could be at all times. He felt the guilt build up inside of him as he thought about how much he had messed up.

If he were the patient, he would be on his way to the Emergency Room. However, he was the doctor and doctors make awful patients. He certainly was not in the mood to be a patient again.

He took the matter up with God instead and prayed that his injuries were not that serious. He needed instant healing. He needed to keep a level head. Most importantly, he needed to stay in the Word before he let his life get totally out of control.

He would keep his injuries to himself and pray to God that no one found out.

CHAPTER TWENTY-SEVEN –
⁓Something Goes Right⁓

*M*ark drove as fast as he could back into town. He pulled up to the apartment building. April was just finishing her morning jog around the park. Mark saw her and quickly got out of his car so that he would not miss talking to her.

"April, wait!" he called, and she stopped and turned around to face him. She saw him grab his left side as he ran up to her.

"Hi, Mark," she said shyly. She let him see that she was no longer upset with him by warmly smiling at him.

"Why haven't you answered any of my calls?" he asked her, out of breath.

"I've been busy, unpacking and everything."

"Can we talk?"

She noted the stressed look on his face. "Sure, what's up?" she asked curiously.

"I know I just met you but I need to ask you a favor."

"What is it?"

"Remember the little girl I told you about? I promised her that I would visit her everyday, but I can't because they have a court order to keep me away," he said as he rubbed his hand over his left side.

"Why?" she asked with concern.

"I don't know; the whole situation is crazy. My father is trying to straighten it out, but until he does, I need someone to look after her. Could you do it?" he pleaded. His pitiful eyes spoke directly to her heart.

"How?" she asked him kindly.

"They have a big sister program at the home. You could sign up to be her big sister. It would only have to be an hour a day," he told her, hoping that she would do this for him.

"Where do I sign up?" she asked with eagerness, bringing a smile of relief to his face.

"At the Family Children's Services Office."

"I will sign up today."

"Thank you, it means a lot to me," he said gently.

"I can tell," she smiled at him.

"One more favor," he said with an inescapable smile.

"What?" she asked with amusement.

"Have dinner with me tonight," he optimistically asked.

She thought about it for a few seconds. "I guess, what time?"

"I'll meet you at your apartment at eight-thirty."

"So late?"

"I have football practice until eight," he told her as he rubbed his left side.

"Eight-thirty it is," she said with a warm smile.

"I hate to run but I have to get a shower and get to a lecture," Mark said as he looked at his watch and shook his head.

"You look like you could use a good shower," she laughed, as she looked him over from head to toe. Mark looked down at himself and remembered that he was still covered with dirt. He looked back at April and smiled.

"I'll see you at eight-thirty," he smiled with a grin.

"Bye," she said as she smiled back into his eyes.

Mark rushed into the building. *Well, at least she said yes. At least something has gone right today*, he thought as he rubbed his painful ribs.

Had she shown a flicker of romantic interest in him? He smiled knowing the answer was yes.

Once in the shower he saw the bruising forming on his upper left abdomen. He cursed himself again. "God, forgive me for being so stupid." When he got out of the shower, he took an old bottle of pain medication out of the cabinet and downed several of the pills.

He hurriedly put on a long sleeve shirt under his hospital scrub shirt so he could hide the red dots on his arms. He put the bottle of pain medication in his jacket pocket. Then he hurried to his morning lecture.

Jeff eyed Mark as he came in the classroom late. Jeff noticed that he looked pale and was sweating when Mark sat down in the seat next to him. That was odd; it was wintertime. What was even odder was the way Mark was squirming in his chair like a child, Jeff thought, *hmmm.*

The day seemed to drag on and on as Mark dealt with the pain. The pain pills were not strong enough to give him much relief. He did not get off work until seven so he quickly drove to the stadium.

At football practice, Mark realized that his ribs were very tight, but he practiced as usual so the other players and his coaches would not realize he was hurting. He tried to convince himself that his ribs were not broken, just bruised.

Mark hurried home to get dressed, but he did not know what he should wear since he had not told April where they would be going. He decided to dress causal, certainly at this hour she did not expect to go anywhere formal.

Mark decided to wear his jeans and a casual dress shirt without a tie. He wanted to look perfect for her. Even if he wore his jeans, he would still look nice, he thought.

He left his apartment and got into the elevator. Surprisingly, he was feeling nervous. The doors opened on the second floor; he walked to her door and knocked.

April opened the door. Mark's mouth dropped open when he saw her standing there in a semi-formal dress, with high heel shoes and her hair elegantly pulled up into a romantic styled bun. She was breathtakingly beautiful. He stood there frozen and admired how stunning she looked.

April saw the expression on his face and could not help but laugh at him. "Come in," she laughed. Mark went in and she closed the door behind him.

"I can go change," he offered, embarrassed at the situation.

"No, it is fine. I will go put on a pair of …uh… jeans," she said as she smiled at him. He could hear her giggling from the bedroom and felt like a fool.

Mark sat down to wait for her, looking around her apartment. He thumbed through the magazines on the coffee table and noticed the scrapbook. A smile crossed his face when he opened it up and saw all the pictures of him. *Someone is a fan of mine*, he chuckled. With a wide grin, he carefully tucked the scrapbook under the magazines.

She was not long and he stood up when she came into the room again. Even in her jeans, she was extremely attractive.

"I'm really sorry you had to change. You looked great in that dress … uh … you look great in those jeans, too," he fumbled for the right words.

"You look great in your jeans, too," she smiled, as she seemed to be enjoying his embarrassment. She loved that goofy smile of his when he was eighteen and she loved it now.

"I don't know what's wrong with me. Believe me, I am not usually this awkward," he told her as he wet his lips.

"I am nervous too, if that makes you feel any better," she admitted, and Mark seemed relieved to know he was not the only one who was nervous.

"That's good … no…. you know what I mean," he said, wanting to smack himself in the head for being so dumbfounded.

"Let's go eat, shall we?" she said as she moved towards the door.

As they drove in Mark's sports car to Nathan's Restaurant, they felt more comfortable with each other and enjoyed their conversation. The crisp cool night air had a romantic feel to it.

When they arrived, Mark was the perfect gentleman. He opened her car door for her, took her arm, and placed it on his as they walked into the restaurant. He held her chair for her to be seated. After looking at the menu, they were surprised when they both ordered the same meal.

"Did you get a chance to sign up for the big sister program?"

"I did. I am now Sunflower's big sister. I did not tell them that you asked me to sign up," she said, not able to take her eyes off him. She was savoring the way he made her feel.

"That's good; they might not have let you be her big sister if they knew I was involved," he told her. She smelled so good, he thought as he leaned closer to her.

"I can see her anytime I want," April said. She did not think he was really listening. His attention seemed to be on her, not on her words.

"That is great. I am so glad you did this for me; it means a lot," he said, unaware that he had taken a hold of her hand on top of the table. He was counting the sparkling stars in her eyes.

The waiter brought their food to the table. It was then that Mark realized he had a hold of April's hand.

"I am sorry, I didn't …," he said as he let go of her hand.

"That's fine. I don't mind; it was sweet," she smiled at him.

He found himself staring at her. Did she notice, he wondered. No, she was too busy staring at him. They ate quietly, smiling at each other between bites. When they were finished eating, the waiter removed the plates.

"How are you doing with all those problems you left behind?" he asked her sincerely.

"I'm still working on them, but I think I have them under control now."

"That's good. I've been worried about you,"

"Thank you, I am doing fine now."

"If you ever want to talk about them, I am a good listener," he volunteered tenderly.

"Thanks," she answered warmly. April looked at her watch. Mark noticed that she was looking at the time.

"Are you ready to leave?" He certainly was in no hurry to end this night. Nevertheless, if she needed to go, he would be a perfect gentleman and take her home.

"Well, it is getting pretty late and I have a big day tomorrow."

"I'll pay the check and we can go." Mark quickly signaled for the waiter to bring them the bill so that they could get on their way.

They drove back to the apartment, enjoying each other's companionship as if they had done this many times before. They no longer felt like they were on a first date; it was as if they were an established couple. Mark was very charming as he made her laugh and smile.

Mark told her more about his relationship with Sunny. April saw the love Mark had for Sunny as he spoke her name. One small blonde-haired girl with curls had certainly won his heart. April was anxious to meet this little girl that had charmed Mark into total submission.

They stood in front of April's door. She was nervously trying to unlock the door, and then she dropped her keys.

"I'll get them for you," Mark volunteered as he bent over to pick them up. As he did, he let out a painful sounding gasp as he felt the soreness of his injured ribs. Slowly he got up, held his ribs with one hand, and handed the keys to April.

"Are you alright?"

"It is nothing." Mark straightened up as he rubbed his hand back and forth across his rib cage and took a slow deep breath. As much as he wanted to hide his pain, it was impossible; the pain pills had worn off hours ago.

April was not fooled. She opened the door, took his arm, and ushered him into her apartment.

Mark decided to sit on a barstool. April watched him carefully, seeing pain cross his face, as he cautiously sat down. He was not hiding anything.

"You don't look fine to me. What is wrong?" she asked with concern as she stood beside him.

He had seen those inquiring eyes of hers before, but when?

"I sorta wrecked my motorcycle this morning, and I think I bruised some of my ribs," Mark confessed as he slowly removed his leather jacket. It seemed extremely warm in her apartment.

"Let me see." She took his jacket from him and set it on the counter in front of them. Mark made no attempt at removing his shirt. Without thinking, April leaned forward and started unbuttoning Mark's long sleeve shirt.

"I'm fine, really."

"Let me take a look," she demanded with a motherly tone, as she worked to undo the buttons. She had cared for his cuts and bruises when they were children; it felt natural for her to tend to him now.

Mark was surprised by her actions. He gently took a hold of both her hands. Now she realized what she had just done and was embarrassed. She looked up into his warm eyes.

"Oh … I am sorry … I don't know what I was thinking," she said as she blushed, feeling his closeness to her.

"It is okay," he reassured her with a smile, and a look of relief crossed her face. Mark continued to undo his shirt. As the last button was free, she carefully pushed his shirt open to expose his ribs.

When she looked at his bare chest, her face took on a concerned look. The left side of his chest was a deep shade of purple and blue.

"Oh, Mark, you really have seriously bruised yourself," she told him with a gasp of alarm. "We need to get you to a doctor."

"I am a doctor," he reminded her with good humor. "I am fine, just sore."

"I do not believe that for a minute," April persisted with a worried face; she was not finding any humor in his injury. He read her face and knew that expression; it was one that at any other time, she might have gotten what she wanted from him.

"Look, I am one of the best ER doctors at the hospital. I'll know when it is time to worry," he reassured her with a teasing smile, letting her know that he had everything under control.

"I have some cream that might help. Do you want me to put it on for you?" she asked him compassionately. She looked up into his face as he leaned towards her, their lips so close.

"If you promise to be gentle," he teased her and she smiled. She could not breathe with him this close to her.

"I'll go get it," she said as she left the room, thankful that the space now separating them would allow her to clear her mind. She brushed her fingers through her hair and took a long slow deep breath. There was no mistaking the way he was sending vibrations to her heart when she was with him.

Mark took a slow deep breath as she left the room. She was tempting his heart with her closeness. He would have to resist the temptations she caused him every time he felt her enchanting eyes grabbing his heart.

Mark removed his shirt carefully. She came back in with the cream in tow and stopped abruptly in her tracks when she saw Mark with his entire shirt off. *Oh, my, what have I gotten myself into now,* she thought as she looked at his masculine body. He was in excellent shape. She felt her body go weak.

Mark realized her dilemma, as she stood there speechless. "It's okay; I'll put the cream on, if you will just hand it to me." He reached out his hand and she placed the cream in it. He opened it and with his right hand, he gently rubbed it over the bruised area.

April watched him, barely able to contain herself from the emotions she was feeling. She wanted to reach out, touch him, and smooth away his pain, just as she had wanted to do after his motorcycle accident several years ago, but she was afraid.

Mark finished and handed her back the tube. He stood up and carefully put his shirt back on. Then he looked down at her. She looked so far away in thought. Concern replaced her beautiful smile. Mark moved his hand in front of her face to bring her attention back to him.

"Promise me, you will not tell your Uncle Dan about my ribs," Mark asked of her.

"Why, Mark, you really should let him have a look at them," April told him with unease, knowing he could be seriously injured.

"Because Dan is very protective of me, he'll want me to stay in bed until my ribs heal. I have so much going on right now that I cannot let this accident interfere with everything. So let's just keep this between you and me, okay?" he begged her with his eyes.

"Did I just hear you say, heal? Are they broken?" she asked alarmed.

"I don't know, maybe fractured, but there is nothing medically you can do if they are," he informed her. "Promise you will not say anything."

"If that is what you want," she agreed, not happy about it. How many secrets had they shared growing up, she thought, Mark Sanders was as mischievous as he had always been.

"I better be going," Mark said tenderly as he picked up his jacket. If he stayed one minute longer, his lips would have found hers and held him captive. "I had a really good time tonight."

"So did I," she said as she followed him to the door.

"I will call you." He opened the door. "Good night," he said, as his eyes looked right into her heart.

"Good night," she said warmly, wishing that he never had to leave her.

Mark closed the door behind him without kissing her. He leaned back against the door, as if to have her close to him for *one more moment in time*. She had leaned on the other side, trying to catch her breath. The evening had been absolutely perfect even if he had not kissed her.

April drifted across the room and sat on her couch. She drew her knees up like she had a habit of doing.

He has done it to me again; he has stolen my heart. So much for my plan, she smiled. *Only this time, Mark Sanders, I will not allow you to break it like you did before.*

Mark had a hard time sleeping that night, thinking about April and Sunny. Every time he moved, he was reminded of his injury.

What was happening to him; had he gone totally weak? In two weeks time, he had lost his heart not once but twice. His life had suddenly become very complicated.

For a man who had always refused to get involved with women, he had let his guard down. What was he going to do now?

One thing was sure, he would get Sunny back because he could not live without her. And April, well, he knew she would be in his future plans, too.

CHAPTER TWENTY-EIGHT –
❦Love Blossoms❧

When Mark arrived early at the hospital the next day, Jeff told him that Dan was looking for him.

"Oh great!" *April must have told Dan about my ribs.* Mark felt betrayed by April. Reluctantly, he went straight to Dan's office to get it over with, certain that Dan was about to chew him out.

Suddenly, he felt condemned, as if he was going to Principal Quarterman's office. He stood frozen in front of the door before he gave a light tap and heard Dan tell him to come in.

Mark reluctantly opened the door and entered the room. Dan was sitting behind his desk reading a chart. He looked up briefly as Mark entered the room.

"You wanted to see me, Dan?" Mark asked with reservation.

"Come in and sit down, Dr. Sanders," Dan instructed him as his eyes remained on the chart in his hands.

Dan never calls me Dr. Sanders. Ok, so April did tell on me. Why did I think I could trust her? He felt busted by Dan's choice of words.

"Why do you look so worried, Mark?" Dan inquired when he saw the troubled look on Mark's face.

"Worried … I'm not worried about anything," Mark tried to convince him. Mark remained standing. The thought of sitting down was too painful to consider; he would stand as they talked.

"I can see by your blood-shot eyes that you had another sleepless night. Do you want to talk about it?" Dan asked with concern in his voice and indicated for Mark to sit down.

"I'm just worried about Sunny living in that children's home," Mark claimed. *Does he know about my ribs or what?* Mark wondered. Mark

223

looked at the low soft chair Dan had pointed at and frowned. He sucked in a deep breath of air and held it in as he slowly sat down, trying success- fully to keep his pain intact so that Dan would not notice.

"If you need today off, I can arrange it for you," Dan volunteered with concern. Mark did not look healthy to him. He started to give Mark's awkward descent into the chair a second thought.

"No, working helps me keep my mind off of Sunny. Besides, this is my last day of rotation in the ER. I have review lectures all next week to get ready for my boards," Mark informed him with a sleepy yawn.

"Do you need something to help you sleep?" Dan offered.

"I could use something to take the edge off," Mark conveyed to him. *Pain –edge, same difference, the pills would work for both,* Mark cleverly thought. Dan wrote Mark a prescription and held it out for him to get.

Mark gave the paper a brief stare. *Oh, man, Dan.* Mark reluctantly stretched forward to get the paper and nearly exposed himself with a gasp of pain that he had to force from leaving his lips. Mark folded it up and put it in the pocket of his scrub shirt. *Dang it, Dan, what are you trying to do to me,* Mark thought as he sucked in what little composure he had left.

"Just remember not to over take these," Dan warned him.

"I won't. You know that," Mark promised.

It was true; normally Mark avoided taking any type of medication. Mark was extremely allergic to so many drugs and was afraid of their severe reactions. He had several half-taken prescriptions, that he was not allergic to, in his bathroom cabinet.

Dan's phone rang and he answered it. "I'll be right there," he said and hung up the phone. Then he got up from behind his desk and looked at Mark.

"I called you in here to ask you if you would mind showing our new recruit around the hospital. She should be here any minute now," Dan enlightened Mark, as he went to the door. Mark remained seated.

"Sure," Mark agreed and Dan left. Again, Dan thought that it was strange that Mark had not stood up and followed him to the door. *Hmmm, what is up with Mark? Guess he is just tired,* he thought as he headed down the hall.

Mark was relieved that Dan had not said anything about his ribs. He had gotten out of that lecture, for now. He took a slow deep breath and rubbed his hand across his chest.

Mark looked back at Dan's desk and saw April's picture. He wondered why he had never paid any attention to it before.

The door opened and Mark turned around slowly. To his surprise and hers, April was standing there in a nurse's outfit. She looked very attractive in her uniform, and Mark was speechless as he stared at her.

Mark remembered now that Dan had told him that April had become a nurse. *So that is why she tried to fix me up last night,* Mark thought with a satisfying grin, as he carefully stood up to face her.

April came in the door, closed it behind her, and stood facing him. "I suppose you arranged this?" she accused him with a candid smile, not believing that this meeting was an accident.

She gave him the head to toe inspection. Mark looked distinctive and handsome in his hospital scrubs, she thought.

"Honestly, I did not remember you were a nurse, until you walked in that door," he defended himself, as his eyes locked on her to plead his innocence.

"So, we can blame this on Uncle Dan?" she grinned at him with a smile that split his heart wide open.

"That would be the correct answer," Mark informed her with humor. "Dan asked me to show the new recruit around the hospital."

"That would be me," April laughed softly.

"I should have figured you were a nurse last night when you came to my aid," he joked with her.

"How are you feeling?" she asked with concern in her voice.

"Better," he replied as he stared at her, making her feel uncomfortable.

"Mark," she said slowly, "stop staring at me like that." She was blushing, her cheeks warm.

"I can't help it; you are so beautiful," he said as he moved closer to her. *What is happening to me?* The very sight of her sent him messages he could not control. He was feeling no pain as his attention was focused solely on her.

No longer could he be the professional doctor and see her as just another nurse. His feelings for her somewhere deep inside of his heart had made that clear. He became sidetracked in his assignment to show her around the hospital.

April felt weak all of a sudden. She wanted to change the subject and pretend she had not heard what he had just said. She was sure she would fall into his arms if he moved any closer to her.

"I'm going to see Sunny today," she said, desperate to draw his attention away from her. It was getting awful warm in Dan's office, she thought as she pushed her hair away from her face.

"That is great," he answered as he moved even closer to her, teasing her with his warm eyes and his handsome smile that she could no longer deny.

April could feel her heart beating as he came nearer to her and their eyes locked. She took a deep breath. She was sure Mark could hear the pounding of her heart.

Mark stood over her and took her soft hands in his, and then he bent his head down to hers. "May I kiss you?" he requested so tenderly.

April thought she was going to melt. She nodded her head yes and lifted her head to meet his.

Their warm moist lips touched softly. His kiss was soft and passionate; she did not want him to stop. She was no longer that little girl in the stable that loved Mark; she was a woman and he was definitely a magnificent man. There was no denying her love for him.

Mark stepped back so he could look into her eyes. Her eyes told him what he wanted to know: she wanted him as much as he wanted her. He put his arms around her and pulled her gently against his firm chest, and then he bent his neck down so he could kiss her again. That kiss sent him to a place that he had never been.

He brushed her long silky hair behind her neck and kissed her neck so softly. Then he just held her close to him to recollect his thoughts. Why was this happening to him; what was she doing to his heart?

He wrapped his arms around her, and hugged her carefully, not wanting to cause her any discomfort. He could feel her heart beating. It all felt so natural to him, to have her in his arms.

He would never get back what they had shared at the dance, but if it were anything like what he was feeling now, he knew why he felt so comfortable holding her and yes, loving her with all his heart.

His eyes conveyed a love that pierced her heart, and in this intimate moment, she gave in to him. Soaking in the love he had for her, she gave her lips to him once more. She was sure she would drown in the depth of the emotions she felt for him. His lips, sweet and intoxicating, caused her knees to go weak, and she was thankful that he held his strong arm around her back as he drew her to his chest.

Finally, she spoke softly, "Mark, we better let go. Uncle Dan might come in and find us like this," she whispered in his ear.

Mark slowly let her go and took both her hands in his and looked at her. The tears of love for him were seen in her glassy eyes. April felt her knees go weak; she was sure she was going to faint so she slid into a chair.

Mark knelt down on one knee and looked in her eyes with love and concern. Those eyes of hers, he knew those unforgettable eyes. Even if his mind could not remember, his heart did. The power her eyes had over him was captivating. She had full ownership of his heart.

Before he knew it, the words he had never said to any woman came out softly with such emotions in them as he gave her his heart in words.

"April, I am in love with you," he spoke passionately, "I know that I have always been in love with you or this would not have happened so quickly. Whatever you and I shared before, the feelings are so strong I cannot deny them. April, you take my breath away," he told her as he easily stole her heart.

April was speechless, but tears of joy filled her eyes. Those were the very words she had waited so long to hear from his lips. *Oh, Mark.*

"I cannot explain it; I knew it that night in the park when we met. It was as if you walked out of my dreams and right into my heart. I have had so many dreams about you and now here you are; you are real. You touch my heart like it has never been touched before," he said as he took her hand in his, and held it to his lips, and kissed her fingers. "I want to share my life with you, April. I feel that in love with you." Tears welled up in his sincere eyes.

"Are you sure ... you love me?" Her voice was shaky. "How can you be sure?"

"I've never felt like this with anyone. All my life I have felt like something was missing in my heart. No one has ever been able to fill that spot. It is as if I was holding that spot in my heart for you. Did my heart know you were out there? I think it did. I think my heart remembers what we shared so long ago, and it would not let go of those feelings. My mind cries out for you when we are apart. I want to hold you and touch you and feel you next to me," he said lovingly. "My mind is consumed with you, April."

"Oh, Mark, you are so sweet," she rejoiced as the tears trickled down her rosy cheeks.

Mark wiped her tears with his hand and kissed her wet cheeks softly, before he captured her lips with his.

She had dreamed of this moment with him for so long. She wrapped her arms around his neck and they kissed. Then she held him closer, broke down and cried on his shoulder uncontrollably as if she was letting out all her pain from the past. She held onto him as if the heartache she felt deep in her soul was to be shared by the two of them in this private moment. It was as if she was crying for what they had both lost a long time ago.

She had to release all her painful emotions so that she could be set free to love him. Her secret would remain a secret; it was better off forgotten, if they were going to start their relationship from this point on.

Mark was not sure why she was crying; he hoped it was because she was happy. He rubbed her back, running his fingers gently through her hair. She lifted her head off his shoulder, and he wiped her eyes and cheeks with his tender hands. She slowly smiled at him and bent closer to him so that he could kiss her.

"I love you, Mark." Her moist lips confirmed her words.

They had found each other again; a love that they had shared so many years ago had overtaken them into a moment they would forever remember.

In their intense moment, they did not realize that the door behind them had opened, and Dan had started to come into the room. Dan was surprised to see them embraced in a kiss, but a joyful smile appeared across his face. After all, he could see he had achieved what he had set out to accomplish. His first attempt at matchmaking had been successful.

Dan stood there quietly; he had to fight back the happy tears as his godson passionately embraced his niece. The tough little boy had grown up and found someone who would love him forever. It warmed his heart to see the love Mark deserved returned by his own niece, April.

Then Dan let the door close with a small bang and walked into the room, acting as if he had not noticed them.

Mark and April looked over at him quickly and Mark jumped to his feet. Mark was sorry that he had moved so quickly as the pain in his chest hit him. He was quick to draw back his hand that was about to grab his chest. April wiped her face and took a deep breath.

"Aren't you two supposed to be touring this hospital?" Dan asked as he walked across the room and sat down in his chair, not looking at them. He was afraid that if he did they would see his satisfaction in their embarrassing moment.

"Yes, Sir, we were just leaving," Mark answered as he helped April up from her chair.

"April, you have been assigned to the third floor for the morning shift. After lunch, go down to the ER and assist Dr. Sanders and Dr. Kirkland."

"Thanks, Uncle Dan," she fondly said as she looked warmly at him, knowing that he was responsible for her new relationship with Mark. Dan looked at her and smiled. The love he had for her was clear; it was written all over his glowing face.

"You are welcome," Dan expressed as he watched them leave the room together. He loved them both very much, and he wanted nothing but the best for them.

Mark introduced April to some of the nurses, Stephanie and Terri. They were in their early twenties like April. Their constant flirting annoyed Mark. They were polite to April but were instantly jealous of the way Mark looked lovingly into April's eyes. *Who does April think she is, stealing Mark on her first day at work?*

Mark had given April the grand tour ending with the third floor. He introduced her to the head nurse, Sally Johnson, not realizing that Sally was April's sister, Debbie's, mother-in-law.

Sally noticed the sparkle in their eyes as Mark and April looked at each other. This would be a heartbreaking day for the rest of the female nursing staff, as Dr. Robert Mark Sanders III was no longer available.

Sally remembered when April had stood at Mark's hospital room door a few years ago. All had wished that Mark would remember her, but he never did. It was apparent that he had regained his feelings for her, Sally thought with a warm smile.

April would be working with Mark's sister, Rebecca and April's best friend, Sharon Johnson. She would be in good hands. Rebecca gave Mark a hearty hug when she saw him. How handsome her little brother was in his hospital scrubs, she thought.

Rebecca was so proud of Mark. She had sheltered him all these years; it was time she set him free. From the way he was looking into April's eyes, she knew that Mark's heart belonged to someone else now. She knew that she would never lose her special spot in his heart no matter who claimed the rest of his heart.

After Mark had introduced April to everyone, he took her over to the lounge area. He looked to see if anyone was watching, and then he kissed her tenderly.

"Where are you going to take Sunny today?" Mark asked her.

"To the park at about five."

"I'll come join you as soon as I can get away from here, then I have football practice at seven tonight."

"Do you think you should practice today?" she questioned him with apprehension, as she gently touched his chest.

"I'm fine," he assured her with a kiss on the cheek, before darting off. If there was a cloud nine, he was definitely on cloud ninety-nine.

April was deeply concerned that Mark was not telling her the truth about the seriousness of his injury. Mark was so high from the love he had shared with April that he was feeling no pain.

That high would not last long.

Chapter Twenty-Nine –
⌐❦Friends❦⌐

*M*ark had gone to work in the ER with Dr. Jeffery Kirkland, one of his very best friends. He was thankful they had only minor patients all morning. The attending and the third year resident assigned to Mark and Jeff had gone to view an extraordinary surgery from the OR observation area.

As the morning went on, the pain in Mark's chest was really making it hard for him to hide his condition. It was harder for him to breathe, but he knew that he needed to breathe deeply and cough as much as possible to prevent his lung from collapsing.

Mark had broken his ribs and punctured his lung in high school, but he did not remember it because he had been in a coma, and by the time he came out of the coma, his ribs were healed.

Mark knew he needed an x-ray, but what would the x-ray tell him that he did not already know. Pain relief is what he needed. He could no longer pretend it did not hurt; he would have to cover it up with pain medication.

Mark went to his locker and got his leather jacket. He pulled out the bottle of Tylenol #3 that he had stashed in it earlier. *These should help ease the pain*, he thought.

Nothing much was happening in the ER. Most of the residents were sacked out or studying in the lounge. The nurses were caring for the two patients with the flu. Mark finished checking on the two and went back to the lounge to wait on the next patient to arrive.

Mark liked working nights when more trauma patients arrived. He was considering going into trauma surgery. However, he was thankful for the quiet ER today.

At noon, Mark went to see if April could have a brief lunch with him. All through lunch, he was uncomfortable sitting in the chair, as the pain got worse. April was very concerned about Mark. He was sweating and he coughed every few minutes, each cough causing him pain. She begged him to let her Uncle Dan take a look at him.

He told her that he felt foolish for wrecking his motorcycle a second time. He told her about the football games coming up, and explained how important it was that he play in those games. She read his deep commitment to his team on his unwavering face.

Mark reluctantly went back to work. Jeff had been watching him carefully. *What has he done to himself this time?* Jeff knew Mark well enough to know he would never reveal his secret. *I'll just watch him closely today*, Jeff told himself, as he tossed a stern look in Mark's direction.

Jeff and Mark were stitching up a patient who had several cuts. Mark dropped something on the floor and bent over to pick it up. When he did, he let out a painful moan.

Mark instantly grabbed his left side in pain. He stood up slowly and looked Jeff square in the face. Mark knew he had been caught. Jeff was frowning at him and shaking his head back and forth with disapproval.

"I'll be right back," Mark told Jeff with a look of self-reproach.

Mark went into the next examining room. He leaned against the gurney and took a slow deep breath. He took his stethoscope from around his neck and listened to his chest.

"Dang," Mark said angrily. He knew what he was facing.

"Let me listen," Jeff insisted as he walked up behind Mark and took Mark's stethoscope from him. Mark turned around to face him. From the look on Mark's face, Jeff knew that Mark had already made his own diagnosis.

"What is it?" Jeff asked him with concern as Mark snatched his stethoscope away from Jeff.

"Pneumo," Mark muttered.

(Pneumo or Pneumothorax, is air in the area around the lungs that can cause the lung to partially collapse. Mark's was due to his injury.)

"What about a hemothorax? We need a chest x-ray." Jeff stated knowing this was nothing to mess around with.

(Hemothorax is blood in the space between the lung and chest wall.)

"It sounds like a partially collapsed left lung; it will heal on its own. I want to relieve the air pressure so the lung will fully re-expand. You can do an aspiration, but not a chest tube," Mark stipulated to Jeff with reluctance.

"Let me call the attending down here," Jeff told Mark.

"We don't need him; you can do this, Jeff." Mark looked anxious. Mark knew that absolutely no one could know that he was injured. He needed Jeff's help; otherwise, his lung would completely collapse.

"First, let's get an x-ray to see what we are dealing with," Jeff insisted. Mark was afraid of what else the x-ray might reveal.

"Just get a catheter and do it," Mark opposed firmly. "Let's just get this done before I change my mind." Mark was extremely agitated that he could not avoid the medical treatment he needed.

When April came down to work in the ER, the charge nurse told her to assist Mark and Jeff, in exam room two. Neither was there, so she looked in the next room. When April walked in, she knew immediately that something was up between the two doctors. She had a feeling it had to do with Mark's ribs.

"What is going on, doctors, and don't tell me nothing," April demanded, reading the annoyed look on Mark's face.

"Dr. Jeff Kirkland, meet Miss April Morgan, our new nurse," Mark introduced them, as his pain-filled eyes looked April directly in the face, connecting them as a couple.

"What is wrong with Mark?" Jeff looked at Mark for permission to tell her. Mark did not look pleased with the situation.

"Pneumo, we are getting ready to do an aspiration," Jeff conveyed to her. Jeff noticed how pretty April was and smiled at her with his playboy look. He would ask her out on a date later.

"What can I do to help?" April moved towards them to be of assistance.

"Get him ready while I get the supplies we need."

"Do you want an IV started?" she asked Jeff.

"No, he doesn't. No sedative either!" Mark told them both firmly.

Jeff looked Mark squarely in the eyes and firmly gave April instructions, "Get him on the gurney and sterilize the area with betadine. I am running the show, Mark. So you better do what I tell you, pal," Jeff told Mark good-naturedly and then he left the room.

Dang him, Jeff thought as he left the room. Mark had pushed the limit before with other injuries, but this time his condition demanded immediate attention.

April put the gurney in a semi-sitting position. Mark was hesitant to remove his long sleeve shirt, not wanting her to see his arms. But there was no getting around it, and he carefully removed his shirt with April's assistance.

The bruising was much worse than last night. She did not say anything because she could tell that Mark was highly agitated. He sat on the gurney and leaned back. She helped him lift up his legs.

"Have you ever done an aspiration before, Mark?" she asked nervously.

"I've performed several on my own in the ER, enough to know that I do not want to be the patient," Mark divulged.

Jeff had returned with the things he needed, and April helped him set up a tray. Jeff looked at Mark with concern.

Jeff took his stethoscope and listened to Mark's chest. Mark had decreased breath sounds and a rapid heart rate, not a good sign.

April carefully cleaned Mark's chest with betadine, and Jeff put on a pair of sterile gloves.

"This better work or you are getting a chest tube," Jeff bluntly told him.

"This will work, trust me," Mark reassured him.

Mark said a quiet prayer. He looked at his friend and gave him the okay to begin.

"Do you want me to talk you through this?" Mark asked Jeff with humor. Jeff smiled slightly. *Just like Mark, he has to be in control. Well, not this time, buddy, you are at my mercy.*

"No, I can handle it. Do you want me to tell you what I am doing?" Jeff asked jokingly. Jeff was tapping Mark's upper left chest with his fingers, locating the spot that sounded hollow.

"No, I know what you are doing," Mark sarcastically remarked.

"This is the part that you tell the patient it might sting, when you know it is going to hurt like heck," Jeff joked as he inserted a long needle with a local anesthetic in it. Once the area was numb, he inserted a larger needle and put in a catheter.

The air from Mark's chest was vacuumed into a bottle of sterile water. Mark seemed to be breathing easier after a few minutes. Jeff listened again to his breath sounds. He really wanted an x-ray and an arterial blood gas done on Mark. Jeff put a pulse oximeter on Mark's finger and turned on the machine.

"Not a word to anyone about this," Mark strongly told them, after the procedure was finished. He knew if he was going to play in the football game on Sunday, no one could know he was injured.

"That is going to be hard to do, when you are on the third floor. I am going to go admit you so we can run all the tests we need. I don't like the way you look so pale and your oxygen saturation level is low," Jeff said seriously, knowing Mark looked too pale.

"I am not going anywhere. I am fine. I feel better already. Just give me an hour and I will be back to work," Mark told him persuasively, as the two of them locked eyes.

"You can't be serious, Doctor Sanders, is that what you would recommend for your patients who have just undergone an aspiration and look like heck?" Jeff wanted Mark to get serious about his condition.

"I am not paying you extra for the lecture, Doctor Know-it-all," Mark answered him back. "I do believe my grade point average was higher than yours," Mark added but Jeff was not impressed.

"That is true. You outranked me in intelligence and stupidity," Jeff stated. Mark smiled at Jeff's witty come back.

"Mark, maybe you should listen to Dr. Kirkland?" April said timidly.

They both turned in her direction and sternly looked at her. Silence fell. She had not been invited into their comedy act. Mark and Jeff were quite the comedians when faced with tough situations. It eased the tension and stress.

Jeff was extremely worried about Mark's condition. And Mark knew that his condition was far more serious, but for now, he would put a band-aid on it.

April did not know what to think as they gave her the evil look for a minute, and then they both smiled and laughed out loud at the same time. Mark grabbed his bare chest and wrenched his face. She realized they were just teasing her. "Real funny, doctors. Mark, I think you should let Dr. Kirkland admit you."

"The woman sides with me. You may have the brains, and the stupidity, but I have the girl," Jeff said victoriously as he put his arm around April's waist.

April and Mark exchanged affectionate smiles. Jeff saw the affection when they looked into each other's eyes.

He frowned at Mark, "What, you got the girl, too?" He regretfully surrendered and let go of April. She went over and took Mark's hand in hers.

"Yeah, too bad, the girl's mine," Mark announced proudly with a winning grin.

"It figures." Jeff cleverly took a syringe off the tray and held it up, catching Mark's full attention.

"But I have the pain medication. How about trading the girl for the medicine?" Jeff smiled with a grin on his face.

"Very funny, give me that. I'll give it to myself. I don't trust you," Mark told him, not amused. Mark reached out to get the syringe. However, Jeff held it up away from him.

"I'll give it to the lady; she can do it," Jeff said as he handed April the syringe and an alcohol pad.

"Left arm, April, we wouldn't want to hurt Mark's precious throwing arm." Jeff half-grinned at Mark and they exchanged a killer look at each other. April just shook her head in annoyance that the two of them seemed to think that this whole situation was one big joke.

April wiped Mark's arm and gave him the shot in his left arm. Jeff looked pleased at the outcome. Then Jeff held up another syringe off the tray, and a wide underhanded-smile crossed his amused face as he looked back at Mark. Mark held his breath; he knew that mischievous look on Jeff's face, all too well.

"Oops, this is the pain medication; sorry, that was the sedative I was going to give you before the aspiration." Jeff grinned at Mark and let out a soft chuckle. Mark quickly sat up alarmed.

"Jeff, what did you just give me?" Mark shouted frantically. Their joking around ended right here.

"Mark, just lay back and enjoy the nap." Jeff smiled with satisfaction at what he had done. Mark lay back as the medicine slowly took effect on his already tired body.

"Don't you touch a hair on my head! When I wake up, you're dead meat, Jeff," Mark told him angrily. The room was spinning, and his eyelids were increasingly becoming heavy, as the medication started to work.

Jeff came closer to the bed and patted Mark on his bare shoulder. Jeff helped Mark turn on his right side and stuffed another pillow against Mark's chest.

"Good night, Mark," Jeff said caringly. However, Mark had already shut his eyes. *Hmmm, the sedative is working very quickly.* Jeff thought with concern; knowing it was because Mark was exhausted. Jeff listened to Mark's chest again. He turned on the oxygen and placed a mask over Mark's face. He turned to April who looked taken aback.

"Start an IV; I want him to have fluids and an IV antibiotic. Get a blanket out of the warmer and cover him up," Jeff instructed her as he removed Mark's boots. "Get me a chart for him." April went to get the needed supplies and did as Jeff instructed her.

Jeff leaned over Mark. "Buddy, what's going on? What are you not telling me?" Jeff asked in a quiet concerned voice. Mark was hiding something and Jeff knew that it was serious. The pit of his stomach churned, as he looked deeply distressed over Mark's condition.

April returned to the room and handed Jeff a chart. She noticed that Jeff was troubled, even though he was pretending to smile as if nothing was wrong.

When April picked up Mark's bare arm, she noticed the small red dots and looked concerned. A sick feeling hit her stomach as she looked at his arm. Jeff looked over at her and they exchanged a fretful look but neither said anything.

April started the IV and covered Mark up with the warm blanket. She touched the side of his face with the palm of her hand and watched him sleep. If Jeff had not been in the room she would have removed the mask and claimed Mark's lips on her own.

When they had finished taking care of Mark, Jeff seemed pleased and relaxed.

Jeff was very attentive in his caring for Mark. April was touched by the closeness that he displayed towards Mark. *Why had Jeff been underhanded about the sedative?*

"Why did you give Mark a sedative?" she bravely asked. Jeff smiled at her warmly; he too had observed how devoted April was in caring for Mark.

"When we were in med school, Mark put a sedative in my coffee to calm me down before our first big test; it knocked me out for the entire day. I told him that I would pay him back someday." Jeff smiled, remembering that day when the two of them had to go to their professor and explain what they had done.

"But seriously, if I had not knocked him out, he would have taken that catheter out and been back to work. My gut tells me that Mark has something else going on with him besides his ribs. He has been losing weight lately and I am very concerned about him," Jeff explained to April with discontent. He seemed in deep thought, thoughts that he did not want to have.

"Have you and Mark been friends for long?"

"We were in high school together. I was two years ahead of him, but we were on the football team together. I went on to college and when he came to college, he skipped his first two years and was in my class. We went on to medical school together for four years, and we have been together since."

"You seem pretty close to him," she said kindly.

"We were roommates. About a year ago he saved my life," he told her with tender emotions as he hovered over Mark.

"How?" she asked as she looked at him. She moved closer to Mark. She took Mark's hand in hers and intertwined their fingers.

"We had gone camping up in the mountains. We were on our way down the mountain on a rough dirt road. We were messing around with our new four-wheel-drive trucks, going pretty fast, trying to get down the mountain before each other," Jeff told her with a trembling voice.

"I was in the lead. I looked back to see where Mark was, and when I looked back to the road, a log truck had pulled out of a side logging road. I hit the brakes but it was too late, the hood of my truck went under the trailer."

"My truck caught fire and the logs leaned down on the cab. My foot was trapped and I could not get out. I thought I was going to be burned to death or be crushed by the logs." Jeff shuddered as he told her the story.

"Mark broke out the rest of the back window and climbed in the cab with me. He took off his jacket and placed it over me. Then he sprayed me down with a fire extinguisher. I was screaming at him to get out. I didn't want us both to die."

"He took out his hunting knife, got down on the floorboard and started cutting away at my boot. I knew he would cut my foot off if he had to save my life." Jeff's eyes were so stressed.

"There were flames all around us now and the logs were making loud crackling noises. The heat from the engine fire was burning the shirt on Mark's arms, but he kept on trying to free me. I thought we were both going to die."

"The other driver would not come anywhere near the wreck. He was yelling for us to get out of there that the tanks were going to blow-up." Jeff touched Mark's arm where the faint scars from the accident were still visible."

"I was telling Mark to leave me, to save himself. He yelled at me to shut up, he was not leaving me. Finally, he pulled my broken foot out of the boot and freed me. He climbed out the back window, grabbed me under the arms, and pulled me out of the truck into the pickup bed. He slid me to the back and carried me in his arms across the road, just before the whole mess blew up, causing us to go flying over the edge of the road, down a fifteen foot incline."

"I don't know how long we both were lying there unconscious. I came to, I looked for him; he was about ten feet from me, not moving, blood running down the side of his face. I thought he was dead. I crawled over to him and shook him. He came to, looked me right in the face and laughed. I lay back and we both just laughed."

"He sat up and wiped the blood from his face with his hand. He studied the seriousness of the situation. I cannot walk. It was freezing. Mark had no jacket on, his shirt was ripped up, from the broken glass in the window frame, and his arms were burned. We could not stay there and wait for someone to rescue us."

"He picked me up under the arms and half carried me up the fifteen-foot embankment. The stupid driver just stood there, screaming. I thought he was in shock. Mark told him to shut up and help us."

"Mark looked over at his brand new truck, his windows were broken out, and the hood was smashed in from a log. He put me in the back of his truck, set my leg, and covered me up with a sleeping bag. He grabbed the driver of the log truck by the shirt, threw him in the back with me, and told him to watch over me. Then he pulled a shirt out of a duffel bag and wrapped it around his head." April took Mark's hand and placed it to her chest.

"He got in the cab, brushed the glass off the seat, and started it up. Amazingly, it still ran. He backed his truck up and turned it around. I thought for sure, we were going to fall off the side again. He drove back up the mountain until he found another way to get down the mountain. We finally got to a little town that had a doctor's office located in a country house."

"He carried me in, put me on the exam table, and told everyone not to touch me. He took the blood-soaked shirt off his head and wrapped his head in gauze to stop the bleeding. Blood was all down his shirt and on his pants."

"True to form, he put his football cap over his bandaged head. He cleaned the blood off his hands. And since the local doctor was out ice fishing, Mark took care of my leg with the help of a nurse named Becky Oliver. I will never forget the astonished look on Becky's face as Mark worked on me. She offered him a job as he fixed me up enough that we could travel the one-hundred miles to get here."

"I heard not too long ago, that Becky was dating Robert Sanders', vice-president, William. Seems Mark is quite a matchmaker." Jeff smiled as he acknowledged the affection April displayed for Mark as he told the story.

"Anyhow, Mark went over to this small town truck dealership, handed them the keys to his truck, and wrote the owner a check for a brand new truck. I could not believe it. Mark looked like he had stepped out of a horror movie and the owner gave him a new truck."

"I guess the owner was a football fan of Mark's."

"He drove all the way back here to this hospital. He carried me in to the ER. Dan insisted that Mark lay down on the other gurney but Mark refused. While Dan was taking care of me, Mark went and took a shower. When he came back to the room I was in, he passed out and crashed to the floor."

"Mark needed fifteen stitches in his head and several stitches on his arms and chest and two units of blood. He had first-degree burns on both his arms. His blood count bottomed out and Dan would not let him leave the hospital. He was black and blue from falling over the edge of the mountain, but he sure was stubborn."

"We spent three days in the hospital in the same room. That's where I learned about his anxiety of small spaces. He was a horrible patient."

"He was climbing the walls. He pulled out his IV and left the hospital to go to football practice. He said he was not letting the team down, because he and I had been stupid. He even played in the Sunday night football game a few days later, with both his arms wrapped in gauze."

"I finally got out of the hospital, and he took me to his apartment and for eight weeks he nursed me back to health." Jeff was remembering their true friendship of endless pizzas and movies.

"When I was finally able to go back to my own apartment, he handed me a set of keys to a brand new four-wheel-drive truck. In case you didn't know it, he's loaded." Jeff winked at her with a smile.

"If it had not been for Mark, I would not have passed medical school. Mark has a brilliant mind, I don't."

"About three years ago my younger brother died of an illness, and Mark was right there for me. I wanted to quit school, but he would not let me. He picked me up and set me straight," Jeff said as tears formed in his eyes.

"Let me tell you a few things about Mark. He does not sleep on his back. He does not like being in small places, he is not fond of the dark, and he hates crawling insects and rats. He is stubborn; he has a temper if you make him feel threatened. He does not always play by the rules; he wants total control of every situation. He loves God. He is very private, humble, and kind. He would give you his last dollar if you needed it."

"When Mark Sanders calls you friend, he'd give his life for you. I owe him so much. I would do anything for him. He's my little brother now, and I have to look out for him, because he does not look out for himself."

Jeff had looked at Mark several times with tears as he told the story. It was obvious that these two men shared a past that bonded their friendship.

"I am very touched," April told Jeff with a kind voice.

"So how did Mark hurt himself this time?"

"Motorcycle accident yesterday." April felt it was fine to tell Jeff the truth.

"It figures. He did that a few years ago; almost cost him his life."

"I know," she said sadly.

"So tell me, who are you?" he asked with interest.

"I'm Dan Morgan's niece. Mark and I were childhood friends; we are just getting to know each other again."

"Any friend of Mark's is a friend of mine," he smiled and held his hand out to her, and they warmly shook hands.

"What are you planning to do with Mark now?"

"I'll let him sleep; he's been exhausted lately. I'll keep checking his breath sounds," Jeff told her with concern. "I'd like to do more, but there is a limit to what Mark would allow me to do without his permission."

"We have plans tonight. I can keep an eye on him while he is with me," April said, trying to make Jeff feel better about Mark's condition.

"It's three o'clock. He should sleep another hour; if his breath sounds stay good, I will let him wake up and leave. If not, I'll have to call the attending down here to have a look at him."

Jeff was torn between covering up for Mark or finding out what was really wrong with Mark.

April's shift ended at four and she went to check on Mark. He was doing better so Jeff told April he would wake Mark up and let him leave at five. Jeff and April both agreed that Mark could use the extra hour of sleep.

April held his hands in hers and prayed for him. "God, please ... let him be fine."

CHAPTER THIRTY –

⌒Heartache⌒

April had gotten off work and had gone to her apartment to change. She was excited about meeting Sunny. She hoped that Mark would be feeling better so that he could join them at the park. She walked to Blanche's and knocked on the door. Blanche answered the door in an uninviting manner.

"I'm April. I am Sunflower's new big sister, is she here?" April said to Blanche. Blanche's eyes grew wide as she looked at April, making April feel uncomfortable.

"Sunflower!" Blanche yelled up the stairs, and then she half smiled at April. *Sunflower is getting way too much attention*, Blanche thought with a startlingly frown.

Sunflower came bouncing down the stairs. April and Sunflower exchanged looks and stared at each other. April knew instantly why Mark had fallen so easily in love with this precious little girl. She was absolutely beautiful, April thought as her heart leaped.

"Sunflower, this here is April; she is your new big sister."

"Hello, April," Sunflower said warmly as she held out her tiny hand and April shook it. Sunny gave April a head to toe inspection. *Hmmm, she's awful pretty, and she must be about Mark's age, hmmm.*

"I thought we could go to the park; would you like that?" April asked her sweetly. Sunflower smiled at her with such lovability. Sunny gave thought to Mark, *hmmm*, her smile widened with her growing thoughts.

"Sure, I'll get my coat," Sunflower said as she grabbed her coat from the rack by the door. April felt uncomfortable as Blanche intensely eyed her.

"Okay, let's go. We should be back at six-thirty," April told Blanche before she opened the door. She could feel Blanche's vigilant eyes on her as they left.

Blanche stood there watching them go down the steps. She was in deep thought trying to recall where she had seen April before. Then her eyes grew wide, she knew, and an uneasy feeling struck her.

April and Sunflower walked to the park quietly. April could not believe how much Sunflower looked like she did when she was a child. Her heart was pounding. Did Sunflower remind Mark of her, when she was his child-hood playmate, she wondered? *Is that why Mark had gotten so attached to Sunflower so quickly?* Once they got to the park, April motioned for Sunflower to sit by her on the bench.

"How old are you, Sunflower?" April asked with the anticipation of hearing Sunflower say she was five.

"I'm six," Sunflower told her. April's face showed disappointment.

"What happened to your mother?" April asked softly.

"She died," she replied sadly, hanging her head low.

"I'm sorry," April told her with compassion. Her heart felt despairingly for Sunflower, or was that feeling for her?

"Can I go play on the swings?" Sunflower asked as she looked back at April.

"Sure, I'll watch you from here," April sweetly told her.

April watched her from the bench. April's heart was filled with sorrow. How many parks had she been to in California looking for a little girl who looked just like she had when she was a child; she had lost count?

When she had first seen Sunflower, she hoped that she had finally found her little girl. Her daughter would only be five, so it was not possible that Sunflower was hers. She would never be able to forget the day she lost her baby. She was only eighteen when it happened. Those painful memories now flooded into her mind as if they had happened just yesterday.

"Daddy, please don't take her away from me! I love her so much! I want to raise her!" April cried as she held onto her newborn daughter with such heartache knowing that her father planned to take her daughter away.

"You have disgraced this family! We had to move away from all our friends and family because of you. I will not have that illegitimate child in my house. You will never ever see this child again, and that is your punishment for your sin. Lewis, take the child from her!" Her father screamed as he stormed out of the room.

"No! NO!" she cried as she tried to fight with her father's right hand man. "Please don't take my baby away from me!" The tears were streaming down April's face. The pain she felt was unbearable.

Lewis had managed to get the baby from her and started to leave the room with her. April ran after him. She grabbed his arm.

"Lewis, wait!" she pleaded. He stopped and turned towards her and saw the tears streaming down her face. He felt compassion for her situation. Lewis was not heartless but his fear of her father was greater. He knew what he had to do.

"I'm sorry, Miss April, but I have to do what your father wants," he told her kindly.

"What are you … going to do … with her?" April stuttered through her tears.

"She is going to a good family; they can't have any kids, Miss April. I know they will love her and give her everything she'll ever need," he reassured her. Each sob touched his heart. He had known April since she was a baby. It hurt his heart knowing what he was about to do to her. Even as underhanded as it was, he still planned to go through with it.

"But I want to love her, Lewis. I will take her away with me. You don't have to tell my father," she continued to plead with him desperately.

"I'm sorry, I can't. We've made all the arrangements. The other couple would tell your father I did not give them the baby," he explained to her sadly. His mind wandered off to the real arrangements that he had made for this baby.

"Oh, please, let me hold her just one more time. Please, I'll give her right back," April begged as she reached her empty arms out for her baby.

Lewis turned and placed the baby back in April's arms. She went back into her bedroom, the very room that she had given birth to her baby. Because her father would not allow her to go to the hospital, she had a midwife attend to the birth.

April had been a prisoner for the last seven months, as her father had forbidden her to leave the house. She had spent most of her time in her room, her only companion being the baby she carried inside her body.

With each movement, she had grown to love it more each day. She had hoped that once her baby was born her father would acknowledge his grandchild and let her keep it.

But Paul refused to listen to her pleading. She had no one to turn to because her mother and her brother, Todd, had been sent to Paris. Her father had told her mother, Tammy, that she had a miscarriage. No one else knew she was pregnant except her father's household employees, and they had been instructed with strict orders to keep an eye on April at all times, not allowing her to use the phone or leave the property for any reason.

April had lived a life of no hope. Her father had promised she could go back to school as soon as she gave birth and gave the baby up. Only then could she have her freedom back. She did not want her freedom; she wanted her tiny baby.

Lewis watched over her now. He hated to see her cry, but he could not disobey her controlling father. The baby had to go. Her father was a powerful man, and Lewis was afraid of what Paul might do if he did not obey him and take the child away from April.

His boss, Paul, was paying a large sum of money for the child to be taken away. Lewis was to do an illegal adoption, since April refused to sign any adoption papers. Then there was the issue of the missing father's rights to this child that Paul wanted to avoid. If April ever told him the truth, Paul wanted no trace of the baby.

It was up to Lewis to find someone willing to take the baby for the child support money without any legal papers and keep their mouth shut. Lewis would be the only one who knew where the baby was located.

"Give me the child, April; please don't make me have to take her away from you again."

April hugged the baby against her breasts and kissed her on the top of her soft head. Her heart was splitting in a million pieces. Nevertheless, she did as she was told. She tearfully placed the baby gently into Lewis arms. Lewis started to leave but April called to him.

"Wait, can I give her something?" April begged, and Lewis turned back to her.

"Sure, I guess it won't hurt none," he hesitantly told her.

April reached into her jewelry box and pulled out a gold chain with a high school class ring on it. She wrote on a piece of paper and put it in the inside pocket of the knitted baby sweater. She had deliberately sewn an inside fabric liner to the sweater with the intentions of hiding things to link her to her baby someday.

Then she placed the ring and chain in a hidden pocket in the liner, careful not to let Lewis see what she had done. She turned to face him. She lovingly put the sweater on the tiny girl, kissed her forehead, and bravely stepped back. Lewis turned and left with the baby in his arms.

April fell to her bed and cried. Choking sobs erupted from her angry soul and spewed hot tears down her face.

The pain was horrendous but there was nothing she could do. She had cried several times a day for months. The pain had followed her for the last five years, especially on August fourth.

She hated her father and knew she had to get out of his clutches as soon as possible.

She had only told her high school friend Jessica that she was pregnant, but she never mentioned having the baby to anyone, not even to Jessica, Christy, or Sharon. It would be her secret for the rest of her life; she had convinced herself. She went on to college to become a nurse.

Her empty heart could never be filled until she found her missing baby. She dreamed about her baby daily and wondered where she was. She was constantly looking for her child, hoping that someday she would have her baby back in her arms.

Now here in front of her was a child that brought back all those painful memories that she was trying so hard to put behind her.

She knew it was not possible for Sunflower to be her daughter. Her daughter was only five, and she was somewhere in California with a good family, not here in a children's home.

Nevertheless, April could not help but be disappointed. Her heart ached all over again as tears fell down her warm cheeks, until her thoughts were interrupted by a small concerned voice.

"Hey, what is wrong with you?" Sunflower asked her kindly.

"I was just thinking how wonderful it would be to have a little girl just like you," April told her sweetly as she wiped the tears from her face.

"That is what Mark says. Do you know Mark?" Sunflower asked hopefully.

"You mean that handsome doctor who calls you Sunny?" April joked with her, causing Sunny's eyes to light up.

"You know him!" Sunny said with excitement as she jumped up and down.

"Yes, I do," April said warmly and smiled at Sunny.

"Isn't he wonderful and handsome? He is going to let me live with him when the courts say I can," Sunny told her proudly with a big grin. *Oh, goodie, this lady can marry Mark,* she thought.

"You really love Mark, don't you?" April asked tenderly.

"Oh, yes, do you ... a ... love Mark?" Sunny asked with anticipation. Was April who God had sent for her Mark, Sunny wondered as she crossed her fingers behind her back.

"Let's just keep this a secret between you and me," April said softly.

"Okay, what is it?" Sunny bent closer to April and put her hand to her ear.

"I love Mark, too," April whispered into her ear, and Sunny jumped with excitement when she heard it.

"God does supply all our needs; it is true!" Sunny smiled, "Oh, boy, now we can be a family, Mark and me, and you!" she said excitedly.

"No Sunny, oh, I am so sorry," April said as she took a hold of Sunny.

"Why? You just said you love Mark," Sunny protested as her eyes became sad with disappointment that she had not found a wife for Mark.

"Love takes a long time to grow into a relationship before you can become a family. Mark and I have to get to know each other really well before we can become a family. It is called dating. Mark and I have only had one date. We need to go on many more dates so that we can get to know each other better." April tried to explain it to her. Sunny looked puzzled as she thought.

"Oh," Sunny said sadly. Time was one thing she knew she did not have. She could not wait any longer; she would have to speed this relationship and dating stuff up some if she could. She liked April, and she would make a good wife for Mark and a good mother for her, she figured, but it was Mark she wanted most.

Just then, Mark came up behind Sunny; he picked her up into the air and hugged her. April saw the immediate affection for Mark in Sunny's bright eyes. Sunny laughed and giggled as Mark teased her. He finally set her down, and she held onto his leg with a hug.

Mark gave April a disapproving smile. He was still miffed at her for helping Jeff with his plot with the sedative.

April stood up from the bench and kissed his cheek. She whispered in his ear that she was glad he was feeling better. That was all it took for her to melt Mark's heart into forgiveness. Mark bent and kissed her lips lovingly and wrapped her body next to his. Sunny squealed with delight when she saw the kiss.

"How is it going, are you gals having a good time?" Mark asked good-naturedly. April and Sunny exchanged looks and smiled. April held her finger to her lips and Sunny nodded in agreement. Mark looked at them questioningly.

"What is going on you two?" he questioned with a suspicious grin. Sunny giggled as she put both hands over her mouth. She would not tell their secret. Sunny winked at April, confirming Mark's suspicion.

"She is wonderful, just like you said," April told Mark warmly as she quickly stole a kiss from him to win back his trust. Sunny just beamed as she watched the two exchanging their love.

"I'm going to go play on the monkey bars; you guys can stay here and get to know each other better," Sunny smiled at them, and then she ran off giggling.

"What was that all about?" Mark asked, sure that he was being set up for something between these two women.

"I don't know," she denied, avoiding his eyes so he would not see through her lie. They both sat down on the bench. Mark took her hand in his.

"Did Blanche suspect anything was wrong when you went to get Sunny?"

"I don't think so, she let Sunny go with me; she did look at me strangely," April said as she thought about the look Blanche had given her.

"Did you notice how much you look like Sunny?"

"I did. She does resemble me when I was younger," April said, "Do you remember me from way back then, Mark?" she asked with anticipation, hoping that he did.

"Sometimes I have flashbacks of us. I don't know if they happened or not." Mark said with regret that his memory of them was gone. He stared out at Sunny as he spoke. He noticed the boy named John standing near a tree watching Sunny play.

"Ask me and I will tell you." She noticed that Mark's attention was really on watching Sunny play. She knew that Mark really loved this child with all his heart, as if Sunny were his own child. Sunny waved at Mark and he returned the wave.

"She sure is cute; do you like her?"

"She is adorable; we hit it off right from the beginning," April assured him. He turned and looked straight into her eyes.

"I've won her over, now I just have to work on you. Will you go out with me tonight after football practice?" he asked, this time his attention was solely on her. She fell right into his eyes and was trapped.

"Same time?" she asked as she melted into his warm eyes.

"Later, around nine. This time you can wear your jeans," he laughed.

"Sure, I will go," she smiled back at him. April loved his warm smile and leaned closer to him to receive the kiss he offered.

"Let's go get Sunny," Mark said as he stood up and held his hand out to help her up from the bench. He was such a gentleman, April thought.

They went over to Sunny, and together they all rode the merry-go-round. They walked hand and hand to the pond. Sunny started playing in the leaves on the ground, gathering them into a big pile. Mark and April helped her, and they all jumped in and rolled around in them, throwing leaves at each other and laughing.

Sunny caught sight of John and headed in his direction to speak to him. A fatherly instinct hit Mark as he watched Sunny laughing with John. Before he could give it much thought April caught his attention.

April dumped a big pile of leaves on Mark's head and got up to run from him, but he pulled her down on top of him. They looked into each other's eyes and stared, and then he bent his head and kissed her with affection. It was a kiss of passion like he had never felt.

She put her affectionate arms around his neck and kissed him back, her moist lips claiming what she desired. He rolled her over so that he was on top and kissed her lips so passionately that waves of love for her washed over him.

Suddenly the flashback of them as teenagers together came into Mark's mind. Mark felt a chill go down his spine and he stopped kissing her. He looked startled as he pulled away from her.

"What is it?" April asked when she saw his serious face.

"We've been here before, together. I have these flashbacks of us here. Haven't we?" he questioned her seriously.

"Once a long time ago," she said quietly, "You kissed me here ... the night of the championship football game."

"No, it was more than a kiss. I can feel it. There was more but I don't know what it was," he said with frustration in his voice.

"It was just a kiss," she said softly.

"Maybe I just wish it had been more. Maybe I wanted you and I to be in love," he said as he got up and helped April up.

"Were we in love then, April?" he asked her seriously, wanting answers once and for all. Before April could answer him, Sunny had run up to them with more leaves.

"Come on you guys, let's go jump in the leaves over there." She grabbed their hands and led them to the pile she had built up with John while they had been talking.

Sunny and April jumped in the leaves. Mark stood back and watched them. He wished that the flashbacks would stop and he could remember it all. He looked at his watch.

"I have to go; I'll see you tonight." Mark waved as he ran towards his car, holding his ribs as he ran. His tumble with April had not helped his ribs any. He was thankful that Jeff had given him an injection of pain medication before he left the hospital.

April and Sunny walked back to the children's home. Sunny talked all about Mark's good points. April knew she was trying to sell Mark to her. She smiled at the sweet child. It would be great if they could be a family. However, Sunny could never replace the void she had in her heart for her own child.

"Sunny, you can never tell anyone that you were with Mark and me at the park today. No one can know that Mark and I know each other or Blanche will not let you go with me. Promise me you will keep this a secret," April told her firmly. Sunny promised her. April promised Sunny that they would go to Mark's football game on Sunday.

They reached the home and stood outside saying good-byes. Blanche was watching them from the window. When she saw them together, she went to her office, took out an old phone book, dialed a number and waited.

"Lou, we have a problem here," she said to the person on the other line.

CHAPTER THIRTY-ONE –
⟡Keeping the Secret⟡

*I*n the football locker room, Coach Walker was sitting in his office going over the plays. The team doctor, Dr. Raymond, knocked on the door and went into the room. Dr. Raymond did not look pleased; he looked concerned. Coach Walker noticed the apprehensive look on Doc's face.

"Did all my players pass their pre-game physical?" Coach asked with unease. He needed all his players to be in top form if the team was going to advance to the Super Bowl.

"All but your star quarterback, Mark. He was a no show, again," Doc told him with frustration in his voice.

"Mark must have had to work late at the hospital tonight," Coach said, not liking that this conversation was about Mark.

"I think Mark is avoiding his team physicals; this is the third one in a row he has missed," Doc told the coach with an irritated voice.

"What's the problem? Mark is a doctor; he'd know if he was having any problems that would bench him," Coach asked without too much concern in his voice.

"That is the problem. Mark knows how to hide medical problems so he can continue to play. It won't be the first time Mark has deliberately played injured."

"Are you aware of any problems Mark is having?" Coach asked hesitantly.

"Mark had lost ten pounds the last time he weighed in. From the look of his baggy practice pants, he has lost more. He has had several nose-bleeds this week during practice, and he is using the oxygen more after he runs plays. I think we need to be concerned, Coach." Doc informed the coach with an unyielding face.

"I think Mark is smart enough to know if he is sick. Mark has always played hurt and come out just fine. He might just have a bug or maybe something has been distracting him lately. Let's not overreact just yet. Don't get so worked up about him, Doc, he'll be just fine, you'll see." The coach tried to sound reassuring.

The truth was the Coach too had noticed that Mark had not been his usual energetic self. He had noticed that Mark was working more with their back-up quarterbacks this week. Was Mark preparing Kevin to take his spot, the coach wondered, because he really was sick? The coach knew that it was critical that Mark play in the next few games, as the team was heading towards the Super Bowl.

"I'd wait for Mark to get here, but I have a meeting at six. If I were you, I would sideline Mark until I can have a good look at him." Doc advised the coach before he left.

When Mark showed up at six, the guys were ready to go on the field. Justin saw Mark come into the locker room and rushed over to him.

"Mark! Where have you been? Doc was looking for you. You missed the pre-game physical at five," Justin told Mark in a frantic voice, knowing that Doc had had a flaming fit that Mark was nowhere to be found an hour ago.

"Is Doc still here?" Mark questioned him as he looked around for Doc, hoping he had already gone.

"No, he left," Justin informed him. Mark seemed relieved that he had gotten out of that awkward situation with the team doctor.

"Thanks, Justin," Mark told him as he patted Justin on the shoulder pad and smiled as if nothing was wrong.

Mark waited until the other players had left the locker room so that he could get dressed in his uniform without them watching him. He did not want anyone to see his bruises.

Jeff had removed the catheter from his chest, but it had bled so much that Jeff had to pack the area with gauze pads and tape them to Mark's chest. Mark carefully removed his shirt, not wanting to disturb the gauze.

"Ahh, man," Mark exclaimed out of frustration when he saw the blood stained pads. Mark could not remove the pads without the fear of his incision bleeding again. The same had happened when Jeff removed the IV from Mark's arm; it had bled too. Jeff had packed the needle puncture with gauze pads, wrapped it in an ace bandage, and told Mark to keep it in place for the next four hours.

Mark would not be able to hide that one, so he slowly unrolled the ace bandage, removed the tape, and pulled the gauze away from his arm. He was thankful the bleeding had stopped. He slowly flexed his arm a few times and watched the sight oozing blood once again.

"Dang, can't I get a break here?" He rewrapped the ace bandage and held his left arm over his head, as he searched through his duffel bag for a long sleeve undershirt to put on under his team jersey with his other hand.

Jeff had been extremely concerned that Mark's blood had not clotted quickly. He wanted Mark to get a CBC blood test, but Mark refused to do it.

Mark told Jeff that he had used aspirin for pain the night before. He claimed that in the dark he had accidentally gotten the bottles mixed up.

"Yeah, right, you expect me to believe that?" Jeff did not believe for a minute that Mark could have been that careless to take a blood thinner when he knew he had an injury that caused bleeding. "Mark, you need to get your head on straight. You are playing with fire here, buddy."

After Mark's persistence, Jeff wrote Mark a prescription for a bottle of pain pills and warned him not to be so careless. Jeff was very concerned that Mark was messing around with his health. Mark filled the prescription at the hospital pharmacy before leaving the hospital.

Once Mark was dressed, he ran to the practice field and went directly to his coach. Mark was apologetic for being late, blaming it on his work schedule. Coach Walker told Mark that he was sidelined for the remainder of the practice since he had missed his physical and was late. Mark respected his decision with disappointed eyes and apologized again.

There was not time for a lengthy discussion over Mark's missed physicals; that lecture would have to wait until later. Coach Walker told Mark to go over and coach the other quarterbacks. "Yes, Sir," Mark responded.

Coach Walker took a deep breath as Mark ran in the direction of the quarterbacks. He did not want to take any chances that Mark would be hurt in this practice. Mark was relieved that he would not have to work hard.

April and Mark went out to eat at Nathan's Restaurant. Mark held her hand as she slid into a curved corner booth, and then he slid in beside her.

He captured her silky smooth hand in his on the table while they waited for their food. Mark admired her pure, wholesome beauty as she sat next to him. He lifted her hand and kissed her fingers with his moist lips as she leaned over and nestled her head on Mark's shoulder.

She was tired; it had been a long emotional day for her. Meeting Sunny for the first time, thoughts of losing her baby, and dealing with Mark's injury had all taken a toll on her. Mark, on the other hand, seemed just fine.

His eyes seemed dreamy as he arched his neck to discover her lips and steal a kiss. He was addicted to the sweet smell of her skin. The dimly lit lights gave the illusion of romance around the booth where they sat. April leaned on him, trying to absorb in some of his energy.

Their conversation consisted of laughing and sharing sentiments of mutual admiration for each other as they savored the way they felt about each other.

"You are so beautiful, April, inside and out. I am so amazed that we have found each other. It is so hard for me, knowing you know everything that has happened between us and I know almost nothing," Mark said with frustration in his voice, as he outlined her entire face with the tips of his fingers, as if he were blind and was trying to discover all there was to know about her delicate face.

"Stop worrying about it, Mark," she reassured him with her warm smile as she soaked in his love for her.

"I am so in love with you, April. This is all happening so unbelievably fast for me. We just met and already I feel like this for you," Mark tenderly spoke as his pulse quickened. He was unable to comprehend the mystery of his genuine feelings for her, the hidden secrets of his heart.

"We agreed to start over; there is no past, just what we make of our relationship now," she reminded him, taking his hand and kissing his fingers with her warm lips in an attempt to distract him from searching for answers of their past.

"I feel like you are the part of my life that was missing for so long." Mark released a slight hint of pain as he lifted his arm over her shoulder.

The genuineness on his face made her realize that there was no turning back; they were heading into an intimate relationship. As much as this was what she wanted with him, her thoughts about her past suddenly scared her.

What if he found out what I did, and could not find it in his heart to understand?

He noticed the troubled expression on her face as she repositioned herself slightly away from him. His eyes invited her to speak.

She was trembling slightly as her reserved thoughts about their relationship consumed her guilt-ridden mind.

"April, what is it?"

"I'm so afraid, Mark," she spoke nervously as her expression fell. Mark noticed that she seemed uneasy in her thoughts.

"What are you afraid of?" Mark looked at her with supportive eyes, afraid of a repeat of the emotions that she had experienced that first day they had been together at her apartment.

"Of losing you ... that you will change your mind about me. What if your memory comes back, and you change how you feel about us?" she asked tearfully. *What if he found out I had a child*, she feared.

"April, look into my eyes; what do you see?" he leaned closer to her, determined to prove his unconditional love for her, once and for all.

"Love," she answered softly as her eyes watered.

"That is right. I love you, and nothing in the past could ever change that." The sincerity in his voice was clear.

"I just don't want to lose you ... again." Her face was so troubled; she had to blink to clear her vision.

"Again? April, tell me what you and I once meant to each other. What happened that has you so apprehensive about us?" Mark wanted to know, yet at the same time he felt his stomach muscles tighten, fearful of the answer he was about to hear from her lips.

"We were good friends ... more than friends, you were my best friend," she revealed, avoiding eye contact with him. Her heart was painfully wishing that she could trust him. If only he was telling her the truth, that nothing could ever change the way he felt about her right now.

"What aren't you telling me?" Mark wanted the truth he felt in his heart that she was hiding from him.

"Nothing ... there is nothing to tell. You know what everyone has told you, that is all there was between us, friendship." April tried to sound convincing, her heart aching that she could not tell him the entire truth and set herself free.

Weariness settled over her heart and he saw it in her eyes. "No, you are hiding something from me. I can feel it; I can see it in your eyes," he said impatiently as he searched the secret places of her soul, trying to read her heart, hoping that she would allow him to enter.

"I dreamed about us a lot, Mark. Of you and me, and our future together as a couple. But, we traveled in different directions back then. I have waited a long time for you to remember me, for us to fall in love once again. It is not that easy for me to open up my heart for fear that you will break it," she said with heartache, wanting so badly to tell him the truth of their past.

"You don't have to dream anymore. I have finally opened my eyes and found you in my heart. I realize there is more to my life than my medical training and football. I have you and I will have Sunny. That is all that is important to me now. You don't have to worry about our relationship. Every minute that I spend with you is a blessing to my life. Nothing will ever change my feelings for you. April Morgan, I love you with all of my heart." His words spoke the intensity of his feelings for her and the sincerity of his intentions to cherish her, and then he leaned over and kissed her.

He wiped her tears and waited for her to smile. When she finally did let a smile cross her face, he kissed her again, and that kiss was the reassurance that she needed. Mark Sanders was a vibrant man and so full of life, and he loved her.

The rest of the dinner was enjoyable, and they went back to Mark's apartment and cuddled together while they watched TV.

It felt so great to have April in his arms. He believed that this was just the beginning of a lifetime with her. If he was dreaming, he never wanted to wake up. Since he found April, everything seemed right in his life. Knowing she was beside him gave him a reason to face whatever he had to face in his life.

April felt the warmth of his body against her and felt so protected in his safe arms. Yet sadness filled her heart, still knowing that she had not been truthful with him.

She knew that if they were to have a relationship it should be based on the truth. Not telling him was causing guilt to build up in her soul and was holding her captive. Nevertheless, she could not risk losing him if he did not understand. She loved him too much to sacrifice losing him now when she had just gotten him back. There was nothing she could do to bring back her child, but she could recapture Mark's love for her. He was the real reason she chose not to end her life on August fifth.

She needed time to heal the pain that churned inside of her. How could she cause Mark the same pain she felt by telling him? Should she spare him the same suffering her heart felt each day?

Would loving him be enough for them, or would the truth drive him far away from her? They needed time to grow in their relationship before she could finally tell him the truth, she thought.

Her agonizing thoughts continued until Mark reached out, took her face in his tender hand, and drew her face to his for an engaging kiss that left them both breathless.

His genuine love for her had poured straight into her heart, until it was overflowing. Finally, she let go of all her fears and freely accepted his love. His kisses sent her body into total submission.

Just as she thought they had gone beyond the point of no return, he took a deep breath and told her that he could not continue. He shared how much he valued his commitment to God and to the commitment of marriage.

They made plans to pick up Sunny for church on Sunday and then have April bring her to the game. Mark wanted both his women at the game to support him.

Chapter Thirty-Two –
∽It is All about Them∾

The next day, April went to pick up Sunny. She knocked at the door and Blanche hesitantly opened the door to let April enter.

Blanche wore a frown across her unpleasant face and smartly remarked to April, "I suppose you came to see Sunflower?"

"I thought we would go shopping and see a movie," April said politely.

"She's got to be back to do her chores by four so you make sure you are back on time," Blanche said sternly.

"Yes, we'll be back by then," April remained polite.

"Don't you be spoiling her none either," Blanche put in strongly.

"I won't," April said calmly.

"All right then. Sunflower, come down here!" Blanche yelled up the stairs. For the time being there was nothing Blanche could do; she would have to let April see Sunflower. The plans to put a stop to this mess were not complete yet. But soon, Blanche anxiously thought, *Sunflower would no longer pose a threat to her.*

April and Sunny spent the morning together, mostly just enjoying each other. It was not long before April realized that she was falling in love with Sunny just as Mark had done. It made her want her little girl that much more. She wondered if her daughter was as sweet and as pretty as Sunny was.

April called to see if Mark was back from his morning football practice. He had just gotten home, so they went over and had lunch with him, and then the three of them went to see a movie.

They had such a good time together. It was hard for Mark to let Sunny return to the children's home. Mark held Sunny close to him as he told her how much he loved her.

April took Sunny back and made her promise not to tell Blanche that she had seen Mark. Sunny agreed to keep their secret. April gave her a hug and promised to come back tomorrow.

Mark and April had decided that it was not fair that they had to wait on the court system to straighten out this mess. Sunny should not be the one punished by keeping her away from Mark. If they had to be underhanded, so be it. Mark would do anything to protect Sunny and provide for her.

April returned to Mark's apartment. She could tell Mark's ribs were bothering him from the morning practice. He looked tired and pale and he seemed rather upset. He was pacing the floor, thinking about something.

Mark was in a pain, but he pretended he was fine. He could not let anyone know what he was thinking about. *Not now, this can't be happening*, he thought as he pulled his shirtsleeves down over his arms when he saw April enter the room.

"Mark, are you sure you are alright?" April asked, concerned that Mark seemed deeply troubled.

"I'm fine," he half told her, knowing that he was not fine.

"Did you take the pain pills Jeff gave you?"

"Not yet, they upset my stomach."

"Come sit down; your pacing is making me nervous."

Mark looked over at her and saw the concerned look on her face, so he went over to her. He tried to hide the pain he felt as he slowly lowered his body to the couch and sat down beside her.

"I'm fine," he lied, "I am just worried about Sunny. It breaks my heart knowing she is over there and not here with us where she belongs."

Her eyes turned sad. "I know; we will just have to be patient," she told him sympathetically as she tenderly kissed his forehead.

"The judge should have been back yesterday, and Sunny should be here with me today," Mark told her with heartache in his voice.

"Did the judge get back?"

"No, he won't be back till Monday, and I have this awful feeling that may be too late," Mark said troubled, knowing things were about to get complicated. He had more to worry about than Sunny.

"Why are you so worried?" April asked anxiously, seeing the tension on his face. If only she knew what was really bothering him, she might be able to help him.

"I do not trust Blanche. Something about her is not right, but I cannot figure out what it is," he said irritably.

"I know what you mean; she acts so strange around me. I get the feeling she does not want me around Sunny either," April expressed.

"Maybe she has figured out that you and I are in this together," Mark said with alarm. He had not realized that was a possibility until now.

"I think she does not like me," April replied.

"How could anyone not like you? Something is not right," Mark disputed.

"Let's pray together." April took his hand in hers and together they prayed for Sunny. April thought back to the many times that she and Mark had prayed together on the football stadium bleachers when they were teenagers.

If only things could have been different back then, she and Mark would not have wasted all those years apart.

They ordered pizza from Bryan's Pizza Joint, since Mark was not feeling up to going out. Mark ate half a piece and tossed the other half in the trash can while April was in the bathroom.

They cuddled on the couch and watched a movie afterwards, and then April went back to her apartment so that Mark could get some sleep.

The next morning Mark told April that he had something he needed to do at the hospital, but he gave April no details. He told her he would be back in time to take her to church.

April went to pick Sunny up for church, but Blanche told her that Sister Jessica had already picked Sunflower up to go to her church.

When April told Blanche she would be back to take Sunflower for the afternoon, Blanche told her that Sunflower could not go with her today. Sister Jessica was spending the day with Sunflower.

Blanche told April that Sister Jessica had been Sunflower's big sister first, and April needed to understand that.

April was not sure what Blanche was referring to, but she got the message loud and clear. Blanche did not want her taking up all of Sunflower's time.

April was afraid to insist she be allowed to take Sunny for fear that Blanche would never let her see Sunny again. So April left and went back to Mark's apartment where he was waiting for her.

April wondered who Sister Jessica was. She thought back to her friend in high school, could it be her? They had not talked to each other since she moved to California. When she got the time, she promised herself she would try to find her old friend.

When April walked into the apartment, Mark stood up from his chair. He had been in deep thought. Something definitely was still bothering him.

"Where is Sunny?" Mark asked with concern.

"She had already gone to church with Sister Jessica," she answered. "We better go on to church or we will be late."

When Mark and April arrived at Mark's church together, Mark's friends were surprised to see he had a woman on his arm as he climbed the steps to go inside the building. They made a good-looking couple and it was obvious they were in love.

Mark's pastor, Pastor Evan Reddick, remembered April and Mark's relationship back when they were in high school. He recalled that for some reason Mark had lost his memory of April just after his motorcycle accident.

April had left a message on his phone a few months later. She had wanted to talk to him, but she never showed up for her appointment with him. Later on, Dan had told him that April's family had moved away.

Mark joined the praise team on the stage. He was singing the praise songs with a new excitement in his voice. Pastor Evan had a feeling it had something to do with the young woman standing across from the stage in the first row. Mark's affectionate eyes never left hers as he sang.

Pastor Evan was glad that Mark had rekindled his relationship with April. Maybe he would have the honor of marrying them someday.

After church, Mark proudly introduced April to the other church members. April had never experienced a church that had so much love for each other. She instantly fell in love with Miss Carolyn, the church greeter.

Miss Carolyn had her arms wrapped around Mark and was teasing him about his new girlfriend. Mark's eyes lit up as he laughed with Miss

Carolyn. If she were twenty years younger, April would have been jealous of Mark's affection for her.

April could not wait to attend again next Sunday. She only wished that Mark could remember that she had already been to this same church with him when they were teenagers. She said nothing to him, knowing how sensitive he was about his memory loss.

Would she stand at the same altar that she had given her heart to Jesus and marry Mark someday? Her heart had never wanted something as intensely as she wanted to be Mark's wife. She felt Mark squeeze her hand, and she looked up into his inviting eyes. His intentions to love her forever were written across his glowing face as he placed a kiss on her forehead before they walked down the church steps. Eternity belonged to them, she thought.

He took her out for a quick lunch and then took her back to the apartment before he left to go to his game. He seemed preoccupied but otherwise he seemed to be feeling fine.

April did not have the heart to tell him that Sunny would not be joining her. She called her Uncle Dan and asked him to take her to the game.

Mark's parents and his sister's family were out of town. They would miss Mark's important game since they had a concert at a Couple's Retreat and they were the lead singers. They promised Mark they would watch his game on TV if they got the chance.

This game was the AFC Divisional play-off game. Mark knew how important it was to win to advance to the AFC Championship Game and then to the Super Bowl.

Mark went back to the hospital again, this time to see Jeff.

Mark would not let his team down.

Even if it meant he had to risk his own life.

CHAPTER THIRTY-THREE –
ᴄ᷐Crossing the Finish Lineᴄ᷐

*M*ark had arrived late for the game. He had called the coach from the hospital and told him he would be late.

The coach had let Mark practice Saturday against the advice of the team doctor because Mark had agreed to meet with Doc on Monday morning for a complete physical. That agreement convinced the coach that there was nothing wrong with Mark; therefore, the coach agreed to let Mark play in the game today.

However, Mark had no intentions of meeting with Doc on Monday; he planned to miss that physical, too. As much as everything about his health had him deeply concerned, he had no choice; he could not risk being side-lined due to his injury.

He would have to withstand the pain and play for the team; there was no other choice in his mind. His teammates were too important to him; he would do whatever it took to take them to the Super Bowl Game.

Things weighed heavy on his mind as he began dressing out for the game in the locker room after the other players had gone out on the field.

Mark sat on the bench in front of his locker and removed the new bandage on his arm that he had just gotten at the hospital. He bent his head forward, prayed with a confused mind, and poured his heavy heart out to the Lord. He prayed that his life was not about to dramatically change as soon as his blood tests came back from the lab.

He blocked the thunderous noises of the crowd out of his mind and focused peacefully on the scripture God placed in his mind and heart. "Fear not for I am with thee."

April and Dan arrived at the game and sat in the family box seats. Jeff was still on duty, so he could not join them right away; he would come when his shift ended.

When the game was about to start, Mark still had not appeared for warm ups on the field with his teammates. April knew Mark had left the apartment in plenty of time so she became increasingly nervous when she did not see him.

During the coin toss, Mark appeared. He seemed fine. He gave her a friendly wave. Wow, he did look great in his uniform, she thought. It all seemed so unreal to her that she was actually dating Mark Sanders, the same man she had watched play football on TV.

He was her little childhood companion all grown up. Her heart was beating rapidly; her hands were trembling as she watched him take his place beside his teammates. "I love you, Mark," she whispered.

April was concerned for Mark as the offense took the field. She twisted her hands together every time Mark came close to being tackled. "Come on Mark, get up, get up, that's it," she whispered, and then she would let out a sigh of relief when he got up after being tackled. She took a deep breath of air as if she was breathing for him. Dan watched April with concern.

When the first half was over, April sat down and rubbed her eyes. Dan sat down next to her. He had been watching her over-protective reaction to Mark's playing. At first, he figured she was nervous because she had never seen him play professional football in person, but after awhile he began to wonder if there was more to it.

"What is going on April? I've never seen you this nervous over anything?" Dan questioned her as she slowly looked over at him. He could read the worried look on her face.

"What do you mean?" she said as she tried to hide her true feelings, wishing she had not promised Mark she would not reveal his secret about his ribs to Dan.

"Look at yourself, April. You look exhausted, and you are so nervous." He knew that she was hiding something that he was sure he did not want to hear her say.

"I'm not nervous, I'm … I'm excited about watching Mark play again."

"Come on, April, out with it," Dan pursued her.

"Uncle Dan, really, that is all it is," she lied, avoiding his eyes.

"April, honey, you have never been able to lie to me. Don't start now; tell me what is wrong with Mark," he said firmly with worry.

"With Mark?" she pretended she did not know what he was talking about as tears formed in her eyes.

"Yes, Mark. I have seen how he has been holding back and been slow getting up after a tackle. What is wrong with him?"

He had April's undivided attention. She was torn between her promise to Mark and telling her uncle the truth. She was worried about Mark's safety.

"Mark had a motorcycle accident. Jeff did an aspiration on his left lung on Friday in the ER. I'm worried he is going to hurt himself more in this game," she cried out, relieved the truth was finally out in the open.

She was crying, knowing in her heart that Mark was sicker than just his injury from the motorcycle accident.

"Okay, honey, it is going to be fine. I'll go down to the locker room and check on him," Dan told her as he got up to leave.

"I'll go with you," April said as she quickly stood up.

"No, you better stay here. The locker room is no place for a lady," Dan told her as he left her restlessly standing there.

Dan hurried down to the locker room. Leave it to Jeff and Mark; he could not trust either one of them. He thought about the two of them using his ER to self-treat each other. He would deal with that issue later. Right now, he was worried about Mark.

After a short frantic search, Dan found Mark. Mark was leaning over a sink, splashing his face with water.

"Mark," Dan called to him. Mark straightened up and slowly turned to see Dan standing there. Mark was pale; he did not look fine.

"What are you doing in the locker room?" Mark asked Dan, but in his gut, he knew exactly why Dan was there.

"I've been watching you. Something is wrong with your chest."

Mark shook his head no. "I'm fine," Mark said calmly, trying to be convincing as he tilted his head sideways and smiled.

"Let me see," Dan demanded, as he came closer to Mark to have a look.

Mark backed away, his face turned serious. "Dan, I said I was fine. I've got to go over the second-half plays with the coach," he retorted as he started to walk away. Dan took a hold of his arm and stopped him.

"Mark, I am serious. I want to have a look at you before you go back out on the field," Dan demanded firmly.

Mark had to think quickly. "All right then … I'll meet you in the training room, but first I have to talk to the coach." Before Dan could object, Mark was off.

By the time Dan realized the game was about to start, he could not find Mark and realized he had been out-foxed. Dan was not happy with what Mark had done. He went back up to sit with April. She was anxious for a report on Mark's condition.

"Did you see Mark?" April asked nervously, not liking the look on Dan's face.

"I talked to him, but he refused to let me have a look at him. Why didn't you tell me that Mark had an accident?" Dan inquired, put out with all three of them for not informing him of Mark's accident.

"Mark made Jeff and I promise not to say anything to you. I am going down on that field right now and tell Mark he cannot play!"

"April, there is one thing you need to learn about Mark, and that is, you cannot interfere when he does not want your help," Dan informed her.

"I just can't sit here and do nothing; he is going to get hurt worse, if we don't stop him," April pouted.

"Mark knows what he is doing. He will be fine; we'll have to trust him," Dan said as he tried to convince himself that was true. In the pit of his stomach he knew that if Mark had avoided a quick exam, he was hurt. Dan planned to have a serious talk with his two interns.

The second-half began, and Mark seemed to be doing fine as he executed plays on the field. April began to relax. She even found herself cheering him on as she had done so many times in high school.

In the fourth quarter, she noticed that it was harder for Mark to get up when he was knocked down. It was obvious to her that he was in pain now, and he lacked the energy he had earlier in the game. He was going for oxygen more often when his team did not have the ball.

The other team got a touchdown after one of Mark's running backs fumbled the ball, and now the other team led by five points at the two-minute warning. This was an important game, and right now, it did not look good for Mark's team.

Mark jumped right back into the game and gave his coach the thumbs-up as he ran out on the field to get the job done. He had full confidence that his team could claim this game. His enthusiasm was contagious as the fans started chanting his name while Mark huddled his offense together.

Mark felt like he had been in this very same position before. The team ran a few plays to move the ball down the field. First down, again, first down, he continued to excel in the plays they quickly ran to move the ball down the field. The crowd was on the edge of their seats, cheering loudly, as the clock was counting down.

With fifteen seconds left, Mark took a deep breath as he looked up at the scoreboard and knew what he had to do. The team gathered around him to form a circle. The crowd continued to yell loudly. The noise in the stadium made it hard to hear what he was saying.

Mark had one chance left. He knew he would have to muster together all his strength and throw the ball over thirty-five yards to his receiver for the touchdown. He could do it, he told himself; he had done it many times before.

Mark called all the players together closer to him, and he assertively called the play loudly, as they held hands in their huddle. "This is it," he told the guys. "We can do this." They believed in Mark, all eyes were on their leader. Mark gave his teammates his traditional encouraging grin as he spoke to God and asked for favor over them.

The crowd was standing with anticipation, chanting Mark's name, for they knew that if anyone could save this game it would be Mark Sanders.

April took a hold of Dan's hand tightly and said a quick prayer for Mark. Dan gave her a reassuring look and prayed.

The players got into their positions. Mark loudly called out the numbers and was hiked the ball. He dropped back five yards with the ball firmly in his hands and looked down the field for his receivers. The one on the left was heavily covered.

Mark raised his hand to throw the ball but a defensive tackler was coming viciously towards him. Mark had to run to the right to avoid the tackle as he continued to look for an open receiver. He could not afford to throw the ball away; he had to wait on an open receiver.

Mark was forced to run back to the left to avoid being tackled. He could hear the crashing sounds of the players hitting together as they blocked for him. The crowd was screaming. He saw an opening up the center. It was his only option; he had to go for it.

Mark sprinted down the field with all his strength. He continued to pray as he ran. The pain was unbearable with each jolt as his feet pounded the ground. He reached out his hand and pushed a defensive player off him. He could not breathe; his head began to spin and his eyes blurred. He jumped over a tackle that was made in front of him.

The crowd watched as Mark slowed down, his legs becoming unstable as he tried to keep his balance. The crowd was screaming, "GO! GO! GO!"

Mark's teammates had managed to block all but one defender who was gaining on Mark. He could hear that player's pounding feet beating against the turf, as he got closer to him. He heard the puffing of the player's heavy breathing, as he was an arms length away, with his arms stretched out reaching for him. Mark knew he was about to be brutally slammed to the hard ground, like a train smashing into him.

Just five more yards. It seemed like a thousand yards to Mark… four … three … two … the defender lunged at Mark, grabbing him around his shoulders. Together they fell over the goal line as the clock ran out of time. Mark was slammed to the ground; his face was pierced with pain.

The referee raised his two hands high into the air indicating a touchdown. The crowd was going absolutely wild in celebration, chanting Mark's name. They had won the Divisional Play-Offs. His teammates were jumping for joy as they headed for him.

Mark had landed on the ball; all the air from his lungs was sucked out. The other player got off him. Mark lay listless for a minute on the ground. All he could manage to do was slowly and painfully roll over onto his back. He tried to remove his helmet so he could gasp for some desperately needed air. His body was screaming in pain.

Before he knew it, he was being pulled up by the front of his jersey by his teammates, who were unaware that he was injured.

They tossed him around and lifted him into the air, slapping him on the back congratulating him. It was not until he collapsed unconscious into their arms that they realized something was wrong with him.

April had seen his limp body on the goal line as she watched the big screen; she saw the excruciating look of pain on his face as his teammates tossed him around like a rag doll. Her worst fear came true when she saw him fall forward unconscious into his teammate's arms and saw them drag him off the field.

"Oh God, Mark!" she said as her heart screamed out in a panic.

CHAPTER THIRTY-FOUR –
∾Against His Will∾

"What do we do with him?" the guys asked each other, fearfully, as they struggled to hold their limp quarterback in their arms.

"Let's get Mark into the locker room! You guys keep the reporters away!" Carlo instructed as he took charge and pulled Mark's limp arm over his own shoulder.

"Get his other arm, Justin," Carlo yelled and Justin did. They held Mark's limp body up and dragged him, like firefighters, toward the locker room. Some of the other team members surrounded them to keep the reporters from entering the locker room.

Dan and April would have to push their way through the crowd to get to the locker room. April prayed as she closely followed behind Dan.

Inside the locker room, in all the excitement of the win, no one else realized what had happened to Mark. Everyone was looking for him, screaming out his name.

"Let's take him into the trainer's room," Carlo shouted over the noise.

"Where is Mark?" They heard the reporters asking, as they secretly went into the trainer's room, closed the door, and pulled the shades. They carefully laid him on the examining table. Carlo removed Mark's helmet.

Carlo found some smelling salt and waved it under Mark's nose. Mark twisted as he regained consciousness. The guys let out a sigh of relief as Mark looked up at them with weak eyes. Mark lifted his hand up, grabbed the front of Carlo's jersey and pulled him down near his face.

"O x y g e n ...... " Mark stuttered as he gasped for air.

Carlo quickly pulled the oxygen mask from the wall above the table, turned the button to the on position, and placed the mask over Mark's nose and mouth. Carlo watched the slow rise and fall of Mark's chest. Mark closed his eyes and started to relax.

"I'll go find the trainer or Doc," Justin volunteered. Mark's eyes opened and he quickly removed the mask.

"No ... don't ... get him," Mark told them in a panic. Justin stopped and looked at Mark's frantic face.

"Why not, Mark?" Justin asked confused.

Mark had placed the mask back over his face. He held his finger up, indicating for them to wait a minute. They stood quietly as they waited for Mark to get more oxygen. Then Mark took the mask off.

"They can't ... find out ... champion ... ship ..." Mark struggled with his words and then he replaced the mask.

"What's he saying?" Justin asked the others.

"I think he means, if anyone finds out he's hurt, he will not be able to play in the AFC Championship Game," Carlo replied. Mark shook his head yes and they understood.

"I don't like it; what if he's hurt bad?" Justin emphasized.

"He's just got the wind knocked out of him. It happens to all of us. Besides, Mark's a doctor, remember, he can take care of himself," Carlo argued. Carlo's clever response was just what Mark wanted him to say to get himself off the hook from the real truth.

Mark took the mask off again. He was breathing easier than before.

"Get me to the showers ... tell the reporters ... I am in the showers." Mark instructed them and then he put the mask on to get some more air.

Carlo removed Mark's cleats and his socks. Carlo and Justin slowly helped Mark sit up and they removed his jersey. Carlo hurriedly but carefully undid the shoulder pads and removed them. Next they helped remove Mark's team t-shirt. In doing so, they exposed Mark's badly bruised side. The sight of it quickly made them nauseated. They saw the gauze and realized that Mark had played in the game already injured.

"Ah, man, Mark, that looks awful!" Carlo conveyed as he thought he was going to throw-up after looking at the painfully disgusting bruises on his best friend's chest and abdomen.

Carlo grabbed a large towel and wrapped it around Mark's torso to hide the bruising. He put another one around Mark's shoulders and let it drape over his chest.

"Man, oh, man, you really took a beating out there," Justin uttered as the other three players looked away from the sight of Mark's injuries.

"Kevin, go get Mark's clothes out of his locker and meet us in front of the showers," Carlo hurriedly instructed him and Kevin left the room to retrieve Mark's clothes.

"Can you walk?" Carlo asked. Mark shook his head yes. They helped him off the table and held onto him until he got some strength in his legs. Mark held his abdomen, as his ribs and upper left shoulder caused him to cringe as he moved.

"Craig and Jerk, you guys follow behind us and don't let anyone touch Mark. Justin and I will clear a path in front of Mark." Carlo instructed everyone to take their positions.

They opened the door and went out into the locker area. It was still wild with celebration. They headed toward the showers through the crowded room. Some of the other players shouted at Mark as they saw him pass by but none of them could get anywhere near him with his bodyguards surrounding him so closely.

"Hey, it's Mark. Where have you been?" Someone shouted and heads turned in their direction.

"Great game!" The players shouted at him as they continued with their loud celebration.

Carlo waved them away as he saw the cameramen and reporters hurrying their way. Carlo pushed Mark quickly into the shower area and told the other guys to stand guard. Jerk went to tell the other players what was going on.

"I'll be fine," Mark told Carlo as he went into a shower stall. They stood guard as Mark continued his shower. Several times, they heard Mark groan in pain.

"Craig, go find Jerk for me and bring him back here. Justin, you go tell the reporters Mark will talk to them as soon as he gets dressed," Carlo instructed them.

Kevin appeared with Mark's clothes. Carlo took them to the shower door and hung them over the top.

"You okay, Mark?"

"Yeah," Mark answered in a twisted painful voice.

Craig came back with Jerk, and Carlo pulled him over in the corner.

"I need some of your pain pills the Doc gave you. Quick, they're for Mark; he's hurting real bad." Jerk pulled the bottle out of his jeans and discreetly handed Carlo the bottle. Carlo pulled a cup from the water cooler and filled it with water.

Mark came out of the shower in his sweatpants and a jersey shirt. His feet were still bare. Carlo took him aside.

"Take a few of these," Carlo insisted and handed the bottle to Mark. Mark looked at the label. Seeing that the medicine was the same prescription as his, he took three out and downed them with the water.

He leaned against the wall for support, knowing the only place he should be going was to the hospital. *I can't do it. I just can't. Not now.*

Dan and April had made their way into the front of the locker room. Dan had tried to convince April to wait outside but she determinedly refused.

When one of the players noticed April, he yelled out loud, "Lady in the locker room; grab your towels!" He shouted and towels were grabbed up quickly. Dan saw the coach and went to him.

"Where's Mark?" he demanded over the noise in the room.

"No one seems to know where he went!" the coach shouted back.

Mark and Carlo came out of the shower area. They were quickly surrounded by reporters and cameramen wanting an interview from Mark.

"Mark!" The news reporters yelled at him. Mark went over to stand by the coach for the interview. He noticed Dan and April but he looked right past them.

"Mark, how does it feel to win your team another divisional title?"

"Unbelievable, but it was a team win."

"Will you take this team to the Super Bowl?"

"You bet, with God and my teammates, we can do it," Mark replied with confidence.

"Some of the fans thought you were hurt on that last play. Were you hurt?"

"I'm fine, I feel great," Mark said with enthusiasm.

"Good luck in the playoffs."

"Thank you," Mark said as he energetically shook hands with a few of the reporters.

Then Mark slid back into the crowd of players, that had surrounded him to keep the other reporters away from him, as they shouted more questions at him.

Word had passed to the players about Mark's injury. They were quiet as Mark passed them. They had great respect and high esteem for what Mark was trying to do for the benefit of the team. Without him, they knew they would have little chance of making it to the Super Bowl.

Mark and Carlo went over to the bench in front of Mark's locker and sat down. Carlo slowly put Mark's socks and boots on for him.

"Thanks for helping me out, Carlo," Mark serenely said to his friend of many years.

"How are you feeling now?"

"The pain is easing, but it still hurts to breathe."

"What's with the bandage on your chest?"

"Motorcycle accident. Hit a tree." Mark told him with humor in his voice, the sly grin on his face turned into a smile. How many times had Carlo lectured him about his reckless riding?

"Darn it, Mark, what did I tell you about your careless stunts?" Carlo said to him with an "I told you so" keen smile and let out a chuckle, as he shook his head at Mark.

"Pretty stupid; you don't have to say it." Mark broke into a wide smile, thankful for the brief interruption in the seriousness of this situation.

"Did you break your ribs?" Carlo asked with concern.

"Uh, maybe, when this place clears out, we'll go get an x-ray and see." If they weren't fractured before, Mark knew they were now.

Mark caught a glimpse of Dan, April, and the team doctor coming towards them.

"Oh, great, here comes trouble." Carlo got the message and quickly stood up as if he was protecting Mark from them. Dan did not give the impression that he was too happy with Mark. The seriousness on Dan's face instantly told Mark, he was in serious trouble.

"You're coming with us!" Dan demanded as he grabbed a hold of Mark's arm firmly.

"What's up? Where are we going?" Mark protested as he was pulled up from the bench by Dan's grip.

"We're going to the training room and have a look at your chest and abdomen," Dan stated firmly. Dan's unyielding look told Mark that he had better cooperate.

"There is nothing wrong with my chest," Mark denied, looking at April intensely with knitted eyebrows. He knew she had enlightened Dan about his injury.

"We'll just have a look for ourselves," Dan stated, looking Mark dead in his eyes.

"Come on, Dan, I'm fine," Mark protested crossly.

"Then you won't mind if we have a look," Dan countered. Dr. Raymond took a hold of Mark's other arm, and they forced him towards the training room.

"Come on, guys, this isn't fair," Mark objected but followed without any further protesting. Carlo followed them into the room, thinking to himself; all that work hiding Mark's injury was for nothing.

"Lie down flat on the table," Dan instructed Mark sternly. Mark did so without complaint; he was not worried; the pills Carlo had given him had taken effect, full effect. *They could drop a ton of bricks on me and I wouldn't feel a thing*, he thought devilishly.

Dan pulled Mark's long sleeve jersey up to his collarbone; a look of disgust was quickly written on his face.

April thought she was going to faint and covered her mouth with her hands. It was much worse than before.

Mark had taken the bandages off in the shower and the sutures from the catheter had bled. The bruising had spread with deeper shades of black and blue. The site was too painful to look at. There was no way that Mark could not be in severe pain.

Dan pulled Mark's arms out of the shirt, and then he took Mark's shirt off to exam the bruising. Dan saw the petechiae on Mark's arms. He reached down by Mark's ankle, pulled up the bottom of Mark's sweatpants, and examined Mark's left leg for bruising and found several.

"Do you call this nothing, Mark?" Dan objected as he looked angrily at Mark. Dan was going to fuss at Mark as if he was Mark's father but only out of concern for him.

"It's not that bad, Dan, I swear. It just looks bad. I can hardly feel it, see." Mark tried to convince them as he pressed on his chest with his fist. April let out a gasp when she witnessed Mark thumping on his abdomen.

"We're taking you straight to the hospital," Dan declared, not convinced at all. Mark had to be faking.

"No, no way, you're not!" Mark opposed firmly as he lifted both his hands up to the sides of his head and pounded his head in frustration. The uncompromising look on Mark's face told them that he meant what he was telling them. He was not going anywhere.

"We need a full set of x-rays," Dan told Mark just as firmly, not about to give into Mark's demand. Mark's fists hit the table with a thud.

"We can do that right here if you both want," Dr. Raymond informed Dan.

Dan gave Mark a pleading look, praying that Mark would bend and give in and let them help him. Dan did not want a fight with Mark and Mark knew it. Out of his love for Dan, Mark had no choice but to give in to this somewhat compromising offer.

"Fine, let's do it here. I am not going to the hospital," Mark repeated unhappily. Love or not, Mark's eyes stared into Dan's eyes to let him know just how unhappy he was about being forced to give in to him.

"Fine, we will do it here." Dan compromised too since Mark was willing to meet him halfway on this. Dan wished that he could avoid this exam but Dan knew that Mark was trying to hide something from all of them.

"Come with us," Dr. Raymond told Mark. Mark got off the table slowly and followed them to the x-ray room and they did a complete set of chest x-rays.

Mark hated doing it, but he said nothing as he stood there in the different positions as they x-rayed him. He did not say a word; his tense face told them just how he felt about doing this.

Then Doc asked Mark to step on the scales. Mark frowned as he stepped on the scales with his boots on. Doc shook his head; Mark was down another ten pounds. Mark rubbed the side of his face in frustration. Doc gave Mark a disconcerting look but said nothing.

When they finished with Mark, he went back into the other room where Carlo was waiting. Some of the other players had come into the room to see what was going on.

Mark did not see April anywhere. He sat silently in one of the chairs along the wall. The guys were standing around or sitting on the floor.

"How's it going?" Carlo inquired. He handed Mark his shirt and Mark put it on. Carlo noticed the gloomy expression on Mark's face.

"They are reading the films," Mark informed him.

Mark looked concerned; he was deeply thinking about what they might find. His secret about his injuries were about to be revealed. His patience was running out. He did not like being forced to do anything against his will.

He had planned to take care of himself once the AFC Championship Game was over. Now Dan had put all the cards on the table, and Mark was not happy about it.

"How did you get all those bruises? You didn't get them all today, did you?" Justin quizzed. Mark and Carlo exchanged looks.

"I wrecked my motorcycle the other day," Mark admitted to them.

"Why didn't you tell us you were hurt? We could have protected you more in the game," Craig expressed.

"You're supposed to protect me anyways," Mark said sullenly. The guys all looked down at the floor with regretful faces. Mark realized what he had done to them. Mark instantly felt guilty for hurting their feelings.

"Hey, guys, I'm sorry. I didn't mean it. You guys, all did great today," Mark reassured them. But they knew he was just trying to make them feel better. They all knew they were guilty of missed tackles and blocks. Mark had been sacked several times during the game.

No matter how poorly they played, Mark had never criticized or placed blame on them. He had been their trustworthy leader and friend. They could always count on Mark to make up for their mistakes.

There was nothing in the world they would not do for Mark, and they knew that he would do the same for them.

It pained them to see his injured chest. They may look like a bunch of apes, but each one of them had a heart of gold for the other. They were faithful companions.

"Come on, guys, stop looking so depressed. I can't stand it … why don't you guys all go home … I am fine," Mark said, wishing that they would not be there to hear about his injuries or something much worse.

They looked up at him, yet no one moved. April came into the room. All eyes fell on her. These guys might not be apes, but they certainly were not blind. April felt uneasy having so many male eyes staring at her all at one time.

"Down boys, she's all mine," Mark said with a smile as he held out his hand for her to come to him.

Mark knew they would respect her now that she was known as his gal. In fact, April would be well protected everywhere she went.

April was relieved to hear Mark was not still mad at her for telling her uncle about his injuries. She could not bear to lose him again. Mark gave her a reassuring look and she moved over to him. He reached out and took her hand in his. Carlo moved a chair over so that she could sit beside Mark.

Mark was getting nervous; Dan was taking far too long. What was Doc telling Dan, he wondered? Mark knew that Dan was unaware of the problems that he had been having at the football practices over the past few weeks.

If Doc told Dan everything and Dan put it all together with what he knew, they would both know what Mark already knew.

Mark noticed that the guys were too quiet, unusual for this rowdy group. If only he could get them to leave. Tension filled the room as they waited. Once again, Mark tried to get the guys to go home but they would not budge.

Dr. Raymond did fill in Dr. Morgan about Mark's lack of energy, his rapid weight loss, his nosebleeds, his dizzy spells. Doc told Dan that Mark had missed his last three team physicals. They both had seen the petechiae and the bruising on his leg. The chest x-ray also revealed Mark had an enlarged heart. They both knew that Mark was covering up an illness.

Dan was able to make an assumption of the diagnosis based on the information he had. A diagnosis that he hoped he was dead wrong.

CHAPTER THIRTY-FIVE –
ᴀFacing the Truthᴃ

ᴅr. Morgan and Dr. Raymond reentered the room. Both had a serious look on their face. They were surprised to see such a large concerned crowd gathered around Mark. The players sitting on the floor stood up. Dan looked Mark straight in the eyes.

"Mark, we have to talk to you," Dan said strongly, hoping to clear the room but no one moved. All the guys remained seated or standing. All ears were listening; the silence sent chills down Dan's spine.

Mark realized that Dan was waiting for his friends to leave. "They are not going anywhere, Dan. I doubt you'll get them to move until they know what you have to say," Mark told him with a regretful voice as their eyes painfully met.

Dan looked uncomfortable; it was all he could do to hold in his emotions. He knew he would have to choose his words carefully. If only he could swallow the lump in his throat, so he could speak.

Mark felt a sick feeling rise in his stomach and hung his head, unable to continue looking Dan in the eyes. Dan moved closer to Mark and put his hand on Mark's shoulder as he spoke to him.

"Mark, you have several fractured ribs; you have fluid around your lung. You are going to have to go to the hospital and have a chest tube put in. We need to run some blood tests right away."

Mark was slowly shaking his head back and forth no, as he listened. Dan took a deep breath before he continued. "Dr. Raymond and I both agree that you are sick. We need to start running tests," Dan told Mark with deep concern on his face.

Mark slowly looked up at Dan and sadly shook his head, no. Mark discreetly held his finger to his own lips for Dan to hush. Mark did not want Dan to say anymore. Dan's distraught eyes told Mark that he was very upset about Mark's condition, which could mean only one thing. It was not good.

April let out a gasp; she quickly hid her face with her hands. Mark gently wrapped his arms around her and offered her comfort, wishing with all his heart that his secret had not been exposed.

Mark regretted that he had allowed his friends to remain in the room. The guys looked dreadful; none of them could say anything. Mark had not wanted the guys to know that he was sick. Mark felt horrible seeing his friends look so distressed because they now knew the truth.

April was crying softly on Mark's shoulder; she knew that Mark's condition was serious, very serious. She could not hold back her tears. She was a nurse; she knew exactly what Dan was thinking. They did not need the tests to know what Mark had wrong with him.

She had seen the bruises, the nosebleeds, and his paleness, his lack of energy, the uncontrolled bleeding, the sweating, his rapid heart rate, and his need for oxygen. Jeff had told her that Mark had lost weight. She had tried to deny that Mark was sick because he seemed so strong and full of life, but now she was forced to face the facts.

The door opened swiftly as Jeff entered the room. His face was panic-stricken, as he stood there half-frozen. Jeff looked devastated as he glanced over at Mark.

Jeff had a medical folder in his hand. Jeff looked straight into Mark's distressing eyes as he held the folder up. Mark instantly understood why Jeff was so upset and quickly stood up and embraced Jeff.

"What's going on Mark, do you have ...?"

Jeff broke down and sobbed on Mark's shoulder. Jeff felt certain he already knew the heart wrenching answer to his question. Jeff's pain shot right through Mark. *How can I do this to him?* Mark's illness was not all about him; it was all about those who would suffer because he was sick.

The football players did not understand what all this meant, but it was not good if a grown man was crying.

Dan took the folder from Jeff and opened it. It contained the results of Mark's CBC blood tests. Mark had gone to the lab that morning, drawn his own blood, and had given it to the lab technician.

Dan left the room in devastation after reading the results. Dr. Raymond went after him to offer support.

April joined Mark and Jeff, and they wrapped their arms around each other.

"It is going to be fine," Mark told them sympathetically. Mark saw the look on the players' faces; many were crying, even though they did not know why.

"What gives? What is wrong with Mark?" Carlo demanded angrily. "We want to know!" Mark looked at Carlo and shook his head, no; Mark could not find the words to say.

Jeff's younger brother had not survived the same illness. Mark could not take the pain away that he knew Jeff was feeling right now. He would not say the unbearable words in Jeff's presence.

Dan came back into the room with Dr. Raymond. Mark stood in the middle of the room. He looked at everyone; all eyes turned to face him. It was all so overwhelming, but he knew that he had to appear strong. He took a deep breath and tried to reassure them.

"It's a mistake; it is something else; there are more tests we need to do before we know what I might have. I want everyone to stop it now. You act as if I am already dead. I'm not, do you hear me? I am fine. This does not leave this room; absolutely no one is to know about this. I am not sick! Does everyone in here understand? Not one word about what happened this afternoon leaves this room! Not one more tear better be shed. I am not claiming this; none of you better either. We have a Championship Game to get ready for and I intend to win it this year."

Mark walked out of the room leaving them standing there in shock. Dan and Dr. Raymond went out into the locker room to try to reason with him. They had to get him to the hospital soon.

Mark had gone over to his locker to grab his jacket. None of the other players in the room said anything to him. His coaches stood along the wall. The room was completely quiet as all eyes looked in Mark's direction. Dan and Doc went to Mark.

"Mark, we need to get you to the hospital," Dan told him sympathetically.

"I have a Championship Game to get ready for; the hospital is out of the question. I can't be sick!" Mark exclaimed as he choked back the agonizing tears that threatened to overcome him, and he banged his fist on his locker. He was feeling trapped.

"I'm afraid, Mark, I am benching you. Mark, you cannot do anything that would put more stress on your heart. Your platelet count is extremely low. You could bleed to death if you were hurt during a game," Dr. Raymond stated.

Mark heatedly turned and faced them. He was in a panic to convince them that he could still play in the game. "We can do a transfusion. I can spend the week building up my blood counts." Mark reasoned desperately.

Dan and Doc were determinedly shaking their head no. Mark looked frantic at the thought of being sidelined. He had to make them understand how important it was for him to play.

"No, don't do this to the team!" he appealed.

"No, Mark, you can't play; your life is more important than playing in that game," Dan answered him. Dan's face was tormented with pain for Mark.

"You don't understand. Those guys in there need me to play in that game! The team needs me; I cannot let them down. This may be the last time they ever get to play football with me. If I have to ... die ... I want it to be playing football, not in some crazy hospital room." Mark choked on his words and walked off. He did not want to discuss this anymore.

The guys had come out of the room and heard Mark. Carlo looked at Dan for answers.

"What is wrong with Mark?" Carlo demanded.

"We think Mark has leukemia or some blood disorder, whatever it is ... it is not good." Dan said hesitantly and left the room, leaving Mark's teammates devastated.

April had tried to be strong for Jeff. The loss of his younger brother to leukemia had almost sent him over the edge. What would he do if he lost Mark, too?

April refused to believe any of this. Mark had the symptoms but the confirming tests had not been performed. Maybe, just maybe, they were all wrong. This just was not happening, she thought. She and Mark had just started their relationship, surely, God would not separate them now, she thought as her knees felt weak.

April met Dan in the parking lot and told Dan she was riding back to the apartment with Jeff. They hoped to find Mark at his apartment. They would try to convince Mark to go to the hospital. Dan stressed the importance of getting Mark to the hospital as soon as possible and told them to call him if they found him.

It was six o'clock when they arrived back at the apartment. Mark's sports car was parked out front. Mark was sitting on the bench in the park. Jeff and April walked over and sat down with him. They sat silently for a few minutes.

"I want you to do everything I need done, Jeff. Can you handle it?" Mark asked him softly. Their eyes met in sadness.

"I'm right here, buddy, you can count on me," Jeff reassured him as he twisted his fingers together.

"I'll help him, Mark," April assured Mark as she took his hand in hers.

"We're wrong, Jeff. I know that everything looks bad right now, but we are going to rule this out. I am not sick; I am just rundown from all this stuff that has been going on." Mark tried to reassure his friend.

Jeff shook his head slowly in agreement, even though he knew in his heart that Mark was extremely sick. Mark needed to be in the hospital right now.

"If we have to do this, let's get it over with so I can get on with my life," Mark said as he slowly stood up, holding his side in pain and caught his breath.

Mark was a doctor. If only he wasn't, he could have walked away and ignored all of this. But he knew that he had no choice, medically he knew he had to go to the hospital.

April and Jeff followed Mark to his car. Mark turned and looked at his friends in despair and they joined together for a group hug.

"We can take my car, Mark, let me drive you to the hospital," Jeff offered.

"No, I'm fine, meet me at the hospital. I have a stop to make," Mark told them.

"Mark, you can't do it," April warned him. Mark pretended not to hear her.

The hospital was the last place Mark wanted to go. He had known for weeks that he was not feeling well, but he never thought it would go this far. Each week he had felt more exhausted which he had blamed on his hectic daily schedule.

When Mark weighed in and had lost ten pounds, he thought it was from his lack of eating. He had no appetite. Once the nosebleeds continued he became concerned. After that, Mark had avoided his team physicals for fear they might reveal something and sideline him from playing.

The final straw was when his blood would not clot, and he saw the petechiae on his arms and the bruising on his legs. Mark knew then that something else was going on.

Mark had gone to the hospital to have the lab work done so that he could treat himself secretly until after the AFC Championship Football Game next Sunday. He even hoped he could hold off treatments until after the Super Bowl was over.

Mark knew that his ribs might be fractured. He had gotten Jeff to give him a shot of pain medication before the game. Jeff had given him plenty of flack but Mark refused to listen to Jeff's advice. Mark insisted that he had to play in the game.

Mark was not sure how Jeff had gotten a hold of his blood test results. He knew that Jeff was not over his brother's death, and the last thing he wanted to do was bring back those bad memories for Jeff.

Mark drove to the children's home and knocked on the door. Katie answered the door.

"Where is Sunny?" Mark asked her with a tone of urgency.

"Upstairs, I'll go get her," Katie answered him. Katie noticed the gloomy look on Mark's face.

It was only a minute before Sunny came bouncing down the stairs, and was in Mark's arms where she belonged. He held her tightly. He brushed her hair with his fingers.

God, I love this child so much. She needs me, God. Don't let the devil take me away from her. He prayed as he held her tight against him.

"I love you, Sunny, don't you ever forget that," Mark told her with a heartfelt voice. Sunny looked at him with her big blue eyes. Mark would remember those eyes and the love she had for him when he was facing the worst of this.

"I love you too, Mark," she told him and softly kissed his cheek. She touched his cheeks with her tiny fingers and rubbed his face. Then she took her fingers, held his earlobe, and rubbed it softly between her fingers.

Mark had tried so hard to smile, but his eyes were so sad. He knew that if something happened to him, Sunny would be heartbroken. He could not do that to her.

Sunny thought something was not right when she first saw Mark. She took her tiny little hands and wiped the tear that fell from the corner of Mark's eye. He kissed her and held her in the safety of his arms.

"Mark," she said softly into his ear, "God will supply all your needs."

He never wanted to let her go.

CHAPTER THIRTY-SIX –
The Patient

When Mark arrived at the hospital, everyone was ready for him. He looked around the room at all his friends who loved him. No one spoke, none of them wanted to believe that he was their patient.

Dan had arranged for those special to Mark to care for him. He wanted to do all he could to make Mark feel comfortable.

It was different for the ER doctors and nurses when they were treating one of their own in the emergency room. Just yesterday, Mark was an ER doctor, and now he was reduced to the patient. Everyone looked at him with such love and compassion.

Instead of giving Mark a hospital gown, April helped him change out of his clothes into hospital scrub pants. He quietly lay down on the gurney. She raised the front of the gurney slightly so that he was not lying completely flat.

April started his IV. When she finished, she placed her fingers in his fingers and held them. He pulled her to him gently, and she bent and kissed him ever so tenderly. She could not say anything; the words would have caused her to cry. In that tender moment, they let their eyes speak to each other and joined their hearts together as one.

Sharon Johnson brought in the blood for Mark's blood transfusion and checked it with the other nurse. April hooked it up to Mark's IV with normal saline and set the drip.

Dan wanted more tests done on Mark's blood. Sharon gently took Mark's other arm in hers, prepared it and then inserted a needle into his vein, and took more blood samples. Mark forced a gentle smile at Sharon as she worked.

Sharon tenderly touched Mark's bare shoulder and looked deeply into his discouraged eyes; she understood how he felt. She would have given anything to be out riding horses with Mark and Carlo right now instead of taking blood from her dear friend.

Mark seemed subdued; he never spoke as they worked hooking him up to the monitors. Jeff knew that deep down Mark hated being the patient and having everyone touching him.

Mark is feeling like a caged animal with no way out, Jeff thought. They had to work quickly before Mark had to have his freedom back.

Mark had made it clear that everything was to be done on his terms. Jeff gave Mark a reassuring look to let Mark know that he was there for him. "I got your back, buddy," Jeff reminded him.

Sally soon announced that Mark was running a fever of 102. She gently wiped the sweat off Mark's forehead with a cool towel.

Dan ordered another IV for meds and an antihistamine. Dan was concerned that Mark might be having a reaction to the preservative in the blood from the transfusion. Mark had a reaction from the blood they had given him when he and Jeff had wrecked Jeff's truck a year ago. Mark was scratching his arms.

Dan was trying so hard to pretend Mark was just another patient but his heart hurt deeply each time he glanced into Mark's downcast eyes. Dan would have to avoid eye contact with Mark if he was going to make it through this difficult night.

The pain pills were wearing off, and Mark felt a great deal of pain in his left section of his abdomen and shoulder. Mark thought about it, what if it wasn't his ribs causing all the pain he was feeling? He knew pain from a spleen injury could be felt in the shoulder area.

Mark looked over at the cardiac monitor and watched it; he had an abnormal rhythm. It crossed his mind that he might have a blunt cardiac injury (BCI) from the motorcycle accident. He had also taken a brutal beating in the football game.

Mark closed his eyes in growing frustration. His pain was increasing, and he was very uncomfortable. He wanted to be positioned on his side. He hated lying on his back. Jeff sensed Mark's uneasiness and raised the gurney slightly higher.

When Mark opened his eyes, he saw Dan watching the cardiac monitor. There would be no more hiding any of his injuries; the pain was getting too severe now. Mark knew he would not be able to get to the pain pills he had in his jacket.

Mark took a deep breath and shook his head back and forth in disbelief that this was really happening to him. He had no choice but to give in and tell the truth about how he was feeling.

"Dan," Mark called to Dan with a pained voice and Dan immediately gave Mark his full attention. "Did my spleen look normal on the x-ray?" Mark asked as he cringed.

Dan looked at Mark's pained face with approval. Mark was an excellent doctor. He felt Mark's left side, and his spleen did feel enlarged. Dan ordered precise x-rays this time for Mark's spleen and his heart.

Did Mark injure his spleen in his motorcycle accident or the game? Did he have a BCI injury, too? Dan wondered with deep concern as he watched the heart monitor. Dan realized that Mark must be in severe pain so he injected pain medication into Mark's IV to give him some relief.

Jeff was ready to do the chest tube. Mark refused any type of sedation. He wanted to be awake if the other test results came back. Mark warned Jeff not to do anything underhanded. Mark did not trust any of them.

The area where the tube would be inserted was numbed with a local anesthetic. An incision was made between the ribs into the chest, and then the chest tube was inserted between the ribs and into the space between the inner lining and the outer lining of the lung, the pleural space. A suture and adhesive tape was used to keep the tube in place. Jeff then applied the large dressing. Blood slowly drained out of it. Dan was thankful that there was only minor bleeding.

The x-rays came back showing that his spleen was enlarged. His heart was also slightly enlarged. Dan took Mark for a CT scan. He stayed with Mark during the scan, and then he waited for the results of the scan while they took Mark back to the ER.

Mark had a small tear in his spleen allowing blood to leak out slowly. That explained the bleeding in his abdomen. Dan hoped that it was small enough that it would heal on its own. They would hold off on surgery. Surgery was too dangerous with Mark's blood counts so low.

What else could go wrong? The spleen enlargement was another serious problem. Dan ordered a platelet transfusion. Dan called Dr. Megan McGuire, the cardiologist on duty, to examine Mark's heart.

It was time for a bone marrow aspiration and a bone marrow biopsy. Was Mark up to the procedures, Dan wondered? Mark had tolerated everything well so far. Dan looked at the clock, eight o'clock. That was about Mark's limit. They had better get things done quickly.

Dan went back to the ER and went into Mark's room. Jeff was sitting on a stool next to the gurney. Jeff looked very concerned. Mark was lying on his right side surrounded by pillows. Mark's fever had gotten higher. Yet, Mark was shaking and they had covered him with blankets. They had put him on oxygen.

Dan gave orders for more IV medications. Mark was not tolerating the transfusion, either that or Mark had an infection that his white blood cells could not fight off. Mark had fallen asleep, once they increased his Benadryl, and Dan was thankful.

The door opened and the Sanders' family entered the room. Dan had called them on his way to the hospital. Dan quickly moved over to them. He gave them the sign to be quiet. Dan did not want Mark to wake up.

"What happened?" Robert asked softly when he saw Mark on the gurney. Robert was flooded with memories of Mark's motorcycle accident. He held firm to Julia as they approached the gurney that held their son.

"Let's go to my office; I need to talk to all of you," Dan told them and they hesitantly left their son to follow Dan.

The news of Mark's possible condition was not taken well. After shedding tears, they joined hands and prayed together before they reentered Mark's room.

Rebecca hugged April when they saw each other. Rebecca introduced April to Robert and Julia. They had not seen April since she was in high school. They would never forget the night April shared a dance of love with their son.

Mark's condition was stable; the blood from the chest tube was minimal. His fever was down. Dan ordered another chest x-ray to check the fluid around his lung and spleen. Remarkably, they looked sound, an answer to prayer.

The transfusion was almost complete. Mark was still sleeping. Dan hated to do the remaining tests but he knew they needed answers quickly. The unforeseen was taking its toll on everyone who loved Mark. Most of the ER staff had gathered outside of Mark's room waiting impatiently for news of his condition.

Mark's friends from the football team had gathered in the waiting room and were nervously waiting for word on Mark. Carlo had come to the room to find out about Mark. Jeff told Carlo what was going on so that Carlo could report to the rest of the guys.

Dan had contacted the hospital's finest specialist in hematology and oncology to come perform the bone marrow aspiration and a bone marrow biopsy. When Dr. Tom Stevenson arrived, Dan introduced him to everyone. Dr. Stevenson specialized in blood disorders and cancer.

Rebecca gently woke Mark up. It took Mark a minute to recall why he was in the hospital with everyone around him. He was sleepy from the Benadryl, and wanted to close his eyes and make everyone go away. Mark saw Dr. Stevenson and knew right away, who he was and what he was doing there.

Mark had done a rotation with Dr. Stevenson over a year ago. Mark had done several bone marrow procedures with him. He never thought he would be one of Dr. Stevenson's patients. Mark was certainly not looking forward to this procedure.

Mark spoke to his parents and reassured them with his fictitious smile that he was fine. Rebecca spoke to Mark before she and her parents left the room. April remained at Mark's bedside, along with Jeff and Dan.

Rebecca stood quiet in prayer; she could not believe that Mark was so sick. Robert held Julia in his arms as they waited outside the door. Mark was not just Robert's son; Mark was Robert's best friend.

When Julia felt dizzy, Rebecca took her to Dan's office to wait. Robert stood against the wall in the hall and closed his eyes in prayer as he waited for the tests to be done on his son. No devil would lie to him tonight; Mark was going to be just fine.

Dr. Stevenson had Mark lie back on his right side. Jeff cleaned the area and covered the area with sterile drapes, and then Dr. Stevenson injected a local anesthetic into the back of Mark's pelvic bone. Mark seemed uncomfortable as Tom did it. April took Mark's hand in hers and squeezed his fingers, more for her comfort than his as she watched Dr. Stevenson begin.

The doctor made a small cut so he could insert a needle. He moved the needle through the bone with a twisting motion. A syringe was used to suck out a small amount of liquid bone marrow. Mark reacted, feeling the pain. It might not have been so bad if he had not watched several of these procedures and could visualize exactly what Dr. Stevenson was doing.

Next, Dr. Stevenson did the bone marrow biopsy. Tom carefully moved the needle further into Mark's bone marrow to collect a second sample called a core biopsy; this was done with a slightly larger needle.

After the needle was pulled out, Tom put pressure on the biopsy site for a few minutes. It continued to bleed, so Jeff took over and applied pressure, until the bleeding slowed, then stopped. Jeff put on a pressure dressing to help prevent potential bleeding. Dr. Stevenson had not anticipated so much bleeding.

The pathologist had come into the room to retrieve the samples. He handed Dr. Stevenson Mark's lab report. Dan leaned over Tom's shoulder to read them. Mark's blood counts were too low.

Mark was getting the VIP treatment. It was nearing ten o'clock. These doctors had come back to the hospital at Dan's request to assist him on Mark's case. All of them knew Mark personally, and none of them noticed the lateness of the hour on the clock, nor did they care.

"While I am here, I want to do a lumbar puncture. As long as we have Dr. Sanders at the hospital and cooperating with us, we need to get all the required tests we need done," Dr. Stevenson told Dan as they stood in the back of the room watching Jeff finish cleaning off Mark's hip.

"I agree. If we can get Mark to agree, let's do it," Dan said, wondering if Mark would allow them to continue.

Mark had turned on his back and sat up slightly. April raised the front of the bed so he could lie back in a semi-sitting position. He looked exhausted and seemed uncomfortable with the chest tube in his side. Dan and Dr. Stevenson approached Mark.

"While I am here, Dr. Sanders, I would like to go ahead and do a lumbar puncture," Tom informed Mark. Mark frowned at him and sighed.

"Dang," Mark responded with aggravation. He looked around the room and was met by everyone's watchful eyes. They had concerned expressions on their faces, obviously waiting for Mark to throw them all out of the room.

"What can I say, just do it and get out of here, this is it, no more," Mark announced. At this point, he was ready to go home.

Jeff got the lumbar kit out and put it on the bedside table. The bed was lowered, and Mark was told to lie on his side in the fetal position. The area was numbed, and the doctor inserted a long thin needle between the lower lumbar vertebrae into the spinal canal and withdrew cerebrospinal fluid. When Tom finished, he applied pressure and Jeff put a bandage over the site.

Mark would have to remain on his back for at least 30 minutes to prevent a spinal tap headache. Dan told him to lay still. He placed the oxygen mask back on Mark to make it easier for him to breathe in this position. Jeff injected a mild sedative into Mark's IV and Mark fell asleep. April covered him up with a warm blanket.

Dan decided he would overrule Mark's request to go home, and he admitted Mark to the hospital. Mark was moved to a private room on the third floor where he would be closely monitored. They were thankful that Mark remained asleep when they transferred him.

Jeff and April both wanted to stay the rest of the night in Mark's room. Julia, Robert, and Rebecca each gave Mark a tender kiss on his forehead before leaving Mark's room.

It was midnight, and there was nothing more anyone could do for Mark now but pray, as they waited for the test results.

Julia was exhausted, and it was decided Robert would take her home where she could rest more comfortably. Dan assured the Sanders' that he would keep them updated on Mark's condition during the night. Robert had Tony fly them back to the ranch.

Dan decided to spend the night in his office. He knew that Jeff and April would keep a vigil over Mark.

During the night, Dr. Stevenson wrote orders for Mark to get another unit of blood, a unit of platelets, IV antibiotics, pain medication, Benadryl and Tylenol.

What would the morning bring?

Chapter Thirty-Seven –
The Test Results

*D*uring the early morning, Mark woke up confused. He was lying on his side on a hospital bed. *What did they do to my side, back and hip?* He thought as he tried to move and the tape on the bandages pulled on his skin. "Ouch!"

His thoughts filled with the memories of the night before. Darkness settled over the room as he closed his eyes to pray that this was all just a bad dream. He sunk deep inside his soul as he remembered the painful expressions on the faces of those he loved. A wave of guilt for their pain swept over him.

A single tear slid down his cheek as his thoughts turned to April. He had promised her forever, not this. "I will love you forever, April. I will never let you go," he whispered as he wiped the tears from his cheeks and touched his chest over his heart.

Then he remembered his last moment with Sunny. He smiled thinking of her words of wisdom. "Yes, Sunny, God will supply all my needs."

There was no way that he would claim any sickness on his body. He removed the oxygen mask and flung it behind his head. "I am out of here; this is crazy; I am not sick." He sat up slightly and leaned on his elbow. His chest and abdomen were sore when he moved. As he let out a moan, he swore that even the pain he had was a lie of the devil.

Mark surveyed his body and discovered that the doctors still had him hooked up to the IV drip, the chest tube, and the heart monitor. He had a pulse oximeter on his index finger. He knew if he took it off, it would sound an alarm, and he could not reach the machine to shut it off.

He felt trapped in the mess of wires and tubes. He pulled the bed sheet up to his neck. He took a slow deep breath and contemplated what his next move was going to be.

He looked over and saw that Jeff was asleep on the recliner in the corner of the room. Was Jeff responsible for having him admitted to the hospital, Mark wondered, slightly annoyed that he could not trust Jeff.

The door opened and April came into the room carrying a cup of coffee. She looked like she had not slept all night. Guilt consumed his heart knowing that he was the reason. She smiled at him as she set the coffee down.

Mark's face lit up knowing he had been rescued. He quietly motioned for her to come over to him. He did not want to wake Jeff up. She joined him on the bed with her legs hanging over the side.

Mark slowly sat up completely on the bed. The sheet fell to his hips, exposing his muscular chest and the chest tube dressing. He leaned forward as far as the tubing would allow him. April, knowing what he wanted, leaned over and gave him her lips. He placed his hand behind her head and gathered her face to his for an intense kiss.

"I am glad you are feeling better," she whispered and kissed him again.

"Take this stuff off of me," Mark whispered back and held up his finger and his arms with the IVs.

"I can't do that. The doctor said to leave them in until he comes back to examine you," she whispered as she kissed him again.

"I am the doctor. I am ordering you to remove them," he stated with humor. She smiled at him with amusement, and then she kissed him again as she touched the side of his face with the palm of her hand.

"Oh really. I am the nurse; what do you plan to do about that?" she teased. Mark mulled over that thought with his eyebrows lifted. *She is about to find out just who she is messing with*, he thought cleverly. He would make her forget that he was supposed to be sick.

Mark looked over to make sure Jeff was asleep, and then he grabbed April, pulled her into his lap, and genuinely kissed her. He dipped her back against the bed, holding her back with both his arms and planted his compelling lips on hers. April laughed as her legs went flying in the air. What drugs had Jeff given him last night, she pondered.

"Mark!" she laughed. He kissed her to keep her quiet.

"Are you two done over there so I can open my eyes?" Jeff joked as he sat up and stretched his arms out. That was one uncomfortable recliner; his back was killing him.

April pulled herself out of Mark's lap in embarrassment. Mark lay back defeated, stuffing the pillow behind his head. Jeff had awful timing! April raised the front of the bed so he was slightly sitting up.

Jeff got up stiffly and walked over to the bed. Mark gave him a disapproving look and Jeff grinned. Jeff turned the pulse oximeter off and removed it from Mark's finger. After he scanned the screen for a normal heartbeat, he turned the heart monitor off. He put the oxygen mask back on the wall and turned it off.

"I suppose you want out of here," Jeff said to Mark.

"Now would be good; we have lectures today. Our boards are Friday. After Friday we will no longer be first year residents," Mark excitedly told April as he freed himself from the wires and the patches on his chest.

Mark was looking forward to his second year of rotations, with emergency medicine being at the top of his list. With football season ending in a few weeks, he planned to devote his full attention to his medical training.

"What about the chest tube and IVs?" Mark asked impatiently.

"No can do, not yet. Let me go see what I can do to get you out of here," Jeff told him and left the room.

Jeff really did not think Mark would be going anywhere soon. However, he certainly was not going to be the one to tell Mark that bit of unwanted information. If Mark thought that Jeff was going to help him break out of jail this time, Mark was wrong.

The phone rang as Jeff left the room and April answered it. It was Robert calling to check on Mark. April handed the phone to Mark. Mark reassured his father that he was fine, and told him that Jeff was working on getting him released from the hospital.

Mark gave his father the run down on his day and promised to call Robert the minute he knew the results of his tests. Julia insisted on speaking to Mark, and again he promised her that he was feeling great, telling her repeatedly not to worry. She made Mark promise that he would come out to the ranch after his lectures.

Jeff went to Dan's office and knocked on the door. Dan opened the door and was disappointed that it was Jeff and not Dr. Stevenson.

Dan had been pacing the floor, looking at his watch, waiting for the test results on Mark. Jeff went in and observed Dan's tense state of mind.

"Mark is awake; he is in a good mood. He looks much better. The drugs Dr. Stevenson gave him seem to be working," Jeff reported as he tried to bring Dan some sort of comfort.

"How is Mark taking all of this?" Dan inquired with concern, fully aware of the history of Mark's hospital anxiety and his determination to stay out of hospitals as a patient.

"He wants out. We have lectures and reviews all week. Friday is our last day as interns."

"That's right; you will start your second year of residency," Dan replied. He knew how hard Mark had worked this year with his internship and his football. *Maybe Mark is right. Maybe Mark's hectic schedule is making him sick.* Dan thought with a tiny glimpse of hope that his godson was just overstressed.

"Did Mark tell you he was sick?"

"He never said a word, but I knew he was hiding something from me when I examined him."

"You should have come to me, Jeff."

"Dan, don't, I feel bad enough already. It was because of me that Mark could not tell us ... you know, after losing my brother ... he'd try to protect me ... he knew I'd lose it and ... and I ... I don't think I can handle this, Dan."

"I understand, Jeff. You are right; Mark hid his illness to spare us. Just like Mark; he is so unselfish."

After waiting an agonizing hour, the phone rang and Dan quickly answered it. He listened carefully and then he hung up. He looked at Jeff, his face drawn.

"That was Dr. Stevenson; he wants to meet with us in his office. He has the test results." Nervously they proceeded to Tom's office. Each step Dan took was in prayer that they would hear encouraging news.

They all shook hands and sat down. Jeff was silently praying as he felt Dr. Stevenson's apprehension to speak.

"Mark asked me to speak to the two of you. His blood tests came back. His red blood cells, white cell count, and platelets are still extremely low. His bone marrow biopsy shows a great reduction in the number of cells in the bone marrow, with a normal appearance of the few remaining cells,"

Dr. Stevenson told them. Dan and Jeff exchanged looks, not sure what they were about to hear.

"It's not that good, Doctors," Dr. Stevenson timidly spoke and the two turned to look at him. There was no way to avoid what he had to tell these two men who loved Mark dearly.

"The bone marrow was clear of leukemia cells; the lumbar puncture was also clear. It is not leukemia. Mark has severe aplastic anemia. Since all his blood counts are already extremely low, Mark has had this for quite awhile. My guess is that Mark has been hiding his condition for some time. Yesterday he dropped way out of normal range, making it impossible for him to hide it any longer."

The room was quiet as Dr. Stevenson took a deep breath.

"I am surprised that he did not bleed to death after his motorcycle accident, or at the football game, with his platelet count so low," Dr. Stevenson informed them grimly. Dr. Stevenson handed Dan the newest lab report, and Dan quickly scanned it and handed it to Jeff.

"Aplastic anemia?" Jeff asked frantically. "Isn't that a rare serious blood disorder? What the heck does all this mean? Is Mark going to be all right?" Jeff asked in despair as his eyes watered. Jeff's body was shaking. He understood blood counts and Mark's were off the wall, way too low!

"I'm afraid it is very serious at this stage. If we do not get his blood counts under control quickly, Mark could die from it. I started treatments early this morning, with two more units of blood and platelets. I was just down there and talked to Mark. He is aware of the seriousness of this disorder. He had training in aplastic anemia during his rotation with me," Dr. Stevenson told them.

Both men were speechless. Jeff covered his face with both his hands and leaned forward in his chair. Dan placed his hand on the curve of Jeff's back to offer comfort. Dan's heart was somewhere in his stomach; he could use some comfort himself.

"Mark did not want to discuss it with me this morning. He just needs time to think about it." Dr. Stevenson continued wishing that he did not have to be the bearer of bad news.

"I'm relieved that it is not leukemia, but this is not much better," Dan agonized. "This is a tremendous blow. Mark is in serious danger."

"What, what is this?" Jeff wanted to know the details.

"His bone marrow is not producing enough stem cells to produce a sufficient quantity of blood cells. His immune system is reacting against the bone marrow, interfering with its ability to make blood cells. Stem cells are no longer being replaced and the remaining stem cells are working less effectively, so the levels of his red cells, white cells, and platelets are dropping," Dr. Stevenson informed Jeff with a serious look.

"On top of that he has the injuries from his accident. His spleen is enlarged, due to the accident or this disorder; we need to consider removing it soon. If he had not had the motorcycle accident we might not have known how low his counts were and ..." Dan could not finish his statement, knowing Mark could have bled out without the transfusions they had given him. His motorcycle accident might very well have saved his life.

"His first blood transfusion did not raise his counts much. I am hoping the units we just gave him will be more successful. He seems to be feeling better. I am going to put in a central line at three o'clock today. Mark is looking at transfusions, immune-suppressing drugs, antibiotics, and growth factors. I have some other things I want to try. If none of these work, he will need a bone marrow transplant," Dr. Stevenson said dreadfully as the men took in the information he was giving them.

"We need to start HLA testing on his family right away. Rebecca is his best chance of a match. His parents would have a 50% or higher rate. His own children would have a slight chance of matching. Does Mark have any children of his own?" Dr. Stevenson asked hopefully.

"Unfortunately not, Mark has no children of his own," Dan sighed.

"The odds of finding an unrelated matched donor are 1 in one million. I will contact the National Bone Marrow Donor Program today," Dr. Stevenson said, knowing that the process of finding a donor took valuable time, time that Mark might not have.

"We also need matched platelet donors right away. His O negative blood is not going to be easily matched," Dr. Stevenson said bleakly, fearing Mark was not going to catch a break. It would take several donors to keep Mark supplied with the kind of blood he needed.

"Mark's father and Rebecca are both O negative. We used his own stored blood for the transfusion yesterday; he has more stored at the blood bank. Mark and his father donated regularly," Dan announced, thankful that they had that blood available to start with.

"I know, I gave him his own blood, but he still ran a fever with it. Mark appears to be allergic to the preservative in the stored blood," Dr. Stevenson told them with concern, knowing that the long list of drugs Mark was allergic to would make it difficult to treat him.

"How did Mark respond to your advice for him?" Jeff asked, knowing Mark was hardheaded when it came to being a patient.

"He listened, but he shook his head the entire time I was talking to him. He said he was going to continue out this week as planned, including the championship football game on Sunday. There was no changing his mind; he was adamant. He desperately wanted to be unhooked from everything, which I did, and he left the hospital with April." Dr. Stevenson filled them in on Mark's unwise plans.

"What, you let him leave the hospital?" Dan asked in disbelief. "You removed his chest tube?"

"The tube was clear this morning. I made a deal with him; he has to be back here at three to have the catheter inserted in his chest. Once we have Mark in isolation, we will continue treatments and keep him in the unit until his counts are stable," Dr. Stevenson exposed his plan to keep Mark in the hospital.

"Isolation, no way, not isolation!" Jeff stood up in a panic. "Mark is never going to agree to isolation, not in a million years! Dan, you know how Mark is about a regular hospital stay; this is not going to work!" Jeff shook his head in despair for his best friend.

"We will have to make it work. Mark's life depends on the treatments he gets in the next few days; he has very few white blood cells to prevent infections. Mark has to be in the bone marrow transplant unit until we can raise his counts," Dr. Stevenson explained to Jeff.

"Jeff, Mark is already running a fever; there is an infection somewhere in his body. It could be his spleen, it is enlarged; he is looking at surgery in the next day or two, once we get his counts up again," Dan informed Jeff.

Jeff was shaking his head in disbelief as he paced back and forth in frustration.

"You are not listening to me! Mark's not going to agree to surgery before the championship game!" Jeff exclaimed miserably, "Mark plays by his rule book, not anyone else's; there is nothing that will stop him from playing in that game!"

"Jeff, Mark is extremely lucky he did not bleed to death after his motorcycle accident or during the football game. If he plays in the game on Sunday, we will attend his funeral on Monday. I am sorry, but that is the way it is," Dr. Stevenson said firmly.

"This can't be happening," Jeff said in despair. "There is no way in heck Mark will miss that game!" Jeff knew they were facing a losing battle with Mark. Would Mark risk his own life for the team? Yes, he would, Jeff feared. Mark was already feeling guilty about the wreck and now this.

"I know Mark's feeling responsible for all of this, but Mark's illness is not his fault. It was only a matter of time before his illness was exposed. I do not think his motorcycle accident was an accident. God works in mysterious ways; it could be that accident happened to make him stop and get the medical attention he needed for his aplastic anemia."

"I was thinking the same thing, Tom," Dan agreed.

"Mark's football season is over. As long as his platelet count is as low as it is, he cannot even get a paper cut; a simple cold could kill him," Dr. Stevenson said strongly, trying to make Jeff understand the seriousness.

"Did you tell Mark all of this?" Jeff asked with hopelessness.

"Mark knows exactly what he is facing. He did a rotation with me. We were treating a patient with aplastic anemia," Dr. Stevenson informed them.

"Were treating? Was he cured?" Jeff asked desperately looking for a positive outcome.

"No, he died during his chemo treatment, from an infection," Dr. Stevenson said regretfully. "However, I have treated many successful cases, most patients respond to some sort of treatment." Those last words were unheard; the word death had struck Jeff between the shoulder blades with a tremendous blow.

The room was silent. Jeff sat back down and tears filled his eyes; he was distraught at the thought of losing Mark. First his brother, now Mark. How could this happen?

"I can't lose him, Dan," Jeff cried inconsolably, placing his hands over his eyes. Dan and Dr. Stevenson went to his side to offer comfort.

"Mark is going to do just fine, Jeff," Dan offered.

"Who is going to tell his parents?" Jeff asked through his tears.

"Mark said he would tell them, they called him earlier this morning, and he promised them he would go out to the ranch." Dr. Stevenson told them.

"He'll lie; Mark will never tell them the truth," Jeff moaned.

"I gave him a booklet to give them. It should help his parents understand what he has," Dr. Stevenson replied.

"What about today? Is Mark in any danger today?" Jeff asked sullenly.

"It's like this, Jeff. When his blood counts go up from the transfusions, he will have more energy, he will feel better, and he will act like the Mark we know. However, when his blood counts go down, he will get tired easily, look pale, be short of breath, and have nosebleeds. He has been coping with his low blood count for a while so the transfusions we have just given him have already made him feel stronger. Other than his sore ribs, he was doing much better this morning. It's his heart and his spleen that have me more concerned."

"Do you know how many times Mark has played injured or sick without anyone knowing, tons of times? He is not going to listen to anything you tell him to do. If I know him, he was going to hide this until after the Super Bowl. He is not thinking about himself right now. He is thinking about the team and getting them to the Super Bowl."

"Jeff, I gave him strict instructions: no football practice. He is not to set foot in this hospital without a mask on. I've taken him off the rotation schedule, he cannot see patients, he has to stay out of malls, restaurants, churches, anywhere the general public gathers, and absolutely no contact with children," Dr. Stevenson educated Jeff.

"This will never work; you've sentenced Mark to prison. Mark is never going to restrict himself from the world," Jeff said despondently, with fear for his best friend.

"Jeff, Mark will follow my instructions if he wants to live. We have to believe Mark can do this. We will all help Mark get through this," Dr. Stevenson encouraged Jeff.

"Mark has this week off for exams, and then you guys can start your four weeks of vacation time. There should be no reason Mark should be at this hospital, except as a patient," Dan stressed.

"That's just it; he's a patient, not a doctor anymore!" Jeff said in anguish.

CHAPTER THIRTY-EIGHT

Living Life to the Fullest

*M*ark had left the hospital with April. He said nothing to her as he drove them to the apartment complex. She sat beside him, biting her lip, trying not to cry. He reached out and put his hand on hers, but said nothing. She placed his hand over her heart and kissed it. He looked over at her and gave her a reassuring smile.

A thousand thoughts were invading his mind. He had just been handed a death sentence if he did not follow everything that Dr. Stevenson had instructed him to do. How was he going to put his life on hold at a time when so many people were depending on him? He felt overwhelmed with all the responsibilities he had to others, so much so that he did not have time to consider his own feelings right now.

Mark's thoughts turned to a former patient, Mr. Wilson. Mark had helped Dr. Stevenson with Mr. Wilson's treatments when Mark had first become an intern.

While in isolation, Mr. Wilson had missed his first grandchild being born, he never got the chance to see her. Mr. Wilson's son graduated from college, he missed that too.

All of the things Mr. Wilson thought he was going to do when he got out of the hospital never happened. Mr. Wilson gave up and inadvertently let AA rob him of living his life to the fullest while he was still alive.

It was the mere fact that when Mr. Wilson found out that he had aplastic anemia, he gave up on life. He lost his faith, blaming God for his illness, and turned into an unpleasant bitter man. Everyday he woke up with an awful attitude, and he claimed every negative aspect of his illness.

Mark had tried to encourage Mr. Wilson and bring him out of his condemnation. Mark entered his room every day with a contagious smile, and a spirit that could raise the dead off their bed.

The young ambitious intern was not about to give up on his patient's health or his pitiful frame of mind. When Mr. Wilson would intimidate the nurses, they called Mark in to rescue them. Mark would put on his best smile and enter the room.

Mark's heart was heavy as he was faced with the realization that it was impossible to help Mr. Wilson accept that his life was still worth living. The devil had a stronghold on Mr. Wilson and filled him with lies. Mr. Wilson could not get past the fate he thought he was destined to have with aplastic anemia.

Although Mark gave constant encouragement, he professionally could not speak to Mr. Wilson about his faith, unless Mr. Wilson was the one who approached the subject. This new experience was very difficult for Mark as a new doctor and as a Christian. How could he mix medicine and his faith together? Mark prayed daily that God would give him the answers so that he could give Mr. Wilson the conviction to seek God.

Finally, Mr. Wilson, fearing the end of his life was near, asked Mark about his belief in God. "I just don't understand you, Mark. What gives you your optimistic outlook on life? How is it that you can love a God that lets people all around you suffer?"

Mark prayed the Holy Spirit would give him the words he needed to say to Mr. Wilson. Mark sat down next to Mr. Wilson, folding his hands in his lap, as he looked him straight in the eyes. As Mark began to speak, his demeanor changed from that of a doctor to a compassionate friend.

Mark explained that God does not permit evil things to come on us to teach us or punish us. He explained that when sickness or suffering comes against us, the devil has trespassed against us. It is up to us to rebuke the devil and seek God's promises of healing that He made at the cross. Mark walked Mr. Wilson through the path of salvation and explained eternal life, and then they cried together.

Mr. Wilson had died peacefully and received his healing. Mark had provided his family with the comfort of knowing their father had received God as his savior.

Now Mark was faced with the same situation as Mr. Wilson. It was his turn to drown in self-pity or have the courage and fortitude to put his beliefs into action.

I can't live like Mr. Wilson did. Mr. Wilson let his limitations overtake his life and stopped living. If I cannot live my life to the fullest despite AA, I do not want to live, Mark thought as he drove.

It was the same feeling Mark had about not walking again. Even if he had never been able to walk again, he still would have lived his life to the fullest, enjoying all that God blessed him with each day.

Nothing would stop Mark from doing the things he wanted to do in his life.

I am not living as if I am dying; I am living to live each day to the fullest. He intended to do just that.

Mark felt that even if people have an illness or a handicap that could possibly keep them from doing the things they wanted to do in life, it does not mean that they have to let it stop them.

Mark's determination to be optimistic in all oppositions of his life would be the stronghold that would give him the assurance that God would inspire him daily with hope and truth.

Mark might have AA, but it did not own him. He planned to have a whole life filled with the joy of living in faith, even if he did have AA. Mark was not succumbing to it; he was overcoming it, in the name of Jesus.

Mark knew that God would be right there to help him get through each day. Mark was determined not to let the devil steal his health or his happiness. Mark was determined not to feel sorry for himself. He planned to continue living normally. Mark would not speak illness over his body; he would speak healing and good health. He would be thankful and celebrate each day God gave him.

I can do both. I can fight this thing and have my life remain the same. I am a fighter; nothing has ever stood in my way before. I can do this with God's help. God proved to everyone that I could walk again. I will prove to them that God can beat this too.

I believe by the blood Jesus shed for me that nothing is going to happen to me. God will fight this for me; this is His battle for me. God does not bring suffering, Mark thought.

Mark believed that with all his heart. God was one-step ahead of him; all he had to do was catch up to Him.

Mark knew that he had to rejoice in his suffering to produce perseverance and hope. God promised him grace and hope and Mark would hold onto that. He would have faith in God and trust Him, no matter what the outcome was for him.

"Blessed is the man who perseveres under trial, he will receive the crown of life that God has promised to those who love him. James Chapter One," Mark recited to April out loud with assurance in his voice and a smile on his face as he looked over at her.

Mark decided that he was giving faith a fighting chance. With his mind made up, he turned the car around and headed to his church. Hand in hand, he and April went to his pastor's office. Pastor Evan Reddick joined their hands and prayed with them, claiming God's promise of supernatural healing for Mark.

As April stood in Pastor Evan's office, she remembered the promise she made to God when she and Mark were teenagers. She gave her heart to God while attending Mark's youth group one Wednesday evening. With Mark on one side of her and her Uncle Dan on her other side, she stood before Pastor Evan and proclaimed Christ as Lord.

Sometimes, she and Mark would spend hours on the football bleachers talking about God's grace. If she missed a Wednesday night service, he shared the message with her. Although her faith was new, she hungered for a deeper relationship with God. She knew that Mark would be there to walk her through it.

However, April never had the chance to learn all there was to learn about her new relationship with God before her father had moved her away to California. Although she wanted to attend church in California, her father had forbidden her, just as he had forbidden her to attend Mark's church with her Uncle Dan.

April felt so much shame when she found out she was pregnant. She was isolated in her thoughts and could not see past the hurt that consumed her. She was sure she had disappointed God. After all, as a child, that deceptive reasoning had been drilled in her head. Her earthly father expected perfection. He would accept nothing less from her. She wanted the loving and forgiving God that Mark had spoke of when they were together on the football bleachers.

Mark was so on fire for God back then that he wanted to witness to all his friends. It was important to him that his friends were saved because he loved them enough to want eternal life for them should anything happen to them. When her thoughts rambled on, she felt that she had disappointed Mark, too, when she had gotten pregnant.

Now as she sat there watching Pastor Evan and Mark together, she knew that she wanted to join Mark in his deep faith and understand everything that he knew about the Bible and God's promises. April's soul was opening up again as she remembered the words that Pastor Evan spoke to her receptive heart so many years ago.

When Mark got back in the car with April, he turned to face her. He seemed relaxed and at peace. His tan face had color once again, and there was no indication that he was sick. His pain medication was definitely working, she thought, as he bent over and faced her.

"I hate this AA illness. I hate everything about it, and I hate what I will have to undergo medically because of it. But this is the end of being in fear of this disorder. It is in God's hands now and I am not taking it back. Every moment of every day is a gift that I receive from God. I love living for God too much to let anyone tell me I am sick or dying." He touched her cheek with his gentle hand.

"I am going to live the rest of my days, whether it is one more day or a million days, in peace. I want you to do the same. I am not hanging out with anyone who lives in fear for me. You have to have faith and joy that I am alive and not fear my death. Our life must continue as if we had never been told I was sick. Can you do that for me? Can you believe that I am not sick?" Mark asked her with such love that she melted in his arms and cried. He held her tight against him. He would give her this one last cry, but after this, no more tears.

"Promise me … you will never leave me," she cried tearfully.

"I promise. I love you so much, April. I am looking forward to our life together. Nothing can take that away from us; you have to believe it with all your heart," he told her compassionately, brushing the tears away from her soft cheeks and kissing her lips tenderly. Mark held her safe in his loving arms. Then she heard his soft voice speak.

"April, it's important to me that you know Christ as your Savior. Have you ever asked God into your heart?" Her encumbered eyes met his as her heart felt sorrow. His eyes were so sincere as he wiped the tears from her eyes.

How could she tell him that the most important day of her life had been the day that she had stood before his pastor with him at her side and claimed God as her savior. Her eyes looked into his, and then she tearfully told him that he had stood beside her on the day that she had given her heart to Jesus right there in his church.

As the final words left her lips, she buried her face in his shoulder praying with all her heart that he would remember that day, a precious moment that had been taken away from him by the loss of his memory.

They went back to the apartment; he took a shower and then went to class. He was more determined than ever that he would continue his life better than it had been yesterday.

There was nothing arrogant about his position on his illness. He was pursuing the promises of God that he knew deep in his heart to be true.

April had taken a shower and changed into her comfortable sweat pants. She sat on the couch with her knees pulled up to her chest and her arms wrapped around her legs, hugging them.

She thought about the kisses that she and Mark had shared. There was no doubting the love he had for her.

If only she was not a nurse and did not know medically what Mark was facing, maybe she could believe as he did in supernatural healing. She knew as a nurse that Mark was facing a battle just to live. She wondered how she could separate her feelings between God's promises and what she knew medically.

She knew that Mark was trying to be so brave for her. He was calling on his faith to see him through this ordeal. Yet, she still did not understand why he was not angry over what was happening to him. How could he be so calm; how could he just accept his illness and move on as if it did not exist? Why had he not shed a tear when Dr. Stevenson gave him the grim news?

She thought about what his pastor had told them. Pastor Evan and Mark had been in agreement together that supernatural healing belonged to Mark. They had laughed together and cut up as if nothing else needed to be said.

They talked about playing golf when the weather got better. Mark invited Pastor Evan to the Championship Football Game on Sunday. Mark was so enthusiastic and energetic when he spoke to Evan about the game.

April had sat and listened in disbelief; she was amazed at the conversation that took place between the two men. The two were so sure that God had everything under control that they could go play golf and Mark could still play football.

She had never experienced that kind of belief in the church she had attended as a child. When someone was sick, he or she certainly did not talk about playing golf.

She tried to remember the things that Mark had shared with her on the football bleachers. If only she had not exposed herself to the doubts, Satan had placed in her mind.

She had lost her child, not to death, but to the unknown. It hurt so deeply, and she wore the scar in her heart. She could not lose Mark.

She no longer blamed Mark for any of the past. Mark had no way of knowing what she had gone through.

She could not help but wonder if she was being punished for her secret. She had lost her child, would she lose the only person she had ever loved, too? Her father had told her that God would punish her for what she had done. Her confusion continued as she battled with her thoughts.

She wished that her faith was as deep as Mark's faith. Mark had opened her heart to the truths of God's words today in Pastor Evan's office. Mark had told her that God was not responsible for his illness or anything else that caused them suffering.

She knew deep down that God would never punish her by making Mark sick. Her father was wrong. He knew nothing about God. "Speak to me, Lord."

She knew she was responsible for the choices that she had made in her life that caused her suffering. She was to blame for the mistakes that she had made. She would claim God's mercy and forgiveness. "God, forgive me."

She knew that the devil was right there waiting for her to lose her faith and her trust in God. Mark's pastor had told her not to open the door to the devil because the devil was just waiting for the opportunity to steal everything God had promised her. She would not let the devil claim Mark away from her.

"You can't have Mark; he belongs to God and to me."

Mark had asked her not to cry but that was impossible. She let the tears flow as she begged God to come back in her heart. Moments later, she gave her heart back to God. She could not wait to tell Mark her decision to join him in his faith and his love for God.

She did not know how she could continue to face Mark without telling him the whole truth about their past. She struggled with what she needed to do. Finally, she decided that the timing was not right. Mark had enough to think about with his illness.

For now, she would have to wait to tell him what he needed to know.

CHAPTER THIRTY-NINE –
ᴄ᷉Trusting Godᴄ᷉

At one o'clock Mark drove out to his parents and gave them the basics of his illness, leaving out the complications of his personal condition in an attempt to spare them from anymore stress relating to him.

Mark sounded so positive and assured them that nothing was physically wrong with him. He looked much better as he stood there and cut up with them in his usual upbeat manner.

Julia and Robert were so relieved to hear he did not have leukemia that they did not hear anything else that he said. Anemia, Mark was anemic as a child; they gave him extra iron, thought Julia with relief. Mark was anemic after his truck accident with Jeff. He had recovered just fine; there was no reason to believe that this time would be any different, his parents thought.

Mark handed them the booklet on aplastic anemia and kissed them goodbye just before he headed out the door.

Robert and Julia sat down together to read the booklet. Julia was soon in tears, and Robert was frantic as he got on the phone with Dan wanting an explanation. "Dan, what is wrong with our son?" Dan had expected the distressful call from them. It was just as Jeff had said it would be; Mark had not been truthful with his parents.

Dan told them about Mark's surgery at three. Robert immediately called his pilot Tony and arranged the flight to the hospital. They wanted everyone from the ranch to be tested for an HLA donor match for Mark.

Mark drove back into the city. The lonely country miles ahead of him gave him more time to soul search. He hated that he had to deceive his parents, but what choice did he have when his mother's tear-jerking eyes encircled his heart the minute he saw her. How could he break her heart and tell her that his life span might very well be shortened?

He was not afraid of this illness. He was not afraid of dying if he was not healed; he loved God. Either God would heal him on this earth or when the two of them met in heaven. Death or no death, God was Mark's healer.

Mark would not ask God why he was sick; he would not blame anyone other than the devil for this illness. There are things we are never to know because we are not God. Mark would have faith to believe in what he did not understand. If it was a battle the devil wanted, then Mark was ready for him. Mark was pressing forward with God.

Mark prayed for patience. He would need it if they wanted to do all those tests and treatments on him. He was not looking forward to the hospital stay. Doctors make the worst patients. He had certainly lived up to that saying before, but he would try harder this time to overcome his anxiety of confinement.

It was from being a patient himself that made Mark a great doctor. Mark understood how his patients felt and he had great compassion for them. He knew that being sick takes away a person's dignity, leaving them feeling vulnerable.

Well, not on his watch. He would never be a doctor who treated just people; he was a doctor who treated each patient as a person with feelings.

Mark let God use him to heal his patients by giving them faith, peace, and hope. Mark was in his medical profession with God. He could do nothing without God's guidance to accomplish God's healings. God had blessed Mark's mind and his skillful hands to bring his patients their healings.

Let the doctors have their way. He would go through the testing and the treatments and continue to live in faith that God would work through his doctors. They would find nothing wrong with him that God could not cure using them as His instruments.

Aplastic anemia was not going to interrupt his life. Mark had made his choice and plan and he would stick with it. He would put on God's armor and stand firm that he was not sick, no way!

After all, this was not about him, it was about his relationship with God. The hardest part of this would be making others believe as he did. Could he convince even April to believe as he did?

That was the end of thinking about aplastic anemia; there was no need to think about it again. On to better things. It was time to start living, and that is exactly what he intended to do as he thought about his amazing *endless love* for April and Sunny.

April was meeting Mark at Sunny's school at 2:30. He would have to hurry. He wanted to be waiting at the gate when her school let out to surprise her. He got there just in time to grab April from behind, turning her around in his arms, and then he passionately kissed her. April noticed that Mark was in a cheerful mood; he had his natural sparkle back in his dancing blue eyes.

"Has she come out yet?" Mark asked excitedly as he kissed her again. Now this is living life to the fullest, he cleverly thought as he felt April's body cuddled next to his.

"The bell is just about to ring," she mouthed the words through a kiss. "Mark, there are parents watching us," April said shyly.

"Who cares, let them be jealous," he said with a laugh.

The bell rang and they watched for Sunny. As usual, Sunny came bouncing down the steps. When she saw them together, she smiled and waved to them with gusto. She quickly skipped to them and gave them a group hug.

Mark picked her up in his arms, and he walked away from the crowd at the gate. He found a bench and sat down with her in his lap.

Sunny noticed Mark's reserved smile as he captured the love in her eyes for him. She had seen that look before on his face when something was bothering him, like the day he lost her.

April stood above them, absorbing the tenderness Mark bestowed on his precious angel as Sunny wrapped her arms around his neck.

"So how was your date?" Sunny asked the two with a clever smile as she crossed her fingers behind Mark's neck. She hoped that the two had finished the dating stuff and were ready to get married.

"We had a marvelous time," April confirmed cheerfully.

"That's good, now when are you getting married?" she asked boldly.

Mark and April smiled at each other and looked back at Sunny. April bent down and whispered in her ear. "He hasn't asked me yet."

Sunny looked up at Mark and shook her head and finger at him. "You have to ask her, Mark," Sunny whispered to him.

"I will, just give me a few days," he whispered back to her. "But it is a surprise, so don't tell her." Mark grinned and gave Sunny a wink as she let loose one of her giggles when he playfully tickled her.

Sunny looked up at April with a wide smile. "Dreams do come true, you know." Her eyes were dancing from the joy she felt in her heart. Finally, her Mark was going to marry April, and together they would be her dream come true family.

April glanced at Mark, her eyes begging him for the hope she needed that he would always be there for them. She bit her lip and held her fresh tears back. Mark gave her a comforting gaze before she turned away to wipe the corners of her eyes.

Katie came up to them and instantly admired the way Mark expressed his love for Sunny. There was no doubt Sunny was so in love with this young couple. If only, Katie thought, somehow Sunny could have them as her parents. If only Mark would marry April, they could adopt Sunny, Katie wished deep in her heart for her little friend.

Then suddenly, a chill swept over Katie as she remembered the ring and her promise to Sunny. That ring held the secret of finding Sunny's real parents. *I have to get rid of that ring before someone finds out the truth,* Katie thought, *Sunny loves Mark and April, let them adopt her.*

"Hi, Katie," April said to her warmly as she exhaled and hid her tears.

"Hi folks, Sunny and I have to go," Katie told them regretfully, as she remembered what Blanche had told her sternly about bringing Sunny straight home after school.

"I don't want to go!" Sunny protested. Mark gave her a stern look of disapproval. As much as Mark hated to let Sunny go, he had to make her understand that she had to obey him.

"Oh, all right," she said sadly. Mark gave her an extra big hug and a sad kind of kiss. April bent down, hugged, and kissed her. Then Sunny saw it, the brief worrisome look that April exchanged with Mark.

She jumped to the ground and took Katie's hand as she observed the couple one more time. There was something different about Mark; something was wrong with him, she worried. They knew something they were not telling her, she feared, but what?

"Good-bye, Sunny," Mark and April said at the same time. Sunny turned and walked away, her head tilted downward.

Mark stood up and wrapped his arm around April's waist as they watched the girls walk off. Sadness filled his heart as he watched them walk away.

There is no way that aplastic anemia is going to rob me of becoming that little girl's father, he thought with determination as the distance between them became greater.

April looked at her watch. It was 2:45; they would have to hurry to make it on time to the hospital. Mark saw her look at her watch, knowing full well why she was doing it.

"They will just have to wait; first I am going to make out with my girl in the school yard. Isn't this where you and I were first friends? Do you want to study biology or chemistry?" he joked as he gently tugged her arm so she would fall into his lap. He sat back down on the bench for another engaging kiss that would linger until he was satisfied that she believed life was just beginning for them.

This time April willingly participated as she encased his face with her fingers on each side of his soft cheeks and accepted the fullness of his mouth on her own.

April thought of the time in kindergarten when Mark gallantly rescued her off the monkey bars when her dress was caught on a bolt. Mark had been her very own brave hero! He had not been one bit shy about having a girl for a friend, and he had been ready to bop any kid in the nose who dared to challenge him on that subject.

Mark was about to get an A plus in the course on how to live one's life to the fullest. No one was going to steal his joy, at least not for the next few minutes, he thought with his clever grin. He held April in his arms, claimed her tender lips, and let her completely hold his heart captive during their *one more moment in time* together.

Chapter Forty –
⌒Angels Among Us⌒

It was just after three o'clock when Mark and April walked into the entrance to the ER.

Jeff was nervously waiting by the door, praying with everything that was within him that somehow he could find the strength to go through this illness with Mark.

Mark was his usual good-natured self as he proudly held April around the waist when they walked in and faced Jeff. The smile Mark held on his face was the same one that was always there when he came to work. Only this time he was not coming to work, he was coming as a patient, Jeff despondently thought.

Jeff handed Mark a facemask. Mark held the facemask in his hand and humbly stared down at it as he twisted it between his fingers. When he looked back up, he saw the fearful expression on April's pale face as she stared at the facemask he held. That mask symbolized what the future could hold for them. Mark's way of life was about to change, starting with one simple facemask.

He knew that he should place the mask over his face, but he worried it would upset April further, and he could not do that to her. He took a deep breath as he tucked it in his pocket and gave Jeff one of his well-known smart-alecky looks as he pretended that all was fine.

"I don't need that; save that for your sick patients." Mark smiled, determined to keep the mood upbeat so they could all survive the true emotions they were feeling.

Jeff shook his head and frowned. He told them that Dr. Stevenson and Dr. Morgan were waiting for Mark in the bone marrow transplant unit.

Mark felt uneasy about the location, but he followed behind Jeff as he led the way.

They got into the elevator, and Mark leaned back against the wall. He crossed his arms across his chest and crossed one leg over the other. Mark started whistling the tune to, "Take me out to the ball game." Jeff's eyes got big as he raised his eyebrows, thinking Mark had gone plumb crazy. Mark thinks this is humorous, Jeff thought as he tried to read the hidden thoughts behind Mark's eyes.

When they came out of the elevator, they were faced with the huge words spelled out across the entrance to the wing. There was no denying what it said. **"Bone Marrow Transplant Unit."** Everything in his life would change once he went through those cold doors. Mark got a serious look on his face as he read the unnerving words, and then he drew a deep breath as Jeff opened the heavy door and they went inside.

All the nurses were wearing masks and gowns as they went in and out of the patient's rooms. The rooms looked like the room Mark had stayed in when he was in the ICU unit, with double sliding glass doors. Mark felt the chill bumps going down his back as he remembered that horrible time in his life.

Mark stood there in a stiff daze; he was contemplating turning around and leaving. April reached over compassionately, wrapped her arms around his body and hugged him to her. She silently prayed for Mark as she used his body to hold herself upright.

So this is how it feels to be a patient in this unit, Mark thought as he felt humbled and swallowed the lump in his throat. The reality of the situation hit him hard. *He was not the doctor coming to treat patients; he was the patient.*

April fearfully slid her hand in his. Mark felt the trembling of her hand and gave her a reassuring squeeze. He looked into her delicate eyes but said nothing at all. He was speaking right to her heart as he smiled to let her know that everything was going to be fine. He would be her strength when she was weak.

Rebecca came from behind the nurse's desk. She nervously smiled at them; she put on her mask and gave Mark a warm hug. The mask she wore hid her heartache for Mark. It was the trembling of Rebecca's hands that caught Mark's attention. He instantly took on his sister's reservations about this whole turmoil.

Mark's smile was gone; he could not speak. There was nothing he liked about this situation. He read the pain in his sister's eyes as she did her best to contain her emotions. He felt himself falling fast into a desolate place he had promised himself he would never enter.

"Follow me," Rebecca said as she led them to a room and slid the door open. She took Mark's left wrist, that had his allergy to penicillin bracelet, and placed a plastic hospital medical information bracelet around it and fastened it. *It was official he was the patient.*

She handed Mark the scrubs that were neatly placed on the bed. She avoided his eyes; she just could not bear to drown in the sadness of his face.

"Mark, you have to take a shower and put these on, and leave your clothes in the bathroom," she spoke to him professionally.

"I know the drill, Beck," he said quietly, as he unwillingly took the scrubs from her and went into the bathroom and closed the door.

His pretend act was harder than he had anticipated. If only his so-called illness was not causing those he loved dearly to suffer right along with him, he could have been more successful in handling the senselessness of this alleged illness that he did not have.

He slowly changed out of his clothes, stepped in the shower and turned the water on. He leaned back against the wall thinking as he let the water spray over his well-defined chest.

I am the perfect picture of health, he thought as he rubbed his hand across his muscular pectoral muscles and flexed his strong biceps. *This is not happening; this really stinks. All of this is so ... unnecessary.* He grabbed the disinfecting soap and chuckled, even the soap stinks. He would go crazy if he did not try to find humor in this situation.

Mark knew that he had to stay strong for everyone. No matter how he felt inside, he would have to do something to make them smile. He knew he needed to reassure them that no devil had control over his body. It was just like Mark to be thinking of the others instead of what he would have to endure to beat this illness. The warm spray of the water across his body, brought thoughts of God's promises to wipe clean anything that came against him.

Jeff had gone to tell the doctors that Mark was in his room. Julia and Robert were sitting in the chairs outside the special operating room for bone marrow patients.

They were quietly holding hands as they thought about Mark's illness. This was a parent's worst nightmare, Julia thought, as she held back her tears. She tried to find the words to pray, but to speak them in her mind was too painful. It meant Mark needed God's help, and she was not ready to acknowledge that he was sick.

Just over a year ago, they had watched their son graduate from medical school at the top of his class. *How could this be happening to their son - not their precious Mark – he did not belong here?*

Julia's tender heart realized that her thoughts seemed almost selfish. How many parents had sat in these same chairs not knowing the fate of their child, she wondered, as she said a prayer for all those that had sat here, before her, feeling as she did about their child?

Jeff went in to the operating room and talked to the doctors, and then he went out to sit with Mark's parents. Jeff's parents had sat in those same seats waiting for news on his little brother. It had been Mark that had gotten them all through the tragic death of his brother. Now Jeff was here again, only this time the tragic illness had invaded the life of his best friend Mark.

Julia saw the pain written on Jeff's face for her son. She picked up Jeff's hand to reassure him. Jeff forced himself to smile at her. Then he found himself burying his face in her shoulder and letting her wrap her consoling arms around him as the unwanted tears spilled out of his grief-stricken heart.

April nervously waited for Mark to come out of the bathroom. Rebecca had given her a mask and gown to put on.

Mark came out, shirtless, in scrub pants, bare feet, and wet unruly hair. His unruly hair fit his defiant mood. His six foot three frame was physically fit, outlined in firm muscles. His form was just a tad underweight, but there was no sickness visible other than the awful bruising on his left side and the stitches where the catheter had been. His mischievous eyes instantly claimed hers.

She wanted to fall into his arms and feel his wet body next to hers, but she knew the rules. He looked at her with a frown when he saw her outfit.

"Not you, too," Mark said with a crooked grin, as he crossed the room to her. He pulled her mask down, kissed her tenderly and wrapped his damp arms around her. She resisted him as she pushed back from him, but he held her arms firmly.

"Mark, what are you doing? Behave yourself," April told him seriously. She was afraid that someone might see them and make her leave the room. Her heart wanted him in her arms where she could protect him from any pain the doctors were about to inflict on him.

Still, she knew the guidelines and procedures for this room. She pulled out of his arms and gave him her stern teacher look of disapproval.

"Look, if I am going to be here, then we play by my rules. I am not giving in to this stuffy environment. I am going to have some fun, got that?" Mark said playfully as he reclaimed her in his arms, brushed her hair off her shoulders, and claimed her neck as his own. If only they were not in this room, she would have gladly given in to his desires.

"Yes, Sir, Mark Sanders, let's hope Dr. Stevenson wants to play by your rules," she smiled as he bent his head close to hers.

"If he doesn't, he's fired," Mark said with humor as he kissed her once again before letting her go.

He looked around the room. His smile disappeared from his face as he gathered in his true feelings about his unfriendly surroundings.

Mark was trying to make light of the situation. Deep down Mark had scrutinized the room and hated it. He could not spend one hour trapped in this room let alone eight weeks or more. *Patience, I have to find some patience quick, Lord,* he said to himself.

April sat down in the chair in the corner and watched Mark closely. If only she could close her eyes and take the two of them to a place far away from here. Some place where the sun came up, rose high in the sky and then the brilliant sunset settled over them as they danced to the love they had for each other, she thought as quiet tears nestled at the corner of her eyelids.

Ten minutes passed. *Why do doctors always make you wait?* Mark thought with a smile. He would have to remember never to make his patients wait when he went into private practice. He thought of the country doctor's office that he and Jeff had gone to not so long ago. He smirked, if all else failed here, he planned to give Becky Oliver a call and run-away to the seclusion the country office would offer him.

Mark paced back and forth, looking out the window several times. He was growing restless waiting. The 10' by 10' room was already closing in on him. He would have to do a lot more praying for patience if they kept him caged in this room. The waiting was stirring his anxiety level.

Mark looked over at the bed and saw himself as an eight-year-old boy with a broken leg. He closed his eyes, trying not to think about the memory of being trapped in the cold, dark, wet mineshaft. That horrible memory was still strong in his mind; it made him feel uneasy.

Lord, help me, I can't do this alone. His eyes grew weak as the waiting continued, and his desire to be in control of his life faded away with each tick of the clock on the wall as time took him on a journey he did not want to travel.

Rebecca had been watching Mark's nervousness while she gathered her supplies. She was thankful that she had been allowed to be reassigned to this unit today.

Mark had not been a cooperative patient at the age of eight, eighteen, or last year at age twenty-three. Mark was accustomed to taking orders from his big sister. She had been his mentor their entire childhood. Everyone was counting on her to keep Mark calm this time.

She put on a brave face and went into the room without wearing the facemask that unnerved Mark.

Rebecca knew she had to act professionally and not as his sister. "I need you to sit on the bed so I can start your IV," she instructed Mark and was met with his determined eyes to be in total control.

"I don't need an IV. Dr. Stevenson will use a local for this procedure," Mark irately told her. *What's the deal? What is Dr. Stevenson trying to pull?* Mark thought as he gave Rebecca his suspicious irritated look.

She received the look and gave him one of her own. This was one time her little brother was not going to get his way, even if her heart wanted to grant him anything he wished.

"I am just following orders. Dr. Stevenson wants an IV; you get an IV," she told him sternly and let him know she was not budging. Mark shook his head no at her as she stared him down with squinted eyes and a frown.

"Robert Mark Sanders, get over here, you are acting like a child," she demanded, not backing down to him as their eyes locked on each other just as they had done as siblings. Silence fell for a brief minute as Mark contemplated giving into her.

"Beck," he squinted his eyes at her again.

"Mark," she stood firm.

With a single laugh, Mark let a smile slip out at his sister as he reluctantly moved over and sat down on the side of the bed, keeping his feet firmly planted on the floor. He frowned at Rebecca to let her know that he was not pleased that he had no choice but to surrender to her.

She picked up his left arm, tied the rubber tourniquet tight, swabbed the area and inserted the needle, then taped it in place. She adjusted the intravenous drip. Then she withdrew two tubes of blood from him. When she was finished sticking him with needles, she stood back and faced him. Mark frowned at the IV. She read his mind, "Don't even think about it, Mark."

"What is taking so long?" Mark asked with annoyance.

"They are going over the lab results. It was a busy day in the lab today. Most of our family came to be tested for your bone marrow transplant," she informed him.

Mark did not seem pleased at all that his family had been involved already. The last thing he wanted was to cause them more pain over this mess.

"What? It has not come to that yet; there are many other treatments to try first." He was confused that they were already talking about doing a transplant.

"You are running out of valuable time to find a matching donor. The test results they took on you this morning are much worse than yesterday; your counts are dropping rapidly. The transfusions did not make much of a difference. Dan said it had to do with your spleen. Your immune system is reacting against your bone marrow; you are not making enough blood cells," she said to him as he just blankly stared at her.

"Are they planning on removing my spleen now; is that why you did the IV?" Mark asked angrily. He did not trust anyone after what Jeff had done in the ER. He would have to watch his own back around everyone.

"I don't know," she told him, avoiding eye contact, not wanting to face him. His spleen had to come out, but could they risk the surgery with his blood counts so low? She knew that the doctors had gathered to plan out Mark's treatment, and Dr. Stevenson would be in soon to talk to Mark about their decision.

"Rebecca, don't lie to me," he glared at her, wanting answers.

"Really, I don't know. I am not sure what they decided." She tried to touch his bare shoulder to reassure him but he held his hands up to indicate, do not touch me.

"I don't understand; I feel better than yesterday." Mark shook his head in confusion, his eyes so stressed as he looked at Rebecca for answers.

"You feel better because of the blood and the medications they gave you during the night," she softly answered him, trying with all her might not to let his eyes make her surrender to him.

Mark's frustration was growing; he was running his fingers through his hair nervously. April came over behind him and wrapped her arms around his bare back. Her heart was breaking for him as she touched his warm skin with the palms of her hands.

"Mark, you need to relax," April said warmly as her hands gently rubbed his sturdy back.

He got up off the bed and stood by it. He could not go far with the IV, unless he took the IV pole with him. He had reached his limit. His patience had flown out the door, and he was about to follow.

"I can't do this; I am going to suffocate in this room," he told them both in a sorrowful voice. He closed his eyes and continued to pray that God would give him the patience that he now lacked.

"I am going to get you something to calm you down." Rebecca turned and went out of the room. Dr. Price had left orders for medications to use on Mark if he became anxious.

Rebecca just wanted to burst into tears. This was her little brother for a patient; she hated this for him. It was her job to protect him just as she had done while they were growing up. She had never forgiven herself for not watching him close enough and letting him fall into the mineshaft when he was eight years old. She was his, Beck, the sister he could always count on to rescue him.

April came around the bed and faced Mark. When he saw her sad doe-like eyes, he instantly forgot his own pain and opened his arms to receive her. She was very gentle; seeing his bruises reminded her of the pain he must be feeling. He sat on the edge of the bed and looked in her eyes like a lost puppy.

"I am so confused; I don't know what to do. I am a medical doctor; I know what is going on here. I need everyone to understand that I have to finish what I have started. My boards are on Friday, the AFC Championship

Football Game is on Sunday, the court hearing is coming up about Sunny. I don't have the time to be sick right now," he told her solemnly. "I have to get things in order before I can ever consider living in this room for eight weeks," he told her with such torment in his voice.

Rebecca came back in the room with a syringe; he waved her back away from him. He did not want it. This time she let him have his way.

"Right now I feel so out of control. Dr. Stevenson has taken my job away; he wants me to quit football. I am confined to my apartment, they want to take my spleen out, do a bone marrow transplant, not to mention chemo and radiation treatments, and I am not even sick. Did you hear me, I am not sick," Mark told them with a serious face. Both just stood there, unable to answer him.

It felt good to let out his feelings. But it changed nothing. Right now, he was not feeling joy in this situation. He wanted to rip the IV out and run as fast as he could out the door before his frustration really came out in him.

Dr. Stevenson came into the room. Tom noted the look of discernment on Mark's face. Rebecca let Tom see that she still had the syringe. He took it from her and without saying anything; he injected it into the access port on Mark's IV.

"We're ready for you in the operating room. First, I have some things I need to discuss with you. Do you have any questions you want to ask me?" Dr. Stevenson asked Mark kindly.

"General or local anesthetic?" Mark asked him, keeping an eye on his sister, hoping to prove her wrong.

"General, I am going to do a tunneled central venous catheter, placing it just under your collarbone. Once I am done, we will x-ray it to make sure it is in the right place. Dan wants another x-ray of your ribs and lung, as well as your spleen. If there is still a hemothorax, he will insert another drainage tube. Dr. McGuire wants to run a few tests on your heart while we have you under the general. She is concerned you suffered a blunt cardiac injury (BCI). Dr. Faye Wilson will perform an intercostal rib block. This will take away some of the rib fracture pain for about 12 hours. Hopefully that will bring up your oxygen saturation as you will be able to breathe easier." Dr. Stevenson informed him.

Mark looked overwhelmed; he had absolutely no idea they planned to do all of this. He just stared for a few seconds, taking it all in. They really had taken him out of control of this situation.

"Wow, what about my spleen? What were you planning to do about it?" Mark asked with annoyance in his voice. Mark looked over at the door and was ready to exit. He was dead serious about leaving.

"Mark, you know it has to come out. Any transfusions we do are useless until your spleen is out. Your counts will continue to drop as your spleen swells. We just need you to sign these papers," Dr. Stevenson told him firmly, but with compassion.

Mark knew Tom was right. If he were the doctor in charge, he would be telling his patient the same thing. He had to think quickly about this. There was no way he could let them take his spleen and still play quarter-back in the championship game on Sunday.

Dr. McGuire entered the room and smiled at Mark. She took her stethoscope off her shoulders and headed towards him.

"My spleen is not coming out today. Next Monday morning, it is yours, but for now, I cannot have an incision that keeps me from throwing the football. No drainage tube either. I am doing fine. That is the way it is going to be; it is not up for debate," Mark said with authority as Dr. McGuire listened to his heart. She did not like the rapid heart rate she heard.

Dr. McGuire was not sure if Mark's heart rate was rapid because he was so agitated or if he did have a BCI. Dan had told her about Mark's panic attacks, so she needed to run her tests when he was calm, which meant putting him under.

Dr. Stevenson was not pleased with Mark's decision. Nevertheless, Tom would respect Mark's wishes. He hated treating doctors, especially the ones as knowledgeable and stubborn as Mark. Mark would be hard to get around, he thought.

"You will be in the recovery room for about an hour. I thought you would be more comfortable sleeping. I planned to start you on your first dose of ATG and cyclosporine, steroids, and antibiotics. They are doing another CBC right now, if your platelet count is below ..." Dr. Stevenson started to inform him.

"No more platelet transfusions until we have a matched platelet donor," Mark interrupted with concern in his voice.

"We have a platelet donor," Dr. Stevenson told Mark.

"Who?" Mark asked somewhat puzzled.

"Your father, he's here ready to do an apheresis platelet donation." Dr. Stevenson was pleased to tell him.

"Did you test my family for an HLA match for the bone marrow transplant?" Mark questioned with concern, knowing that his father could be a match and medically, the bone marrow donor should not donate platelets.

"You have really done your homework. We have tested your parents; they are both only a 50% match. Robert has your blood type and can donate platelets. Your mother is not compatible. We are using the blood you had stored at the blood bank for right now."

"Rebecca is a one-antigen mismatch, five out of six; she is the closest related donor we have found. April was surprisingly a one-antigen mismatch also; she will be our second choice, so we will not let them donate blood for you. We will try to find you a matching donor."

"Kevin Brown and his mother Rose will also be able to donate platelets. Jeff, Dan, Maria, Thomas, Charlie, Pedro, Carlo, and all of your teammates were not matches." Dr. Stevenson informed Mark.

"So we don't have a perfect match?" Mark said with disappointment. His GVHD percentage increased with an unmatched donor. (Known as graft-versus-host disease)

"I am going to start you on a G-CSF drug. It will cause your healthy stem cells to leave the marrow and enter your blood, and then we will do a process called leukapherisis. If we end up doing chemotherapy or radiation therapy, we can transplant your stem cells back into your body," Dr. Stevenson said with confidence.

"I have complete trust in your judgment. You're the best, I am glad you are on my team ..." Mark responded.

"But?" Dr. Stevenson interrupted.

"Let me finish out this week. I am going home tonight to study for my boards. If I don't take the boards on Friday, it will be six more months before I can take them." Both doctors frowned at Mark's request.

Dr. Megan McGuire compassionately touched Mark's shoulder. "Mark, your heart is unstable right now. I do not want you to do anything to put more stress on it. We need to find out why your heart is enlarged and start treatment for it."

Dr. Stevenson's face pleaded. "Mark, I need you to stay in isolation. We need to monitor you for reactions to all these powerful drugs. Most of these drugs will take several hours intravenously. You will have to have them over the next few weeks. Cut me a deal here."

Mark noted the ghostly expression on April's face. He would never allow his pain to be her pain. Somehow, he had to spare her the fear that Dr. Stevenson's words had inflicted on her. If he did not take any of this seriously, maybe she would relax; at least it was worth trying. He gave her a playful smile, but got no response from her.

"April stays with me during my surgery. I'm out of here in the morning, in time to go to my lectures. April stays here with me tonight, and I can kiss her anytime I want, otherwise, no deal." Mark grinned as he tried to make them think he had not taken any of this information seriously.

Whatever they had given Mark to relax him was working, they thought. The truth was that Mark had started praying, and God had spoken His words of healing to Mark. Mark looked peaceful as he once again stood firm, he was not even sick; he had nothing to worry about.

"It's a deal. You have to be back in this room as soon as the lectures are finished; now let's go get started," Dr. Stevenson said.

Dr. Stevenson was not pleased at all with Mark's decisions, but he knew that with Mark, he would have to take whatever he could get.

An apheresis donation involves giving one component of blood, usually platelets, but also plasma or red cells. During the apheresis proce- dure, blood is drawn from your arm and passed through a collection kit in a blood-separating machine that separates and collects the platelets, plasma, or red cells and returns the rest of your blood to you. It is an extremely valuable donation. http://www.bloodnj.org/apheresis.htm

Everybody's bone marrow has a certain type. It's kind of like blood- typing. Bone marrow cells have certain proteins or "antigens" on the surface of the cells. They call these proteins Human Leukocyte Antigens (HLA). There are six HLAs that are important when you match someone's bone marrow. Each person receives three from their mom and three from their dad. That is why they look at sisters and brothers first to see if anyone matches. Since the mom can send any three of her six and the dad can send any three of his six to any given kid, it is not often that a single sibling will match his brother or sister, 6 for 6. The chances are 25%. http://machleu-kemia.homestead.com/HLA.html

Petechiae (pronounced pet-TEA-key-eye) are tiny, flat red or purple spots in the skin or the lining of the mouth caused by abnormal bleeding from small blood vessels that have broken close to the skin or the surface of a mucous membrane. Petechiae may spread over a large area of the body within a few hours.

Petechiae spots range from pinpoint-size to BB-size and do not itch or cause pain. They are different than tiny, flat red spots or birthmarks (hemangiomas) that are present all the time. Petechiae do not turn white when a person presses on them.

Petechiae that develop quickly over a few hours may mean that a serious infection or lack of platelets (part of the body's defense against bleeding) has developed and requires immediate medical treatment.

http://my.webmd.com/hw/health_guide_atoz/stp1380.asp?navbar=hw80304

Chapter Forty-One –

A Single Ray of Hope

April kissed Mark before Dr. Stevenson led him to the operating room, then she went to get dressed to go into the operating room with Mark.

Mark stopped to get a hug from his parents and Rebecca before entering the room. He hated that they looked so worried; their pain reflected in their distressed eyes. Mark would have done anything to spare them the pain they were feeling because of him.

Jeff stood against the wall, facing away from Mark. There was no way that Jeff could face his best friend with his eyes so swollen from the tears he had just shed.

Mark slowly turned his head in Jeff's direction. His gaze fell on his friend, and sadness filled his heart knowing the pain that Jeff was suffering. As much as Mark wanted to embrace Jeff, he decided it would be better not to say anything to him while Jeff was so upset.

Rebecca noted Mark's hesitation to speak to Jeff and understood. Jeff needed more time to adjust to Mark's illness. She sympathetically took Mark's arm gently and led him inside the operating room.

Dr. Faye Wilson, the anesthesiologist, shook Mark's hand and then gave him a warm hug; she was from Mark's church. Sally Johnson had come to be the head scrub nurse. Dan and Steven were planning to do the surgery and to assist Dr. Stevenson.

"The splenectomy is out; Mark has refused to let us do it until Monday." Dr. Stevenson disappointedly reported to the others. Dan's face showed disappointment. How was he going to save Mark's life if Mark would not let him? It was so much easier when Mark was a little boy, and Dan could tell him what to do.

Steven pulled off his surgical gloves angrily and stepped out of the room. They had hoped to slide the surgery in before Mark had a chance to refuse it. Now there was nothing more Steven could do for his hardheaded brother-in-law. The other surgical nurses left the room.

April had put on her surgical mask and helped Mark carefully lay down on the table. Dr. Faye Wilson hooked him up to the monitors. She placed an oxygen mask over his face. Sally placed a surgical sheet over Mark's legs up to his bare waist.

Dan led the group in a prayer as he held Mark's hand in his, the same hand that he had held when Mark was a small boy. As far as Dan was concerned, Mark was his son. April held Mark's other hand in hers.

Mark was just 24 years old. All his life he had been expected to act more mature than his actual age. Nothing could have prepared him to understand completely what he was facing; not even being a doctor would grant him the understanding of how to deal with his illness, Dan thought.

Then Dr. Wilson injected the general anesthetic into Mark's IV. Mark's eyelids got sluggish, and he welcomed the sleep that quickly came. April continued to hold his hand as she spoke encouraging words into his ear.

Sally handed Dr. Stevenson Mark's latest CBC report. Dr. Stevenson ordered another platelet transfusion. A second IV was started.

Dr. McGuire hooked Mark up for an EKG and then she did an echocardiogram. She injected Mark with a medication to bring his heart rate under control. She was satisfied that his enlarged heart was from his aplastic anemia and not from a BCI. Mark's heart had to work harder because of his low blood counts; this meant that he had AA for quite a while, which had enlarged his heart.

Dr. McGuire did not want to take any chances that it could have been a BCI. She told Dr. Stevenson that Mark was not to play football or lift heavy weights. His tachycardia still had her concerned. (1)

They did an x-ray of his spleen, and it was still enlarged but there was no more bleeding seeping from it. April knew that Mark had received his first healing.

Dr. Stevenson believed Mark's enlarged spleen was causing the reduction in his peripheral blood count. Dr. Stevenson felt that his spleen was responsible for the transfusions not working. He was concerned it might rupture at any time. A football injury to his abdomen could be catastrophic.

Dr. Faye Wilson did the intercostal rib block. They took another x-ray to make sure the injections did not allow air in his chest. The block would make it easier for Mark to breathe without as much pain.

The transfusion was almost finished, so Sally prepared the area on Mark's upper chest for surgery. They were preparing for excessive bleeding; they would give Mark a unit of his own whole blood.

Dr. Stevenson made two incisions, one over the vein where the catheter was inserted and the other where the catheter emerged from the skin. Dan had to suction the blood from the incisions so that Dr. Stevenson could continue.

He placed the catheter beneath the skin between the two incisions. Then he gently threaded the catheter into the vein. They took an x-ray to make sure everything was correctly located. He placed two small stitches, one at each end of the tunnel. They waited for the bleeding to stop from the incisions. Then he put a dressing on the incisions.

"Remind me to tell Mark he cannot go swimming with this catheter. I do not want him to get an infection," Dr. Stevenson told Dan.

Sally drew two tubes of blood for the lab. She left the room with them.

Dr. Stevenson started the new medications one by one, waiting 30 minutes between them. The others would drip into the catheters for the next several hours. Dan covered Mark up with a warm blanket. Now they would watch him carefully for reactions.

Dan loved Mark like a son; it was unbearable to see him lying there so helpless. He touched Mark's forehead and prayed. God, please spare his young life.

Shortly after giving Mark a small dose of ATG, his face and neck flushed, his heart rate became irregular; he had difficulty breathing. When his blood pressure dropped, they knew he was going into anaphylaxic shock. They immediately began treatment to reverse the reaction. For the next 30 minutes, everyone was extremely tense as Mark continued to struggle breathing.

Mark's reaction was worse than any reaction that Tom had ever experienced with an AA patient. Dr. Stevenson was thankful they had taken the precautions and had Mark in the OR where they could quickly treat him.

Tom and Dan knew that Mark would have to be given extremely small doses gradually to reduce his body's severe reactions to the ATG. Both men held grave faces as the thought of Mark rejecting the drugs he needed to beat AA could only lead to one conclusion. If Mark could not tolerate these treatments, he would be in serious trouble.

Earlier in the day, Dr. Stevenson had met with Dr. Raymond and Coach Walker in his office. By now, the entire team was waiting for answers.

"As far as I am concerned, Mark's football career is over, until we can get his blood counts under control. It may take up to a year before he recovers from this. One cut could cause a major bleed, which could mean instant death for him.

"Mark is determined he is going to play Sunday. That has to be his decision. You can bench him; or play him for shorter periods of time; that is your decision."

"You need to meet with all the players and inform them of Mark's condition. No one with a simple cold should be anywhere near him. Set up a shower and toilet stall just for him. He is not to drink from the water cooler. Stock bottled water for him to drink on and off the field. He is not to eat or drink after anyone," Dr. Stevenson warned.

"Limit all contact. No tackling, no high fives, no hand slaps, no backslaps. Tell your players to keep their hands off of him," Dr. Stevenson warned the men.

"Any signs of bleeding, from the nose or mouth, he goes straight to the hospital. If he plays Sunday, Dan, Jeff, and I will all be there. We will have everything we need to treat him quickly. Robert will have his helicopter on standby to transport him if we need to do that."

"Mark does not want the media to know he is sick. I know this will be impossible, but let's keep it quiet as long as possible."

"I want you to go through your players medical charts and find players with type O negative blood. Contact them and have them come to the hospital today to be tested for a platelet match. If they have any family members with the same blood type, I want them to come as well."

"Get in touch with the other team's coach and let him know about Mark's condition. Ask him to help us find a donor for Mark."

"If you have any questions, here is my card." Dr. Stevenson stood up and shook everyone's hand.

April had gone back to Mark's apartment to get his medical books. She noted that one of his medical books was open to blood disorders. So Mark had known all along that he was sick, she thought, her heart aching, knowing the burden that Mark had been carrying alone to spare all of them.

Then she noticed the most important book of all; Mark's Bible lay open near his pillow. She picked it up and read where he had left off reading. Touched by the words, she cried as her heart received the comforting words that Mark had discovered.

"By God's stripes I am healed. No sickness will come against Me!" Mark had written in pen.

April and Jeff would stay with Mark tonight. Jeff really needed Mark's help with the studying. She gathered a few things Mark might need.

How could this be happening to them? After all they had been through to be together and now this. *Why, God, tell me that?* It made no sense to her as she held Mark's things in her hands.

She took the Bible with her as she went into the living room. Seeing another one of his medical books lying on the coffee table, she set the other books down, so that she could pick up the book and see what it was about. After thumbing thought it, she decided to leave it on the table. When she picked up the other books, she unintentionally left the Bible sitting there on the coffee table.

She stopped and talked to the Browns and thanked them for coming to the hospital. Rose had made cookies, but April told her that Mark was not allowed homemade food.

She put everything in her car. She was driving along the park, and was about to pass by the children's home, when she saw Sunny sitting outside on the steps. She stopped abruptly. Sunny ran to her car. She looked depressed.

"Hi, Sunny, give me a hug," April said as she got out of her car. Sunny hugged her weakly.

"What is wrong, Sunny?"

"I miss Mark. He didn't look very good today, is he sick?"

"Mark is sick, Sunny. He is in the hospital right now, but he is going to be fine, don't worry about him. I am taking good care of him."

"Can we go see him right now?" Sunny begged. "I'll go tell Katie I am with you." Sunny ran inside before April could say anything. She came out a few minutes later.

"I can go, let's hurry," she said excitedly, thinking of seeing Mark.

April did not have the heart to tell her no. The doctor had told Mark, no contact with children. Mark was making all the rules; maybe he could get away with breaking this one.

Mark was taken back to his room to sleep off the last effects of the general. When he woke up, he had mild pain in his chest where the catheter had been placed. He was hooked up to several IV bags of fluids containing his new medications. The IVs in his arms were still in place. He was hooked up to the heart monitor and had oxygen prongs in his nose.

Rebecca came in the room to check on Mark. He was still drowsy as he turned onto his side and wrapped the pillows around him. Rebecca carefully arranged the tubing and wires for him. She noted that he was pale.

"Mark, how are you feeling?" Rebecca sat on the bed beside him. She was wearing her facemask. She put the head of the bed up slightly for him.

"Is that mask really necessary? I am not doing chemo."

"I don't want you to catch anything from me."

"Where are the folks?" he asked sleepily as she took his hand in hers and embraced his fingers.

"They flew back to the ranch. Mom is not taking this very well." Rebecca looked deep into her brother's eyes with sadness.

"Everyone is over-reacting. I am fine; all I needed was some sleep. So, how did everything go?" he asked hesitantly.

"You gave us a scare, but you are just fine. All your x-rays were good; there was no fluid around your lungs, and your spleen has not gotten any larger since your last films. You are scheduled to have it out on Monday," she told him warmly; she noticed that he seemed uncomfortable.

"I'm feeling sick to my stomach," he told her as he moved around in the bed trying to find a comfortable position. He was itching all over. She handed him a plastic pan and went to get him something to calm his stomach. She came back and injected the medication into the access port on his IV.

She took a cool washcloth and wiped his forehead. He seemed better after a few minutes. She gave him a drink of water from his water pitcher. He took a sip of the water, then he made a strange face and set it back down.

April knocked on the door and came in. She had her sterile gown on over her street clothes. Mark gave her a warm look. She smiled back. She did not move from the doorway.

"I'll let you two be alone." Rebecca smiled at them and left.

April walked slowly to the bed. Mark thought she was walking strangely. When she got to the bed, she stepped aside. Sunny jumped out and yelled surprise. She too had on a child's sterile gown and a tiny facemask.

Mark grabbed Sunny up on the bed and rejoiced at having her in his arms. Mark instantly forgot how sick he was feeling when he saw Sunny. He pulled her facemask down so it sat under her chin. He wanted to see her bright smile.

April sat down on the bed with them. The three looked like a precious family, hugging, tickling, and laughing. Their hospital surroundings were quickly forgotten in their rejoicing of being together in this celebration of having each other.

Dr. Stevenson came in the room and looked at the three on the bed. What caught his eye was the child on the bed. Mark and April both noticed that Tom's complete attention was focused on Sunny as he stared at her.

Would he make Sunny leave? April feared. Then she quickly prayed that just this once, Dr. Stevenson would allow Mark to visit with Sunny.

"Mark, I thought you and April did not have a child?" Dr. Stevenson asked confused. Dr. Stevenson's face lit up with excitement as he looked back at Sunny.

"What do you mean?" Mark asked somewhat confused.

"Your little girl here could be the key to your HLA match," Dr. Stevenson told Mark with encouragement.

April turned as white as a sheet. She had not thought about that. Mark looked at Sunny with a big smile and then at the doctor.

"This is Sunny; she will be my adopted daughter soon." Mark set the doctor straight as he hugged Sunny to his chest, wishing with all his heart that Sunny was his own child.

Dr. Stevenson still looked confused as he saw the resemblance between all of them. Sunny and April favored each other, and Sunny definitely had Mark's blue eyes. She was the mirror image of the couple.

"Hello, Sunny," Dr. Stevenson said and shook her hand gently.

"Hello, are you going to make my Mark better?" she asked in her sweet voice that no one with a heart could possibly deny.

"I sure am," he smiled at her and then he faced Mark. "Mark, do you need anything? I was about to head home." Dr. Stevenson asked caringly as he continued to wonder about Sunny.

"I have everything I need right here," Mark smiled warmly as he hugged Sunny closer to him, making her giggle in delight.

Dr. Stevenson saw the obvious love that Mark had for this little girl. Sunny was certainly the best medicine Mark needed. If only Sunny had been Mark and April's natural child, she might have been a perfect bone marrow match for Mark. Dr. Stevenson shook his head back and forth, as that thought crossed his mind.

"Good-night, Sunny," Dr. Stevenson said with a friendly smile, yet a hint of disappointment was heard in his voice.

"Bye," Sunny cutely waved at him keeping her other hand securely around Mark's neck.

Dr. Stevenson turned and went out of the room. When he saw Sunny, he thought he had found Mark's miracle. Right now, Mark's life needed a miracle. Dr. Stevenson stopped and instructed the nurses to allow Sunny in the room with Mark as long as she was wearing a child's facemask over her face.

April told Sunny it was time to go, and she took Sunny back to the children's home. April stopped at her apartment to cry. She had not realized that Mark would have a chance of an HLA match with his child.

If only I knew where our child was, April thought with despair. Mark's life might depend on her finding their daughter. How was she going to face him; how was she going to tell him the truth? She tried desperately to call Lewis, but was told that he had gone out of town.

Marty from housekeeping came in Mark's room and emptied the trashcan. He had on his facemask so that Mark could not see his face. He cleaned off the nightstand by Mark's bed. Then he picked up the water pitcher and asked Mark if he wanted fresh water.

Mark told him yes and Marty took the pitcher into the bathroom. He suspiciously took something from his pocket and placed it in the pitcher, and then he went and got Mark fresh ice and brought it back and handed it to Mark.

Mark drank from the pitcher; he handed it back to Marty and thanked him. Marty left the room with an evil smirk on his face, satisfied at what he had done.

Jeff came into Mark's hospital room with his pile of books and plopped them on the table. Jeff looked at Mark on the bed. It hurt his heart to see his friend like this, but he forced a smile.

When Mark told Jeff that Dr. Stevenson had mistaken Sunny as his own daughter, Jeff told Mark he needed to think seriously about having his own child, the sooner the better, if he wanted one.

"With Chemo treatments, you may not be able to have your own children," Jeff told Mark with concern, knowing that Mark wanted a family someday.

Mark had already thought about the possibility of never being able to father a child. He did not want April to have to give up having children if they were married someday.

Mark had planned to ask April to marry him before all this mess started, but now it did not seem to be the right time to ask her. More than anything, he wanted to be her husband, her soul mate, her spiritual leader, the father of her children. He wanted to hold her in his arms and protect her for the rest of her life.

It pained him now that he might not be the man she deserved. He would never imprison her to him if there was any possibility that he was not going to survive aplastic anemia. She deserved to have her first relationship with her husband, and if he could not guarantee he would live a normal life, he would not ask her to be committed to him as his wife.

Jeff saw the pain in Mark's face as he explained his thoughts about April. Jeff was speechless but offered his friend a reassuring hug.

April came back to the hospital to find the two men studying. Mark's spirits were upbeat considering his current situation.

Mark insisted she lay on the bed while he and Jeff studied at the table. Mark removed all the lead wires to his chest so that he could sit at the table.

April frowned at Mark as he unhooked everything. Mark was certainly going to be a challenging patient, April thought as she watched him act like a schoolboy heading for the playground as he jumped off the bed. She handed him his water pitcher and watched as he gulped down a drink from it.

She had fallen asleep quickly. When she awoke an hour later, she discovered that Mark had stretched out beside her and had his body curled around hers. His closeness felt right. Even if they were not joined together as husband and wife, she would lie in his secure arms tonight.

Her mind gave way to thoughts of them. Would she stand across from him and vow her entire heart to him? She prayed that one day she would lie in his arms in the solitude of their own home. She knew that he would then love her with every inch of his body, heart, and soul. She felt his peace with every breath of air that he drew, and then she went back to sleep in his protective arms.

Jeff planned to spend most of his time studying that night while April cuddled in Mark's arms on the bed. He looked over at the two. Both had fallen asleep in the comfort and security of each other. Jeff claimed victory for him. Mark would one day take April as his wife. He closed his weary eyes and fell asleep.

It had been a long day. What would tomorrow bring?

FYI- HLA testing done on children of Aplastic Anemia parents. Since Mark would pass 3 of his 6 antigens to his child, he would need for his child's mother to just happen to have and pass the other 3 that he already had to their child.

This would give that child a 6-6 match with Mark. The doctors would only test the child if the mother had three of Mark's six antigens.

Dr. Stevenson knew that April had 5 of Mark's 6 antigens. There was an 83% chance of them having a child that matched Mark perfectly. Mark's only miracle left.

CHAPTER FORTY-TWO –
Finding Faith to Battle the Darkness

April had awoken around ten to find Mark feeling extremely sick. She got off the bed and woke Jeff up to help her care for him.

Mark had broken out in a sweat, yet he was cold and shaking violently. He was in the fetal position holding his stomach. He complained it was hard to breathe. He had hives all over his body. This was a sign of rejecting the drugs, or so they thought.

Mark had severe stomach cramps and a relentless headache. April tried her best to comfort him. She wrapped him in blankets and ran her fingers through his damp hair, desperately trying to comfort him.

Her comfort was short lived as he quickly grabbed the pan from her as the sick feeling he had became a driving nausea and it welled up in his throat. The blood drained from Mark's face as he continued to empty his stomach. April knelt on her knees behind him and held his back in her arms. Please God, stop his suffering, she begged with all her heart.

He continued to moan in pain, holding his forehead with both hands and rocking back and forth. The pounding was as if a thousand little hammers were attacking him. Once again, his empty stomach convulsed to rid itself of the burning liquid, but he produced nothing as he shook from head to toe. Then he had a nosebleed and coughed up blood.

He wanted them to stop the drugs they were giving him. They were killing him, he thought, as he suffered unbelievable pain. His frustration increased as the pain seized all his strength to tolerate his desperate condition.

He determinedly grabbed at the one remaining IV in his arm. He frantically wanted to stop the lethal drugs invading his body.

"Mark, you have to leave your IV in!" Jeff and April tried to calm him down and prevent him from using his other hand to disconnect the IV. However, they were unsuccessful as Mark proved to be too strong for them and finally he managed to rip the IV out of his arm. Satisfied, he lay back exhausted from the battle. He held his head with both hands and prayed for the pain to stop.

Jeff was in a panic; this whole scene was a reminder of his little brother's unsuccessful battle. Jeff called Dr. Stevenson, begging for relief for Mark. He looked over at Mark and tears swelled in his eyes. The feeling of helplessness consumed him.

How could he watch Mark die? There was no way that he could handle the kind of suffering that Mark was going through. He wanted to run as far away as he could and block it all out.

Suddenly, an unexpected strength came from out of nowhere and instead, Jeff reached out his hand, took Mark's hand, and squeezed it tightly and gave Mark what little comfort he could offer. Jeff was astonished that his touch amazingly calmed Mark's breathing down.

Jeff looked up and searched Mark's uncommonly clear eyes. Mark was quietly praying between the waves of pain that relentlessly assaulted him. Oddly, Mark was not cursing God; he was praising God. Jeff knitted his eyebrows together. How, how could Mark be praying like this, Jeff wondered as he watched Mark continue to shake violently, and he heard the stuttering sounds of words form from Mark's lips.

"God please, please God, please, please, please God." Mark's voice was barely understandable. "Thank you, God, thank you. Lord of heaven and earth … as I stumble through the dark, I will call your name … reveal your heart to me."

April rubbed Mark's forehead and ran her fingers repeatedly through his hair. She begged again that he find the peace he was seeking from God.

Sally disconnected the new medications in his catheter. Mark was unable to tolerate them at this time. Once again, Mark's reaction was abnormal, not one that Dr. Stevenson had seen other AA patients experience. Mark had Dr. Stevenson completely baffled.

Dr. Stevenson ordered medications to counteract the ones Mark had been allergic to and told Sally to call him back in thirty minutes with a report on Mark's condition.

Sally administered them into his catheter. She gave him a strong pain medication and placed an oxygen mask over his face. She put him back on the heart monitor and called Dr. McGuire for orders. Everyone waited nervously for the drugs to work.

An hour later, he was more relaxed and able to fall back asleep. Sally drew blood and sent it to the lab. Sally told April that Mark would probably be sick for a few days from the drugs they had given him. Dr. McGuire arrived and stabilized his heartbeat.

Jeff was afraid to go to sleep. He wanted to keep a watchful eye on Mark. He picked up one of his books to study. He was unsuccessful; his mind was on the scene that had played before him. How did Mark find it in his heart to praise a God who let him suffer like he had? The same God that had let his brother die. Jeff thought about his own inadequate relationship with God.

It was Mark who stood on God's side. Somehow, Mark believed he was on God's varsity team. Mark never blamed God, never resented Him, and one way or another Mark endlessly trusted God.

Jeff thought God had deserted him when his brother died, but Mark had stood firm and claimed God was the one holding him up. Jeff wanted to believe in Mark's kind of God. He prayed God would show him how he could believe as Mark did.

I don't want to be on your second string team, God, move me up to varsity with Mark. Heal Mark, God, and I will trust you. I'll bat a hundred percent if you will do this for me, God. Jeff continued to have a one-way conversation with God until he had fallen back asleep on the recliner.

However, April was unable to fall asleep right away. She kept thinking about what Dr. Stevenson had said about Sunny.

If only she and Mark had had a child, that child would have a chance of being a perfect match. The truth would have to come out. Their child would have to be located. Would Jessica's new parents give her up to them? Would Mark ever forgive her for letting go of their child? She would try to call Lewis again in the morning.

She reached over to get a drink from Mark's water pitcher but she accidentally knocked it on the floor. She picked it up and threw it away. She went and got him a new one.

Tuesday morning came. Mark had been sick again at midnight and then again at three A.M. so they gave him additional medications to help calm his stomach and a stronger pain medication in an effort to relieve some of his stomach pain.

April was in a panic as she watched Mark suffer. She hugged him to her and tried to offer him comfort while they waited for the medications to work. He drifted off and stayed asleep in April's arms for the remainder of the early morning.

Sally gave Mark another round of medications at six-thirty and hoped that he would remain asleep. Then she went into the nurse's lounge to get a cup of coffee and offer up a prayer for Mark.

Dr. Stevenson came to the hospital early to check on Mark. All deals were off. Mark was too sick to leave the hospital. Now all Dr. Stevenson had to do was tell Mark that.

Dr. Stevenson quietly slipped into the room only to find April sleeping on the bed alone. Jeff was asleep on the recliner. Mark was not there. Mark's IV tubes were dangling from the pole. After checking the bathroom and finding Mark's scrubs in the shower, Tom knew that his patient had deserted.

Dr. Stevenson woke up Jeff and April. They were as surprised as he was to find that Mark had disappeared. Jeff looked at his watch, seven-thirty. He gathered up his books in a hurry and headed out of the room. Lectures were at nine. Knowing Mark, that is exactly where they would find him.

April too fled quickly; she headed back to the apartments. Mark's car was there. She went to his apartment and used the key he had given her to unlock the door.

CHAPTER FORTY-THREE –
The Power of Love

*M*ark was on the couch studying. April was very upset with him for scaring her and she stomped over to him. He looked up at her and smiled as if nothing could possibly be wrong. That made her madder. He smiled again; she was so cute when she was mad.

"What do you think you are doing?" she asked sternly.

"Studying?" he teasingly answered her as he held up his book.

She grabbed the book out of his hand. She was fired up. "Mark Sanders, you make me so mad!" she said harshly.

Mark put his arms up and crossed them, to protect himself from the book she was about to clobber him with. She threw it on the floor instead.

He saw an opportunity and took it. He grabbed her arms and pulled her onto the couch on top of him. Before she could protest, he had her locked in his arms and was tenderly kissing her.

Her anger quickly evaporated as his kiss left her completely breathless. Her heart leaped wide open as his arms encased her against his chest. April ran her fingers through his hair and caressed his face in her hands.

"Mark, you feel like you have a fever," she worriedly said, as she remembered what Sally had told her and cast him a somber look.

"The only fever I have is for you," he spoke cheerfully, kissing her again, as he disregarded her words and concentrated on the sweet taste of her neck.

"No, I am serious. You have a fever," she said as she moved, and when she did, she accidentally elbowed him in his chest. Mark jerked in pain and groaned. She carefully slid off him onto the floor.

"I'm so sorry, Mark, are you alright?"

Mark rubbed his ribs and then slid off the couch beside her on the floor, and pushed the coffee table away from them.

He turned his body toward hers; he put his arm across her, and lifted himself up on his arm so he was over her, looking down at her delicate face. He studied her face and she studied his, each of them thinking of the love they had for the other.

"I love you, April Morgan," he said sweetly with such love in his voice. They were so close to each other, their noses almost touched.

"I love you, Mark Sanders." She lifted her hands up to cup the sides of his face, and they kissed with such passion she thought she was going to dissolve.

As he continued passionately kissing her, she could hear and feel his heart beating for her. The truth of his love for her was in his tender eyes as he stared deeply into her inviting eyes. She reached up and felt the outline of his jaw with her fingertips. She smoothed his day's growth on his face with the palms of her hands.

He reached up and ran his finger down the bridge of her nose, and then he outlined her lips with his index finger. He wanted to sketch every inch of her body.

The touches of his tender hands on her were warm and gentle. Tears swelled up in her eyes, as she felt so much love for him. She closed her eyes as he kissed her neck and sent uncontested waves throughout her body.

As her hands felt his bandage under his shirt, her mind was suddenly flooded with the horrible memories from the night before. Fear instantly filled her heart, and her body became taut as she lost interest in loving Mark.

Her hands remained loosely around his back as he teased her neck with tender kisses. She took a shallow breath to keep her tears in check as her mind filled with sadness.

He had endured relentless pain just hours ago as he begged God for peace and mercy. God had answered his prayers this time and delivered him out of his darkness and gave them this exclusive time together.

What if I never get the chance to be with him again? She could scarcely breathe now as that fear pierced her heart. What if they never got the chance to continue dating, or worse, what if she never got to marry him?

She knew that death could unfairly steal him away from her at any moment. April could not bear the thought that this romantic moment alone with Mark might be her last. She had waited six long years to have him back in her life. She held him closer and relaxed her body against his.

More than ever now, she needed Mark to love her so she would know that he was hers forever. As his tender kiss brushed against her lips, she silently prayed with God, asking Him to spare Mark's life so they could have an eternity of loving each other.

Then, tearfully, she remembered Mark's promise to God. The question was, at this very tranquil moment in time, was he remembering? More than ever, she wanted to honor his promise, but her convictions were shattered as she continued to have thoughts that she might never have these kinds of moments with him again. Her heart trembled.

Every moment alone with him was on borrowed time. She closed her eyes again as her uncertain thoughts gave way, and she was willing to forget his promise. She freely let herself become absorbed by his love in this tender moment that not even death could take away from them.

She melted into his very existence with her and cleared her mind of all thoughts except the ones to love him back with every fiber of her body. She would not hold back as she claimed his face in her hands and drew him to her lips.

For those brief minutes, they were able to forget they had no control over what the rest of their future held for them. They enjoy this moment in time with each other in the gentle quiet innocence of their kissing and touching and loving each other with their hearts.

Mark's flesh had wanted more, but he would not let himself take her as his own, not now, not unless he married her first. He drew the line of their intimacy and did not cross over it, much to her disappointment.

She now wanted to capture every part of him in order to give her a lifetime memory of him to keep with her when he was gone. His words of love for her filled her mind as he promised to love her forever.

The alarm clock that Mark had set went off, and Mark turned over on his back. He did not want to move; he wanted to keep April in his arms forever. However, he knew he only had thirty minutes to get to class.

Besides, April was making it impossible for him to keep his promise to God to wait to explore the pleasures of husband and wife until after they were married. *Thanks, God, for the alarm, we needed it,* he thought with a warm smile. Then he promised himself not to let things get so out of control in the future.

"I have to take a shower and go to my lectures," he told her as he got up. He held his hand out to her and helped her up off the floor. Disappointment showed on her face, as she was not willing to give him up so soon. He gave her a consolation kiss on the forehead.

Then he went into the other room to shower. His stomach started wrenching painfully, and he folded his arms against his stomach, refusing the sick feeling, until it passed.

He gave thanks for his time with April, being with her had been a blessing with no pain, no sickness. Even as brief as it had been, he was grateful.

He took the pain pills that Jeff had given him and prayed that he could fool everyone into believing that he was fine. He had thrown up blood just before April had entered his apartment.

He prayed he could have a few more days to get everything he needed to do, done, and then if he wasn't already healed, he would surrender himself to Dr. Stevenson's care.

April made coffee and soft buttered toast while she waited for him. She leaned against the counter in deep thought about her time with Mark on the floor. After giving it serious thought, she was thankful that Mark had honored his promise to God and waited. She cherished the thought that he had respected and loved her enough to wait. She quietly prayed that she would be given the chance to love him completely on their wedding night.

Mark came out dressed, with his wet hair neatly combed. April could not help but notice how handsome he was as he stood there and admired her beauty. His playful smile lit up the entire room as he headed in her direction and took ownership of her in a hug and placed a soft kiss on her cheek.

He sat down at the bar next to her. He looked at the toast but did not touch it.

"Dr. Stevenson was not pleased with your exit this morning," she told him with those teacher eyes of hers.

"He will get over it," Mark joked as he played with a strand of her hair. "He told me yesterday I could go to my lectures."

"That was before you got so sick last night. Are you going back to the hospital after your lectures?" she curiously wanted to know.

"I told him I would; I'll keep my promise," he responded as he stared into those eyes of hers that put him back under her alluring spell. He leaned over, swiped the hair from her neck and kissed her. He knows just how to charm his way out of trouble, she thought.

"I don't understand why you are in such a good mood this morning after what happened to you last night," she stated simply as their lips met. "You were so sick last night."

"I choose to get out of bed every day and have a positive attitude. I tell myself each morning: this is going to be a great day. Having you in my arms this morning on the floor proves that it works." He smiled as she blushed, and he stole a kiss.

"Really, Mark, I just don't understand how you can be so positive."

"It's like this, I had symptoms of the flu last night, thousands of people have the flu today, and I am not one of them, so today is going to be a great day. I am not living according to what happened yesterday. God gave me a new day, and it is up to me to enjoy it."

If his statement was not convincing enough, his warm kiss on her soft lips was. This time she took control before he sent her on another skyrocket of emotions.

"I am going to get Sunny after school and take her to the park, and then we will come see you," April said cheerfully. He had her hand in his and kissed each one of her fingers tenderly. This was a great start to a wonderful day, he told himself with his dazzling smile.

"That sounds great. I will think about that all day," he smiled as he continued to tease her with his playfulness.

"Eat your toast," she laughed as he made her quiver from his enticing touches.

"I can't even look at it. My stomach is messed up. I can't even keep water down," he admitted to her seriously, as he stopped touching her. She could hear the concern and frustration in his voice even if he was trying to hide it from her. If he was worried, something must not be right.

"Call Dan, he'll give you something to calm your stomach," April offered. She reached up and combed his hair through her slender fingers.

"I plan to get something before I go to the lectures, so I better hurry. Remember, today is a great day, because I love you!" he said as he got up. He kissed her cheek, grabbed his keys, and was out the door.

April was amazed at Mark's good humor. He really had given this whole situation over to the Lord and found humor in it. Although he hated everything there was about the hospital, he was being good natured and cheerful about it with her.

She found it hard to keep her smile when she was alone. She sat and prayed that she too could have Mark's positive outlook on life. She touched her warm lips, closed her eyes and thought of him.

He had given her another memory she never wanted to forget.

CHAPTER FORTY-FOUR –
❦Holding On to Hope❧

*M*ark had gone to the review lectures. His pain medication had worn off quickly. He was very uncomfortable. His ribs hurt, his stomach was burning, and his skin still itched, so he got up and went into the hall. Jeff followed him out.

"Are you all right?" Jeff asked with concern. Mark was very pale and sweating.

"It is so stuffy in there. I am going to get some fresh air and come back," Mark told him. Jeff wanted to follow him but Mark insisted that Jeff go back to the room without him.

Jeff reluctantly went back inside the room, and Mark went outside the building. He walked off campus to the main street where the small shops were located.

His stomach was churning now in fierce waves, as the devil reminded him that he was sick; he could not deny it at this moment.

He came to a jewelry store and looked at the rings in the window. His heart wanted so much to go in and buy April an engagement ring, but he could not do it to her.

He could not trap her into whatever uncertainty lay ahead for him. The sweat was running down the side of his face; he was feeling sicker as he thought.

He leaned on the window for support and saw a gold necklace. Then he had a flashback of him putting his class ring on April's finger. Then it was gone. He closed his eyes. He was dizzy; the ground under him was spinning. That was all he remembered before he hit the pavement.

He heard voices speaking to him, he heard sirens blaring, he felt someone touching him, but he could not respond before everything around him went black.

When he woke up, everything was fuzzy, but he could make out the figures in front of him: Dan and Dr. Stevenson, Rebecca and Sally. He was back in isolation.

He was hooked up to all the machines and monitors, IV lines in his chest catheter, and oxygen prongs in his nose. His stomach was screaming relentless pain. Had they removed his spleen, he wondered? The wall clock was at two o'clock; he had lost four hours of his day. He closed his eyes and went back to sleep.

April had gone to pick up Sunny after school. They went to the park. They sat on "*Mark's Bench*" as Sunny called it.

"How is Mark?" Sunny asked, sad that Mark could not join them.

"Mark is doing better, but the doctors want him to sleep all day so he will get stronger," she told Sunny warmly and hugged her.

"So we can't go see him?" Sunny asked sadly.

"Not today," April told her. Sunny cuddled closer to April.

"So did he ask you yet?" Sunny asked hopefully.

"Ask me what?" April smiled at the little devilish matchmaker.

"To marry us," Sunny laughed.

"Not yet, but I have a feeling he will." She smiled and tickled Sunny.

"Oh, goodie, I can't wait."

April held her closer. She needed to fill her arms with the love of this small child.

"I've been thinking, Sunny, how would you feel if I asked the courts for custody of you since they won't give you to Mark?"

"Oh, could you, do you think you can do that?" Sunny said excitedly.

"My chances have to be better than Mark's and it's worth a try."

"I really love you," Sunny said as they hugged.

Then she had run over to the monkey bars and April watched her play. That same boy from the other day joined Sunny. April was glad that Sunny had a distraction so that she could sit on Mark's bench and think about her uncertain future with Mark.

She thought of their morning together on the floor, with tears in her eyes. Seeing him helplessly lying in the emergency room a few hours later had opened up her fears of their future together. Would she lose him before they could share the love they had for each other? Why would God bring them together just to let them be separated by death? Now she wanted to cry for having that awful thought. She knew that Mark would be so disappointed in her brief lack of faith.

Later, April took Sunny back to the children's home.

April had tried to find Lewis; no one knew where he had gone. Her father was out of town too. She would have to wait to find their child. April had gone by the hospital to check on Mark.

Mark had an infection. He had several nosebleeds and continued to throw up blood. They were giving him massive doses of antibiotics through his chest catheter. His blood count had not improved much due to the bleeding. Therefore, they gave him another blood transfusion. Now they would have to wait and pray that his condition would improve.

His family went in and out of his room throughout the day. His pastor had come and provided the family with much needed prayer. Pastor Evan reminded them to keep a positive attitude for Mark.

Steven would not do the surgery Mark needed without Mark's permission, and Mark refused to give it to them. Mark continued to claim he was not sick. He tossed in the bed in pain; his hair was damp from the fever he had, but he would not give in.

He claimed he was playing in the football game on Sunday and there was no changing his mind. Everyone felt very frustrated as they stood there watching him suffer.

Dr. Stevenson tried to give Mark the medications he needed to stimulate blood cell production but once again, Mark got violently sick from them, and they had to stop giving them to him. They finally sedated him and let him sleep.

Those drugs had side effects that most AA patients could tolerate. However, Mark's body was rejecting them stronger than any other patient Dr. Stevenson had ever treated. Dr. Stevenson did not understand why the drugs were making Mark so sick. What had caused the lining of his stomach to rupture? It just did not make any sense.

Dr. Stevenson knew that without a bone marrow transplant, Mark's condition would rapidly get worse. Mark would become dependent on blood transfusions. Each transfusion would decrease the success of a bone marrow transplant. They had to find Mark a matching donor soon. If only they had caught his condition earlier, they would have had more time to treat him.

April stood by his bed and brushed her fingers through his damp hair. She prayed the words that Pastor Evan had given her. She thought about all they had been through in their life together. It tore her heart out to see him going through this kind of suffering. She kissed his forehead softly but he did not respond.

Robert had told her that Judge Thompson had refused to give Mark temporary custody of Sunny. Robert told her that Mark's condition would prevent him from gaining any type of future custody. How could they tell him the news without jeopardizing his condition? She would call Robert back and see if he could get her temporary custody.

Mark desperately wanted them to be a family. Would they be able to include Jessica when they found her, April wondered?

If only she had told him the truth in the very beginning about the night they had shared in the park. Although they both had not planned it to happen that night, it had happened and it had been beautiful. She had freely given Mark her heart and body in a moment that she would treasure for the rest of her life. Somewhere out there, they had a little girl.

April would have to wait until she talked to Lewis before she could break the news to Mark. No one seemed to know where Lewis had gone. Had her father done something to him? Lewis would not be the first person who had disappeared working for her father.

If she did not find Lou, she would never find their child, she feared.

Chapter Forty–Five

⟨Never Stop Giving Up⟩

Wednesday came and Mark had not improved much. Every time he ate the hospital food or drank the water from his water pitcher, he became violently sick. He could no longer hold down any food and stopped eating.

In what they thought was his state of delirium, he claimed the hospital water was contaminated with poisons. He would only drink from the sports bottles he had April get for him out of the vending machine. No one would take him seriously; after all no one else in the Unit was sick from the water.

Every time Marty came in the room with a new water pitcher, Mark poured it out in the bathroom sink and threw the container in the shower. Marty frowned when he saw the empty sports bottles in Mark's trash can, but he said nothing to Mark about it.

Mark continued to have severe reactions to the medications they were desperately trying to give him. They had no choice but to discontinue them. He had lost 5 pounds in two days.

Dr. Stevenson had never seen such a severe reaction to these medications. Why did Mark have to be the one patient in a million that rejected the medications he needed to get well? Tom thought with frustration as he watched Mark's health decline.

Mark had missed the review lectures. How could this happen to him? He had worked so hard; he was the leader of his class. April was beside herself. Mark did not deserve this. Why do bad things happen to good people, she questioned? Mark told her it was the work of the devil.

Even as sick as Mark was, he was still refusing to give up everything he wanted to do this week. He was determined that he was taking his boards on Friday, and he was playing football on Sunday. No one could reason with him.

Mark was convinced that all he needed was for them to stop all the drugs and to let him out of the hospital, and he would get better.

"I wasn't sick until I became a patient in this unit; something is not right. Let me go home and I promise you, I will get better."

Dr. Stevenson finally gave in and stopped all the new drugs. Nevertheless, fearing Mark was facing severe dehydration, he wanted to keep Mark in the hospital and on IV fluids until the vomiting stopped.

Mark would have to remain on the antibiotics since his white blood counts were so low. Tom ordered another round of platelets and red blood. They began searching for more platelet donors; Mark's dad and Mrs. Brown were not enough. Mark refused to let Kevin Brown donate for him since Kevin would be playing quarterback in Mark's place in the Super Bowl.

Mark knew the devil was having fun playing with his life. Nevertheless, the devil was not going to win this battle, Mark determinedly told April. He studied for his boards and went over the playbook for the game on Sunday while sitting on the bathroom floor in front of the toilet. He continued to grip the bowl every twenty minutes, as April held his back and wiped his forehead with a cool washcloth.

After two hours, Dr. Stevenson gave him enough medications to knock him out again. Dan and Jeff removed his books, picked him up off the bathroom floor, and put him back in bed. Once he was settled, they hooked him back up to the monitors and placed an oxygen mask over his face.

Dr. Stevenson stood with Dan and Jeff and observed Mark's condition, and then he shook his head in disgust and left the room.

April had talked to Robert about her getting custody of Sunny, and he had agreed to give it a chance. Robert told her there was absolutely no chance of Mark getting custody of Sunny. Sunny would never be Mark's daughter, he told her as his heart broke for Mark and for Sunny.

Coach Walker had a meeting with Coach Kelly from the other team that they were playing on Sunday. Coach Kelly told him that he had met with his players, and they all agreed that the game Sunday would be played in Mark's honor.

Mark was well respected by all the teams in the NFL. Cards and flowers poured into the hospital for Mark. He sent all the flowers to the nursing home.

The news media had picked up the story and invaded the hospital lobby. Dr. Stevenson attended a press conference. He made a plea for the public to be tested for a bone marrow match for Mark. Every player in the football league was tested. No match was made. Several players were matches for other patients waiting for transplants and agreed to help them. Mark had served his public in bringing new awareness to volunteering to be a donor.

All the players on Mark's team showed up at the hospital to donate blood. Mark's illness had produced a public awareness of the blood donations needed to save lives.

The reporters wanted to know if Mark was playing in the Championship Game. Dr. Stevenson told them that it was still not clear what Mark would do.

Wednesday night Mark was awake and feeling better. The vomiting had stopped, and he was able to keep down the water from the water bottles April brought for him.

Mark joked with April that she was the only medication he needed. April cuddled with him on the bed, and they watched a movie before falling asleep in each other's arms.

Early Thursday morning, Mark was sitting up, drinking soda from a can. He was still refusing to eat any of the hospital food. His fever was lower. His blood counts were up from the blood units he had received over the last few days.

Someone was always in or near the room to keep an eye on him. They did not want to take a chance that Mark would leave the hospital on his own.

Jeff came in the room to study with Mark. He gave him the notes from the last two days of lectures. They would spend the day and night cramming. Jeff knew that Mark was only doing it for him; Mark would have no trouble passing.

By mid morning Mark was hungry; he was allowed to eat the soft foods Julia had brought him from the ranch. He had been receiving nutritional fluids in his IV since he stopped eating. His skin tone had returned to normal. His platelet count was slightly higher from the transfusions.

Mark never doubted God's healing powers. If only the others would believe as he did, he thought as he took a knee on the bathroom floor, prayed for complete healing, and thanked God for the day.

April went to spend the afternoon with Sunny. As soon as she left the room, Mark decided to test his abilities.

He got out of bed, did strengthening exercises, and walked the halls that afternoon for an hour. Sally handed him his facemask when he rounded the nurse's station for the first time. He agreed to wear it if she agreed to let him out of his room.

Things were finally going his way. He felt much stronger with each passing hour. He had a great attitude. He claimed victory over AA. Mark planned to walk all over the devil. The devil had no authority over his life.

Some of his teammates sneaked into his room to visit him, which boosted his spirits even higher. Mark was throwing the football around with them in the room. He was even more determined to get out of there when Sally threw all his friends out of his room.

April returned to spend the night with him. They dined on food from Nathan's. He actually ate it, which surprised everyone. April rejoiced as he made her laugh with his upbeat sense of humor and played with her feet under the table during the meal. He certainly was feeling better!

She knew that he would sleep more soundly if she were in his arms. She had been right. Mark was peaceful the entire night.

The plan was to release Mark in the morning with Jeff at his side. They would let Mark attend the boards and after they were over, he was to return to the Unit.

Mark had different plans after the boards; he was going back to his apartment and wait for April to bring Sunny to him for a visit.

Then he would return to the Unit. His terms, of course, it was just like Mark.

CHAPTER FORTY-SIX –
⌒The Circle Around the Ring⌒

*F*riday morning came. Mark and Jeff had to be at the board-testing site by seven am. Mark had gotten up at five-thirty; he had already taken a shower and was ready.

He was lifting hand weights when Dan came into his room and told him Dr. Stevenson wanted him in the examination room. Dan frowned at Mark as he took away the hand weights.

Dr. Stevenson and Dan examined Mark and determined that he was healthy enough to leave the Unit to take his boards.

His blood counts were below normal but higher than when Mark had first been diagnosed with aplastic anemia. He was feeling stronger than he had been before he was admitted to the hospital earlier that week.

Mark convinced them that he was physically strong when he optimistically flexed his biceps in his arrogant way, pointed to them with his finger, and stated that he was in perfect physical condition. There surely was nothing wrong with his facial muscles as he grinned in his typical contagious way, trying to coax a smile out of them.

Both doctors shook their head at him, but deep down they both were thankful that he was feeling better, and he still had his witty sense of humor after all that he had gone through in the last few days. Mark read the hint of doubt they had on their faces.

"Listen here, either you have faith or you don't. Either you believe in healing or you don't. You have to be single minded. I believe today is going to be another great day. What about you two, you guys gotta stop treating me like I am sick, and start claiming my victories. Don't stand in my way. Don't take away my dreams just because you are in fear of what

Satan thinks he can do to me. Believe me; Satan is not going to whip me. So how about you two joining forces with me and believe with all your heart that God is in control of my life."

For one so young, for one who had been through so much in his short life, Mark was sincerely filled with a heart for God, Dan thought, as he looked into the eyes of an altruistic compassionate twenty-four year old man with admiration. Then he looked over at Tom. "Mark is right. Today is a new day, and Mark will find his victories, starting with his boards."

The men joined hands and prayed over Mark. Mark gave them each a warm hug and thanked them for all they had done for him.

Tom gave Mark his pain medication and three antibiotics. Mark would not allow them to give him another unit of blood because he did not want to take Benadryl and be sleepy during the test.

Dr. Stevenson gave Jeff instructions for Mark's care, as well as additional medications to be given at lunchtime. "If Mark shows any signs of stress, Jeff, I want you to bring Mark back to the hospital immediately." Mark shook his head at their over-protectiveness.

April framed Mark's face with her fingers and tenderly gave him a good luck kiss. Everyone in the Unit cheered them on as they headed down the hallway. Mark turned and gave them the thumbs-up. The grin on his face was clear; he was ready to face the world.

Mark's spirits were a great deal higher. He seemed like his old self, or was he just putting on a show for them, the doctors wondered as they watched him float down the hallway and exit out of the doors to the Unit.

Mark was higher than a kite as he knew that God had given him the strength he needed to be walking out of the hospital today. With God on his side, he could do anything, and he was ready to ace this test.

Mark had taken the boards and finished early. He was feeling great; he knew that he had passed the test. He was no longer an intern and he was looking forward to his second year of residency with more responsibilities. He gladly gave the credit to God as he humbly said a prayer of thanks before standing up from his seat.

Mark gave Jeff the thumbs-up before leaving the classroom and then headed out into the fresh air. What a beautiful day to be alive, Mark thought with a smile as he got into his car and opened the sunroof and rolled down all the windows.

Mark decided that he would go to football practice at two. Why not, he was feeling great, and April was not expecting to meet him until four o'clock. Today he planned to resume his life and live it to its fullest.

April had picked Sunny up from school and gone to the park. She loved to watch Sunny jump about and play. She sat on "Mark's Bench" and watched her. Mark would be home in about an hour, and she would take Sunny to see him. That thought brought a warm feeling to her heart.

"I've been looking for you!" A strong furious voice came from behind her, causing her to jump. She looked up and was surprised to see her father standing there. She quickly stood up and faced him.

"Father, what are you doing here?" she demanded.

"I thought I told you never to return here!" he retorted.

"It's okay. No one remembers; no one knows why we left. I have not told anyone what happened here," she said frantically as her legs felt weak.

"I want you to pack your things and come home right now before someone finds out the truth!" he forcefully demanded with anger that clearly steamed off his face.

"I can't. I have a job here, and an apartment, friends and Grandma and Grandpa Parker, Debbie and her kids, and Todd. I can't leave all of them."

"You don't belong here!"

"Why are you doing this to me? Haven't I already paid the price for my mistake?" she said with terror in her voice.

"I came because I was worried about you. How could you come here, after what happened to you?"

"I'm fine; Uncle Dan is looking after me."

"What about the boy, is he here? Did you come back here to be with him again?" he demanded answers.

"I have not seen him. I told you he moved away from here."

"You are lying. Who is he?" he demanded with hatred in his eyes.

"No, Father, I will never tell you that!" she screamed back, her whole body shaking. "Not after you said you would kill him!" she declared in a panic.

"I still would, April, do you hear me!" he threatened.

"Yes, I hear you. You do not have to worry; he is not here!"

Sunny ran up to them at that point. Paul's eyes opened wide when he saw Sunny grab a hold of April. The two of them stood side by side. Sunny was the mirror image of April when she was a child.

Sunny stared up at him. She did not like this man; he was upsetting April.

"Who is yelling at you, April?" Sunny asked fearfully as she grabbed a hold of April's leg and hid behind her.

"It's okay, Sunny, this is my father." Sunny did not like the man. Nevertheless, she would use her good manners that Mark had taught her.

"Hello ... I am Sunny," she said shyly, and timidly held her hand out to him but he did not take it. Paul just stared at her with anger on his face.

"Go play, child!" he said sternly and frightened her. She retreated back behind April and held tight to her legs.

April bent down to her. "It's okay, Sunny, go play." April removed Sunny's little hands from her legs as she gently pushed Sunny's shoulders toward the playground. Sunny did not want to leave April, but she obeyed and walked away slowly as she kept an eye on April.

Her father is mean, Sunny thought. She would sit on the merry-go-round and watch over April. From behind a tree, the boy John appeared and kept a close watch as well.

Paul was infuriated. April looked him straight in the face.

"I know what you are thinking, Father. She is not mine; I am just babysitting her. But I wish she were mine; I wish you had never taken my baby away from me!" she cried out. This was the first time she had spoken to her father about that awful day, five years ago.

"I did what was best for you; you should be thanking me," he blurted back at her.

"You broke my heart!" April cried with such pain in her voice.

"I did not break your heart, that boy did, when he got you pregnant!"

"He loved me, Father! Don't you understand, he loved me?"

"Don't say that. He used you and then he dumped you," he contradicted.

"That is not true; he doesn't even know. I never told him I was pregnant. If he had known, he would have married me; we could have been happy. But I couldn't tell him because of you," she cried, knowing what she had given up all those years with Mark, because of her father.

"No, I would have killed him first before I let him marry you," he insisted.

"That is why I never told him; that is why I can never tell him the truth!" April expressed with sorrow. It was true she could never tell Mark. She could not risk her father harming him. Mark would never know he had a child with her.

"You protected him?" he screamed at her.

"You gave me no choice. I will never let you hurt him!" she shouted at him.

"If I ever find out who he is, he will pay for this!

"He is not here. He moved away, so go home, Father. I do not want you here," she cried, tears streaming down her swollen face.

"How can you say that after all I have done for you?"

"You broke my heart, and I will never forgive you for that, never!"

"I will be at your grandparent's house. I am not finished with you yet, you can be sure of that," he said before he walked away.

April sat down on the bench. She could not stop shaking; she had never stood up to her father before. She had to act fast. She quickly took Sunny back to Blanche's and then ran home.

Katie was waiting for Sunny when she came in the door. They went up to their bedroom so they could be alone.

"I have a surprise for you," Katie said excitedly.

"What is it?" Sunny asked sadly. She was still upset about April.

"Remember that ring that your mother must have given you?" Katie asked with excitement in her voice.

"Yeah, so?" Sunny said softly with sad eyes.

"It was from my high school. The ring had a date on it, and the initials M.S. on it, and a football on it. Which means M.S. played football!" Katie said excitedly.

"So," Sunny said, not caring anything about it. Her mind was still focused on April and her mean father.

"So, I went to the school library and got the old yearbook out for that year and the only M.S. in the book was your Mark Sanders! Do you know what that means, Sunny?" Katie exclaimed.

"I'm not sure," Sunny said puzzled.

"Mark Sanders has to be your real father! And whoever he dated, must have been your mother. I think she was April Morgan. Because there was a picture of them together in the yearbook and they were looking into each other's eyes with pure love. And besides, you look just like April, so it has to be her!" Katie told her with excitement in her voice.

"But why didn't they tell me?" Sunny asked tearfully.

"Because somehow I think they really don't know who you are. April just moved here. They must have given you up for adoption, and then those people dropped you off here or something like that," Katie told her.

"Mark never would have given me up!" Sunny cried tearfully. "I have to go tell Blanche; she'll have to let me live with Mark now."

Before Katie could stop her, Sunny ran out of the room shouting for Blanche.

April had rushed home and as she was running, she thought. *My father loved me once and wanted to protect me, until he found out I was pregnant.*

She had told her father that her baby's father did not know she was pregnant. She said that he was a college boy she had met at a party. Her father said he would kill whoever had done this to her. She had refused to tell him who he was.

Now she had to protect Mark. If her father knew she was dating Mark, and Dan told him that she had dated Mark in high school, he would figure it all out and he would try to hurt Mark. She could not let that happen.

April had to warn her Uncle Dan not to tell her father about her relationship with Mark. She picked up the phone and called Dan's office. His secretary told her that Dan had gone to see his brother at her grandparent's house. She had been too late. She had to get there before Dan did and stop him from telling her father about her relationship with Mark back when they were in high school.

Mark had gone to football practice at two against the advice of Dr. Stevenson. He felt so good to be where he belonged, with the guys. He was doing what he did best, and it made him feel normal again.

His teammates rushed over to him when he came out on the field in his practice uniform. The reunion was touching; none of his teammates thought they would ever see him back on the field again.

After an hour of playing quarterback, he was tired. He had trouble breathing and had to go into the locker room for oxygen. Paige took charge of his care and sat with him while he regained his strength from the oxygen.

Doc kept a close eye on him as well. It would be so hard to sideline Mark on Sunday and take away from him the very reason that he existed: to be a quarterback.

It all seemed so unfair; why was this happening to someone who had always given his best to the team? Doc knew Mark would have the answer to that question. Doc was sure Mark would say something about the devil stealing what belonged to him. The team could always count on Mark to lift them up out of their troubled times with his wise words from God.

His teammates had not touched him. They all protected him like over-grown watchdogs. Mark had gotten them to this championship game and they owed him. They anxiously waited for him to return to the practice field.

When Mark came back out twenty minutes later, he worked with Kevin Brown on key plays. The team would need Kevin after Mark had his surgery on Monday.

Mark planned to be back before the Super Bowl Game, but there was a strong possibility that he would not be able to play in that game. Well, with God, nothing was impossible. Maybe he could slide through surgery and be back on his feet, he wishfully thought, but medically the surgery would sideline him for weeks. He was not going to think about that possibility.

Mark worked intensely with Kevin for about thirty minutes, each play becoming harder as he grew tired. Frustrated, he walked off the field and went back to the locker room for another round of oxygen. He ate the banana Paige gave him, but refused her help with the oxygen. Instead, he took a quick refreshing shower, gathered his positive thoughts and went home to see the joys of his life, April and Sunny.

It was just before four o'clock when he pulled up to his apartment building. Mark looked over at the park and noticed that April was not there with Sunny where she had told him she would be until he got home. That is odd, he thought as he looked around for her. When he parked his car, he noticed that April's car was gone.

Something did not feel right, but he could not figure out what was causing the uneasiness he felt as he went in search of the women he loved.

CHAPTER FORTY-SEVEN –
∽The Truth∾

*T*he phone was ringing when Mark opened the door to his apartment. He hurried to answer it.

"Hello," he said. It was Sunny. She was upset, and it was hard for him to understand what she was trying to tell him.

"Mark … I … need … hurry … taking me away …" she cried tearfully. But before Sunny could finish, they had been cut off. What was going on, Mark thought puzzled, what was Sunny trying to tell him, and why wasn't Sunny with April?

The doorbell rang and Mark opened it. It was Carlo. The coach had sent him to check on Mark, but Carlo was not about to tell Mark he had been sent.

"I was worried when you left practice so early so I decided to come by and see if you were okay," Carlo told Mark with concern in his voice.

"I'm just tired, that's all," Mark answered. "Listen, Carlo, I'm in a hurry. I was supposed to meet April," Mark said anxiously.

"You're getting pretty heavy with April again?" Carlo snickered. Mark stopped dead in his tracks and looked Carlo straight in the face.

"What do you mean, again? What was there between us before?" Mark asked angrily. Mark wanted some answers and he wanted them now. He was fed up with all the secrets everyone was keeping from him.

"You know, the night after the State Championship Game, at the park?" Carlo said, unable to avoid Mark's demanding eyes.

"You know I don't remember that night; what did happen at the park that night?"

"I don't know how you could forget that night, wow, you gave April your class ring and you two went off by yourselves, and you know …

well, uh, the guys and I took off and left you two alone and you uh, well, you two had a good time and then you passed out on her." Carlo was fidgeting as he told what he knew. Mark looked surprised. Just what was Carlo trying to tell him?

"Don't you understand? I do not remember anything about that whole day, come on Carlo, tell me what you know; this could be important! I have to know the truth now, stop talking in circles and tell me what happened?" Mark demanded.

"You gave her your class ring, you fooled around with her, you were drunk, and you passed out. She came and got us and the guys and I took you to my cousin's. We got even more plastered, then I dropped you off at your house. Thomas sobered you up so you could race in that race that almost killed you. Wow, Dr. Morgan told us you had forgotten some things, but I never thought you'd forget about something like what you and April did," Carlo said in a huff, glad the truth was finally told to Mark about that night.

"C'mon, are you sure?" Mark asked in disbelief. There was no way anything could have happened between April and him. He did not believe what Carlo was saying was true.

"Well, I thought you made out that night, but I didn't actually see it happen. Don't you know; didn't April ever tell you?"

"No, April never said anything. Listen, Carlo, I have to go," Mark said in a hurry and quickly grabbed his car keys off the counter and ran out the door, leaving Carlo standing there looking dumbfounded.

Mark rushed over to Blanche's and pounded on the door. Katie answered the door.

"Where's Sunny?" he asked in a hurry.

"She's not here. Blanche took her somewhere. Sunny was kicking and screaming, and I'm so afraid!" Katie fretted.

"Where did she take her?" Mark asked confused. *Why was Katie so upset?*

"I don't know; they just rushed out of here so fast. Here, Sunny told me to give this to you before they left."

Katie handed Mark the class ring on the gold necklace. Mark looked down at the ring and saw that it was his.

He had a vivid flashback of himself putting the ring on the chain and putting it over April's head; he had done it in the park, just as Carlo had said. He stood puzzled as he stared at the ring.

"It's your ring, isn't it?" Katie said as she startled him back to reality.

"What?" Mark said, still thinking about the ring.

"Is that your ring?"

"Yes, but where did you get it?"

"It belonged to Sunflower's mother."

Then he remembered the ring had been too big for April's finger, so he had put it on her gold chain and pulled it over her head. He had given this ring to April. *How did Sunflower's mother get it from April,* he wondered.

"You said it belonged to Sunflower's mother, how did she get it?" he asked confused.

"That's right. Sunflower's mother gave her that ring when she was a tiny baby," Katie told him with a smile.

"That's not possible. I gave that ring to April," he reasoned.

"You don't understand? Sunflower had that ring when she was brought here five years ago. It was hidden in the liner to her baby sweater."

"Five years ago, what? Sunny is really only five, not six, are you sure?" he questioned. Katie confirmed the answer with a positive nod yes.

"As sure as I know that you are Sunny's real father, and April gave that ring of yours to Sunny," Katie announced proudly.

"Her father … what? My God, that's it, it has to be, but why didn't Sunny tell me about this?"

"Sunny just found out today. I'm pretty sure April is Sunny's mother, and she don't know Sunny is her kid. When Sunny told Blanche that you were her real father, Blanche took her away," Katie worriedly told him.

Mark ran back to his car and drove back to the apartments to get some answers from April. It was all coming together. You made out with her; you gave her your ring, Carlo had told him. She came to the hospital after your accident, and her family just picked up and moved, Dan had told him. She had stood there in his hospital room and cried when he did not remember her.

That is why she acted so upset with me when she came back here. She and I, we have been together … was it possible … was it true … do we

377

really have a child … what happened that night in the park, he thought, *how did it happen? April has a lot of explaining to do.*

He rushed to her apartment. Her door was wide open. He hurried inside, took a quick look around, and saw that her phone was off the hook and hanging off the desk. Mark could feel something was terribly wrong. His heart was pounding. He felt sick but he refused to give into the nausea that swept through his stomach.

He saw that her phone book was opened to Dan's office number. He picked up the phone quickly and called there.

"Is Dan there? … Did his niece, April call there? … What did she want … this is very important … Her Grandma Parker's house … Where does she live? … Thank you." Mark hung up quickly.

"Something is wrong; I can feel it," he said as he ran out and went back to his car. Adrenaline quickly filled his blood stream; his chest was pounding. "What is going on? Where's Sunny; where's April?"

He drove about five miles out when he saw flashing lights around a sharp curve. He saw the skid marks on the road. *Was there an accident*?

He slowed down as he passed. He did not want to stop, but then his doctor instincts made him pull over to see if he could help. He jumped out and called out to the police officer that was standing by his car trying to use his broken radio.

"Do you need any help? I'm a doctor?" Mark asked in a hurried voice.

"There is a car down in the ditch. The passenger is injured; my radio is not working," he yelled back to Mark.

Mark quickly ran over and started down the ditch. It was getting dark, but the full moon was out. The minute Mark saw the car he knew.

"Oh, no, it's April's car!" he thought as he stopped breathing and rushed to it. Adrenaline filled his veins.

April was in it; she was unconscious. She had a small cut on her forehead that had bled down the side of her face. Mark felt his chest stiffen in fear for her. He quickly prayed she would be alive.

The officer joined Mark. "You said you are a doctor?"

"Yes, go up the road about five miles. There is a white farmhouse on the right, the Parker place. That is her grandparent's house; her uncle is there. He is a doctor too. Go get him and bring him back here. I may need his help," Mark instructed as he examined April for other injuries. The officer left in a hurry.

The cut appeared to be from her fingernail. *She must have braced for impact,* Mark thought. There was no broken glass in the car. There was very little damage to the car. He felt no broken bones. The airbag must have knocked her out.

April moved her head and slowly opened her eyes. She moaned.

"April, can you hear me?" he asked as he wiped the blood from the side of her face with his handkerchief. Then he kissed her face to let her know that he was there.

Her eyes opened wide then she heard Mark's voice. She looked up into his frantic face, and started breathing faster.

"Mark! Oh, Mark! My father knows; he's going to ..." She closed her eyes and tried to catch her breath. Mark thought she was delirious. He continued to examine her for other injuries.

"April, you are all right, just calm down and breathe slowly," he told her as he held her neck in place. She reached up and placed her hands on his.

"My father ... is here ... he knows about us," she managed to say, as she drew his hands away from her neck.

"What are you talking about?" Mark questioned her.

"He will kill you; he knows now," she whimpered in fear.

"What does he know? What are you trying to tell me?" he anxiously asked.

April was emotionally crying, fearful of the words she was about to say to Mark. She did not want to hurt him, but the truth had to be told. There was no time left.

"He knows ... that you got me pregnant ... it happened the night of the Championship Game ... in the park," she cried.

Mark stood back in shock. It was true then. He put his hand in his pocket and pulled out the ring. He leaned back down to her.

"The night I gave you this ring?" he asked as he placed the ring and necklace in her hand. She took one look at it and panicked.

"Mark, where did you get that ring?" she cried out anxiously.

"Sunny had it."

"No," April shook her head frantically, "Sunny could not have given it to you," she said with tears.

"Why not? I don't understand?" he asked puzzled.

"I gave that ring to our baby girl," she tearfully explained, trying to make Mark understand.

"Isn't Sunny our child?" he asked her, confused that she was clueless that Sunny was her child.

"No, Sunny is six … our child is only five," she said as she started fading in and out of it.

"Katie just told me Sunny has lived with them since she was a baby, and that she is really only five-years-old."

"What?" April asked in disbelief as she looked into Mark's strained face. "What are you saying?"

"What did you name our baby?" he asked sternly.

"Jessica Parker, after my Grandma Parker and Jessica Morton," she cried.

"Sunflower's real name is Jessica Parker. My father's investigator told us that was her real name," Mark explained to her, as he remembered what Robert had told him on Christmas day.

"It can't be … oh Mark … how can that be true?" she cried so distraught, not believing it was possible. *Was Sunny really her Jessica?*

Mark realized that April had not known the truth about Sunny. Everything was just one big confusing mess.

Mark's mind was racing with questions. *Why had Blanche lied about Sunny's age, and why had she taken her away when she found out the truth about her parents?*

He was worried that Sunny was in some kind of danger. He had to find her quickly. He had to get to Sunny, but he did not want to leave April behind. He looked anxiously for the police car, but it was nowhere in sight. He ran his fingers through his hair in frustration.

"April, can you move? Does your neck or back hurt?" he asked her in a hurried voice.

"I'm fine. I think I can get out, if you help me," she said weakly. Her mind was spinning with everything Mark had told her, but she was not hurt.

Mark helped her slide carefully out into his arms, and he carried her to his car and helped her in. She lay back against the seat. He put her seatbelt on quickly. Mark ran around to his side and jumped in the car. He turned the car around in one swift movement, causing the wheels to spin, and raced back into the city.

"Where are you going in such a hurry?" April asked weakly.

"Sunny called me. Something was wrong but I could not understand her. When I went there, Katie told me that Blanche had taken her away. We've got to go back there and find out where they went," he said with anxiety.

"Oh no," she sighed, as fear overcame her.

"What?" he asked her firmly.

"My father, he saw me with Sunny. Mark, he has taken her! He must have figured out she was mine. Oh Mark, what are we going to do?" She fearfully cried, knowing that her father had already taken Sunny when she was a baby. What had he done with her now?

"Why would your father take her?" None of this made any sense to Mark.

"Because he took her away from me after she was born, and he told me I would never see her again," she cried, tears streaming down her face.

"We'll find Blanche and get some answers," he assured her. He had a sick feeling in his stomach that told him that something was terribly wrong. He remembered the words Sunny had tearfully said to him on the phone.

He looked over at April; she had closed her eyes, and her cheeks were wet with tears. He loved her, but he was angry she had not told him about their child.

If only they had been able to put the puzzle pieces together sooner.

How did all this happen? He was not even sure what was happening.

CHAPTER FORTY-EIGHT –
◦Outraged◦

*D*an and Paul Morgan arrived at the scene of April's accident with the police officer. They quickly got out of their car and ran down to April's car only to find her missing.

"I thought you said my daughter was here?" Paul shouted at the police officer.

"She was right here. I left her with a young man who claimed he was a doctor," the officer said flabbergasted.

"Was he well built and had dark sandy blonde hair, driving a blue sports car?" Dan inquired, thinking the man had to be Mark.

"Yes, I think he was that football player they have been talking about," the officer answered, wondering how Dan knew that.

"It is all right, Paul. He was Mark Sanders, the young man we were just talking about," Dan assured him.

Just minutes ago, Dan and Paul were talking together over old times at April's grandparent's house. Paul really did not want to have this conversation with his brother. The two of them had never been close to each other. They just tolerated one another.

Dan had been the good sheep of the family, always seeing the good in everyone. Paul had sowed the wrong seeds in the wrong ground. Still, Dan treated him fairly and worshiped Paul's children as if they were his own.

Ted and Jessie Parker had welcomed their son-in-law back into their home. They prayed daily that Paul would find salvation in God.

"What are you doing here, Paul? Did you come on business or to see the kids?" Dan asked his brother Paul.

"I came back to find April. Her mother and I have been worried about her," he stated. Paul did not tell Dan why he had really come, and Tammy had no idea where Paul had gone.

"April is doing fine. She is working at the hospital, she is dating, and she has a really nice apartment," Dan informed Paul with a smile.

"She's dating?" Paul blurted angrily.

"Don't tell me you still don't allow April to date. She's twenty-four, Paul," Dan teased as he remembered how over-protective Paul had been with his daughters.

"No, she can date. I'm over that," Paul lied. "So, who is she dating? Is it anyone I know?" Paul had to trick Dan into giving him information about this man who was dating April.

"Do you remember the young boy that I took under my wings about twenty years ago? You remember; April used to go with me to his house out in the country. His name is Mark Sanders," Dan said proudly, thinking of the young couple affectionately.

The name Mark Sanders was the last name Paul thought he would hear. Paul held his anger; he needed more information from his brother.

"That's right, Mark. April mentioned him; didn't they date back in high school?" Paul suppressed his anger.

This time Dan was surprised that Paul knew. April must have finally come clean about her relationship with Mark to her father, Dan thought.

"They made quite a couple back then. They seem to have picked up where they left off. Brother, I think it is wedding time again," Dan kidded Paul with humor.

"Did April ever date anyone else other than Mark?" Paul asked with intentions to deceive his brother.

"No, why?" Dan asked, puzzled at the question.

"You know how protective I am of my girls. I was just wondering," Paul lied. The anger was building up. April had been lying to him all this time. He had warned her not to be friends with Mark Sanders.

"Well, you don't have to worry. April has picked a good one. I think you will approve of this relationship," Dan said with pride.

"Why is that?" Paul asked, desperately trying to conceal his growing anger.

"Mark is everything you could ever hope to have in a son-in-law. Mark and April are trying to adopt a little girl right now, so it should not be long before they get married and you have an instant granddaughter," Dan happily said.

"This little girl, where did she come from?"

"She lives in a children's home. Now that I think of it, you should know the woman that runs the home. Her name is Blanche Richards. Isn't she the sister of your assistant, Lewis, or was his name Lou?" Dan asked, thinking back to when he had met them.

"I never met her," Paul lied. Dan looked confused.

Paul got up from the table to get a drink of water, but what he really wanted to do was figure this all out without Dan getting suspicious.

April and Mark, that girl that looked just like April did when she was a child, and now Blanche and Lewis.

Did Lewis give April's child to his sister? Had Lewis told April where her child was and that is why she came back here, to claim her child? It was Mark Sanders who got my daughter pregnant. Mark will pay for that.

The more Paul thought about the whole situation, the angrier he became.

Mark was also the quarterback that was causing him problems with one of his business deals. Had Lewis messed that up, too? If Mark was still able to walk, Lewis had not done his job. The price on Mark's head had just gone up, Paul thought angrily. Paul turned to his brother.

"I have an important call to make, I will be right back," Paul stated and left the room quickly. He went into the other room, picked up the phone, and called Lewis' private phone.

"Lewis, I thought I sent you here to take care of business with that quarterback, Mark Sanders?" Paul said angrily, but quietly so Dan could not hear him.

"It's not that easy, too many people are always around Mark. But I have inside help now at the hospital. Don't worry, boss, Mark Sanders will not play in the game on Sunday; he'll be too sick." Lou declared firmly.

"Well, he's not sick now; he's got my daughter. You messed up, Lewis. Do you hear me?"

"I'm on it, boss, uh ... he won't be playing in no game ..."

"Lewis, what did you do with April's child when she was born?" Paul asked angrily. There was a brief pause on the phone line.

"You know, I gave her to that family you have been paying child support to," Lewis answered, he was afraid of telling Paul the truth. Paul would kill him if he found out where April's baby really was.

"Don't lie to me, Lewis. You gave her to your sister, and you have been stealing my money. You idiot, April is here. Did you tell April where her child was?" Paul demanded answers.

"No, April don't know nothing, boss," Lewis guaranteed him with a shaky voice.

"Well, it won't be long before she does!" Paul retorted angrily, his face the tint of a blazing fire.

"I know, boss, my sister, Blanche, uh, called me. She realized who April was, and she figured out who the father of her kid was, somehow. She got scared that the truth would come out, so she took the girl. You don't have to worry none, boss." Lewis told him in a panic, fearing Paul.

"I don't believe this!" Paul yelled, "how could you be so stupid!"

"It's okay, boss, no one will find out. I've taken care of her," Lewis claimed, fearing his life was over now that Paul knew the truth.

"What …?" Paul started to say, but Dan had rushed into the room and grabbed Paul by the arm.

"April's been in a car accident; we have to hurry," Dan told Paul in a panicked voice.

"Lewis, I'll call you back." Paul slammed down the phone and raced out with Dan.

Now back at the accident scene, his daughter had disappeared with this Mark Sanders guy. Paul was absolutely furious! *When I get a hold of him, I am going to break both his legs,* Paul thought angrily.

Mark was the one who was messing up the gambling bets on the AFC Championship Game. Was Mark playing or not? Lewis had told Paul that Mark was injured and in the hospital. Not even the press knew where Mark was.

They had inside information about Mark's condition from *Lewis' girl-friend,* who was a *nurse* at the hospital. But if Mark was injured, what was he doing out of the hospital, and what was Mark doing with his daughter?

"Mark must have taken her to the hospital; let's go there," Dan said as they rushed back to their car and headed to the hospital. When they got there, they rushed into the emergency room only to find out that Mark and April were not there.

"Let's go up to my office and wait," Dan suggested.

"If he's done anything to harm my daughter, I will kill him!" Paul stormed.

"What are you talking about? Mark would never harm April," Dan disputed, shocked that Paul would say those words.

"It doesn't matter, all that matters is we find April," Paul growled angrily.

When Mark Sanders showed up, Paul planned to hurt him; that would solve one problem. It would keep Mark from playing in the Championship Game. No one would blame him for hurting Mark after what Mark had done to his daughter, Paul justified as his face hardened.

Chapter Forty-Nine –
⮾Ripped Apart⮿

*M*ark stopped his car in front of the children's home and hurriedly started to get out. He was tense and extremely worried that something awful had happened to Sunny.

"I want to go with you," April begged him, as she grabbed his arm before he got out of the car. Mark saw the look of determination in her eyes to go with him.

"Are you sure you are okay?" Mark asked with concern for her, knowing she could have unseen injuries from her accident.

"Yes, just help me," she mumbled weakly, determined to follow Mark.

Mark got out, went around to her side of the car, and opened the door. He gently helped her out. She was wobbly; he put his arms around her waist and helped her up the stairs. He impatiently pounded on the door. Katie answered it.

"Is Blanche back yet?" Mark asked in a panicked voice.

"No, she didn't come back," Katie tearfully told him, as she shook her head no. Mark noticed her tear-swollen face.

"Where is Blanche's office?" Mark inquired gently as they went in. They followed Katie to the office and went into the room. Mark was looking for clues that would tell him where Blanche had gone with Sunny.

"Wait out here, Katie. Knock if Blanche comes back." He instructed her, as he quickly thumbed through the papers on Blanche's desk as April watched over his shoulder.

Mark went to the file cabinet and thumbed through the files until he found one that said Sunflower. It was empty; he threw it on the floor. He looked through the other files; he found one labeled J.P. in the very back and pulled it out.

April leaned closer to him. He opened it as his heart picked up a stronger beat. There was a slip of paper in it and Sunny's medical records. Mark opened up her medical records; Sunny was type O negative. She matched Mark's blood type. Would she match his tissue type, he briefly thought?

Then Mark opened up the tattered slip of paper and read it. "Your name is Jessica Parker. You were born August fourth, at six A.M. I wish I could keep you but I can't, but I will never forget you and I will always love you. I will find you someday, but until I do, have a wonderful life and be happy. Love from your mother, A.M."

"This proves Sunny is ours!" Mark excitedly explained to April with pure joy in his voice. "Sunny is my daughter!" He saw that April was about to faint and reached out just in time to catch her, but instead they both fell to the floor. Thankfully, Mark hit the floor on his right side.

April looked up into his eyes and very weakly said, "I wrote that letter; Sunny is ours." Then she passed out.

Mark got up slowly, rubbed his ribs, and opened the door. He carefully picked April up in his arms. He took a deep breath, ignored the pain he felt, as he carried her out to his car, and drove quickly to the hospital.

A thousand thoughts filled his mind as he thought about Sunny. Would he get a second chance to be her father, if only he could find her? He felt the wetness of the tears that fell down his cheeks. He felt an endlessness of sadness fall over his heart. Sunny belonged to him; he had a daughter somewhere out there in the darkness.

Mark carried April into the emergency room and laid her gently down on an examining table. Mark's friend Jeff saw him come into the hospital and followed behind him. Jeff noticed that Mark was sweating and pale. He grabbed Mark's arm with deep concern.

"What happened? Where have you been? Dr. Stevenson has been trying to find you. Dr. Morgan is looking for you and April. He said there had been an accident. April's father is up in Dan's office with him. They wanted me to call them if you came here. What the heck is going on, Mark?" Jeff asked Mark in a panicked voice.

Mark had been examining April quickly, checking her pupils, her breathing. He was deeply concerned about her but his heart was crying out for Sunny. What had happened to her? He had to find her.

"Take care of April, Jeff, she has a concussion. Get a CT scan just in case. I'll be right back," Mark said as he rushed out of the room before Jeff could stop him.

Mark quickly headed to the elevator. He banged the up button with his fist and waited impatiently for the doors to open, banging the button repeatedly until the doors finally opened. He went in and punched the third floor button. He had to think, what was happening, what was he going to do? His mind was overwhelmed.

"Sunny, hold on. I am coming for you. God, you got to protect her for me, tell me where to find her."

When the doors opened, Mark rushed to Dan's office and flung the door open. Dan quickly stood up from behind his desk. Paul was on his feet quickly too. Mark slammed the door behind him.

"Mark!" Dan exclaimed, alarmed at Mark's forceful entrance.

"So you are Mark!" Paul said angrily and grabbed the front of Mark's shirt by his fists, with all intentions of hurting Mark. Mark forcefully pushed Paul's hands away from him, knocking Paul backwards.

"Are you April's father?" Mark questioned him angrily.

"What have you done to my daughter?" Paul yelled at Mark with a voice that tore into Mark sharply.

"She is in the emergency room. What have you done with my daughter?" Mark demanded desperately.

Dan looked confused. *Mark's daughter, what was Mark talking about?*
"Calm down you two," Dan told them.

"Where's my daughter!" Mark shouted again looking Paul straight in the face with anger. "Give her back to me now!"

"What are you talking about?" Dan asked Mark, confused.

Mark's untrusting eyes never left Paul's face. "I know that Sunflower is really Jessica Parker, my daughter, and your brother has taken her!" Mark blurted out.

"What are you saying, Mark?" Dan asked baffled.

"He doesn't know what he is talking about!" Paul yelled.

"I don't have all the pieces yet but I know that five years ago April had my child, which is why they moved to California. That child is Sunny. I am her father, and your brother has kidnapped her!" Mark lashed out and had to grab a breath of air when he finished speaking.

"Is that true, Paul?" Dan questioned Paul, knowing deep down if Mark said it, then it was true.

"You moron, you got my daughter pregnant and then you left her high and dry. I had to pick up the pieces!" Paul grabbed Mark by the shirt and forcefully threw him against the door.

Dan instantly panicked when he saw the pain on Mark's face as Mark hit the door. Mark had the wind knocked out of him and felt faint for an instant.

"I told her I would kill whoever had done this to her, and I am going to kill you!" Paul screamed at Mark as he pinned him against the door. If Lewis could not finish the job, he would hurt Mark himself.

"Paul, let Mark go, are you crazy!" Dan yelled at him as he grabbed Paul's arm, pulling him off Mark. Paul reluctantly let go. If looks could kill, Mark would have fallen to the floor dead.

Mark's face held a distant look. "I never knew April was pregnant; she never told me!" Mark insisted, but then those words he had just said hit him squarely in his heart. The reality of the truth crushed the air from Mark's chest; he had gotten April pregnant. Mark suddenly lost his fight at that moment as he thought about what he had done to April. "Oh, God, what did I do?"

"You forced yourself on her; why did you do it?" Paul shouted loudly, looking Mark dead in the face.

"I didn't … I don't know … how it happened, I can't remember it." Mark thought for that brief second that Paul had every right to be angry at him for getting his daughter pregnant. Then he thought about Sunny. It was all his fault that Sunny had suffered all those years. "Oh, God, what did I … I do?"

Paul shoved Mark in the chest again using both his hands and pushed Mark back against the door, screaming at him like a lunatic.

"You got her pregnant, and you can't remember it!"

What have I done to April? Mark thought about those words as he felt his back hit the door. Mark knew he deserved to have Paul beat him to a pulp.

Paul attacked Mark again, this time swinging his fists in the air at him. Mark was angry but he did not want to fight this man. Paul was April's father, as much as Mark hated him for what he had done to April and Sunny, he had to respect him. After all, Mark thought he deserved the beating Paul was about to give him. The punch hit Mark in the right side of his stomach; its force bent Mark forward. Mark grabbed his chest with both hands. Paul moved in to hit Mark again.

"Paul, don't!" Dan yelled at him, as he grabbed Paul and held him away from Mark. Dan was surprised that Mark just stood there and did not defend himself.

"Stop it, both of you! This is getting us nowhere, now sit down and let's talk about this!" Dan demanded as he forcefully pushed Paul down into a chair to keep him away from Mark.

Mark staggered over to Dan's desk. "Just tell me where you took Sunny!" Mark pleaded in a weak voice; he was still bent over in pain, one hand holding onto Dan's desk for support and his other hand holding his abdomen.

"I did not take her anywhere!"

"Sunny is missing ... she was dragged away by Blanche, and no one knows where they went," Mark informed them through his pain.

"What?" Dan asked as he looked over at Paul for an explanation.

"April said he did it," Mark told Dan weakly.

"I did not do it! Lewis, he must have taken her," Paul replied.

"Who is Lewis? What does he have to do with this?" Mark asked as Dan gently placed his hand on Mark's back with concern.

"Paul, tell Mark the truth, tell him what you have done with Sunny!" Dan demanded. "I want you both to calm down so we can figure this mess out, for Sunny's sake we have to work together."

"Lewis works for me. He is the one who took April's child when she was born. I never asked him where he had taken her. I did not care. I never thought he would be stupid enough to bring her here to his sister's house. I guess he has taken her somewhere else. I do not know what he has done with her," Paul admitted.

"Will he hurt her ... is she in danger?" Mark fearfully asked in pain. He held his breath waiting for the answer.

"I'm not sure what he will do with her," Paul claimed. "I'll call him and find out, and then we can get her back." Paul sounded somewhat calmer.

"I don't trust you, why would you go to any trouble after all you've done to keep her away from April?" Mark asked, unconvinced that Paul was telling the truth.

"I've seen her. She is my granddaughter, and I have seen the way April loves her. It is not what I want, but I am not going to stop April now from having her child."

However, Mark did not believe that for a minute. He feared Paul was up to something; he would not trust him.

The phone rang. Dan answered it. He listened carefully, shaking his head with concern. Dan looked over at Mark.

"Mark, that was Dr. Kirkland. April is calling out for you. He cannot calm her down, so you better go to her."

"I'm going, too," Paul said as he stood up to leave behind Mark. Mark stopped and looked Paul straight in the face.

"No, April asked for me. She does not want you. You stay here and call Lewis and find my girl, or next time I'll tear you apart!" Mark shouted at him.

"Don't you dare threaten me!" Paul said angrily.

"Go on, Mark, get out of here. I will deal with Paul, and we will find Sunflower," Dan instructed as he followed Mark to the door. "I love you, Mark, now go to April."

Mark turned and left. He rushed down to the emergency room. He leaned against the wall to catch his breath. He opened the door and immediately went to April's side. She was crying uncontrollably when Mark entered the room. He sat on the bed and held her in his arms.

"Please, don't hate me, Mark," she sobbed, thinking Mark would never forgive her.

"Why didn't you tell me that you were pregnant? Why didn't you tell me we had a child?" he asked softly, rubbing her hair gently between his fingers. Her suffering caused him immense pain. He sucked in a breath, his chest stiff.

"I wanted to tell you, but my father said he would kill the man who had been with me. I had to protect you. When I went to the hospital to see you, you could not even remember my name. So how could I tell you I was pregnant with your child?" She held onto him and cried. He felt her anguish deep down in his soul.

Mark closed his eyes and held her tightly in his arms. Sunny had been ripped from April's arms, and now she had been ripped from his. They had both lost their child. He just wanted all of this to go away.

How was all this possible?

CHAPTER FIFTY –
⤳Safe in My Arms⤲

*M*ark closed his eyes; part of his memory came back as he recalled the day that April had come into his hospital room. It had been two months after his accident. Julia was in the room with him. April had tentatively come into his room. He had stared at her as if he had known her, but he could not remember her name.

"Hi, Mark," she said shyly. She seemed so tense.

"Do I know you?" he asked kindly as he sat up in his bed to face her. Her face looked shocked that he had asked that question.

"It's me, Mark, April," she mumbled as her eyes watered.

"I'm sorry, I don't remember you. Do we go to high school together?" Mark asked her warmly, noting her uneasiness.

"What are you saying, Mark? Don't you know who I am?" She looked bewildered.

Mark slowly shook his head no. He did not want to hurt her feelings. There was something familiar about her that spoke to his compassionate heart, as her tears escaped one at a time down her cheeks. He thought for a minute about lying to her and telling her that he did remember her, if that would take away the tears that slid down her soft face, but what could he say about them? He did not know.

"But you and I, we ..." She looked over at Julia. She knew that Julia was listening so she could not say what she had to tell him. She turned back and looked at Mark, her eyes pleading for him to remember her.

"We danced together at your birthday party, we ... we met after the game, in the ... we were in the park," she said softly in despair. Her tearful eyes were trying to find a connection to his.

"I don't remember that night; it's all a blank. I am sorry," he sadly told her with regret, wishing he could somehow take away the sadness that showed on her face.

"How could you, Mark, how could you forget us!" she cried as she ran from the room. Mark was left feeling empty inside.

Julia had tried to get Mark to remember the dance, their friendship with each other as children, but it had all been a blank, wiped clean from his mind.

Mark got extremely upset when the memories of her would not return. He felt as if part of his heart had died when he thought about her. It was as if they had broken up, yet he did not understand why he felt that way. He fell into a depression and closed the part of his heart that he knew belonged only to her.

No one had understood why Mark could not remember April. She was the young woman he was so in love with just months ago.

Mark's doctor had told them to let his memory come back on its own, so no one forced his memory of April. Everyone thought he would remember her and everything would return to normal. But before they had a chance to reunite, April moved away and Mark filled his life with other things.

Now here he was, holding her in his arms, loving her with every fiber of his soul. He had fallen deeply in love with her the moment they had met in the park a few weeks ago. It had been as if he had known her all his life, and as it turned out, he had known her all his life. Why had he blocked her out of his memory? Did it have to do with what had happened that night in the park?

April was torn apart; crying desperately for the child he never knew existed. She moved out of his arms and lay back down on the bed, looking away from him. Mark brushed her hair back from her face and kissed her tenderly. He wiped the tears from her cheeks softly. *She cannot even face me*, he thought in despair.

"My father had Jessica taken away, didn't he ... she's gone ... I've lost my baby ... I want my baby," she cried before she drifted off to sleep.

What have I done to her? She carried my child, gave birth, and then was forced to give up her baby, our baby. The pain she must have suffered because of me. No wonder she acted as she did when we met again. How she must have hated me all those years, Mark thought.

He lay down beside her on the gurney holding her while she slept. She was restless as she whimpered; calling out Jessica's name. She began tossing her head, slowly at first, and then she woke up screaming for her baby.

Mark tried to calm her by holding her closer, kissing her forehead. She continued fighting him, hitting him with her fists, screaming for her baby. Mark had tears in his eyes as he felt her pain deeply in his own heart.

Mark loved Sunny from the very first day he met her and to lose her was inconceivable. He gathered April back in his arms, and she relaxed against his chest. Then he closed his eyes and prayed that God would give him the strength he needed to get them both through their pain.

Mark was concerned that April was referring to Sunny as Jessica, a baby, and not as Sunny, a little girl.

April's father opened the door and looked in. Mark yelled at him to get out and to leave them alone. Paul left the room without making a scene.

Dan came in the room. He was worried about these two. Dan was more concerned about the punch that Paul had given Mark in the abdomen. Mark could be bleeding internally; he needed to be examined.

Jeff came in the room. He put something in April's IV. "Mark, we are ready to move April to her own room," he kindly said to his friend. "I gave April something to calm her. I can't give April anything to make her sleep, not with her concussion." Mark shook his head in understanding.

Mark got up slowly and laid April down gently. Jeff unlocked the gurney, and he and Mark moved it out of the room. They took April to her room. When they got there, Mark picked April up off the gurney and carried her to the bed.

Mark gently covered her with a blanket. Then he lay down beside her, wrapping his arms around her body. Dan and Jeff stood watching sadly.

"Mark, it's late. You are beat; you have to get some sleep. I want you to come with me so that I can check your spleen and see if Paul did any damage." Mark did not look up. He did not care what Paul had done to him.

"I'm not leaving April," Mark said faintly but firmly.

"We are doing everything we can to find Sunny."

"Did Paul talk to Lewis?" Mark questioned as he looked up in hope that they had found his daughter. His begging eye caught Dan's heart and twisted it in half.

"Not yet, son, but he will and this will all be over," Dan said to Mark's pain-stricken eyes. Their eyes held as Dan absorbed Mark's heartache. Dan could not find it in his heart to tell Mark that Lewis was not answering any of Paul's calls.

"Just find her, Dan, bring her back to us," Mark said with such sadness.

Mark continued to look at Dan for comfort the way he had done as a child. Mark's eyes were extremely blood shot; he was pale and sweating.

I have to get Mark back to the Unit; he needs his medications for the day, Dan thought, wishing he could take away Mark's pain.

Then Mark looked over at Jeff's worried face. "I'll stay with her, Jeff; you go home and get some rest."

"You need to get some rest yourself, Mark," Jeff softly pleaded with him.

"I'll be fine, go home," Mark said quietly, as he held onto April with no intention of letting her out of his arms.

Jeff looked at Dan for permission to leave the room. Dan shook his head and the two of them went into the hallway. Both looked concerned.

"I don't like how Mark looks," Jeff told Dan with concern.

"Go call Dr. Stevenson and see what he wants us to do," Dan replied.

Dan went back into the room and looked at Mark. Mark looked so exhausted and stressed. Mark's fever must be back the way he was sweating.

"Mark, I am worried about you. I want you to go up to the Unit and let Dr. Stevenson have a look at you," Dan requested with deep concern.

"I'm fine; I am not going to the Unit," Mark said with conviction.

"Mark, you need to get some sleep. You cannot keep going on like this all night," Dan pleaded with him. Mark got off the bed, held his chest, and slowly walked to the door and opened it. He faced Dan; his eyes were so weary. Dan moved in his direction.

"Mark, you look like you are in pain, let Jeff have a look at you," Dan emphasized. Dan just wanted to hold Mark in his arms and protect him from all the heartache he was feeling.

"I am fine, Dan, just leave us alone. Tell the nurses not to come in here tonight," Mark peacefully told him. He was too weak to look Dan in the face. His pain was not physical; it was his heart that was tormented not knowing where Sunny was.

Dan took the door from him. Mark turned to walk back to the bed. Dan stood watching him. Mark was so drained of energy, as he tried to walk back to April's bed, his legs became unstable, and the blood drained from his head. He lacked all physical strength. Mark knew he was going to black out so he lunged for the chair beside April's bed, but he could not reach it.

Dan realized Mark was blacking out, and he grabbed him from behind and caught him. Dan lugged Mark over to the spare bed and set him down on the edge.

Mark sat for a minute with his head bowed forward. Then he looked into Dan's worried eyes. Deep down he knew Dan was right; he had to take care of himself to ensure he could take care of April. But he had no choice, April needed him right now; she came first.

When he felt he had regained enough strength, he stood up slowly, unsure if his legs would hold him up. Dan held his arm, ready to catch him again.

"I'm fine; I just lost my balance," Mark told Dan as he walked unsteadily back to April's bed.

"Like heck you are. Your body is completely drained; you are exhausted. I want you to lie down on this bed over here and get some rest before you injure yourself!" Dan demanded strongly.

Dan was very concerned about Mark's health and wished that he had insisted that Mark had stayed in the Unit today.

"I'm going to call Jeff and get him to come back up here and have a look at you," Dan told him sternly. Mark needed medical attention whether he wanted it or not.

"I'm just stressed and tired; there is nothing physically wrong with me. Tell Jeff to go home. I'll go see Dr. Stevenson tomorrow morning," Mark insisted.

"Mark, I am dead serious. You need medical attention right now; you have to think about your health," Dan maintained.

"April needs me. She is so distraught over Sunny; I have to be here when she cries out. If I go to sleep, I will never hear her. I have to be her strength until she can cope on her own," he said weakly, leaning on her bed for support.

April cried out Mark's name, and Mark turned back to her and held her hand. He was so tender with her. His heart just poured out to her.

"It's all right April, I'm right here," he reassured her so tenderly.

"Tell me you still love me," she sobbed, needing him to say the words.

"April, I love you so much. I will always love you. You don't have to be afraid; I'll be right here." Mark leaned over, placed his cheek next to hers, and wrapped his arms around her and gathered her like a rag doll to his chest.

Mark was going to do all that he could to bring April comfort. The power of their love would be all that they had left to survive the heartache deep within their souls for their missing child.

CHAPTER FIFTY-ONE –
❦Help Me Find My Way❧

$\mathcal{T}$he door opened, and Robert and Julia started to enter, but Dan motioned for them to go back into the hallway and he joined them. Julia looked worried as she fell into Dan's arms and he gave her a reassuring hug.

"What are you doing here at this hour?" Dan quizzed them.

"We could not wait at home any longer; you never called us back," Robert reminded him. In all of the confusion, Dan had forgotten his promise to call them back. He had called them earlier and had briefly told them what was happening, promising to get back with them as soon as he knew more information.

"All we know is what you told us on the phone."

Julia's eyes told of tears shed on their way to the hospital. "We cannot believe that Mark is a father and we have a granddaughter, and she is Sunny. Is it true that Sunny could be a donor match for Mark?" Julia continued as her heart stopped still. She felt as if her heart could not beat a single beat again unless Dan spoke the words she wanted desperately to hear. Sunny could save her son's life.

"Yes, it is incredible how things have turned out," Dan confirmed as he gathered Julia in his arms again and gave her a comforting hug.

Robert was unable to express the words that pulled at his mind. The judge had declared Mark an unsuitable candidate for Sunny's adoption. Robert would have to appeal that decision as soon as possible. Somewhere out there in the darkness of this night was his granddaughter, and he would do everything possible to bring her home to his son safely.

"How is April; was she hurt badly?" Julia asked with concern.

"No, she has a concussion. She is emotionally distressed over the disappearance of Sunny though. It is Mark I am worried about; he is suffering from extreme exhaustion. He has truly been incredible the way he has handled April's mental state. He is so compassionate to her needs; that he does not realize that he is jeopardizing his own health."

"What can we do?" Robert volunteered as Sally Johnson joined them.

"Do you need anything, Dr. Morgan? Should I go in there and care for April?" she inquired. She gripped Julia's hand and gave it a caring squeeze.

"Bring me a mild sedative in a syringe. I'm afraid the only alternative we have is to forcibly sedate Mark, since he is so determined to endanger himself," Dan informed them all. He could not let Mark continue like he was doing.

"I'll be right back," Sally said.

"Can we try to reason with him first?" Julia pleaded. She knew how angry it would make Mark if they sedated him against his own will. Her eyes showed panic as she imaged the fuss that Mark would execute if they try to sedate him. Mark would definitely put up a fight to the end, and she just could not stomach upsetting Mark even more than he already was at this moment.

"Go ahead and try, Julia, but at this point, nothing we say is going to matter to him," Dan voiced, as he opened the door and led them into the room.

Julia grasped Robert's hand as they entered and witnessed the indisputable despair of Mark's heart for April and Sunny.

Mark was sitting on the bed, his legs hanging over the side of it. He was holding April's hand in his as he hunched over her. He briefly looked up at his parents.

"Hello, Mark," Julia spoke warmly to her son, as she approached the bed. Robert stood back, afraid that his strong presence would put unwarranted stress on Mark. Mark did not say anything as they entered. He continued staring at April. He was overwhelmed with grief and guilt.

"Dan told us what happened. I am so sorry April was hurt. May I sit with her while you get some sleep?" she volunteered gently as she placed her hand on his shoulder with love.

Mark reached up and placed his hand over her hand. She lifted her other hand up and touched his hand, connecting them together in this heartbreaking moment between a mother and son. Yet she realized there was nothing she could do to take away his pain.

"I can't sleep, Mom, not 'till I know where Sunny is, not 'till I know they haven't hurt her," he said quietly as tears rolled softly down his face. The pain in his heart poured out instantly as his mother gathered her arms around his back and held him like a child.

"Oh, Mom ... they took my little girl," he tearfully cried out.

"I'm sure they are not hurting her, Mark. We have to believe that in our hearts. But in the mean time, Mark, you have to get some rest," she encouraged Mark gently as she fought back her own tears. It hurt her deeply to see Mark in such emotional pain. Mark turned around and looked into his mother's eyes with remorse.

"I'm so angry, I feel so helpless. I love April; she is my life." He touched his fist to his heart. "I cannot leave her; she needs me here with her. I did this to her. Don't you see ... she is suffering because of me?" he mourned as fresh tears fell. Julia wiped the tears from his cheeks and held her hands on his face so that he was forced to look her in the face.

She took a deep breath and gathered her own tears back, trying to be strong for her son. "There is a bed right over there. I will sit with her while you sleep. I will wake you up the second she starts to stir," Julia encouraged him with her soft protective voice, the very voice that he had always obeyed when he was a child.

"I don't know," Mark said as if he might give in.

"Please, Mark, I'm so worried about you. Let me help you," his mother said warmly with love for her son. Mark turned back to April.

"You promise you will wake me?" Mark asked quietly.

"I promise. I'll sit right here by her," Julia promised.

April started to stir at that moment, her eyes opened wide with fright.

"I want my baby ... where is my baby ... Mark!" she muttered. Mark brushed her hair back and held her in his arms, trying to calm her. "Jessica ... Jessica," she cried softly against Mark.

"Shhh ... it is okay, April, I'm here," he told her as he tried to soothe her fears about their child. The same fears ripped at his heart as he visualized Sunny's innocent face.

Julia stood quietly; she had been so close to getting Mark to go to sleep. If only April had not woken up.

Sally came into the room. She stood back by Robert. Mark tenderly rocked April in his arms speaking tender words of comfort. She finally calmed down and fell asleep. He gently laid her down on the bed.

Mark turned and looked at everyone. His anger had returned after seeing how destroyed April was, knowing he was the reason that she was grieving for their child. No one spoke as they witnessed the lines of stress form on his distraught face.

"Why are you all just standing there?" he said angrily, wanting to be left alone to grieve with April.

"We are all concerned about you and April," Julia explained to him.

"We'll be fine. How many times do I have to tell you that? Just leave us alone," Mark pleaded, avoiding Julia's eyes.

"I will sit with April now, and you can get some sleep, and everyone will leave," Julia said warmly, hoping that Mark would calm back down and agree. Mark's ears could not deny her concerned voice for him. He took a slow breath and wiped his face.

"It's okay, Mom, you and everyone can go. You all need your sleep too, so just go, please," he softly begged her calmly. It was just like Mark to be concerned about them, Julia thought of his unselfish qualities.

"Mark, you are the one who needs the sleep!" Robert said firmly, then he quickly realized his strong voice threatened Mark, even though that was not his intention. "Please, Mark, everyone is concerned for you."

Mark did not want to hear anymore; he just wanted them to leave him alone with April.

"I told you, I don't need any sleep!" Mark said put out. He was frustrated that they would not listen to him. How could he make them understand that he just wanted to be alone with April? Why couldn't they understand that and leave?

Mark got off the bed quickly to stand up so he could get rid of them, but his legs would not support his weight, and he collapsed to the floor.

Robert and Dan both had tried unsuccessfully to grab him as he fell. They quickly moved to his side. They helped him up, holding him under his arms as they led him to the extra bed.

"I am not lying down!" Mark shouted at them as he tried to break away from them. They held him firmly as Dan told Sally to bring him the syringe.

Robert forced Mark down against the bed. Robert put his full weight against Mark's chest and held Mark's wrists with his hands against the bed. Mark tried to put up a struggle, but he was too weak to fight his father's strength.

"Don't fight us, Mark!" Robert begged him.

Sally handed Dan the syringe. Mark saw it and resisted more, trying to free his arms from his father's grip. "Don't do it, Dan!" Mark yelled at him frantically, his eyes wild. "Don't do it, please don't, Dan!"

"You leave me no choice, Mark," Dan told him firmly.

"April needs me, don't do it!" he screamed out frantically, refusing to give up his struggle.

Sally rolled up Mark's long sleeve shirt and helped hold Mark's arm down firmly against the bed as Dan injected the syringe into Mark's arm.

"Nooo ...." Mark voiced as he felt the needle pierce his skin and the sensation of the medication warm his vein. He rolled his head back and forth in frustration against the bed.

They held Mark until he was still. It was not long before Mark gave up his struggle and closed his eyes and was quiet. They lifted his legs up on the bed and pulled the blanket up over him.

Mark knew he could fight the drug but he did not have the strength to fight Dan and Robert, so he pretended to be asleep. It worked; they all left the room.

Mark struggled to sit up. The drug was working quickly. He grabbed the handrails to the bed and pulled himself up using all the strength he had left. Then he slowly stood up, still holding the railing. He grabbed the nightstand and made his way carefully to April's bed. He lay down beside her; he slid his right arm behind her neck, and cuddled her next to him.

He could not fight his fatigue and the sedative any longer; he fell asleep.

Julia returned to the room to sit with April, but when she saw them sleeping together, she quietly left the room. She and Robert decided there was nothing more they could do and chose to go home. It had been an exhausting day, dealing with Mark's illness and the loss of their granddaughter to the unknown was more than she could handle.

Dan called Jeff to come up to the room to examine Mark. He wanted a sample of Mark's blood. Jeff came up and together with Sally, they went into April's room.

Jeff took his stethoscope from around his neck, he put it in his ears, and then he slid his hand between April's back and Mark's chest. He placed it on Mark's chest and listened, and then he placed it on Mark's back.

"He sounds good."

"Let's get some blood from him," Dan gave his order to Sally. She had everything he needed on the bedside table.

"Let's get his shirt up. I want a look at his chest, be gentle, I do not want him awake," Dan said. He was concerned about Mark's spleen.

Dan gently lifted Mark's arm that was around April's waist, and slid Mark's arm out of his long sleeve shirt. Jeff helped Dan pull Mark's shirt up to Mark's neck, exposing his back and left side. They both gasped when they saw the bruising on his back and arm. They both looked at each other in disgust.

"Did he get these from football practice today?" Jeff asked, forgetting that Dan was not aware that Mark had gone to practice today. "Uh …."

"What do you mean football practice?"

Jeff did not respond to the frustrated look on Dan's face.

"I just don't know what I am going to do about you two knuckleheads, this is it, Jeff! You and Mark are going to start following the rules around here, or I am going to toss you both out of my program!" Dan sighed as he shook his head back and forth.

"I've let things slide because Mark is like a son to me, but no more, either he starts listening to us, or I am going to knock his head off."

Nevertheless, as soon as Dan looked back and saw Mark lying there defenseless on the bed with April in his arms, his heart went weak. He knew that everything Mark did was out of his self-sacrifice for those he loved.

Dan looked back at Jeff and noticed the remorse on his face. He realized that this whole situation was out of Jeff's control. No one had control, which was the whole problem.

"I'm sorry, Jeff. I am not handling Mark's condition any better than you are. This whole mess is more than any of us can handle. A father wants what is best for his son. I want Mark to surrender to us medically, and all he wants to do is live his life as a normal twenty-four year old. I made him a promise not to stand in his way, but I cannot keep that promise, Jeff. Do you understand; I am his doctor right now, not his godfather?"

"Dan, I know ..." Jeff really wanted to avoid the subject so he changed it. "What about the bruises?"

"Paul knocked him against a door and hit him in the chest. I am sure that is how he got them." Dan's stomach churned as he remembered what Paul had done. He felt miserable as deep concern showed on his face. The truth was. *Paul could have killed Mark today.*

Dan examined Mark's spleen and determined it was still about the same. Mark made no jerking motion when Dan pressed on his spleen. Dan was thankful Paul's blows had been on Mark's right side and not on his left side.

"His heart sounds fine; he has good breath sounds," Jeff thankfully relayed. "We need to find out what his blood counts are."

"You're right, let's get the blood, and then we'll go from there." Sally took blood from Mark's arm and sent it to the lab.

They decided it was better for Mark to sleep there with April. Sleep is what he needed. They could not risk another battle with him if they tried to move him to the Unit away from April.

Dan injected the medications Dr. Stevenson had ordered for Mark. Sally brought in the IV fluids, hung them up, and hooked them to Mark.

When Mark's blood tests came back, they gave him a unit of blood and a unit of platelets.

Jeff returned to the ER to sleep in the staff call room. Dan went to his office and slept there so he could keep an eye on them during the night.

Sally Johnson would also keep a close eye on April and Mark. She covered them with a blanket and turned the light down low before she left the room.

Then she stood against the door and prayed for divine protection over the couple.

Chapter Fifty-Two –
⮜The Night in the Park⮞

*M*ark found himself dreaming of the past. His mind was racing, as he relived those forgotten days.

He and April were riding Thunder together; she had her arms affectionately around him. She was his childhood playmate, his very best friend. They were climbing trees, fishing, swimming in the pool, going on his endless adventures, and caring for his homeless animals.

April was in the stables with him after his grandfather died. They were holding each other so tenderly, she being the only one who understood his broken heart. Then he went away to school and lost track of her.

Carlo had brought them back together in his senior year. It was as if they had never been apart the moment they stood before each other speechless, absorbed in the love they had for each other.

April's father had forbidden their relationship, and she wanted friendship, no more than that, but it turned into so much more as they spent quality time together.

Mark and April were having lunch together at school. He was at the water fountain with her, laughing, talking, and sharing his day with her.

They spent hours on the football bleachers talking about their future dreams. Then, there she was at his eighteenth birthday party. The splendid vision of her had stopped him in his tracks as he realized that she had possession of his heart. They were dancing cheek to cheek, his fingers spread open to embrace her slender waist. They gave the impression of being deeply in love. Then he kissed her passionately on the lips to seal his eternity with her. They were king and queen at the homecoming dance. He had secretly taken her there.

April stirred and Mark briefly opened his eyes and then he went back to sleep.

At the Championship Football Game, he had kissed her on the sideline. The game had been exciting, the score stayed close, they had to come from behind. With seconds to go, Mark had gone back to pass, no receivers were open. He ran the ball for an amazing touchdown.

The crowd cheered loudly, chanting his name. The gun went off; they had won a State Championship Game! Excitement filled the stadium as everyone ran onto the field, screaming, hugging, and slapping hands. Mark was the center of everyone's attention. College scouts bidding to speak to him swarmed him.

However, his thoughts were exclusively on finding April as he frantically looked for her through the crowd. He jumped up to see over the reporters around him, hoping to get a glimpse of her. They made eye contact with each other briefly, but he could not get to her, in the mass of players that were now squishing him between them.

"April, wait!" he shouted out as he waved at her just before his teammates lifted him up on their shoulders and carried him towards the locker room. They carried him away from the one person that he wanted to share this spectacular moment of his life with tonight. "April!" he turned his body in her direction and pointed to the parking lot. She nodded her head in agreement.

His adrenaline was rapidly flowing throughout his body from the excitement of the moment. He had done it; his future as a quarterback was secured, and he was about to rekindle his relationship with the woman that had jump-started his heart in ways that he could never have imagined.

The guys had gotten a cooler and filled it with beer before the game and had hidden it in the showers. When the coaches went into their office, the guys sneakily took it out, ready to begin their victory party with their star quarterback.

The players cheerfully gathered around Mark. They handed him a drink, forcing it into his grip. At first, Mark turned them down, knowing it was wrong to be drinking.

"Guys, I don't think ..."

"C'mon Mark, let's celebrate!" One of the players reached over and pulled the tab off the can for Mark. Then the other players toasted him with good cheer. They toasted the victory. "To Mark! We are the State Champions!"

Mark's mind filled with uncertainties about what they were doing, not wanting the drink, wishing he were with April. But this was an important time for his teammates; he did not want to offend them in their victory celebration.

"My dad is buying me a truck for winning this game!" Blake expressed in an over-zestful voice. His words sent Mark's mind spinning in a downward spiral.

This was supposed to be a special night, his night, where all his hard work in football for the last four years would reap its reward. Angrily, Mark thought of his father's inexcusable absence. His father had missed the most important night of his life, Mark thought from the pit of his churning stomach.

"Darn him!" Mark felt his anger rise up as his face got heated. His heart turned hard thinking about all the times his father had disappointed him. Mark took the drink, squeezing the can tightly between his forceful fingers and toasted his teammates.

"Great game, men, to us!"

The vision of his father's disapproving face stirred his anger that much more. This was one time his father would not steal his victory, he thought with determination, as he took another drink. He held the can up high with one hand as he toasted.

"To you, Dad, wherever your sorry self is at!" Then he took another drink as the anger consumed his wrenched heart, and then he discreetly threw the half-empty can in the trashcan. "I hope you're proud of me … Dad." He softly expressed his remorse as he sucked back his disappointment in what he had just done.

The team had showered and gotten dressed. When Mark came out of the locker room, they were secretively waiting for him outside the building. Mark was hoping to sneak away; he had made plans to meet April at the park, and that was where he was heading, when he felt someone grab him.

His friends had other plans intended for him. They grabbed the front of his football jacket and dragged him away from his car. They took him out on the football field. Their harebrained drinking continued, as the players celebrated with laughter and fooling around on the field.

Mark unwillingly was the center of their attention, as they reenacted the winning play. Mark was feeling good now as the alcohol entered into his system.

Mark's mind was focused on thoughts of April waiting in the park alone for him. He wanted to share his victory with her, just as they had shared every important moment of their lives with each other, when they were younger.

Finally, Mark broke down and told Carlo that he had to leave and meet April at the park. That was a huge mistake. The guys decided to go with him. They surrounded him, grabbed hold of his jacket and forced him to go where they wanted him to go. They were laughing hysterically.

Mark lightly protested as they shoved him around, but he gave in to their fun so he would not hurt their feelings. When they reached the parking lot, they pushed Mark into the backseat of Carlo's car and drove to the park. They rowdily laughed as they kidnapped their reluctant quarterback.

The drinking continued as Carlo drove entirely too fast. They opened a can of beer and shoved it in Mark's hand. Mark knew now that his friends had stepped over the line; they were uncontrollably drinking and carelessly driving. Mark was convinced they were all about to die or kill someone. He quietly prayed for their safety as Carlo continued to drive.

Mark was regretting his choice to drink with the guys. He sat quietly as he looked down at the can he held in his hand. *If only I had said no.* It was too late to undo what he had done. If only he had stood up to what he believed in and not submitted under pressure to drink with the guys.

Even though Mark had taken small sips at a time, he was beginning to feel the effects of the alcohol. His system was not used to the alcohol. It would not take much to have an effect on him, especially since he had not eaten all day.

As the car swerved, Mark feared they would all die on the same night that they had won the most important game of their life.

When they arrived alive at the park, Mark gave God a silent praise. As they emptied the car, Mark begged the guys to leave him alone with April. Carlo had gotten blankets out of his trunk.

"We'll go over by the fountain and party while you and April do whatever it is you are going to do." Carlo laughed as he threw Mark a blanket. "Here, you might need this, Romeo," Carlo laughed; they all laughed as they formed a buddy line and staggered off to the fountain.

Mark brushed off their sly remarks. Mark had no intentions of doing anything with April but talking to her or taking her out to get something to eat.

Mark found April sitting on a bench by a lamppost. She was still in her cheerleading sweater and skirt. Her hair was pulled back in a ponytail. She was absolutely beautiful sitting there in the scenic moonlight. He was instantly drawn to her loveliness as he sat next to her on the bench.

"I'm sorry I'm late. The guys wanted to celebrate the victory and I couldn't get away from them," he apologized as his eyes were frozen on her appealing face.

"It's okay," she said shyly. April was truly gorgeous in the lamplight; Mark was melting deep inside her eyes.

"Wow, what a game. Wasn't it great!" Mark said excitedly as he flashed her a charming grin. He still felt pumped, his heart beating steadily. He wanted to share his excitement with her.

"You were great," she said bashfully, her eyes inviting him into her heart. She knew that she needed to be careful to avoid the temptations that came with weaving him into her heart while he was so thrilled to be here with her.

"I have you to thank for that, you got me back in the game with that kiss."

"You're welcome," she smiled tenderly.

"You want to walk down to the pond?" he asked her as he stood up, unsteadily at first, as he awkwardly regained his sea legs. She knew then that Mark was under the influence.

"Sure," she said with a smile, and he held out his hand to help her up. His hand was so strong and warm as it embraced her hand.

She had never seen Mark drink and wondered why he had done it tonight. He must have been pressured by the guys after tonight's win, she thought, wishing that he was more sober.

They walked hand in hand to the pond as Mark staggered a few times and she grabbed her arm around his waist to hold him steady. It was darker by the pond, but the moon was shining over it, making it very romantic, as the rays of light danced across the water. The winter ducks were floating smoothly across the glassy water.

Mark laid the blanket on the ground. They both sat down. "Are you comfortable?" he asked with concern when he noticed that she was shaking. It was cold outside; of course, she had to be cold. He thoughtfully took off his football jacket and wrapped it around her shoulders.

"Thank you," she said sweetly, her eyes meeting his eyes tenderly; she drew a breath as she joined her heart to his. *Oh, Mark, I am so in love with you*, she dreamingly thought, wishing that the words could escape her lips.

April looked so stunning in the moonlight, Mark thought again. He could not deny the love he had inside his heart for her. He noticed she was still shaking. He bent closer to her and wrapped the jacket around her more securely. Her eyes captured his as he moved closer to her. He bent his face to hers in an exquisite moment of his affection for her.

"May I kiss you?" he petitioned her in a moment of weakness. She favorably agreed with a shake of her head. Mark kissed her lips so softly, so gently, as he held the back of her head in his restful hands. He wanted to melt as he drew her face to his yearning lips.

She positioned her arms around his neck as they continued to kiss again. He pulled her hair out of the ponytail and smoothed it out with his hands. Her hair felt so soft and silky as he ran his fingers through it.

"You are so beautiful, April. I am so in love with you," he softly expressed his undeniable feelings as they poured out of his heart for her.

"I love you, Mark," she let the words tenderly spill out, knowing that there was no turning back, she wanted to belong to him. They kissed again so tenderly, neither knowing the boundaries those innocent kisses were opening. She seized his face in her warm hands as she claimed him as hers.

"I feel like my veins are on fire," he expressed to her as he kissed her again. This time the kiss lasted longer, taking in the unfamiliar feelings of such an emotional bond with her.

He took a few deep breaths to recover. "I have thought about that night we danced at my birthday party so many times. I wished that night that you would fall in love with me. But you never spoke to me after you left me standing there alone. Why?" he sincerely asked, wanting to know why she had not returned his love for her.

"I was already in love with you before that dance, Mark. I loved you in the stables that day Carlo took Sharon and me out there," she informed him tenderly.

"Why didn't you tell me?" he asked as he pushed back a lock of her hair and framed her face with his thumbs.

"I was afraid you did not feel the same way about me," she softly spoke to his heart, choosing not to mention her father's involvement in her aloof behavior.

"I did. I thought my heart was going to jump out of my chest when I saw you. I knew I was madly in love with you," he replied lovingly and gained a striking smile from her. His words were so sweet; she heard the truth of his feelings in his voice.

Tears formed in her eyes, "Oh, Mark ... my heart had already exploded when I saw your eyes again that day. I loved you back when we were childhood friends. I have always loved you, Mark Sanders," she admitted to him as their eyes melted together during their confessions of their hidden emotions. This was the very moment that she had been dreaming about all these years.

Mark took off his class ring. He knelt on one knee gallantly as he charmingly faced her. He took April's tiny hand and placed the ring on her finger. It was way too big, but it did not matter. This ring would be a symbol of his unending commitment to the girl he loved. He wiped back a joyful tear, gathered a breath of fresh air and spoke.

"April Morgan, will you be my girl, will you promise yourself to me and only to me forever and ever?" he delightfully asked with such love.

Tears formed in her eyes. "Yes, **my prince**, I promise myself to you, until we part from death," she replied enchantingly as she knelt on both her knees in front of him. They held each other and sealed it with a kiss. He had joined their hearts together in this wondrous moment.

Mark took off her gold necklace from around her neck and put his ring on the chain. Then he placed the necklace over her head and adjusted it around her neck.

"It is official, April Morgan. You belong to me." He leaned over to kiss her and lost his balance, knocking them both down on the blanket. They both laughed, but then they both became very serious as this serene moment took them to a place they had never known.

Mark put his arms around the back of her neck, supporting her head in his hand, and kissed her. He had never felt this kind of passion. The desires they felt for each other were overwhelming.

He wanted to resist his urges but his flesh had taken control of his better judgment. His heart had opened up, and he wanted to love her forever. He reached out and gathered her snug against him in an embrace.

April had her arms wrapped around him, kissing him, kissing his neck. He could feel her warm breath on his neck. He could feel her heartbeat against his chest. Never had he known such intense feelings as the ones she was sending him.

Mark removed the jacket off her shoulders and let it fall behind her. He pushed the jacket under her head to support her neck, considerate of her comfort.

He held her, he touched her; she responded as she placed her hands under his shirt and touched his chest. Then she outlined his face with her affectionate hands and kissed him. She was driving him wild, yet everything was slow and tender as they advanced into the unknown of loving each other.

The desire to love her burned deep inside of him. He could not shake the feelings that consumed and diverted his mind from what he knew to be right. Any perception of what was about to happen to them was the furthest thought from his mind. Otherwise, he would have realized that the true desire of his heart was to be faithful to a commitment that he had made with God.

It was too late to turn back; he wanted to love her completely. He had tried to hold back, but there was no turning back what was happening to his heart.

He looked deep into her calming eyes. Did she know what was happening to him; did she want him too? "Do you want me to stop?" he asked her passionately. She did not say no. She kissed his lips and invited herself into his soul.

She wants me as much as I want her, he thought sincerely. She touched his warm skin with her enticing fingers on his back. She was not resisting him; she was encouraging his desires.

He was passionate and gentle, as he loved her with his entire heart. It all felt so wonderful and natural. Did she feel as in love as he did? He told her repeatedly, "I love you. I love you." She repeated those same words peacefully in his ear as he held her close, joining them together as one.

Then breathless, Mark lay down beside her, taking in all that had just happened between them. His mind was racing. It was then that he heard her whimpering softly. *She was crying*, he thought fearfully! Suddenly he felt very ill. His head was swimming with emotions. *What have I done*? Then reality hit him. His stomach was on fire. He had done the unthinkable, the unimaginable, the unforgivable act that he had promised he would reserve for his wedding night. The very night that he had dreamed would belong to the two of them someday.

He had hurt her. He wanted to die. He wanted to undo what he had done, but it was too late. This should not have happened, he thought in anguish. How had he let things get so out of control?

He wanted to comfort her. He rolled over on his side and placed his arms around her. Something that should have been so special for the two of them, was not, that is what he thought. He could not breathe knowing what they had just done.

"I'm so sorry, April ... I didn't mean to ... hurt you ..." His head filled with blood as the alcohol over took him. "A ..." he tried to say but he fell back unconscious.

April had not had a chance to tell him how she had felt about what they had done.

Later, the guys had taken him to Carlo's cousins and they had gotten plastered. This time Mark did all the drinking on his own.

He wanted to wipe the night out of his mind.

Life did not matter, he had hurt the girl he loved more than his own life.

CHAPTER FIFTY-THREE –
∼Lies of the Devil∽

Sally had come into the room early that morning to check on the couple.

Dr. Stevenson had ordered for Mark to have another unit of blood during the night. He had to keep Mark's counts up. Sally had given Mark his medications and prayed that he would be able to tolerate them.

Mark and April both seemed restless. Mark was sweating; she wiped his forehead with a cool cloth. She took April's vital signs. Should she take Mark's, she wondered; she did not want him to awaken.

Mark seemed to be breathing heavy; she raised the bed slightly higher to help him breathe easier. Sally gently touched his hand in affection for his young life. How much more would he suffer, she wondered as she went out to the nurse's station to pray.

Mark's dream became a nightmare as he continued to hear April crying, the park became dark, cold, and scary. He had left her alone there as his friends gathered him up off the ground and took him away.

Mark opened his eyes. He had broken out in a sweat; he was terrified. His breathing was labored as he tried to sort it all out.

He was in shock from the reality of the dream he had. Was it a dream? No, he knew it was the truth of that forgotten night. Mark was in total disbelief that he had done such an irresponsible thing to April. They had been together, and for the last six years, he had no clue that he had taken her innocence away from her or from himself due to drinking.

Unfortunately, Mark only remembered the tears that April had shed, and those fallen tears cut through him like a sharp twisting knife, inflicting insurmountable damage to his vulnerable heart. What did I do that night? *Was I so drunk I date raped her?* he thought in anguish.

He did not remember the tenderness of their love that they had shared. He could only remember the tormenting end of the dream. He wanted to throw up; it made him physically sick thinking about the heartache he had put April through these last few years.

The unbelievable anger was welling up inside of him. *I must have done it, which is why April never told me about what happened that night. That is why she avoided me when she came back to town.*

He continued to think irrationally. The devil had taken over his mind and was filling it with terrible lies, in hopes of crushing his longevity of faith.

That is why I got so drunk at Carlo's cousin's house afterwards. I was trying to drown out what I had done. I was trying to block it all out of my mind.

He thought that was just what he had done. He had destroyed his memory of his precious April to keep out the pain of what he had done to her. *The doctors had been right; he had been suppressing his memory of that night because he wanted it to vanish from his memory forever.*

Mark remembered when he told his father in the emergency room, that he wanted to die. He was remembering that weekend in tiny pieces; the pain he had felt then was all coming back in waves.

Mark pulled his arm out from behind April's neck carefully. He was appalled at what he had done to her. He could not live with himself.

I do deserve to die for what I did to her. I got her pregnant, and I went on living as if nothing had happened while she lived in a nightmare of pain and suffering, all because of me.

All because of a choice to drink that night out of anger at my father. I caused all of this mess. This is all my fault!

Mark remembered how his grandfather had warned him against doing things to get back at his father.

I failed. I broke my promise to my grandfather, he thought with deep agonizing remorse. "Oh, Papa, I am so sorry."

Mark pulled out all the IV lines that were inserted into his catheter. *How did they get there? Dang those doctors; I can't trust anyone around here. What medications did they give me this time,* he wondered.

How could April ever forgive me? Have we been living a lie, these last few weeks? How could she let me touch her after what I have done to her? He tormented himself.

In the last few weeks they had done nothing more than kiss and innocently touch each other, saving themselves for their wedding night. Mark had been raised to respect women. His grandfather had always asked his grandmother if he could kiss her. Mark had his mother's gentle ways; he had his grandmother's compassionate heart.

Why, why did I drink that night and end up doing something so awful to April. I loved her so much, how, how could I have done this?

His mind raced with unsettling thoughts. This was unthinkable and stood against everything that he valued. His walk with the Lord all these years, had it been nothing more than a lie? *Have I been living a lie?* He thought he had been living an obedient life. He knew he was a sinner, but this was more than a sin in his mind.

Mark continued to torture himself with the untruths the devil was telling him. The door to his soul was wide open for the devil to enter and destroy him. Mark was allowing the devil to take this opportunity to steal away his faith by attacking his mortal flesh. His peace had turned to anger.

Mark continued to think as he paced the room. He was running his fingers through his hair in frustration. Tears stung at his eyes in the depth of his sorrow.

Sunny is paying for my mistakes. For the last five years, she has done nothing but suffer because of me. Is she suffering now? What are her kidnappers doing to her? Oh, God, where is Sunny?

Mark's rage was overwhelming. He violently knocked everything off the nightstand causing a small crashing sound as the things hit the floor.

Dan rushed into the room when he heard the crash. Dan saw the results of Mark's rage all over the floor. Mark stood there, with such anguish in his eyes and the dampness of tears on his face. Dan had never seen Mark this upset. Dan rushed to him and looked into Mark's suffering eyes.

"What is it, Mark, what happened?" Dan asked with alarm. Mark pushed by him and rushed to the door. Dan was able to grab his arm and twist Mark back around.

"What happened, Mark?" Dan demanded again.

"I remembered what happened that night. Oh … Dan … I date-raped her!" he shouted in torment as tears filled his broken heart. Then he pushed Dan aside and ran out the door. Dan was too astounded to move.

Then Dan saw Paul. Paul had been standing at the door; he had heard Mark's full confession.

CHAPTER FIFTY-FOUR –
ᴂGod's Amazing Loveᴂ

an saw the look of rage on his brother's face. Dan grabbed Paul by the upper arm and pulled him in the room. April was still sleeping soundly on the bed. Dan was thankful that she had been spared Mark's outburst.

"My office, now, do not say a word," Dan whispered to Paul angrily. Dan went into the hall and walked down to his office. Paul had followed. When Paul entered the room, he shut the door behind him.

"I heard Mark admit it, Dan, he raped my little girl, and I am going to have him arrested!" Paul yelled angrily. Dan looked at him with disgust.

"Haven't you already done enough? That young man never could have raped her, not in a million years! Mark does not know what he was saying," Dan relayed to Paul strongly, and then he picked up his phone to call Robert.

"Mark is dead. Do you hear me, he's dead!" Paul stressed angrily as he left the room in a storming rage. Dan had yelled after him but Paul left.

What luck, Paul thought. *Mark will go to jail and not be able to play in the football game. This was better than hurting him. Mark's team will lose the game and I will win my bets.* Paul celebrated his thoughts with a cunning grin.

Paul had planned to place all his bets on Mark's team to win Sunday, but with the polls favoring Mark's team to win, no one was betting against Mark's team to lose.

But when Lewis gave Paul the heads-up tip that Mark was in the hospital sick, Paul cashed in quickly and bet against Mark's team for Sunday's game. Paul had major money invested in this game three days before the public became aware that Mark was sick. The betting odds on the game had taken a dramatic change when the news conference released a statement saying that Mark had been hospitalized and the odds were not in Mark's favor of playing.

When Lewis called back later and said that it was uncertain if Mark was playing or not, Paul could not handle the pressure of losing all that money. He could not allow Mark to play.

Paul's anger at Robert Sanders came flashing back. Robert had messed him up in a business deal costing him a million dollars, and now his son, Mark, was going to do the same thing. It was more than Paul could tolerate. The thought of losing all that money pushed Paul into unthinkable insaneness for revenge.

Paul had to stop Mark somehow, and so he sent Lewis to do the job. The word was; Mark was sick with some kind of illness. Lewis would just have to make sure that Mark Sanders stayed just sick enough that he could not play. And so began the plot to poison Mark using several hospital employees Lewis had connections with.

Robert came to the phone, and Dan told him what had happened. It was too unbelievable. It was not possible, they both agreed with conviction. Now they had to find Mark and convince him that he had not done anything to hurt April.

"I know Mark. If he thinks he raped April, he is out to destroy himself; we have to find him quickly. Dr. Stevenson gave Mark his treatments very early this morning through his catheter, and I am afraid of another reaction. We have to find him; he will need his medications to counteract those reactions," Dan stressed to Robert frantically, as he paced back and forth while on the phone with Robert. Dan knew Mark would need nausea and pain medications as soon as the ones they gave him in the hospital wore off.

"I will go to his apartment; maybe he went there to sort this mess out," Robert urgently replied to Dan.

Mark had run back to his apartment. He knocked everything off his top shelf. He beat his fists angrily against the wall, the pain and guilt so overpowering. His heartache for Sunny and April caused his anger and rage. His disappointment in himself had sent him on this rampage. His heart was wrecked, smashed into a million pieces.

He loved April so much it hurt to breathe thinking he might lose her. How could she ever forgive him? He could not live without Sunny, not another day could pass without her in his arms. He intensely cried out as he held both hands against the wall and hung his head down in despair.

"Why … why is this happening, why is the devil doing this to me?" Mark felt his body go weak. His emotions hit the pit of his stomach like a fierce tidal wave.

Mark felt sick. He held his stomach, as he went over to the kitchen counter, and got the pill bottle Dr. Stevenson had given him for his upset stomach. He took several and waited for the feeling to pass as he leaned over the sink praying he would not be sick.

How could I have done this to April, he said with denial, as his heart was tearing in two, *how could this have happened? And Sunny, where was she? What has Lewis done with her?*

Then he took the pain medication he had, his hand shaking as he lifted the water glass to his lips. He accidentally dropped the medicine bottle on the counter and the pills spilled out. He hated these drugs; they were a reminder to him that he was supposed to be sick. He swiped them across the counter onto the floor in a fit of anger.

The pain inside of his heart hurt much worse than his physical pain from his injuries, but he could not deny that the physical pain was overtaking his life. At this moment, he was faced with the reality that he had aplastic anemia. He was frustrated and emotionally drained.

Mark looked over at the empty coffee pot. The thought of coffee made him sick but he knew he had to have something to keep him awake.

In desperation to continue functioning, he opened the cabinet drawer and got out the pills that Jerk had given him. He briefly looked at the label. Unsteadily he lifted the glass back to his lips, spilling drops of water down the front of his shirt as he tossed the pills into his mouth. *These stimulants will keep me awake*; he tried to reason with himself, as he took several of them.

As a doctor, he should have known better, but he was not thinking like a doctor. Mark had been so preoccupied with what he had to do today, that he was not thinking logically.

In his state of mind at that moment, he might not have cared that mixing those drugs together could be dangerous to him. The devil was working overtime in his mind and winning his battle against Mark. Mark had just given the devil the upper hand to destroy his life. The devil had come to trespass, steal and destroy Mark.

Then Mark went into the living room, and he saw it sitting on his coffee table. Its presence hit him with such force as he stared down at it. His Bible lay there on the table. It was not in his bedroom where he had left it. It was as if God had placed his Bible on the table where Mark would find it when he needed it the most.

God spoke to Mark's mind in a gentle voice and reminded him of the truth of the cross.

The second Mark saw his Bible he realized that he was not handling this situation according to God's Words. He realized that his anger and rage was nothing more than the work of the devil.

Seeing his Bible stopped him dead in his tracks, as if God had gently slapped him in the face and said, "Son, what are you doing, have you forgotten Me?"

Mark knew most of God's words and promises in that Bible. Mark felt God's incredible love for him in that instant as he stared down at his Bible. His Bible had always given him comfort.

God continued to speak to Mark's hurting heart with the Words that Mark knew all too well. Believe in Me, believe in the Words I have given you. You have been forgiven for your mistakes by My blood that I shed for you on the cross. I am right here with you. Fight for what you believe in your heart to be true. Stand strong and fight the enemy who has come against you.

Mark knew he had let the devil in to destroy him. Mark knew that he should have gone to the Lord first and not acted as he had. It was Satan that wanted him to feel hopeless and worthless.

Mark picked up his Bible and held it tight between his fingers. Then he held it to his heart and cried quiet tears of remorse, as he fell to his knees and told God how sorry he was for forsaking Him in his time of need.

Mark's anger swiftly left him, and he was filled with the peace that only God's love can supply. Mark let the humbling tears fall, thinking how

God had already forgiven him for all his mistakes by dying on the cross for all his sins.

God reminded Mark that he was not saved by the good he did. He was saved by the blood, which God had freely given him. God had forgiven, cleansed, and made him whole, at the cross.

The lie that Mark had lived all these years was thinking that he had to be perfect and not make one mistake. He opened his Bible randomly, asking God to give him a word to speak to his heart. His fingers turned to Romans and he read a passage that he had underlined sometime in his life.

Romans 3:23-26, God puts people right through their faith in Jesus Christ. God does this to all who believe in Christ, because there is no difference at all, everyone has sinned and is far away from God's saving presence. But by the free gift of God's grace all are put right with Him through Christ Jesus, who sets them free. God offered Him, so that by His sacrificial death, He should become the means by which people's sins are forgiven through their faith in Him.

Mark was released of the perfection he thought he needed to have to live for God. Mark's need for perfection had come from needing his earthly father to love him, not from his heavenly Father. Mark knew better, God's love for him was unconditional; all he had to do was claim God as His Savior.

God had not put Mark in bondage to be sinless. God had loved Mark, knowing he would make mistakes in his life. Mark was a sinner and God still loved him. God said, "I forgive you and I call you Mine."

Mark was finally set free to let God love him for who he was. Mark realized that his mistakes as a teenager had already been wiped clean a long time ago.

Mark had honored his commitment to the God he loved and trusted, and he would continue to live for God. Mark thanked God for reminding him that we have all sinned, and we all have been forgiven. Mark sat and prayed. Mark felt God's loving arms wrapped around him as he listened to what God had to say to his heart.

Mark would stay in faith and believe that God was a healing God. God would fight the enemy who wanted to bring Mark down. Mark's mortal flesh was at war with the devil, and Mark planned to battle the devil to the end.

Mark would have no ill effects from the drugs he had taken. God had delivered him from them. God had placed His shield of protection over Mark.

Mark was thankful that when he made bad choices, God was there to protect him. Mark wiped his tears with the back of his hand. Then he sat on the couch and closed his eyes in quiet prayer.

Mark made his praying all about God and his relationship with God. Mark asked for God's forgiveness and mercy for the way that he had handled this situation.

Once Mark had done that, he was released instantly of his pain and was able to have peace again. Mark truly believed that God would take care of Sunny for him. God would bring Sunny back home to him safely, and God would restore his relationship with April. Sunny was in God's hands now, and with that comforting thought, he no longer had to live in fear for his daughter's safety.

Mark was now relying on his deep relationship with God. He put his love, faith and trust in God to handle this situation for him. Mark was now humbling himself before God. God immediately gave him the strength to finish what he had to do today.

Kevin, who lived across the hall with his parents, came in the open door. Kevin was unaware that Mark had been back in the hospital the night before. He looked around at the mess.

"What happened in here, Mark, did you get robbed?" he asked with concern.

"No, what are you doing here?" Mark responded.

"It's Saturday. We have practice this morning, remember?" Kevin reminded Mark. "I thought we could ride together, Mark," he added as he noticed that Mark seemed out of it.

"Mark!" Kevin yelled to bring Mark back to earth.

"What?" Mark responded. Mark was not ready to stop thinking about all God had in store for him.

"Practice, let's go," Kevin told him, pointing in the direction of the door.

"Right, let's go," Mark agreed, and he followed Kevin out of the room.

CHAPTER FIFTY-FIVE –
Fighting the Enemy

*R*obert arrived shortly afterwards and found the apartment unlocked. He held his breath, not knowing what to expect, fearful of what Mark might have done to himself.

He slowly entered the apartment and discovered the mess left behind by Mark. He looked around and found the pill bottles turned over on their sides on the counter, and the pills scattered on the floor. Frightened of what Mark had done, he quickly called Dan.

"Mark has been here; the place is a mess! I found some pills here. Dan, I am scared; they look like Mark has been in them. I have a bad feeling about this, Dan," Robert exclaimed desperately wanting to know if Mark's life was in danger from taking those pills.

"Bring the bottles to me and we'll find out what he has taken." Dan instructed Robert and then hung up the phone. His fingers were shaking. "Please, God, if Mark did anything stupid, send him an angel to protect him."

Paul came into Dan's office unannounced.

"I called my old friend, Captain Nelson, from the police department. Do you know Grant?" Paul asked Dan with an attitude that Dan did not like.

"I know him. I want to know why you are doing this, Paul?" Dan asked him angrily.

"Because Mark Sanders is not about to get away with what he did to my daughter!" Paul said vindictively.

"This is crazy, Paul!" Dan yelled at him.

"You may think so, but you did not have to move your family away from the shame of what Mark did to April," Paul retorted back angrily.

"Mark did not know April was pregnant, and I do not care what Mark said, he did not rape her. There is absolutely no way Mark could have done that!" Dan insisted firmly.

"He did! I know my daughter; she never would have done it willingly," Paul disputed.

"Stop it, whatever happened between them is over. They were only eighteen years old. They did a foolish thing, but April loves Mark, she has always loved him. It is about time you realize you cannot control her life any longer," Dan said unnerved.

"I lost Debbie to her foolhardiness; I won't lose April," Paul insisted.

"I told you to let Debbie marry the man she loved but you insisted she marry someone you preferred. No wonder she ran off and got married to Phil behind your back. Besides, Phil is a nice young man, you should be thankful for that. Paul, you are losing your children with your foolishness," Dan warned him.

"Phil is a bum, but at least he did not get Debbie pregnant," Paul angrily replied.

"Phil is not a bum and you know it. Why can't you just accept the men your daughters love and stop all this nonsense?" Dan responded. Dan's eyes wanted to cut Paul in half for his ignorance. Phil was a professional baseball player, well respected. Sally Johnson was Phil's mother and Dan had great respect for her family.

"I know what is best for them!" Paul arrogantly retorted.

"How can you act so uncaring? How could you have made April give up her baby, your grandchild?" Dan shook his head in disbelief. "How could you have lied to Tammy and told her that her grandchild was dead? I just do not understand you, Paul!"

"What is done is done. I had to do it for April's sake," Paul said with the slightest hint of remorse.

"April is in a hospital bed unable to function or cope because of what you did to her! I had to sedate her this morning. When she woke up and found Mark gone, she was hysterical thinking she had lost Mark. Is that what you want for her life, Paul, grief and pain? Mark loves her far more than you could ever love her," Dan said sternly.

"Don't you think I know that? I have seen April with Mark. I am trying to find their child. Can I help it if Lewis has disappeared?" Paul stated as if he might actually care.

"What has Captain Nelson done to find Sunny?" Dan inquired.

"I haven't told Grant about Sunny. I hired a private investigator to find Lewis and Blanche. We cannot have the media getting a hold of this story," Paul announced.

"I don't believe you, Paul. You call in the police to report a rape that never happened, but you did not call them to report the kidnapping of your own granddaughter, because you do not want the media to get a hold of that story. What do you think the media will do with the rape story? Mark is a public figure; you may have just opened a box of dynamite. This could get very ugly if the wrong people handle this situation," Dan said, shaking his head in disgust.

Robert walked in the office and nervously handed the pill bottles to Dan, and then he saw Paul. The two exchanged hatred looks. Dan took the bottles, read the labels, and shook his head.

"I was afraid of this," Dan informed Robert.

"What's wrong?" Robert asked anxiously.

"If Mark took an overdose of these, he could be in a lot of danger," Dan explained to Robert. Both men felt deep concern for Mark rise up in the pit of their stomachs.

"Great, now I found out that Mark is a drug addict. I'm sure Captain Nelson would be interested in knowing that information, too!" Paul arrogantly said with a sarcastic tone that got the full attention of the two other men in the room.

"Mark is not a drug addict, and you are not going to mention this to Captain Nelson. Do you hear me, Paul?" Dan responded angrily as his blood pressure rose.

"What does Grant have to do with any of this?" Robert asked, giving Paul a detestable look, knowing the man was capable of doing anything fraudulent.

"I told him what your son did to my daughter. I've pressed charges against Mark, and Captain Nelson has a warrant out for Mark's arrest," Paul informed Robert.

"That is insane!" Robert yelled at Paul, "I will deal with you later!"

Robert grabbed the phone and called the police department. Paul hurriedly left the room. Dan was thankful he did. Robert would have beaten Paul to a pulp.

Robert talked to Captain Nelson and told him that Paul was insane. Grant calmed Robert down by explaining that he had not done anything on the case since both Mark and April were eighteen at the time it happened.

Unless April was the one to press charges, nothing further would be done on the case. Grant assured Robert that the public would not hear the story from the police department.

Dan lightly sedated April. Her grief was out of control. She had lost her child, and now she believed that she had lost Mark too. Dan did not tell her what Mark had told them for fear it would upset her even further. Besides, Dan did not believe a word Mark had spoken.

Dan would tell her later today, when she was a little more stable. He knew that it would have to be April to calm Mark down and speak the truth to his heart.

April had come to the hospital when Mark was in the ICU. There had been no indication that Mark had raped her. She had only been upset at him because he did not remember her, which was understandable. Dan had seem the undeniable love that April held in her heart for Mark that night.

Dan was disappointed that April had not told him the truth about being pregnant. If she had, he would have helped her. If only he could turn back the time, he thought. Mark and April could have married and raised Sunny, and none of this would have happened. Dan did not blame April or Mark; he blamed Paul for this whole mess.

Mark and April's love for each other started from childhood. Mark had always been so tender with his little companion. He had treated her like a china doll and protected her. If only life had not taken them on an unexpected turn of events, they would have had the last six years together.

There was not a hurtful bone in Mark's body. Whatever Mark was feeling was false, caused by the drugs he was taking. The sooner this mess was cleared up the better, Dan thought as he went to speak to Dr. Gina Price. Maybe Gina could reach Mark and help him sort out his feelings.

Later, Dan called April's sister and brother-in-law, Debbie and Phil. Dan let them know what had happened to April. Debbie told Dan she would call her mother, Tammy, and break the news to her about Sunny.

No one knew where Mark had gone. When Dan told Dr. Stevenson about the pills, Tom assured Dan that Mark would be fine. They had to trust that Mark would only take what he needed for his pain and nausea. Mark will turn to God; Tom reminded Dan of Mark's deep faith.

Dr. Stevenson told Dan how important it was for Mark to have his stem cells removed today, since they had no matching donor. They could not wait until tomorrow since Mark still planned to play in the football game.

Dr. Stevenson was excited that Sunny could be the link in saving Mark's life. They had to find Sunny and test her as soon as possible. Mark's blood tests were not improving.

They would have to do the bone marrow transplant. Or Mark would die.

CHAPTER FIFTY-SIX –
∽Final Arrangements∾

hile Mark and Kevin were driving to the stadium, Mark was in deep thought about what had just happened to him at his apartment. Mark realized that he had not humbled himself before God as he promised he would, when he first learned that he had aplastic anemia.

Mark had put aplastic anemia in his hands thinking he was strong enough to handle it all on his own. How wrong he had been. He was making a mess of things because he had not turned to God for help when things got out of control. Mark had a lot to think about with all that had happened to him in the last few days of his life.

Mark was not claiming it, but he knew his final days might be numbered. It was his responsibility to get everything in his life in order. Mark did not want to leave things left undone or unsaid. He wanted to speak words of encouragement to his family and friends in a way that would give them the strength they would need should something happen to him.

Mark trusted God for his healing; yet he did not want to miss the opportunity to say his final thoughts to those he loved before the game tomorrow.

It was not about saying the word, good-bye; it was about leaving a final impression of how important God was in his life. Something he should have been doing all along. He needed to let his family and friends know that he had no regrets about his life. All of them had been blessings to him, and he had lived a full life because of them.

If we had one minute to say all the things we needed to say to those we love just before we died, what would we say? So why wait, say them today, and tell them how important they are to you. Treasure each minute of your life as if it will be the last impression other people will have of you. Mark had lived by those thoughts once.

He wanted everyone to say, "Mark Sanders knew how to live life to the fullest and he loved God right up to the end," which is what he planned to do.

Then Mark thought about the final words that his grandfather had spoken to him when he was eight. His grandfather had prepared Mark's heart with faith-filled words that would bring Mark comfort when his grandfather did die.

"Find happiness. Life is what you make of it, Mark." Those were the words that Mark had cherished his entire life. His grandfather's words had given him the encouragement to be a strong, yet a charitable man and to have a heart for God.

Mark had to let April know how sorry he was for what he had done to her that night in the park. He loved her more than his own life. He wanted to give her forever, and be there when she trusted God with their future.

An awful thought swept over his heart like a cool breeze: he might not get the chance to be a father to Sunny or know what had happened to her. That reflection hurt his heart more than any pain he had ever felt. He wiped the single tear that fell as he thought of his Sunny.

Losing Sunny hurt more than knowing that his body was rejecting all the treatments they were trying. Without a successful transplant soon, without his blood clotting, with the high risk of an infection, his enlarged heart, or his spleen rupturing before surgery, he might die within the next few weeks. He could no longer deny that, he was a doctor after all; it was medically possible that his life could end soon before Sunny came back to him.

I trust You, God, tell me what to do, he thought. If he thought medically, did he not trust God to heal him? Was he being double-minded? Was he surrounding himself with people who spoke death over him and not healing?

Mark was confused and searching for answers. He needed to talk to his pastor today and find solid ground with someone who believed in his healing, and Pastor Evan was just that person. Whatever happened tomorrow in the football game, Mark trusted God to handle it for him.

Mark had met with his lawyer while he was in the hospital and had everything in order so that he could play on Sunday. He knew that any one of his doctors could prevent him from playing in the game. He was hopeful that none of them would stand in his way. Everyone knew how important this game was to him and to his team.

The coach had called an early meeting with the rest of the team to discuss the game tomorrow concerning Mark. The meeting took place before Mark and Kevin got to the stadium.

Coach Walker told the team how important it was to protect Mark. Since Mark had his heart and mind set on playing, the coaching staff agreed to honor his wishes and let him play part-time. Mark's playing time would be limited but he would get the chance to play. The coaches did not plan on having Mark risk his life.

This could be Mark's last professional football game, and they did not want to deprive him of the chance to play in an AFC Championship Game.

After all, Mark had been the one to bring the team to this Championship Game and he deserved to play. As much as Mark was doing this for the team to help them win, they would do it for him and let him play.

This had been a hard decision to make; the coach was counting on the other team going easy on Mark. He put the final decision to prayer and found peace with his decision to allow Mark to play.

The team was subdued, but Carlo reminded them how Mark felt about pity and how mad it would make Mark if they all fell apart. Carlo advised them to act normal and pretend that nothing was wrong with Mark. For many of them, this would be very hard to do. They knew that Mark was willing to risk his life for them by playing in this game.

When Mark showed up with Kevin, no one said anything about the meeting. The locker room was filled with the anticipation of the upcoming Championship Game. Mark too set aside everything that had happened the night before and pretended that nothing was wrong.

This might be his last practice with the guys he loved, and he wanted them to remember how much they meant to him. Mark looked around at each one of them, his buddies for life. That was right, his buddies for life, he smiled.

Mark had not given up the battle yet. Medically it might be over, but Mark was not living medically, he was living supernaturally or so he thought.

There was the usual upbeat fooling around as the players got dressed to go on the field. They were playing jokes on each other. When the men got too loud, the coach came out of his office and told them to knock it off with the noise. Deep down he smiled, glad that they were spending quality time with Mark.

The men had hung a big sign up on the shower that had been set aside for Mark, which said, "April Morgan's Private Nursing Service, enter at your own risk."

There were endless jokes about Mark's new relationship with April. The bachelor had been roped and hung.

"How many penalties did it take to win her?" Kevin laughed.

"Off sides, I'm sure," Carlo added.

"Pass interference – 15 yards!" Justin laughed. Mark just shook his head at them. He would let them have their fun.

"I bet he can't wait for that honeymoon touchdown with her," Jerk added and everyone busted out laughing.

"Real funny guys." Mark broke a half smile at them as he took his shirt off without thinking, to put on his team t-shirt and then his shoulder pads. The players looked away and the room got quiet.

Everyone quickly pretended to be dressing, so that Mark would not notice they had looked away. Seeing his bruises and the catheter had reminded them how sick Mark was and it affected them deeply.

Mark noticed the silence and his heart sunk. He loved his teammates for trying to be strong for him.

"Hey, guys, I am not married yet. We can still have some good times," Mark said as he changed the subject.

Mark got them started all over again acting crazy. Maybe he should have been quiet, because they were losing it again laughing.

They even discussed Mark's wedding on the 50-yard line. Instead of tuxedos, they would wear their football uniforms. They would line up in two rows, and April would walk down between them on the 50-yard line. As she walked by them, they would raise their helmets up in the air.

They lined up and acted it out. Jerk got a towel; he put it on his head like a veil, and pretended to be April. Jerk walked down the path between the guys, swaying his hips back and forth, waving his hand like a lady. Mark thought Jerk did a good imitation of a woman, maybe too well, Mark laughed to himself.

"Hail to Princess April. Long live King Mark," they shouted, as they had taken their helmets and demonstrated what they planned to do.

"Remind me not to invite any of you to my wedding," Mark half-laughed.

When they started making plans for his honeymoon, Mark blushed; they were getting a little too detailed. He got up from the bench and waved them off. They all laughed at Mark's expense because they loved him.

Deep down Mark knew that if there could have been a wedding, they would have been the perfect gentlemen. They would have treated April like a china doll. He hoped that when he was gone, they would look after her for him. Maybe even one of them would marry her and give her everything she deserved.

Mark was saddened thinking about that, until Jerk started making kissing noises and pretended that his arm was April's face and he was kissing her.

"I love you guys, but you are not going on my honeymoon. I think I can handle that myself," Mark told them in fun. They all laughed.

The coach came out and told them to line up and take the field. It was nine o'clock. He had given them plenty of time to spend with Mark.

The coach went to Mark with a downcast face.

"Listen, Mark, I want you to take it easy today. Let Kevin have the ball today, ok? I am saving you for tomorrow."

"Sure." Mark relinquished his quarterback position to Kevin with nobility, fully understanding the coach's awkward position.

They went over the key plays for the game, and Mark diligently worked with Kevin, preparing him for the game. Mark had total confidence in Kevin as he coached him. At 10:30, they went in the locker room and changed out of their practice uniforms.

Afterwards, the coaches and the team had a team family grill-out, and Mark joined them for that festive get-together.

Mark tried to keep his mind off April and Sunny, but uninvited thoughts crept back into his heart when he saw everyone there. Many of the players had their entire family there. Would Mark ever have his family? Would April ever forgive him? Would they find Sunny? Those questions wrapped around his heart, and he had to take a deep breath and regroup with God.

Every time the guys saw Mark drift off with a despondent face, they did something funny to bring him back to them. However, it was standing on God's Word that put the smile back on Mark's face and allowed him to enjoy his time with the team.

Mark stepped back and reclaimed God's promises once again. At the next team grill-out, both April and Sunny would be there with him. He was confident of that optimistic thought, especially when a single *dove* landed on the grass in front of him. God had sent him a vision of peace, and Mark gave God praise.

It had been a good morning with the team, and Mark was thankful for their companionship, but he was getting tired. The medications had worn off. Mark asked Kevin for a ride back to the hospital.

When they were leaving the field, the reporters swamped Mark. Mark was very gracious and looked confident.

"Is it true that you have aplastic anemia and need a bone marrow transplant?" a reporter asked him.

"Yes, that is true," Mark answered them.

"Have they found a matching donor?"

"No, not yet," Mark answered upbeat.

"Are you playing in tomorrow's Championship Game?"

"Yes, I am playing," Mark said with confidence.

"Aren't you too sick to play?"

"My throwing arm feels great. I just had a great practice," he told them.

"Is your life in danger, if you play?"

"No, not unless I throw too many interceptions," he grinned and gave them his devilish smile. The reporters laughed.

"Do you think your team will be able to win if you are sidelined?"

"Yes, they are the best team playing tomorrow," he said with assurance.

"Thank you, see you at tomorrow's game," Kevin said and then waved his hands in the air to let the reporters know that the interview was over.

Interception = When the quarterback throws the ball to the other team instead of his own team. Not a good thing to do!

Chapter Fifty-Seven –
⌒Role Model⌒

*M*ark asked Kevin to take him to Toys-R-Us. It was something that Mark did before every home game. They went in and they each grabbed a shopping cart. Mark was spinning the cart around the store, having a good time with Kevin, as they went to the sporting goods section.

Mark filled the carts with footballs. Every aisle they went down, they were followed by young fans in disbelief they were actually seeing Mark Sanders. Mark grinned at Kevin. It was the price of fame, but when it came to being a role model for young kids, Mark was glad to do it.

Mark paid for the footballs, then autographed several of the balls, and handed them out to the appreciative kids. Mark took two netted bags of footballs and put them over his shoulders as they went to the parking lot, his fans still trailing behind them.

Mark stuffed the footballs in Kevin's car. He spoke to the kids before they left. He reminded them to follow their dreams, to work hard in school, and to love the Lord.

When they got to the hospital, they carried the footballs in with them. They went into the ER. The TV was on in the waiting room. Mark's picture was on the screen. Kevin grabbed Mark's arm to stop him so he could watch what they were saying about Mark.

"This just in from our local news source. Quarterback Mark Sanders, who was diagnosed with severe aplastic anemia, will play in tomorrow's Championship Game. In an interview today with Mark, here is what he had to say." They showed the clip with Kevin and Mark.

"We have called in expert medical doctor, Janelle Brooker, to get her view on the situation. The question is, should Mark Sanders be allowed to play in tomorrow's game? Here is what Janelle had to say."

"Absolutely not. Mark is currently in stable condition; however, medically, he should not be encouraged to continue playing football. It would be unsafe for Mark to engage in any type of strenuous activities such as football."

"I guess she's not a fan of our team. Our opponents must have put her up to that interview to keep me from playing." Mark laughed as he pulled Kevin's arm forward; he had heard enough. Kevin resisted; he wanted to hear more.

Janelle continued, "Mark Sanders needs a bone marrow transplant right away. Mark's illness has brought forth the public's awareness to be tested for a bone marrow donor. Please consider doing it for Mark and for others just like Mark. **If you cannot donate your bone marrow, please donate blood.**"

Janelle's final sincere words captured Mark's heart, and once again, reality of his illness stuck hard. He took a deep breath to compose his thoughts back to a more positive way of thinking. "Okay, so maybe Janelle is on my side."

Mark smiled at the kids and the people in the waiting room who were pointing at him saying, "There he is, Mark Sanders! Mark!" Mark waved and pointed to the TV and with a smile, he said.

"That woman doesn't know what she is talking about. Do I look sick to you?" He cheerfully winked at them and proceeded to walk to the doctor's station.

Jeff was on duty. Yeah, it was Jeff's first day as a second year resident, Mark thought with envy, knowing he should be on duty right beside Jeff.

"Where the heck have you been?" Jeff asked Mark in a panic knowing that everyone was looking for Mark.

Mark held up the footballs and grinned.

"Shopping," Mark responded with a comical smile. Kevin held up his bag and played along with Mark.

Jeff did not seem impressed as he shook his head in disapproval at Mark and hoped that Dan was not around to knock Mark's head off for his newest stunt.

"Just what are you planning to do with those?" Jeff inquired, afraid of the answer he knew was sure to follow.

"Hand them out in the children's ward," Mark answered without a doubt, with his typical crafty grin that usually caused Jeff to succumb to his plans. Not this time; however, Jeff was not responding the way that Mark had hoped.

"Like heck you are! You know you are not allowed in the children's ward." Jeff protested in disapproval. Mark might be willing to risk catching some illness, but Jeff certainly was not willing to lose Mark to a bunch of sick kids.

"Jeff, you know the routine when I have a home football game. Those kids are not going to be able to go to the game tomorrow. I just want to give those kids a smile and give them something to tell their friends, that's all." Mark explained calmly, hoping that Jeff would understand the compassion that Mark had in his heart for those children. Instead, Mark was met with Jeff's stern eyes.

"Don't blame me if you get in trouble. Dr. Stevenson is about to tie you to a tree. Your father and mother are upstairs talking to Dr. Stevenson right now. Dan is having a nervous breakdown. Stop fooling around, Mark. I don't care what your motives are; stay away from those kids!" Jeff emphasized by the seriousness in his voice.

"All you doctors need to get a life," Mark affirmed with a grin, as he tilted his head to the side to tell Kevin they were moving out.

"Bye, Jeff. If you want an autographed football, you know where to find me," Mark said with humor. Yet a sense of sadness filled Mark's heart, knowing that Jeff could not look past his illness and see things through his eyes. No longer was Jeff on the same page as Mark. Mark was about living and giving back. Jeff was about claiming aplastic anemia and putting Mark in a glass box.

Jeff put his hands on his hips. He was steamed at Mark's recklessness with his life. He picked up the phone, called Dr. Stevenson, and told Tom where he could find Mark. It was the first time Jeff had betrayed Mark, but someone had to stop Mark from his own destruction. Jeff was not about to lose Mark as his best friend.

Kevin and Mark got into the elevator. Mark maintained his grin. "Look here, Kevin, there are always going to be bad days. We can give in and lie down and claim it, or we can choose to get up, brush it off, and make something better happen." Mark was serious during this conversation with Kevin.

"Yesterday was a day from hell, but today, well, I'm going to live my life better than it has ever been. Great things will happen to me today; you just watch and see what happens."

Kevin nodded his head in agreement but his mind was not as convinced. Mark was facing death, nothing could happen that would change that fact, Kevin thought. Mark is just grabbing at straws here; his life right now stinks, if you asked him.

"There are sick kids in this hospital that need someone like us to lift them up out of their miserable situation, and that is a responsibility that you and I owe them. When we walk in there, their little faces will light up and they will briefly forget why they are in this hospital." Mark expressed from his heart. The two men got off the elevator and walked to the children's ward.

Kevin was speechless; his heart was touched by Mark's unselfishness. *So who is going to make Mark forget he is sick*, Kevin thought, just as Mark turned and faced him.

"It's all about their smiles, Kevin, that's your reward for doing this." Mark enlightened him.

Mark asked the nurses to round the kids up into the playroom, while he visited those who could not get out of bed. He asked for a facemask to wear in the rooms where the kids might have something he could catch.

These nurses knew the routine well, as Mark often visited the children's ward and entertained them as he handed out autographs before a home football game. Everyone got busy getting the children together in the playroom. The excitement of Mark's visit quickly spread throughout the unit.

Mark and Kevin were throwing a football back and forth in the hallway as they went in and out of rooms talking to the children.

Finally, the nurses were ready for them to talk to the children in the playroom. Mark chose a child to play catch with and Kevin chose his. They were having a good time tossing the ball back and forth. The joy on the children's faces was why Mark did this with them. Mark knew many of them by their first names. Kevin was amazed at the sight of Mark playing with the children.

One of the children over-threw the ball into the hallway, and when Mark turned around to get the ball, he saw Dr. Stevenson standing there with his arms crossed, his eyebrows knitted together. Oops, Mark had been caught.

Mark stood frozen, his mouth dropped open, as he looked straight at Tom. The corners of Mark's mouth lifted, and he gave Dr. Stevenson a wide grin and the "ok, so you caught me" devilish smile of his. Mark lifted his facemask and replaced it over his face to hide his guilty expression.

Dr. Stevenson shook his head in disapproval, but a smile crossed his face when Mark winked at him on his way back into the room with the football. Mark and Kevin signed the footballs and gave them out to the kids.

When they finished, Dr. Stevenson caught Mark's eyes. Tom had his finger pointed out at him and indicated for Mark to follow him. The serious look on Tom's face told Mark that he meant for him to come right now.

Mark stood up and told the kids good-bye. The kids all jumped up and down, telling him to have a good game. Mark waved good-bye and gave a few high fives. Those kids gave him more joy than he could ever give them. The kids quickly surrounded Kevin as Mark went to speak with Tom.

Dr. Stevenson was not mad at Mark, not after watching the smiling faces of the children with him. Nevertheless, he was not about to let Mark know he understood why Mark had risked going in there with the children to brighten their spirit. Tom was in awe at Mark's ability to bring joy to all those he came in contact. Mark had a God-given gift of compassion.

Still, the risk was too great that these children could make Mark sick. It was time to let Mark know who was in charge. Mark stood in front of Dr. Stevenson like a child facing the principal after committing a serious transgression. Mark undid the top strings to his facemask and let it fall down against his chest.

"Dr. Sanders, you belong on this floor with these kids. You fit right in," Dr. Stevenson declared, trying not to smile.

"Thank you, doctor, I take that as a compliment," Mark half-chuckled, as a smirk broke out on his face.

"Were you planning to visit the Unit anytime today?" Dr. Stevenson inquired with a stern face.

"Later, give me, say, half an hour. I have another stop to make," Mark keenly answered back, as Kevin joined him.

"See to it you don't get lost on your way to the Unit," Dr. Stevenson responded smartly as he walked away shaking his head.

"I know the way, thanks, Doc," Mark called after him with humor. Tom shook his head as he headed to the elevator.

"These doctors around here need to relax more," Mark said to Kevin as they walked into the main hallway.

Mark genuinely thanked Kevin for his part in their comedy act with the kids. Mark hoped that Kevin would realize that being a public figure meant he had responsibilities such as remembering that sick kids need his attention too.

Mark knew that he was about to hand over his famous status to Kevin, and he wanted to prepare Kevin for the total responsibilities that came with the fame he would gain when he replaced him.

Mark shook hands with Kevin and told him that he would see him later. Then Mark went to thank the nurses for their help.

CHAPTER FIFTY-EIGHT –
⊷I Believe in You and Me☙

*M*ark's next stop was to check on April. He walked down the hallway to the elevator. As he passed a room, he heard the announcer on the TV saying they had an important announcement about a "Missing Child" in their area. He stopped dead in his tracks and went into the room. He stared up at the TV.

Sunny's picture was on the TV screen. *That is my child on the screen,* he thought in despair. Mark had to face the reality that Sunny was missing when he saw her picture. He instantly felt sick and quickly went into the bathroom to throw up. He leaned against the wall as he sat on the floor in the bathroom and prayed that April had not seen the announcement. He did not know that the alert had gone out that morning.

Mark's humor and calmness were gone. He was once again filled with guilt and sorrow. "Oh, God, help me." Losing Sunny was more than he could handle alone.

God gave Mark a word of assurance that Sunny was going to be just fine. Sunny was with Blanche, and as much as Mark distrusted Blanche, he knew that Blanche would never hurt Sunny. He would give Lewis and Blanche the ransom money, as soon as they asked for it, and they would set Sunny free unharmed.

When he felt overwhelmed, he desperately continued to seek God's strength. He got up, splashed cold water on his face, and tried to step forward with God, but each step was as heavy as his heart felt.

When Mark came out of the bathroom, he apologized to the child and left the room.

Mark could no longer face April; he stood against the wall to catch his breath. He held his hand over his heart. His chest was so tight he could not breathe; he was suffocating, but not from the lack of air. It was from the pain in his heart from losing Sunny.

Nurse Ashley saw Mark leaning against the wall. She saw the look on his distressed face, and feared something was wrong with him.

Ashley had worked with Dr. Sanders while he was doing his rounds in the Pediatric Unit. She loved and respected him. Not many men would treat sick children the way Mark did, with such kindness and compassion.

She had heard the rumors about Dr. Sanders and the new nurse. She had seen the news reports on Mark, so she was aware of the turmoil that he was facing in his life.

Ashley went to him and asked him if he was all right. She respectfully called him, "Dr. Sanders." The gentleness in her voice spoke to Mark's heart, much like April's voice.

In that moment, Mark's heart spoke to him to go to April. He looked at Ashley's face and knew what he had to do. He would reclaim what was his. He thanked Ashley with a gentle hug and went to find April.

Mark hurried to April's hospital room. When Mark opened the door, he saw that April was sitting up. Dan was holding her hand.

Their eyes met, she reached her arms out to him, and he quickly grabbed her up in his arms and sat on her bed. They embraced. April cried against Mark's chest as he held her in his secure arms. Dan slipped quietly from the room.

"I am so sorry, April. Can you ever forgive me?" he asked tearfully. His heart was breaking from the hurt he felt.

"You have nothing to be sorry for. Dan just told me what you told him. Mark, how could you call what we did rape? What you and I shared that night was warm and beautiful," she tenderly told him.

"But I remembered you crying afterwards; I hurt you," he mumbled as he looked away, unable to face her. She gently cupped the sides of his tormented face and turned his face so that their eyes fell into each other's.

"I was crying because I was so happy I had finally captured your heart. You made all my dreams come true when you loved me the way that you did. You were gentle and affectionate. When I was cold, you warmed me up," she touched his face to let him feel the warmth of her love for him.

"We sat in the moonlight, we talked, we kissed, we touched each other so tenderly, and we expressed our love in so many ways. Mark Sanders, you stole my heart, nothing else, that night. I pledged myself to you and you to me. You gave me your ring as a sign of your commitment to me. I wanted you so much I thought my heart was going to explode." She kissed his forehead softly.

"I was scared and had mixed feelings at first, but I could not deny your love for me. You asked me if I wanted you to stop and I told you no. I touched you and encouraged your feelings. It was my fault. If there is anyone that needs to be blamed for that night, it is me," she tried to reassure him.

Mark was unable to speak. He prayed what she said was the truth. She was so sincere as she spoke to his heart.

"We were childhood sweethearts; we belonged together the moment we met. We lost our way through the years, but never did I ever stop loving you when we were apart." Her eyes spoke her words of love for him.

"If I could change anything about that night, it would have lasted longer. That we could have talked about what we did. That you would not have passed out on me. I wish you could remember how much we loved each other, just as it happened. I wish that all the guilt you feel right now would disappear. If only you could be in my head and see that night the way it so beautifully happened."

They fell into each other's arms and both cried. She looked him in the face, her eyes pleading to his heart. She ran her fingers through his hair. His absence from her had given her time to reflect on their uncertain future together. Her fear of his death had filled her mind with the desperate thoughts and desires she was about to reveal to him.

"Mark, please, take me back to the park tonight. Let me show you how it happened. I do not want you to die without knowing and feeling the love of that night between you and me." Her eyes begged him. She kissed his lips and wiped his tears from his cheeks.

"I would die inside if I thought you never had my love completely the way it should have been for us. Please, Mark. Please do this for us." April begged him with all her heart as she pulled him into her desperate arms and kissed his neck softly.

What they had done that night in the park was wrong. Even as beautiful as April had described it, it should never have happened. He could not repeat the same mistake with her. He could not take her as his own when she did not belong to him by marriage. He was going to have to tell her that she needed to save herself for her future husband. As much as it was tearing his heart out that it would not be him, he had to tell her. He pulled away from her slightly so that he could look her in the face. He struggled to say the words.

"April, there will never be a future for ... " Mark tried to say as his eyes watered. She put her fingers to his lips to hush him.

"Don't say that. You are my future whether you are alive or whether you are just a memory in my heart. Please, Mark, I need you to do this for me before it is too late. Take me away with you tonight, and let us have one more moment, one more memory of us."

If he said no, it would break her heart. He stood up and kissed her tenderly on her forehead. She held his hand in hers, until he gently pulled them apart. He let her go.

"I have to go for another treatment. I will be back around six to pick you up, but April; I have to think about this. We will be together tonight but not in the way you want; I just can't," he told her sorrowfully.

He turned and headed to the door, not turning back around to look at her desolate face, knowing that he would not be strong enough to do what had to be done.

He closed the door behind him and stood against the door. How many times would he break her heart? When would it all end?

What scared him more than anything was the fact that April had not said one word to him about Sunny. Just as he had blocked out the memory of the night in the park, he feared that April would suppress her memory of their child.

She had painfully lost her child again, and she was desperately seeking not to lose him, too. Her entire mind was consumed with her unending love for him; he was all she had to hold onto right now.

Tears formed in his eyes with that lingering thought.

CHAPTER FIFTY-NINE –
∽A Mother's Tear∽

*R*obert and Julia had arrived at the hospital at noon to meet with Dr. Stevenson. They wanted Tom to be straight with them about Mark's condition.

Dr. Stevenson told them that he had never seen a patient with aplastic anemia have a case as severe as Mark's. Tom did not understand it at all. Most aplastic anemia patients responded to some form of treatment and lived a relatively healthy life. Mark would not be one of them. What made his case uncommonly different? Dr. Stevenson could not explain it.

Dr. Stevenson told Julia and Robert that Mark's blood counts were at a dangerous level. Mark was abnormally allergic to the drugs needed to treat his condition. His body was rejecting all the medications they had given him. Other than a perfectly matched bone marrow transplant, there was nothing more Dr. Stevenson could do to save Mark's life.

"Mark's chances of coming off the football field alive tomorrow if he plays aggressively are not very good. Mark will have to play conservatively. One blow to his spleen could cause massive bleeding we might not be able to control," Tom informed them. They listened intensely as Tom continued.

"Mark believes there will be no grass stains on his uniform tomorrow. However, this is a serious game, and Mark is surely going to make physical contact with the defense at some point." Robert nodded in agreement; this game determines which team goes to the Super Bowl.

"Mark's heart is still enlarged and weak due to his aplastic anemia. Even standing on the sideline watching could be dangerous for Mark if he does not remain calm during the game. Let's face it; there is no chance of

Mark doing that," Tom said as he shook his head back and forth, knowing that Mark was not going to take a backseat in this important game.

Tom regretfully told them they needed to prepare for the end of Mark's life; it could happen as soon as tomorrow. His soft words cut through Julia and Robert's hearts. Julia grasped Robert's hand firmly as she let out a heart-wrenching gasp.

"When Mark gets here today, sedate him, Tom. Keep him under sedation until the game is over," Julia tearfully pleaded with Dr. Stevenson as she begged him to save her son's life. "Oh, God … I can't lose my son … please, Tom … sedate him." Her desperate tears fell, knowing that in just hours her son could lose his life.

Dr. Stevenson could not bear to look her in the face as he remorsefully reminded her that it was Mark's wish to be with his teammates and on the field playing tomorrow. They had to honor his last wish.

Julia cuddled closer to Robert as the words that Tom spoke continued to rip at her heart. Tom felt the need to offer her some sort of hope.

"Mark does not plan to die tomorrow, and I will do everything in my power to make sure he doesn't. We will all be there to give Mark immediate medical attention if he requires it."

Tom reminded them that Mark did not want to die like those he had seen die in the hospital, without fulfilling their dreams. Mark wanted to live out his dreams.

"Mark feels like this; if he surrenders to a hospital room, he is surrendering to aplastic anemia and not to the life that he feels God has in store for him."

"Even if Mark does not play in the game; there is a good chance that he would die anyways in the next few weeks or months if he does not get a matching transplant."

Even with the transplant, Mark was allergic to several of the drugs needed daily to prevent a rejection. One way or the other, Mark was probably going to die from the complications of aplastic anemia. Not playing in the game would only buy him a few months if they did not find him a matching donor.

There was a chance that his heart could give out at anytime. "Each week that passes, Mark will get weaker, and his heart will finally give out. I am not looking forward to the risks he will encounter with his surgery on

Monday. Mark is a ticking time bomb; we just do not know what to expect with him."

Dr. Stevenson explained that Mark's football career was over after tomorrow. "This will be Mark's last chance to play professional football. We have to give Mark his last chance; he deserves to be on that field tomorrow."

Dr. Stevenson would not deny Mark the opportunity to have one more chance at living out his dream. Mark had been born for this moment tomorrow. During his entire life, Mark had been a hero to those his life had touched.

Mark would be a hero for making the public aware of the need for bone marrow donations when he stepped on that field tomorrow. He had already saved several lives.

Dr. Stevenson looked at them both with sincerity. "Mark deserves to have his family support him in his decision. You need to celebrate his life while he is still with you. God has blessed both of you with a fine young man, and if God wants to call Mark home, you should be honored," Dr. Stevenson justified.

Dr. Stevenson explained that he was going to spend the rest of the day building up Mark's system with treatments, as much as Mark could tolerate. Jeff would be at Mark's side for the next twenty-four hours in case he needed assistance.

Tom wanted Robert to donate his platelets so he could give them straight to Mark. Fresh platelets would be more effective.

Tom had already built up the blood bank with O negative blood just in case they needed it tomorrow.

"If I had a son, I would want him to be the image of your son. You have been so blessed to have Mark as your son," Dr. Stevenson told them. "I will miss him if things go wrong tomorrow … he keeps this hospital in good spirits during times we would all like to forget. Through all of this, Mark has held his head up and made us smile."

It was extremely emotional for Dr. Stevenson to talk to the Sanders, with Julia sitting across from him crying during the entire conversation. Tom stood up, shook hands with Robert, and hugged Julia. Then Tom prayed with them.

The phone rang; it was Jeff. Tom just shook his head as he listened to what Jeff had to tell him about Mark.

Now Dr. Stevenson knew exactly where he could find Mark. Tom left his office hoping he could convince Mark to come back to the Unit, and get started on his last treatments before the game tomorrow. Tom prayed he could build Mark's system up enough to withstand the game, but he knew that Mark needed a miracle more than those treatments.

Jeff had informed him that Mark was in the Pediatric Unit. *Doesn't Mark listen to anything I tell him?* Dr. Stevenson thought as he walked down the hallway. It was just like Mark to be where he was not allowed, in order to benefit others.

Julia and Robert went to the donation room. Dan suddenly entered the room; he looked as white as a ghost. He had to speak to Robert and Julia right away. They knew that something had happened the minute they saw Dan's white face.

Half an hour later, Mark knocked on Dr. Stevenson's door. Tom gave Mark the fifth-degree for being late: it was two o'clock. Dr. Stevenson explained to Mark that his father and mother were in the donation room. Tom told Mark that he could go speak to his parents while he had the nurses get everything ready for him.

Mark walked into the donation room. He stood tall and handsome; his outward appearance looked healthy and he seemed in high spirits. Julia jumped up to hug him. She did not want to let Mark out of her yearning arms. He very tenderly kissed her forehead.

"Thanks, Dad, for the blood," Mark said with a gentle voice, as he looked into his father's eyes with love. Who would have guessed that his father would be the one to provide Mark with his life saving blood? Mark stood humbled as he stared at him.

Grandfather would have been so proud of his father, if he were here, Mark thought. *I will have to tell Grandfather how it all turned out when I get to heaven.* Thinking about seeing his grandfather again made Mark humbly smile.

"I would do anything for you, Son," Robert said as tears formed in his eyes. Mark shook his head to acknowledge that truth. It had taken eighteen years to win his father's love but once Mark did, the two of them had made up for their lost time together as father and son.

Mark now depended on his father's relationship with him and deeply respected him. Mark was thankful that God had moved in Robert's heart and deepened their relationship as a father and son.

Dr. Stevenson came in the room. Tom was touched by the parents' obvious affection for their son. He wished more than anything that he could have given Robert and Julia more hope.

It was Mark's emotional state of mind that Dr. Stevenson was the most concerned about. Mark was carrying the weight of too many decisions on his shoulders. How overwhelmed he must be feeling trying to deal with everything and everyone. Mark's unselfishness caused the burdens he was toting. If only Mark would stop trying to be so strong for everyone else. *Mark needs to be the patient and let others carry his burdens while he concentrated on getting well,* Tom thought.

The nurse had just finished unhooking Robert.

"We are ready for you, Mark," Dr. Stevenson said warmly. "Robert, I will be back in a few minutes to check on you." They would begin processing the platelets for Mark's transfusion.

"We are taking the helicopter back to the ranch. Your family would like for you to come out and eat with us tonight. How about it, Son?" Robert asked Mark softly. It was evident that he loved his son as he stood a foot away from him and touched his shoulder.

"Sure, I will bring April with me," Mark agreed. "I will call you and let you know how everything went here," he told them and gave his father and mother a hug.

"Mark, I love you," his mother whispered in his ear and then she let go of her little boy, freeing him to be the man that he had become.

"I love you too, Mom."

His words came softly from his heart, feeling the dampness on his shirt where his mother had left behind her tears.

Chapter Sixty –
☙Letting Go and Finding Peace❧

$\mathcal{M}$ark followed Dr. Stevenson to his room. Mark sat on the bed and removed his shirt. The bruising had not faded any; on the positive note, it had not spread.

Dr. Stevenson introduced Mark to Christy Edwards. She would be his nurse. They exchanged friendly greetings. Christy smiled at Mark as she placed her mask over her face. She handed him a hospital gown but he handed it right back to her.

Mark wanted to stay in his jeans today, just in case he needed to leave quickly. He knew that everyone was praying he would change his mind about the game and have the operation instead.

Mark certainly has not changed a bit since high school. He still has to be in charge, Christy thought with a grin as she remembered the star football player that she had cheered for in high school. She had continued to watch him play professional football; she was definitely a big fan of his.

Dr. Stevenson and Dan tried to safeguard Mark and carefully select those who took care of him. Mark posed a delicate situation with his celebrity status; they had to protect his privacy and his dignity.

Christy was an old friend of April's, and they felt certain that she would be able to handle Mark's temperament and his confidentiality.

Mark had requested that Rebecca, April, or Sally be in charge if he needed any delicate nursing care. It was hard emotionally to be a doctor and a patient at the same hospital where everybody knew you. Thankfully, everyone had maintained a professional relationship with Mark, helping him feel comfortable as they provided him with their care.

Christy took Mark's blood pressure and temperature, while Dr. Stevenson listened to his heart and lungs. Christy put the oxygen monitor on his finger. His oxygen saturation level was low.

"This is what we are going to do. We are going to build you up as much as possible. I am going to hook you up to the infusion pump and give you a good meal through your catheter. Then we'll do a transfusion of whole blood and platelets, plus your usual cocktail of antibiotics, and Benadryl," Dr. Stevenson explained to Mark.

Mark listened carefully, knowing that he had to make this treatment work if he was going to play tomorrow. His stomach was still messed up from the last treatment they gave him. The thought of throwing up for the rest of the day was not a welcome thought, but he knew he could not take the Benadryl or the nausea medication and stay awake.

Dr. Stevenson saw the look of frustration cross Mark's face. "I am going to give you something to relax you so you will sleep through this treatment. Maybe you won't be as sick to your stomach and you can keep things down."

If only Mark's body would not reject the medications and the nutrition, he could beat this, Dr. Stevenson thought frustrated.

"I am out of here by five, not one minute later, no Benadryl either; I have too much to do tonight," Mark informed him knowing he had to keep his date with April and his parents, they were counting on him.

"I had planned for you to be here all day and all night, if you plan on leaving in three hours then we will have to start an IV and use it too," Dr. Stevenson stated with disappointment in his voice.

"I got a date, and I am not breaking it," Mark stated with certainty, but with good humor. He had to keep his humor.

"You are back here after the date, got it?" Dr. Stevenson insisted, but he was thankful that Mark was in a good mood. Just like Mark, he was making light of what could be his last attempt at saving his life.

"I am not promising you anything this time; you have three hours to start with." Mark was adamant. "You can do an IV but I don't want the sedative either. I'm so tired, if you would get out of here, I'd fall asleep on my own."

"Lie down and let me feel your spleen," Dr. Stevenson instructed. Mark lay down flat on the bed. Christy removed Mark's boots for him and then pulled the blanket up to his belt buckle.

Dr. Stevenson felt Mark's spleen, and disappointment showed on his face. Mark's spleen was still enlarged. Just one blow to it and Mark could bleed to death. Dr. Stevenson shook his head in disappointment. *Can't this kid get a break*, he thought, frustrated that nothing had worked for Mark. He placed an oxygen mask over Mark's face.

As much as Dr. Stevenson wanted to give Mark a lecture about the game, he remained quiet. Mark had to go through with his plans regardless of the outcome. Tom knew that it had not been an easy decision for Mark to make, and he planned to support Mark.

"Christy, start an IV, left arm, give medications thirty minutes apart, slow drip, watch for reactions, have the Benadryl on hand just in case Mark needs it."

Tom gave Christy the okay to hook Mark up to the pump. He stood watching Christy do her job and then he left the room. He planned to keep a close eye on Mark. After Mark had experienced severe reactions to the medications and to his transfusions, Mark had never gone without the Benadryl before a treatment.

Mark remembered Christy from high school. She was one of the cheerleaders. In fact, she was one of April's friends, Mark thought with a smile, amazed that he really did remember that fact. Maybe his memory was coming back.

Christy took two tubes of blood from Mark and then hooked up his platelets. She started the IV in his left arm and injected his first medication, and then she hooked up the fluids. She pulled the blanket up over him.

"Thanks, Christy."

Christy's eyes fell compassionately on him. "Mark, I am sorry. I cannot imagine how devastated you must be feeling right now, with this illness, losing your child, and having to play in the game tomorrow. If I were you, I'd crawl in a hole and never come out. I have to hand it to you, Mark, you always conquered the impossible, and I believe with all my heart you will come out on top tomorrow too."

Mark pulled his mask down so he could speak. "Thanks, Christy, I'm fine. God is handling everything for me. I have no fears about tomorrow; in fact I am as excited as I was when I played in the Rose Bowl."

"You hold on to your dreams, Mark, you deserve them." She bent down, accepted a warm hug from him, and helped him place the mask back on his face.

Once she was finished hooking Mark up to everything, she left the room. Her prayers would remain with Mark.

Mark rolled over on his side and stuffed the pillows under his head. He was just about to fall asleep when the door opened quietly. Mark looked up to see who had entered his room. Once he saw that it was Marty, from housekeeping, he closed his eyes.

Marty discreetly came in and started cleaning around the room. He had on his facemask. Mark thought Marty must be new at the hospital. Mark could not remember seeing Marty around the hospital before the other day when Marty had come in his room several times.

Marty cautiously viewed Mark and quietly picked up his water jug, and as he did, Mark opened his eyes. Marty took a quick breath as Mark looked in his direction.

Thinking quickly, Marty asked Mark if he wanted fresh water and Mark told him, no. Marty seemed frustrated as he set the water jug forcibly back on the table and left the room in a huff. Mark thought that was odd behavior, as an uneasy feeling came over him.

Jeff came in the room and told Mark that he was staying in the room while Mark was there. He went over, plopped in the recliner, and opened up the magazine he had in his hand. Mark grinned at him. Jeff was going to drive him crazy with his hovering, but Mark loved him just the same.

Ten minutes later a wave of nausea came over Mark. "Jeff, I'm sick!" He pushed back his oxygen mask, and he quickly slid off the bed and grabbed the IV poles as he hurried into the bathroom. Jeff was at his heels, helping him with the IV lines.

Mark splashed his face with cool water and took a deep breath as he gave thanks that the nausea passed without him having to throw up. God had won another battle for him; he smiled as he looked in the mirror. "It's You and me today, God," he remarked, satisfied that God's armor was brand new and was surrounding him.

Mark looked behind him and saw Jeff's distraught face in the mirror. Jeff's face claimed Mark's death. The look on Jeff's face was more than Mark could bear. Mark shook his head no, as he covered his eyes with the palms of his hands, and then he slowly ran his fingers from his forehead down his cheeks to his chin, as he leaned over the sink.

Mark slithered to the floor as the second wave hit the pit of his stomach with a driving force. He clutched his stomach with both arms and again he refused to give in and be sick. Jeff handed him a cool washcloth and a drink of water.

Mark sat in the stillness that surrounded him and leaned against the wall as he buried his mind in victorious thoughts even as the burning in his stomach placed a final thought he had avoided until this dreaded moment.

Everyone was claiming his death; none of them understood how he could not accept the fact that he was going to die. His heart grew heavy. *Lord, they think I am being arrogant when I claim I am already healed. How can I get them to see past the natural and see the healing God that You are?* Tears wanted to form in his eyes, but he held firm and refused their entrance.

He thought about all those that loved him and the unnecessary torment that giving in to his illness was causing them. Then he thought about April as again his stomach reminded him that medically there were no drugs that could save him, his body was rejecting even the antibiotics.

"Jeff, I need you to look after April for me ... you know, if God has other plans for me and I don't get better. Promise me that you will love her for me ... make her forget about me so that she can be happy. And Sunny ...." He stopped short as no words came. Mark did not have to say anything. Jeff understood the pain and the darkness that Mark had just let escape from the hole in his heart.

Tears swelled up in Jeff's eyes. "I will love them for you, Mark. I promise you, and I will make them happy. Now let's get you back in bed." Jeff wiped his face of his tears, helped Mark up off the floor, and untangled the IV lines.

Jeff unhooked the medications that poured like poisons into his best friend's veins. They exchanged no words with each other. Mark was somewhere in his own tangled thoughts, having pity on Jeff and yet angry with him for his lack of belief.

Jeff knew death all too well. He had seen it in his brother and he was seeing it in Mark. He sat down in the recliner with all intentions to dwell on Mark's losing battle.

However, when he looked over at Mark, different thoughts came to his mind. He saw Mark running like the wind with the football and scoring. Mark had won the game. Mark's face spoke life, not death. Jeff realized how wrong he had been to throw in the towel when Mark was still winning one small victory at a time. He had let Mark down.

"Mark, I'm sorry. I still got your back; we are going to beat this thing, buddy, you and me. We are going to do it, together."

"Thanks, Jeff, that means a lot to me." Now his team was complete, God, April, and Jeff.

Mark lay back down on his side to sleep. *God, show me what I need to do to make the others believe.* His prayers sent him into a peaceful sleep.

He had only been asleep for about an hour when his memories of his past life started flowing back to him.

Mark remembered when he and April had given their hearts to each other when they were just children. He remembered their childhood together. He remembered his senior year when he had fallen in love with her. He remembered standing beside her as she gave her heart to Jesus. He remembered the night in the park. There was nothing frightening about anything that had happened in the park that night; it had been tender and beautiful.

He remembered everything just the way it had happened. When he woke up, he had peace in his heart. April was the first and only woman he had ever loved. He had never hurt her; he had only loved her. God amazingly had revealed the truth to him.

Carolyn Taylor from housekeeping came in the room and looked around. There was nothing for her to clean-up. She seemed particularly puzzled and went out to check to see if Mark's room was on her list to clean. His room was on her list. That was strange, she thought, she would have to check with her supervisor.

As Mark lay there, his mind was on what April had said. What was he going to do? What if he really did not live through the game tomorrow, he thought? Tonight might be their last memory of each other. What memory would he leave her with tonight? His heart was so torn. The battle continued in his mind, as he lay there deep in thought.

What about Sunny? He had to make things right with her. He was her father, and he wanted her to have his name.

Mark talked to Jeff and Jeff left the room. Mark picked up the phone and made several important phone calls. There were things he needed to tell the people that he loved. Mark spent the next two hours on the phone talking to people.

Mark's family had assembled and decided how they wanted to spend their last precious night with Mark. Tonight the family would gather for one last family dinner. Maria and Martha got busy in the kitchen and planned Mark's favorite dishes.

Everyone was busy getting things ready for Mark. Thomas dusted the dining room and put out the fine china. The whole house was buzzing with excitement. This would be a homecoming no one would ever forget. They would make this night very special for Mark and celebrate his life in style.

Mark called his pastor to speak to him. Mark fought the tears as he spoke to not just his pastor, but to his friend. Mark wanted to make sure that everything was set the way that he wanted it to be done. Mark did not want someone else doing this final task. He had never had to make these kinds of arrangements before, and he felt extremely nervous about having to do it. The two men prayed together at the end of the conversation.

Mark called his mother on the phone to let her know about his final plans. When he told her what he wanted, she fell into a chair and cried. He told her that he had made all the arrangements with his pastor so that she did not have to worry about taking care of that detail.

She sat on a chair; her heart was bursting as the tears fell. She had not expected this news. Julia had many calls to make and so little time. When the time came, Julia sent the limo to pick Mark and April up from the hospital.

Mark's final call was back to his lawyer to make sure that all the paperwork he had requested was completed for him to sign. Thirty minutes later the papers arrived and Mark signed them.

Dr. Faye Wilson and Dan came into Mark's room, and Dr. Wilson did another intercostal rib block so that Mark could breathe easier without pain. Then they took Mark to be x-rayed.

As the pair fussed over him, Mark encouraged them to go out together and get to know each other better. Mark worried about Dan not having someone to fulfill his life. Mark knew that if he did die, it would be extremely hard on Dan. He wanted Dan to have someone like Faye to be there to bring him comfort.

When five o'clock came, Mark was on his way back to his apartment. When he got there, he opened the door to find that someone had already cleaned it spotless.

He went into Sunny's room and picked up the t-shirt that she had worn. His eyes became teary as he held the t-shirt to his heart. He had made her promises that he had not been able to keep. If only he could take her small hand in his hand and hold it, he would hold on tight and never let her go from him again. He knelt down beside the bed and prayed for her.

He packed a small duffel bag of the things he would need for Monday after his surgery. He included Sunny's t-shirt. Then he took a shower and got dressed.

He was claiming his life. Mark was sure that God was going to spend a little more time on him, just as the song on the radio was playing as he drove to the hospital.

*FYI – an intercostal rib block, numbs the pain from the rib fractures; giving Mark the strength to do what he needs to do tonight.

CHAPTER SIXTY-ONE –
∽Draw Me Close to You∾

The intercostal rib block had done its trick. Mark was feeling great. The blood transfusions and his platelet transfusions were working as well. Mark gave thanks to God for his continuous healing.

Mark was not claiming death; he was claiming life. Mark knew that his life was in the hands of God. Whatever happened, Mark was ready to accept his fate and he knew in his heart that he was going to find victory tonight.

Mark made one last important stop before going back to the hospital to get April.

When Mark got to the hospital, he opened the door to April's room and went in. He was handsomely dressed in his tuxedo. April's mouth dropped open when she saw how magnificent he looked. Her prince had arrived, she warmly thought.

Mark was absolutely edible, and she rushed to claim his scrumptious lips to satisfy her hunger for him. She noticed the glow in his eyes as she caressed his clean-shaven face.

Mark handed her a dress bag that he had gotten out of her closet, and he gave her a make-up bag he had found in her bathroom at her apartment.

"I wasn't sure what you would want to wear. I found this dress bag in your closet and thought it would do for tonight," Mark explained to her with a brilliant smile.

Mark told April that they were going out to eat dinner at his parent's home, and it was to be a formal dinner party. He said they did not have time to go back to the apartment to change. First, he said he had a stop to make before going to the ranch.

April took the bag into the bathroom to change. When she unzipped it and saw the white gown, her face was bewildered. She had worn this same gown to his eighteenth birthday party. She wanted to cry; the tears welled up and threatened to fall. How could she wear the dress that had been so special on that night and not agonize when he did not remember it? Her heart was breaking.

"Oh, Mark …" she whispered, choking back her tears.

April thought back to that magical night when she had worn this dress, and Mark had held her safely in his arms. Tears slowly fell as she thought of the love they had shared on that amazing night. That was how love was supposed to be for them. How could she get that moment back?

April had already taken a shower and was ready to go to the park. Mark had ruined all of her plans for them tonight. Her heart was torn. She would just have to bear it for his sake. This might be their last night together.

April had wanted Mark to take her to the park tonight. She wanted him to remember the night that they had shared so intimately. She wanted him to remember the love they had exchanged between them that night.

Her tears that night were from the love she felt for him after he had made love to her. She knew at that moment that the two of them shared the same heart and would forever be one. If only she had been able to let him know the love her heart was pouring out for him, before he had passed out.

If only they could have that night back. But Mark had made other plans for them tonight. He would never know how it felt to love her completely; his death would take that away from them. "No, I can't let that happen; no … I will never let him go until he has loved me … he has to love me tonight." Her tears fell as she melted her face into her hands so that Mark would not hear her crying.

If he had forever to live, then she could honor his commitment to God and wait until they were married to love him. However, tonight might be his only night left with her. If he did not love her tonight, tomorrow would be too late. She just wanted to continue crying, but she brushed back her tears and put on a brave face for the man she loved.

April closed her eyes and prayed. "Please, God, forgive me for my thoughts … you know my heart is breaking for Mark. Lord, if You plan to take Mark from my life, Lord, let me have this *one more moment in time* with him."

When April came out, she was breathtaking, just as Mark knew she would be. He stood admiring her beauty. His voice filled with complimentary words that dazzled her heart into submission. She would surrender herself to him.

They went to the door and into the hallway. He picked her up and held her in his muscular arms. Her prince was finally carrying her off into the sunset.

Mark had carried April out of the hospital in his arms. She had her arms wrapped around his neck; her head lay on his shoulder. He smelled so wonderful, a fragrance that she would treasure.

The limo was waiting outside for them. Mark gently set her feet on the ground and helped her into the limo. He gave Thomas a nod and got in beside April. Thomas drove them to the park.

"I thought we would stop here for a minute first," Mark told her warmly as he leaned over and stole a kiss.

Mark got out and got a blanket from the trunk. He opened her door and helped her slide out of the limo into his loving arms. She was confused as she looked into his mysterious eyes.

What had happened to the family dinner? Maybe he had changed his mind and was going to surrender to making love to her after all? Her heart began to beat faster thinking that Mark had changed his mind.

Mark carried her down to the pond. The moon was high in the sky; its brilliant rays reflected in the water so romantically. He carefully put her down so that she was standing in front of him. She had never seen such joy written on his face.

This was the very spot that he had made love to her for the first time. April's heart felt the love she had for Mark burning deep within her.

Mark took the blanket and smoothed it over the ground. He knelt down in front of her on one knee. He took her hand in his, brought it up to his lips, and kissed it tenderly. He took a deep breath, searching for the words he wanted to say. He said a silent prayer first, and asked God to bless this moment.

Her soft beautiful eyes watched with affection. Then he gently pulled her to him and embraced her body to his. She sat down on his knee. She noticed Mark's hesitation and knew that it was up to her to show him her love. She wrapped her arms under his jacket and hugged him to her, feeling the warmth of his back with her hands.

The snowflakes softly sprinkled on them. Mark and April would not feel the coolness of the night. The warmth they shared between their bodies would keep them warm. Slowly they dropped to the blanket as she kissed him.

She spoke so softly with passion in her voice, as she was face to face with him on the blanket.

"You were all I ever wanted. That night brought us together and sealed us together in our destiny to be forever joined as one. Nothing could ever change that one moment we shared because all my dreams had come true," she told him with such love in her voice, as she was gently touching his smooth face with her slender fingers.

"You were gentle, compassionate, considerate, loving, oh so loving, Mark. There is nothing that I would ever take back from that night, except that its memory was taken away from us when you did not remember it," she said as he drowned in her sparkling eyes. Her breath on his neck as she kissed him sent him warm chills. She continued speaking softly.

"That night gave us a child. A child that I cherished the moment I knew that I had a part of you growing inside of my womb. If I could not have you, I had Jessica to love for all those months we were separated." He kissed her fingers, as he held her hand in his.

"I wanted to tell you with all my heart. I did tell you so many times when I pretended that you were beside me on my bed. I had all our memories of us together locked in my heart. No one could take those away from me." She touched his face where the single tear had fallen. She kissed his lips and ran her fingers through his soft hair. She continued to speak to him softly.

"I never stopped loving you, never. For the rest of my life, my heart will love only you; no one will ever take your place. You are my first and only love. I will never love anyone like I have loved you." She drew him closer to her so that his lips could join hers. She whispered in his ear.

"Please, Mark, give me that night back. Give us that chance to make love the way it should have been. Love me, Mark, make love to me right here where it all began for us. Give yourself the same memory I have so that forever we will be joined as one." Her heart pleaded to his.

His body was screaming for her, to hold her, to have her safe in his arms forever. If he was going to have a heart attack, it would be now here with her.

If he died, he would never get the chance to share her life. They would never get to love their child as a family. The tears were gently falling down his face; he loved her so much.

Mark had not shed a single tear about his illness until this moment. It was this moment, when he realized all that death would take away from him. She cuddled closer to him and let him cry softly into her chest. She was whispering words of love to him, comforting him with her gentle touches.

His mind was swimming with emotions, what he wanted to do and what he had promised himself he would not do to her, tugged at his mind. She was making it so difficult for him to resist her love. She wanted one more memory with him. Now was not his turn to say no.

She did not deny him that night so long ago; she gave herself freely to him. He would give her this night; he would not deny her. Forever she would have this memory of them. He would give her one more memory of them together. He closed his eyes and once again spoke to God about his decision that he had made earlier.

Then he suddenly pulled away from her and sat up. He helped her sit up. A sad look of confusion crossed her face as she thought he was denying her what her whole body desired. She wanted to cry out to him and beg him to make love to her.

Mark got up and helped her to her feet. He reached into his jacket pocket; he felt the silky box and pulled it out. He slowly knelt down on one knee and took her hand in his.

Her eyes met his warm blue eyes as he smiled up into hers. She wanted to say something, but he put his fingers to her lips. He took a deep breath and sucked back the tears forming in his eyes and was ready to say the words he intended to say earlier before he was interrupted.

"It's my turn to talk, April. I have always loved you. Today in the hospital I remembered it all, everything. From the first time, I pulled your pigtails, 'till the time we shared our first kiss at my eighteenth birthday party. That was the first time I saw you in this very gown." He fondly smiled, and she realized he had picked this gown out for her to wear tonight on purpose.

"I thought my heart was going to burst out of my chest when I saw you standing across the room in this dress." New tears formed in his eyes.

"God wanted us to be together from the very beginning." He kissed her hand so tenderly.

"I have had a wonderful life, but my life would not have been completed if I did not have you," he said lovingly, fighting back his tears and this time he brushed her tears away.

"April Elizabeth Morgan, I would be honored if you would be my wife. Will you marry me?" he asked tenderly, as he held up the magnificent diamond ring.

April was speechless as she looked at the ring he held. Mark waited for her to answer, as he smiled at her. Finally, a brilliant smile spread across her face, when she finally caught her breath. She placed her hand affectionately on his heart. At this moment, she knew she owned his very heart forever.

"Yes, oh yes!" She said in tears of joy and he stood up, took the ring, and placed it on her finger. She fell in his arms and they hugged. They kissed with such affection. Finally, she stood back and looked at the sparkling ring.

"Did I mention I would move heaven and earth for you? God has blessed me so that I can financially give you anything your heart desires, and I am going to give it all to you, starting right now," he told her devotedly.

She did not understand what he was talking about as his eyes beamed with love for her. She was completely swept away by the happiness that covered his face as he looked into her wondering eyes. He smiled as he pulled her gently back into his arms and hugged her. She could hear his heart speaking to hers.

"April, I would give you anything to make you happy. I am going to give you *one more moment in time* with me, one more memory of my *endless love* for you. I never want this night to end for us." His voice was so sincere, she knew that everything she had ever dreamed of was about to come true.

Mark turned away from her and yelled up the hill.

"She said, 'Yes!' She said, 'Yes!' " He yelled with joy.

From over the hill, screaming and clapping was heard. April looked at Mark with a huge question on her face. Who were all those people and what were they doing here, she thought. She looked deep into his sparkling eyes. "Mark?"

"Did I mention that tonight would be a beautiful night to get married?" He glowed with the thought of marrying her.

April's eyes got big. "Oh, my stars, Mark!" She thought she was going to faint. Mark held her up against him. He was just bursting with joy; he was so happy.

"Are you ready?" he asked her affectionately. She shook her head yes.

"We are ready!" Mark yelled up the hill, and then he took one last lingering kiss from the woman who was about to become his wife.

This was how love was supposed to be. Nothing could take tonight away from this couple, as they would pledge their love for each other.

April heard Mark's sister singing, "*Nobody Loves Me Like You Do,*" as they stepped forward to join their lives together.

Movie Song "Nobody Loves Me Like You Do" by *Whitney Houston*
Like a candle burning bright, Love is glowing in your eyes
A flame to light our way, that burns brighter everyday
But now I have you. Nobody loves me like you do.

Chapter Sixty-Two –
⁓My Endless Love⁓

*S*uddenly the trees lit up with tiny white Christmas lights. The whole park took on a magical appearance. Mark's teammates came down the hill, all in tuxedos and being perfect gentlemen. They formed two straight lines across from each other.

Mark's buddies for life were so touched by the sight of Mark and April standing there in front of them, that they shed tears of pure happiness for them. Mark smiled at them; there was no doubting the friendships between them.

Carlo unrolled the white carpet on the ground between the two rows of men. Each player took out a tiny candle and lit it, holding it out in front of them, as they stood at attention.

Mark took April's arm and escorted her onto the carpet and hand in hand, they gracefully walked up the hill to the gazebo. April thought she was going to melt as she looked into Mark's magnificent eyes as they walked. He had created the perfect atmosphere for an exquisite wedding.

The gazebo was outlined with hundreds of sparkling candles and beautiful white and pink roses. Mark's pastor stood in front of the gazebo holding a Bible. The guests were sitting in white chairs covered with baby's breath and roses. Bouquets of elegant flowers were everywhere.

Dan came to Mark and April; he too was wearing his tuxedo. Dan gave them each a heartfelt embrace. Dan was glowing with love and joy for April and Mark.

"This is where I go take my place. April, I love you so much." Mark kissed her soft cheek. "The next time I kiss you, we will be husband and wife," he told her tenderly, his face radiant with happiness. He felt very much alive.

Mark attractively walked up the aisle and took his place beside Jeff, Carlo and his father. His three best men were each beaming with the pleasure of sharing in something so special to Mark.

At that moment, a *dove* gently landed on the gazebo, and Mark felt the presence of his grandfather in his heart. Mark tightly pressed his lips together to keep from crying tears as his heart was overwhelmed with all that was happening. It was his father's loving touch on his shoulder that brought him a smile.

Mark remembered his wise words to Kevin earlier that day. Today was going to be a great day, but never in his wildest imagination had he thought it would be the happiest day of his life. He wanted to drop to his knees and thank God for making this night possible.

Debbie, Rebecca, and Sharon came to April and helped her out of her jacket. They placed long white silk gloves on both her hands. Then Debbie held out an elegant long sleeve, floor length, white jacket with diamonds and helped April slip into it. They put a beautiful silk veil on April's head.

Debbie handed April an exquisite bouquet of flowers. Dan stepped forward and placed her hand on his arm.

The women stepped back to admire the perfect vision of beauty. Never had they seen a bride as beautiful as April. Rebecca rejoiced at the woman that her brother had chosen to be his wife.

April stood facing Mark. He was everything she could ever want in a husband. His adoring eyes stared into hers. Her heart was pounding, as she knew she was seconds from becoming his wife. This was it, the moment that all her fairytale dreams would come true.

It was time to line up as the processional music began to play. Rebecca got her two sons in order, each handsome in their small tuxedos, each holding a white laced pillow, which held the expensive diamond wedding rings Mark had chosen.

"April, choose your maid of honor," her sister, Debbie said. April chose her. A warm hug was exchanged between the two sisters.

"We will be the bridesmaids," Sharon volunteered.

"Now all we need is a flower girl," Rebecca said.

Instantly April's heart dropped. Tears quickly formed in her eyes as she thought of Sunny. April sadly looked at Mark. She could not do this without Sunny. Her heart was now heavy and shattered. The joy had been taken from her. *Oh, Mark,* she cried inside her heart as a tear slowly trickled down her face.

Mark's face had an overwhelming astonished look about it. He was quickly coming towards her. He seemed in a panic to reach her. What was wrong? Had he felt her heart crying out? When he reached her, he took her hand and slowly turned her around and held her in his arms.

There standing behind her, under the lamppost next to "Mark's Bench," was Julia. Standing next to Julia, and holding her hand, was a tiny child, dressed in a long white dress with lace. On her head was a ring of tiny white roses. How precious she looked, as she lifted her tiny hand and waved at them.

Mark ran to her, picked her up in his arms, and hugged and kissed her. He never thought he would ever see her again, and his emotions came pouring out.

Julia kissed Mark's cheek and hugged the two of them. It was a mother's joy to see her son reunited with his precious child that he loved more than his own life. This truly was a homecoming no one would forget.

Mark's eyes were full of questions. This whole wedding had been his plan, but who had found Sunny; how did she get there? Julia just looked at him with love and a warm smile. She would tell him the whole story later.

April had been unable to move, frozen in disbelief. Dan held her arm tighter for fear that she might faint. Her arms ached to hold her child in them.

Mark quickly carried the child to her mother, and together they rejoiced and gave thanks to God for bringing their daughter home to them.

The entire family had gathered around them to share in their joy. Thankful prayers were uplifted to the God that had made it all possible.

Sunny looked up into Mark's happy eyes, took her small hand, and touched his cheek ever so gently.

"God does supply all your needs, Mark," she said so sweetly, as her face glowed with the love she had for her father.

Then Sunny held up her other hand. In it was a small piece of paper wrapped in white ribbon. She handed it out to Mark.

Mystified, he took it from her; carefully he unwrapped the ribbon, and unrolled the paper so he could read it. He was stunned at the words he read. He drew a deep breath.

His lips quivered and tears formed in his eyes. He looked into April's awaiting eyes and softly spoke.

"It is Sunny's HLA test results. She is a perfect match," he spoke in tears.

The three hugged and kissed each other in their happiness. *God had supplied all their needs. All in God's time, He had supplied their miracle.*

Sunny broke the rejoicing up by announcing it was time for them to get married. "Let's get married," she announced with a giggle and they did.

Her beloved Uncle Dan escorted April up the aisle. Her face was radiant with joy as she reached her magical prince. Mark, so dashingly gorgeous, took her hand in his and they faced their pastor. Sunny stood enjoying the excitement of the moment, beside April.

Pastor Evan warmly thanked everyone for coming. He thanked the Lord for the many blessings that April and Mark had just received.

Then he held the microphone out to Mark and stepped down. Mark stood on the step to the gazebo. He lifted his hand out to April. She took his hand, and together they gracefully went to the top and stood.

Mark turned to face her and looked lovingly at her. She was stunning and radiant; she was God's gift to him. She was the woman he had prayed God would send him.

Then he held up the microphone and spoke to all those who had come to share in their happiness. Mark looked into April's loving eyes and smiled.

"I want to dedicate this song to my bride and to my daughter." Sunny came up and joined them. The music began to play. Mark sang with all his heart, "Endless Love" by Lionel Richie, to April.

April joined him in the second verse. Together they expressed their *endless love* for each other; in life and in death, they would forever be one. God had supplied all their needs, all in God's time.

Two hearts - two hearts that beat as one.

BOOK TWO –
ꙮOne More Moment in Timeꙮ

*I*f you enjoyed the first book, the second book will be sure to capture your heart. It will make you smile, cry, laugh, get angry, find faith, forgiveness and hope as you engage in Mark's life and warm your heart with his determination to have One More Moment in Time with all those that he deeply loves.

Mark is determined to win his battle and take the path of endless love with the woman who gives him strength, peace, love, and joy in his life.

You will not be able to put this captivating book down once you begin reading. The story's intensity and your curiosity will keep you fueled to know more.

The continuation of the Romantic Wedding, Wedding reception, Wedding night, Sunday morning, The Church Service, and the Championship Football Game are included in this intriguing book.

Will Mark survive the Championship game? Will Mark recover from his illness? Will he have the family he always prayed he would have? Experience the drama, the love and the surprise ending to a love story of Endless Love in *"One More Moment in Time."*

If you would like to purchase a copy of Book 2: *"One More Moment in Time."* Contact: endlesslovebookorders@yahoo.com
Type - Request of Book Two – in the subject line

** **Disclaimer – All the medical treatments, conditions, and terms may not be entirely accurate.** This book is not intended to provide medical advice or suggestions for treatments. This book was not written in the present time of 2007. The story is fictional, with drama, to bring life to the story.

Mark's aplastic anemia condition is <u>offset by other health conditions</u> that Mark has; therefore, **his case is very unusual**. You will learn more about the uniqueness of his condition in Book Two; *"One More Moment in Time."*

If you have any of the medical conditions that Mark Sanders had in this book, please seek medical attention and advice from a medical doctor.

Mark Sanders is a **fictional character**. His story is fictional with the intentions of bringing awareness to *aplastic anemia* and *bone marrow donations*. His love for the Lord is an inspiration to those who have aplastic anemia or any illness.

Authors Notes About Aplastic Anemia:

Since writing this book, I have become deeply aware of the courage and resources families like the Sanders' need if they are to challenge aplastic anemia. Please help the thousands of families fighting bone marrow diseases by donating your blood, platelets, and bone marrow. To do this, contact your local Red Cross and hospital to find the blood center closest to you. And please help fund research by contacting the Aplastic Anemia & MDS International Foundation at (800) 747-2820 or <u>www.aamds.org</u>.

Your generous response will help save someone's life.

APLASTIC ANEMIA & MYELODYSPLASTIC SYNDROMES
CAN STRIKE ANY PERSON, OF ANY AGE, ANY GENDER, OR ANY RACE, ANYWHERE IN THE WORLD

Aplastic Anemia and Myelodysplastic Syndromes are non-contagious and often fatal blood diseases that occur when the bone marrow stops making enough healthy blood cells. Although all of the causes are still unknown, they have been linked to toxins and viruses that we are in contact with every day. Research is desperately needed because more people than ever are being stricken with these disorders, and there is no one cure that is guaranteed to work for everyone. We are making progress in the fight against these diseases—every year the chances for survival are increasing, thanks to advances in medical research. You can help the thousands of patients battling this disease by: donating your blood, platelets, and bone marrow; financially supporting our research efforts to treat and cure Aplastic Anemia, myelodysplastic syndromes, and other bone marrow diseases such as PNH.

To receive more information, contact them today!

APLASTIC ANEMIA & MDS INTERNATIONAL FOUNDATION, INC.
Providing Global Support, Education & Research
P.O. BOX 613 ANNAPOLIS, MD 21404-0613 U.S.A.
TEL: 410.867.0242 800.747.2820 FAX: 410.867.0240
help@aamds.org www.aamds.org

Final Words of Encouragement

Good morning Liz,

*Y*our book is very well written – top quality literature. The messages you share, reveal, and let the reader discover are what they need to know. They need to know about God's love, forgiveness, and faithfulness. They need to know, as shown in your final thoughts, that God supplies all our needs. Life is about living to the fullest.

Mark always lived his life to the fullest—in football, on his motorcycle, as a doctor giving the best to others, and to April and Sunny. He always gave all of himself. He was willing to give of himself in football for his team at the end of the story even if it meant losing his life.

Everything that you wrote in the story had purpose and was well said.

Just as Mark stepped out at the threshold of life and death with great faith, knowing that God supplies all our needs, you need to step in faith and move forward with your book. God inspired you to put these words on paper. Others need to be given the opportunity to read this message that God has for them.

Liz, you need to get it published, God will work out the details and you know that. I support you.

Again, I thoroughly enjoyed reading and editing this beautiful work. You cannot hold back what God has inspired within you. It was very, very, very well done. Move forward.

Teresa Manczyk – editor and friend

∽Words from your Author∽

Thank you everyone for making this book possible. I love each one of you that took the time to read my book, either by e-mail, on copy paper and now by paperback. I am taking a faith-walk as I share this book with others. I am in prayer, that it will touch your hearts. I look forward to hearing from you. Be Blessed. Elizabeth A. Ryan – endlesslovebookcomments@yahoo.com

About your Author –
Elizabeth A. Ryan and her four children and three grandchildren make their home in Georgia. She is an active member of Believer's Church and serves as the director of the children's Bible story room. She owns a Christian based Home School called, "Noah's Ark Christian Academy." She enjoys working with small children and helping them develop a heart for God.

My heart goes out to all of our **Military families**. I understand first hand, their dedication to this country in their commitment to serve. My son, Justin, is in the Air Force. During his tour in Afghanistan, I spent many sleepless nights, working on this book, waiting for him to come online so that we could spend a few minutes together. Thank you and God bless all of you and your families.

Endless Love Book Editors -
Deborah Edwards, Faye Adams, Kathleen Ford, Kittie McGuire, Marcia Price, Melanie Williams, Susan Hershey, Suzy Schmitz , Teresa Manczyk

"Endless Love" A Romantic Christian Love Story Series that draws you into the life of Dr. Mark Sanders, a brilliant and attractive young man who is determined to find the meaning of true love.

This captivating book is filled with romance, action, drama, passionate characters, intense plot twists until the unexpected heartfelt conclusion.

Mark's faith walk is challenged when life takes him on a path of intricate hardships and inconceivable heartache. Mark's determination leads him on a breath-taking journey as he discovers how to stand on God's promises when faced with death.

When his beliefs are challenged, will Mark find peace and love? Can Mark overcome the enemy's deceitfulness and embrace life's joy?

This story will warm your heart and restore your faith as you witness Mark struggle to uncover the truth, find love, and grant forgiveness.

An epic love story to read in front of a crackling fire.

Kittie McGuire

Printed in the United States
99560LV00003B/39/A